P9-CFE-571

The Reckoners

Doranna Durgin

TOR®
paranormal romance

A TOM DOHERTY ASSOCIATES BOOK
NEW YORK

This is a work of fiction. All of the characters, organizations, and events portrayed in this novel are either products of the author's imagination or are used fictitiously.

THE RECKONERS

Copyright © 2010 by Doranna Durgin

A Tor Book
Published by Tom Doherty Associates, LLC
175 Fifth Avenue
New York, NY 10010

www.tor-forge.com

Tor® is a registered trademark of Tom Doherty Associates, LLC.

ISBN 978-0-7653-6164-6

First Edition: February 2010

Printed in the United States of America

0 9 8 7 6 5 4 3 2 1

With thanks to:
my fun editor Heather Osborn and Melissa Frain, agent
Lucienne Diver, glossary assistant Adrianne Middleton,
and early readers Julie Czerneda and Kristen Britain.

Not to mention cats for being cats.

Author's Note

The Winchester Mystery House is the most fascinating place *ever* . . . a unique chronicle of one woman's struggle to come to terms with the events of her life. It is not, however, completely open to the public or even to curious authors who want to get things right. So while I looked into the house's public areas with glee, you know what I did with the rest of it? No, seriously. *I made it up.* Also with glee. Just so you know!

The Reckoners Cast

Our heroine: Lisa McGarrity (Garrie), a natural reckoner, once mentored by a ghost named Rhonda Rose.

Our hero (or is he?): Trevarr, half-human bounty hunter from another dimension

Our hero's bond partner: Sklayne, an energy-based creature of curiosity and appetite, often appearing as an Abyssinian cat.

The Bad Beings: the Krevata, a clan of semi-ethereal rogue demons dabbling in powers beyond their control, who also plot revenge against Trevarr.

Reckoner crew: Lucia Reyes, spiritual empath
Drew Ely, ethereal historian
Quinn Rossiter, researcher and trivia master

Guest star: the Winchester Mystery House

Glossary

atreya: heart partner.

atreya vo: atreya mine.

atreyvo: bondmate.

blood token: a powerful clan object.

caray: a Spanish interjection, meaning "!!!"

chakka: a parasitic darkside entity that invades smallish predators and hulks them out, then controls them in a hunt for atypically large prey for its own consumption.

chicalet: Lucia's nickname for Garrie, based on Spanish *chica* and the English diminutive, not to mention an allusion to a certain brand of wee gum.

darkside: a place vague in Garrie's understanding, from which invading entities come. They all have the same flavor to her. She has thought of it in terms of spiritual planes rather than dimensions. This may change.

darksiders: entities that come from the darkside.

The Eye: a dimensional travel tool.

The Gatherer: a hunting tool; it detects energies and can "store" and transport beings in an ethereal state.

eatsll: a nasty living substance from Kehar.

fark: Every culture seems to have a word for this.

ghosties: what Garrie calls ghosts.

Kehar: Trevarr's world.

Kirkhirra: a record of clan history kept in knots and formed into a ceremonial belt. The most complex macrame *ever.*

krevata: a clan of semi-ethereal demons, particularly ill-formed and excitable.

memory stone: one of Trevarr's clan objects. He seems to have the responsibility of carrying his people's important things.

nibblers: darkside entity, an aggregate creature that nibbles away at the energies of other beings.

reckoner: those who take care of a final reckoning for spirits who need it; specifically someone who can manipulate ethereal breezes to accomplish this, although Garrie considers her team to be reckoners beside her.

spive: air-based darksider entity.

The
Reckoners

1

Underestimate an angry spirit only if you want to become one.
—Rhonda Rose

Here, little ghosties...
—Lisa McGarrity

Lisa McGarrity eased into the brand-spankin'-new patio home in northern Albuquerque. The ultimate in desert chic, still unfurnished and unoccupied . . . she could almost hear her breath echo.

It also steamed. Albuquerque summer night's heat, and her breath steamed. Never a good sign. From within the house, something went *plop*. There was a gooey quality to that sound. Not a sound the average person should be familiar with.

And since when have you ever been average? Never. Not since Rhonda Rose found her. Not since she'd realized she had an inside track on things dead and things dying and things that shouldn't have been there at all. Or that she had the responsibility to protect not only the living, but much of the once-living and even the never-living. Once upon a time, Rhonda Rose had opened the door to her power . . . and taken away her innocence, all in one fell swoop. Once upon a time.

And now . . . ?

"I'm getting out," she said over her shoulder.

Behind her, Lucia Reyes quite sensibly stood just outside the entry of the fancy new home, her flashlight bouncing off the high ceiling. In this business, unexpected problems often came from above, and Lucia had been on Lisa McGarrity's team long enough to learn that lesson well.

Lucia was slender and leggy and gifted with exquisite angles beneath Hispanic features, a tidy J-Lo ass, and the generous budget to clothe, adorn, and otherwise showcase her attributes. She said, "If you're getting *out,* you're going in the wrong direction." She tossed back her hair, a naturally haughty gesture, as she glanced meaningfully at the doorway.

Lisa—Garrie to her reckoner team—raised a self-conscious hand to her own hair: dark nut brown streaked with electric blue, short and spiky. Not bad, actually, if only those spikes had come from styling instead of her lamentable habit of clutching her hair.

Inside the house, something else went *plop.* It sounded larger than the first.

Lucia said, "Still the wrong direction for getting out."

"*After* this." Garrie shot her a quick scowl, extending her awareness into the empty house along with her flashlight beam. Penny-ante reckoner work—new haunting on new construction. Didn't mean they could take it for granted. "Don't tell me you didn't see it coming. This is the most exciting gig we've had for weeks, and that's just because we've got our spooky flashlights."

"Well," Lucia murmured, glancing around the spacious house, "it's got the actual ghostie vibes going on. That's a big step above knocking water pipes."

"Right. Exactly why I'm getting out." Never mind the twinge of guilt as she said it, or the familiar, starch voice of Rhonda Rose reminding her *This is what you were born to do.*

But I'm not doing it, Rhonda Rose. I'm not doing it.
Not really.

Lucia was scary-good sometimes. Her tone dry with self-awareness, she asked, "And what are you going to do, walk away from yourself?" None of them could exactly walk away from their unusual skills, Garrie most of all.

"Hey, chicas, c'mon." Drew Ely shadowed the doorway just behind Lucia, hopelessly geeky in spite of—or perhaps because of—his attempts to be oh-so-hip. Lank hair of an indeterminate color, eyes to match, complexion just getting over the whole becoming-a-man thing. Of late he'd been experimenting with the one-day stubble look, and it really wasn't working for him.

But he was a real wizard at reading the history of any given space. And he'd just saved Garrie from mustering a response to Lucia, so points for that. Cautiously, Garrie moved into the house, making room for Drew to enter with Quinn Rossiter on his heels.

Garrie, head reckoner: trained by her own personal invisible friend from childhood to communicate and influence spirits all of natures. Lucia, their spiritual empath. Drew, their historian. And Quinn, their memory-gifted researcher, tall and broad-shouldered, eyes a deep clear blue, hair a crisp blond that always fell naturally into whatever style he'd chosen. The three of them were the support team to Garrie's reckoner muscle, giving her the information she needed to work fast and clean.

Or not so clean. From out of thin air, a glob of sticky, stinky ghost poop landed on Garrie's cheek. "Gah," she said, and swiped it off, flinging it away with the casual skill of long practice. Since her midteens, she'd been doing this. And with Rhonda Rose at her side, most of it had been a lot more exciting than . . .

Ghost poop.

"Someone's mad," Lucia said.

"Please don't tell me you had to use your superpowers to figure that out." Garrie moved cautiously into the great room—beamed ceiling far above, corner fireplace way down there somewhere, arching rounded doorways to bedrooms, open into the kitchen. If there was ghost poop, there was anger.

"This place is phat," Drew decided, just behind the curve in cool factor as usual. "I bet you could get a deal on it after we clear it."

Garrie didn't answer. She had her own perfectly good condo, smack in the middle of the city's university area. Everything she could possibly want within walking distance and plenty of eccentric, benign spirits to keep her company. "You guys pulling in any clues?"

"The whole *angry* thing," Lucia offered.

Drew shook his head. "The history is muddled to the max."

Garrie could understand that. "All this new construction material, pulled in from all over the place." She took a deep breath, inhaling that peculiar scent of disgruntled spirits that only she could perceive. "I know you're here," she said out loud, words to focus the unspoken communication she broadcast to the house. "Get real, *everyone* knows you're here. Quit throwing spitballs and let's talk."

The straightforward approach. Rarely successful, but always worth a try. This time it netted her a faint but definite spiritual glower, as though impotent pieces of power had mustered righteous offense. No more effective than being hit with pats of soft spiritual butter. "Ooh," she muttered. "Eeek."

Quinn moved into the room, circling around and squinting at the walls—visualizing the structure, running his mind over all the possible connections and influences. "It's not *all* new," he murmured, touching the textured wall paint.

Somewhere in the house a door opened. The reckoners, as one, turned to look at Garrie. She shrugged. "Just supposed to be us." She thought this particular batch of spirits had thrown their drama quota into the ectoplasmic yuck, so that left something more earthly. But . . .

"There's way more than one," she realized out loud,

distracted from the noise of the door. She felt it plainly enough, now that she'd puzzled it out—the weird fractured pieces, a kaleidoscope of personalities. All of them annoyed, but none of them truly powerful. Not darkside entities, just disturbed echoes of those who had once lived in the flesh. They needed her help as much as the man who'd hired her.

Down the hall, shadows in shadow . . . something moved. Yet a deeper layer of shadow, flashing along the wall.

Quinn said, "I think—" and then stopped short at the screeching yowl that cut the night.

Drew jumped, whirling, his flashlight painting wild, bobbing patterns of light across the walls and archways. "Shee-it!"

"Touch*eee*," Lucia murmured to Garrie. She could afford to be complacent. She was the one who always walked away without a single splot of ghost poop on her person. The *only* one.

Garrie slanted her a silent *cut the kid a break* and reached down the hall, pushing out her bubble of awareness. *Nothing.*

"Cat," Quinn said, matter-of-fact and preoccupied with his walls.

And there it was. Loitering at the end of the hall, tail held high and undulating smugly enough that even Garrie, the noncat person, could see its self-satisfaction. "Who let it in?"

Silence from her team. Loud silence. Until a voice not at all familiar to any of them said, "I did."

They all startled. Ghosts didn't vocalize. The occasional whispery noise, the faintest of moans . . . not deep, strong voices.

And they didn't appear at the end of the hallway, solid and tall in the shadows.

The cat ran to the new arrival, wound briefly between his ankles, and faded away into a corner. Garrie didn't hesitate—she lifted her flashlight so the beam shone directly on the man's face.

He can't be for real. Not with a black leather duster over a shirt with leather panels and crisscrossed lacings, pants with front panel styling that might have been stylish a hundred years ago, calf-high boots much scuffed and secured by a row of outside buckles. But he was also far too solid to have come with this particular house. And far too reactive to the flashlight—a pained squint, a futile effort to fend off the light with one hand.

Of course he had half-finger gloves to complete the picture. Of course he had thick straight hair past his shoulders, shorter front strands softening his features with just the right amount of careless.

"Ay-yi-yi," Lucia murmured.

No kidding. But Garrie wasn't looking for reasons to linger in a house where the dead hosts had decided to impress the living with their ghost poop. "This is a private party."

He didn't seem impressed. "You mind?" he asked, a hint of an accent in even those two words. He moved his upraised hand to shield his eyes. "The light?"

"I don't mind a bit," Garrie said, and kept the flashlight beam where it was. Drew's laugh came muffled and more than a little nervous. The cat, invisible in the shadows, yowled in response. It made Garrie's spine tingle.

"Garrie," Lucia said, latching onto Garrie's arm, unspoken words so familiar that Garrie didn't need to hear them. *Garrie, be nice. Garrie, don't chase the hottie away until we figure out if he's a good or evil.*

Garrie scowled. "You know damned well it never turns out well when we run into cute games."

Lucia made a face at the truth of this statement, but then her expression brightened. "There was that goth wannabe who thought his gran was possessed. That wasn't too bad."

"Gran had *Alzheimer's*. It was *tragic*. And what about the others? The reporter who made us look like idiots in prime time, the actual idiot who thought he could steal our skills if he just tried hard enough?" *Trying hard enough* had involved surgical instruments from some ancient collection. No, when they came on all clever like this, there was always some hidden price.

"No games," the man said, moving closer. Garrie kept him in her light. "Desperation. I need your help."

"Funny, that's what the guy with the surgical instruments said." Garrie sidestepped another falling blob of glop. "In case you hadn't noticed, we're in the middle of something here." She sent out a silent mental radar sweep, hunting spiritual pings and listening with half her attention while the other half considered just how problematic their leather-clad, cat-toting visitor might be. She jerked in surprise when one of the pings came back from the visitor in question.

"Adobe," Quinn said abruptly, as if their work hadn't been interrupted by the cat, the man, and the conversation. "The mud. *Old* mud."

The man cleared his throat. "Hello?" His voice still sounded tight. "The light?"

Garrie lowered the beam to his neck. She dug into the back pocket of her jeans and pulled out a worn business card, which she flicked down the hallway at his feet. "Bad timing, mister. You want to talk business, give me a call."

"It's the *mud*," Quinn said.

"The adobe?" Drew headed instantly for the door, grabbing the excuse. He hadn't been with them for the whole incident with the surgical instruments, but he'd heard plenty enough about it.

Their interloper left the card where it fell. He might have spoken, had the house not subtly *shifted*. Garrie felt it; Lucia felt it. And the man looked over at the empty kitchen in alarm.

From outside, Drew called, "Yes! It's the mud!"

The house made a noise like someone's last breath. Silent demands plucked at Garrie's attention. Irritation at being ignored, promises to up the ante, a crude image or two—

Lucia gasped, fully distracted from their visitor. "Garrie—"

"I feel it," Garrie said grimly.

"Containment?" Lucia said, slinging her Burberry tote from her shoulder, hand ready to plunge inside.

"Size large," Garrie said, holding out her hand without removing her attention from the kitchen. She switched her flashlight off and jammed it into the holder on her cargo belt; she'd need both hands now, and her inner sight was more important than her physical sight anyway. Lucia slapped the bag into her hand, flexible and plastic. Easy zipper. Double layered.

"Is that—" the stranger started, not bringing himself to finish the sentence.

"Yes, yes, the all-purpose Baggie, coated inside with a secret blend of eleven herbs and spices." And it was, too. The plastic gleamed with the petroleum jelly base, and the grit of the ingredients prickled against her fingertips, from juniper and lilac to garlic and leek. "Now be quiet. Or better yet, go home. Call me tomorrow." It wasn't hard, herding minor, fractured spirits into containment with ethereal breezes . . . but it took concentration. Serious concentration.

"I can't," the man said, moving closer. Garrie touched the stun gun also conveniently hanging at her side and otherwise didn't take her attention away from the entities gathering in the kitchen. Invisible, angry entities. "Tomorrow is too late."

Too bad she had the skepticism of experience. "Go. *Away.*"

Drew ran back inside, stopping so short that he skidded on the tile. "You coming? You got 'em? 'Cause it's the adobe plaster, all right. Quinn says if we get 'em and the mud, we're good till he figures out where the mud came from. Near a wash somewhere, probably. Flash flood—"

"Makes sense," Garrie murmured. She sensed only pieces because these beings had been scattered across a wide area, the adobe mud harvesting only a partial presence of each spirit. "No wonder they're mad."

"Will you just—" the man said before running out of words, voice hard with what might actually have been desperation after all.

"Everyone's got a mad on," Lucia said pointedly. "I'm going outside. What about—?" And she nodded at their interloper.

"That's his problem," Garrie said. She reached inside herself, opening the door that held in her own inner light. *Here, little ghosties . . .*

"He could get slimed . . ."

"I'm right *here,*" the man said. "And I'm on a tight schedule. A very *tight schedule.*"

"The word *very* only weakens your meaning," Garrie said, finding the coalescing spirits as dim spots in her inner eye, gathering toward the kitchen. "Ask any English teacher." All that wiring, all those appliances . . . always a favorite spot. *Here, little ghosties . . .* She lured them in, knowing better than to try to reason with such fragmented entities; she let her energy build, spiraling through her grounding in an Escherian swirl. Once she got close enough . . .

Someone grabbed her arm. Not gently, and not quite hard enough to hurt. From the doorway Lucia yelped in surprise and belated warning, and a deep voice in her ear said, "A very, *very* tight schedule."

She opened her eyes, shocked to see even in the darkness that his eyes weren't quite right, to see with her lingering inner vision that his aura wasn't quite . . . *expected.*

And then she realized that he still held her arm, and in the background she heard Lucia's dismay and Quinn's dramatic here-we-go groan, and Drew's emphatically spat curse. She glowered right into his gaze, saw the instant of surprise there as he read her expression—read it quite well, in fact, as she lost the leading edge of her temper and unthinkingly drew down the already spiraling energy to fling him away, giving him a psychic King Kong shove that was a stupid waste because it only worked on spiritual entities except *damn* if it didn't shove him right back against the nearest wall hard enough to elicit a grunt. And then, even more utterly unexpected, radiated back out from him twofold, passing right through Garrie and into—

The kitchen.

For an instant there was silence. And then Drew said, "Shee-*it*," and Quinn said, *"Garrie,"* and Lucia's voice rose half an octave as she shouted, *"¡Caray!* Run! Oh, *crap!"* and Garrie felt the spiritual fury raising the hair at the back of her neck and then down her arms and she mouthed her own silent curses as she sprinted—

Too late. Far, far too late.

2

Don't forget to check under their skirts.
—Rhonda Rose

It's your own fault.
—Lisa McGarrity

Garrie still smelled. She still smelled *bad*.

Partly the acrid scent of displaced and disgruntled spirits, partly ghost poop. She tugged at the wet hair behind her ear, despairing that she'd ever wash it truly clean again. Maybe she should head to the twenty-four-hour grocery, get some deskunking pet shampoo. She needed another run anyway.

It's your own fault. She hadn't listened to Rhonda Rose. Not that Rhonda Rose was around any longer, but she'd heard enough of those axioms to last a lifetime. And she hadn't checked under the guy's skirts.

Metaphorically, of course. But she'd lost her temper, made assumptions . . . paid for it. Damn, she was losing her edge. Too many easy jobs, too few even of those.

"I'm getting out," she said. "If you were still here, Rhonda Rose, you would totally agree."

Though if her longtime tutor and companion had still been here, Garrie would still be in the thick of it. Still be in her prime, young and fierce. A reckoner to be reckoned with. A reckoner actually filling the needs of more than just a few isolated spirits who needed help anchoring themselves. Most people thought a lingering spirit needed to let go; Garrie knew better. They needed to complete whatever connection they'd lost.

But she wasn't the only one who could handle the lightweight work. Plenty of mediums at work there, some who didn't even know what they were doing. The priests, for instance—she wasn't sure they'd ever catch on. She sure didn't plan to clue them in. And she herself didn't fit the mold.

Twenty-five and over the hill. Time to get into something different. The university area was a bustle of activity . . . of service jobs. She slouched back in a bed way too large for one person, surrounded by squishy pillows and plush animals with her laptop balanced against her legs. "Here's a beautician's school," she commented out loud to the plushies. "Think they'd even let me in the door?"

None of the stuffed animals responded. Just as well. That would be a bit too much even for a reckoner.

She'd dealt with the displaced spirits at the patio home, of course. She'd gone back in and rounded them all up while they were still weakened by that blast of retribution they'd flung all over the house, little pushes and tugs of ethereal breezes with a surgeon's precision. There'd been no sign of the man. No sign of the cat. Big surprise.

Quinn had already taken a scraping of the mud, all the while Lucia apologized for not warning Garrie when the stranger had grabbed her. "He was so fast . . ." she kept muttering, and Garrie told her to forget it. Lucia hadn't been the only one taken by surprise. Besides, they had the spirits and they had the mud. Quinn had gone off to research the adobe plaster supplier and would return the spirits to their proper location come daylight, while Garrie had already severed their ties to the adobe at the patio house.

There'd been only a twelve-foot strip of property between that patio house and its equally chic, equally new neighbors. She wondered if anyone had complained about the pyrotechnics. More than likely, no one had noticed at all.

"If I'm not going to make a real difference," Garrie told the plushies, "I'd rather paint nails. Or change car oil. Or run the tram up and down Sandia Peak all day long."

She threaded her fingers through short, wet hair and tugged in the frustration of it all. And the plushies said nothing.

Sklayne stretched his awareness into their new location, sheltered by an unfamiliar spreading bush. ::green sharp smells, twittering dry feathers, hard glossy beetle—:: A satisfying crunch and swallow, beetle no more.

"Think *cat*," Trevarr said, his tension battering at Sklayne's edges.

Sklayne knew *cat*. Sklayne had done *cat* in the darkness not long ago. Sleek reddish feline, leggy and much with the ears. Sklayne held his mind still, *pushed;* he expanded to encompass everything and anything before abruptly shrinking back to the *cat* shape. Now . . . vision of washed-out colors with sharp edges up close, fuzzy edges across this green expanse of manicured growth. Scents just as sharp, just as stingingly dry—and the recently consumed beetle had left its own aura. A prominent needled branch caught Sklayne's attention; he sniffed, then delicately rubbed his face against it even as it bent out of his way. "Mrow," he said; an experiment.

"Very convincing." Trevarr stood tall beside him, shaded beneath a pampered cottonwood, squinting into the too-bright sunshine of this place even through his newly acquired sunglasses. Trevarr in disgrace. Looked much like Trevarr not in disgrace, but felt . . .

Tension. Guilt. Determination.

Trevarr ignored the brush of Sklayne's thoughts. "Now behave yourself, and let's go deal with this."

"Mrrp," Sklayne said, and liked that one even better. He found their target—not very large, not in the least aware of them. Sitting on a curvy wooden bench in the shade, bent over a printed binding. ::Get herrrr,:: he added.

It sounded like a purr.

3

Untidy humors spill everywhere.
—Rhonda Rose

It's a sticky business.
—Lisa McGarrity

In the distance, a siren wailed. Drivers honked at one another, pedestrians cried out in surprise as a cyclist swooshed through their ranks, and birds fluttered in the city plantings with only a cocky chirp or two to give them away. The city's universal color scheme—appointments in bright turquoise, coral, and sunrise orange—made an impact even on eyes that had grown up with it.

Garrie closed hers, the big book of vocational opportunities still propped on her crossed legs. The brisk clarity of this block park beside her condo had drawn her here long ago—long before the condo had even gone up. Here the ethereal breezes ran quiet, making it easy to keep track of unusual activity. Safe to run in; easier to relax, to concentrate on other things.

Something blipped against her perception—her personal ethereal radar. Something unfamiliar—not unpleasant—and then gone again, detectable only as the faintest hum off to her left.

Not that she wasn't wary of first impressions. After

all, Rhonda Rose had terrified her upon first meeting, swooping down with the outraged righteousness of a spirit who believed the ten-year-old had known what she'd been doing, making ethereal waves. And in the end, she hadn't been terrifying at all.

Although that had been the end of any pretense of normality in Garrie's childhood. No more shrugging off the invisible friends; no more ignoring the ethereal breezes just because no one else could feel them. Instead she had a unique mentor, guiding her through a world both thrilling and dangerous. First the easy encounters, the quick victories over diffuse entities. And then the life-threatening battles to stop tragedies the mundane world had never even noticed looming.

If she'd known where it would all lead, would she have given Rhonda Rose that second chance? Or *pow, out of the ballpark*? She could have done it. Even back then, she could have done it.

Thoughts of how it had been versus how it was now . . . far too familiar. Garrie let go a big sigh and muttered, "Same old, same old," to herself. And then she felt the shift in the hum off to her left and targeted it, turning her head so by the time she opened her eyes, she looked straight at the source. And she said bluntly, "That's close enough."

He still radiated that *not safe* vibe. Last night she had attributed it to circumstances, but today . . . Today it was plainly attached to him. In the daylight, she half expected to find an artistic two-day stubble to go along with the attitude— but his face was smooth, his hair pulled back to let the bright Albuquerque light skim its hard angles. Hard . . . still determined. He wanted something, and he wanted it from her.

But out in the park, broad daylight, witnesses everywhere—what was he going to do, anyway?

Not that she'd let him try. When he didn't heed her warning, Garrie sent a shove through the breezes, a puff of ethereal wind. A reminder. A reminder to herself, too—not to take this one for granted. Not when he could perceive her manipulation of the breezes. Not when he was affected by them.

He stopped short, stiffening against the push until she let it die down. "You're farking prickly."

"You think?" She considered it. Prickly. Not necessarily a bad thing, in her world. *Farking?* There was no telling.

A sandy red cat with copious ears and deep reddish points sauntered past her bench, tail high and quivering; it hesitated only a moment before jumping lightly to the slats beside her. Right. The cat. The cat that was somehow his.

She didn't even look as she nudged it away, ignoring its *mow!* of protest. "I bet *farking* isn't something you say to nice girls."

That seemed to take him back more than anything, standing there almost close enough to loom, way overdressed for this summer morning with his head tipped in a way that made Garrie believe he was squinting behind those trendy sunglasses. Then, as though he was at a loss for just how to respond, he simply spread his arms away from his sides slightly, that universal signal of *I mean no harm.*

Right. How naive did she look, anyway? She took an ostentatious sniff of the dry city air. *Ghost poop.* "Still got the smell going, I see."

He shook his head almost imperceptibly; his mouth twitched in what was probably annoyance. In that moment, Garrie thought that if she were smart, she'd be running. If she were smart, she'd pay attention to the danger vibes.

Except this was *her* park. And he'd already found her twice.

She suddenly regretted her outfit of the day. A tight spaghetti-strap tank top beneath an equally snug bodice, low-slung cropped cargo pants below . . . she abruptly felt smaller. Smaller than him; smaller than the usual her. She tucked her knees up, turning the book into a shield, and then cursed at how she'd given herself away.

If he noticed, it didn't show. "I still need help. Your help."

The cat again jumped lightly to the curved wood slat seat, its tail high and vibrating in another precipitous claim to the bench. Just a damn cat . . . but the cat came with the man, and this was *her* turf. Garrie crowded it back off the bench. "Tomato juice does a pretty good job."

"You know that's not what I mean." He lifted his head momentarily at the sound of a jet far overhead, barely audible over the generalized noise of the university area, and relaxed only when it faded.

"Right." She lifted an eyebrow, a skill gained through many hours of practice in front of a mirror after her first exposure to Classic *Star Trek*. She'd stay cool today—not annoyed, not taken off-guard as she'd been the night before, letting her temper get the better of her. Rhonda Rose had taught her that much. *Untidy humors.* And she'd been right, as the mess of the evening before had proven. "Though I'm surprised to see you here. Short on time and all that. Not to mention the probability that, you know, I've already totally had it with you."

He took a step closer—might have taken another if she hadn't given him another reminder, ethereal breezes ruffling the long tail of his duster. Annoyance shifted his features, as fleeting as the breeze. "Short on time, yes. It twisted my reasoning. It was a mistake to approach you last night."

"You think?"

That annoyance again, and something else . . . a hint of desperation? "I still need to talk to you. I'm new here—"

She snorted, mixing it up in a laugh; she almost dropped her book. "That's not news to me, by the way." Even without that accent. Part Russian, part German.

"Amanda Myers recommended you."

Now *that* got her attention. Amanda lived on the West Coast, had once had the worst infestation of nibblers Garrie had ever seen. No longer. Satisfied client . . . someone she trusted. And not someone who would give her name to a pretender.

He took a chance and a step closer. "What I saw last night . . ."

She laughed, a short and bitter sound. "Last night was nothing." Not false modesty. She meant it. She'd rather deal with a mansion of darkside nibblers than a house of spirits so fragmented that the best they could do was fling poop. Once she'd focused, it hadn't been hard to corral the unwilling spirits, not even while drenched in the ectoplasmic goo.

"Nothing," he repeated, and looked at her book with sudden comprehension. "You're thinking of quitting—"

She frowned at him. "I'm looking for *something*."

"Ah." He smiled, suddenly confident. "I can show you that."

Damned if she didn't believe him. Garrie had no trouble recognizing someone who lived in the unseen fringes of society. She had enough practice seeing just that in her bathroom mirror. Someone who might be in touch with the unusual.

He let her think about it, and said, "If it weren't *something,* do you think I'd still be here after last night?"

Good point. She frowned at him for a long moment. She thumbed the pages in her book. And finally she nodded to herself, and to him. "Garrie," she said. "You can call me Garrie. And for now . . ." she smiled, beatific with the thought just now striking her. "For as long as it takes to finish the ice cream you're about to buy me, we'll talk."

4

Know who you are, lest you lose yourself.
— Rhonda Rose

Take a flashlight.
—Lisa McGarrity

Standing in line, waiting for ice cream . . . Garrie quickly
learned that Trevarr had no gift for small talk and no
inclination to fill the silence. Left to her own thoughts,
she wandered away from the concerns of the near future to those of the past. The *way it had been* versus the
way it might have been. The way it probably *had* been
for everyone else. But being a reckoner . . .

Garrie thought it was like being a child star, except
without the fame, the restricted hours, or the perks. No
ponies in her childhood; no limos or tutors or nannies.

Her parents hadn't even known what she was doing.
Bad grades? Obviously, since no matter how hard she
studied, her schoolwork suffered. Certainly couldn't
be because she'd been up half the night convincing the
ghost of a rabid skunk not to spray the ethereally gen-
erated virus on the neighborhood pets. Because who
believed in ghosts? And if there were ghosts, they sure
wouldn't come in the form of rabid skunks. *Contagious*
rabid skunks.

The things she'd missed . . . all because of the re-
sponsibilities of her gifts. The need to protect those
who had no idea they were even in danger. The need to
help the restless find peace. The need to ground herself
with endless exercise of all kinds. No pajama parties;
no dances. No late-night make-out sessions by the Rio
Grande. No prom.

"I missed my senior prom," she informed him, waiting

for the clerk behind the ice cream bar to finish blending ooey-gooey Oreo and double-fudge mix-ins with her mint ice cream.

Her companion didn't respond—not ignoring her; simply not having a response at all.

Not that she'd expected one. No one could have possibly followed her train of thought, and his single-mindedness was evident enough. "You sure you don't want some ice cream?" she said. "Because don't think you're getting any of mine." His shoulders shifted as though the notion truly startled him. With sudden impatience for the sunglasses, she said, "Take those off, if you want to talk to me."

He dug into his pocket, pulling out a money clip of worked metal just a shade too light for silver. *Platinum?* Who had a freaking platinum money clip?

As if he saw her looking, he peeled off a bill and jammed the rest back into his front pants pocket. He put the bill on the counter and said, "Something simple. White is probably best."

"Vanilla?" the clerk asked, a strand of lank blond escaping her hair net and disbelief escaping her voice.

"White?" Garrie asked, and wrinkled her nose at him. Sure, he had an accent . . . but his English was far too good for *white*.

"White," he said firmly, with no evident need to make explanations or excuses. And then he looked down at her. "My eyes are not good in this sun."

"We're not in the sun," she pointed out. She'd deliberately brought them here to the shady side of the street. "And I'm not talking about this if I can't see your face." Not if she had to guess the subtle expressions being hidden by those dark shades. "I'm perfectly happy to eat ice cream and go back to my reading. Your little teaser . . . just not that good."

But it was good enough, and she let out a breath when he gave the slightest of nods, half his attention on the ice cream cone Garrie accepted as he indicated a take out bowl for himself. And then he looked away—and to her surprise, she felt the faint wash of manipulated energies. Unfamiliar energies, outside her experience—and so faint she lost the memory of the sensation before she could put a name to it.

Maybe she'd grown too used to being the only reckoner in the Land of Enchantment.

As if it hadn't been a topic of discussion at all, he lifted the glasses with one hand, folded them against his shoulder, and tucked the earpiece into a buttonhole of the toggle-fastened coat. Then he looked at her, one eyebrow raised so naturally that she instantly knew he'd never had to practice it in front of a mirror at all.

His eyes were eerie liquid silver, pupils nearly hidden in irises tarnished dark around them. She hadn't expected it; she'd thought hazel or brown by his coloring. She didn't try to hide her reaction. "Well, no wonder," she said, and took her ice cream cone to the glass-topped sidewalk table where she'd left her book, perching on the edge of the wrought-iron seat.

He didn't ask her *no wonder, what?* He had to know the impact of those eyes. That they'd draw attention, that they'd distract from conversation. Sun-sensitive. Right. She looked straight at them and said, "This is as patient as I get. Talk to me."

He'd been contemplating his flimsy plastic spoon, but looked up when she spoke; his eyes were hard, cold metal. Something brushed against Garrie's legs; she didn't have to look to know the cat had found them. Not that it surprised her. Not after so many years of wrangling things everyone else in the world pretended not to see.

She caught a drip off the edge of her cone and said, "C'mon, then. We talking posthuman spirits? Animal? Darkside goodies pulled in by some fake séance medium who never expected a response?"

He pondered the question—and this time, because she could see those eyes, she knew he wasn't simply ignoring her. After a moment, he said, "Imports. Mixed with naturals."

Different terminology. Okay, she could deal with that.

He added, "More than you've ever seen in one place."

She laughed shortly, a jerk of her head that left ice cream smeared over her chin. Without haste, she reached for her paper napkin and wiped away the blot of sweet green. "You're making assumptions."

"Yes," he agreed. "And no. If this weren't big—"

"Mow!" the cat interrupted, putting its paws on his thigh.

Without any obvious thought, he scooped a tiny sliver of ice cream and held the spoon down for the cat while its raspy pink tongue made quick if delicate work of the morsel. He said, "Have you heard of Winchester House?"

She laughed. "Who in the business hasn't?" Self-proclaimed ghost hunters, real-life sensitives, and the rare full-fledged reckoner . . . they all knew of the Winchester House in San Jose. The unbelievably huge, rambling, twisting maze of a house with its inexplicable architecture, rooms inside of rooms, rooms without doors, without floors . . . it had been built by Mrs. Winchester, a woman obsessed with the people killed by her father's invention: the Winchester rifle. The house was her ode to them, a soothing balm to her own soul . . . a place to confuse spirits into endless wandering . . . inadvertently, a place they called home. And it had never been confirmed, not even unofficially, that it had done the trick. Commercial ghost hunters weren't allowed anywhere near the entrance or extensive gardens; sensitives couldn't bring themselves to get anywhere near the place. And reckoners . . .

Reckoners had bigger things to worry about.

Or at least, this particular reckoner had once had bigger things to worry about. The very fact that mention of the Winchester House had intrigued her, had caught her attention . . .

Garrie dropped her forehead against the table and gently banged it on the glass. She was pathetic.

"You're getting ice cream in your hair," he said.

She lifted her head to glare at him. "It'll add to my charm," she snapped, knowing just whom to blame for this additional reminder of how much her life had changed since Rhonda Rose had moved on. "What *about* Winchester House? They can't want a cleansing. The whole purpose of that place is to gather ghosties."

"It's gone awry," he said simply. "Twisted. They're only beginning to realize it. Their spirits have been peaceful, adept at living unseen. Not any longer. The small troubles they've had—a lost tourist or two, difficulties in the gardens—are nothing as to what will happen if the situation is not resolved."

She took an unnecessarily vicious bite of the ice cream, braving brain freeze for the satisfaction of it. And as she rolled the Oreos and mint in her mouth, she watched him. Watched his quicksilver eyes, still wincing now and then from the flash of sunlight off a passing windshield or side-view mirror. Watched the tight set of his mouth, for the first time noticing the small scar beneath his lower lip that looked as though he'd once had an offset piercing.

All she found was sincerity. More sincerity than the situation required, truth be told. More intensity. More at stake, somehow, than a lost tourist or a sagging garden. *Things unsaid. Things that mattered to him.* "What's your part in it?" she asked abruptly. "Why do you care enough to come to Albuquerque and track me down not once but twice?"

He sat back in the wrought-iron chair; it creaked in

protest and she suddenly realized that he was bigger than he looked. By then he'd stabbed that flimsy spoon into his softening ice cream and said, "There are generations of spirits in that house. No one's ever cleared them. No one's managed them at all. What do you think will happen if they turn? Do you suppose the house will hold them? Do you think even San Jose can hold them?"

It took a moment for the impact of such potential to hit her. The magnitude of it . . . the raw, wild consequences. Something inside her thrilled to it, enough to inspire guilt. One did not thrill to impending disaster. "You think it's that bad?"

"Would I come to Albuquerque and track you down *not once but twice* if I didn't?"

"Depends," she said, keeping her tone light, "on who paid the bill and how bored you were at the time."

The man smiled with no humor whatsoever, a dark, tight expression. "You'll have to take my word on that. But tell me if I waste my time. I only have so much of it to find someone who will help."

Pride stung, Garrie said, "There's no one as good as me. And you still haven't told me why you care. You, personally. Care."

"I owe someone," he said flatly. No prevarication, no hedging. Just that.

"I need to think," she said just as abruptly. With one future sitting in her lap in the form of a career counseling book, and another sitting across from the table from her.

It doesn't have to be that simple. There's always another session at whatever school wins the McGarrity vocational lottery.

"I have to think," she repeated.

"I don't have long." For someone who'd come looking for help, he was fond of that warning tone.

"Right, right. The end of San Jose as we know it." Flippant words, but too close to the truth—*his* truth, anyway—to judge by his subtle wince. Or maybe someone had just flashed another reflection of sunlight his way. "Give me your name . . . let me know where to find you. I'll get back to you."

"Trevarr," he said, and stood, pushing the spoon-impaled ice cream aside. "And I'll find you."

Lucia's jaw dropped, revealing expensive, pretty white teeth. "He said that? He seriously said that? How very James Bond of him." She made a purring noise, slouched in Garrie's favorite chair—white with narrow green stripes and the best sink-into-me-stuffing ever.

"Don't toy with him," Garrie said sharply. "He's not safe. He's not telling me everything, and I don't know if I believe what he *is* telling me." She put her mug of iced horchata on the rug beside her, leaning back against her not-so-favorite chair. Homemade by Lucia's auntie, the cinnamon-spiced rice milk had been cut by real milk for Garrie's gringo taste buds, and it was her favorite comfort drink in the whole world. Not doing much good on this particular day.

Lucia's oh-so-perceptive eyes narrowed slightly, accenting their almond shape. "And yet you're thinking of doing this? Because don't try to bullshit me. I know you, chicalet." She said it *cheeklet,* and only used the nickname for good effect.

Garrie scowled back at her. "Yeah, I am." She lifted the vocational book from the coffee table before her and let it drop back down onto a pile of fashion magazines—most of them Lucia's, as if providing such things would change the casual-funky nature of Garrie's wardrobe. "Look at this. I'm actually thinking about trotting off to CAD-enhanced drafting courses, or some computer tech thing! Or what the heck. There's picture framing. I kind of like the sound of that."

Lucia shuddered delicately. "If it's a money thing—"

"Don't even go there. I'm good for years if I'm careful. Rhonda Rose lived in a time when a woman was at the mercy of society. No way she was going to let me splurge the income from those early gigs. Jeez, if she'd been born in our generation she'd have a CNN show on investing by now. *Rhonda Rose Knows!*" Garrie gave the book a baleful nudge. "It's just . . . I've got to do *something*. Something *challenging*."

"I don't think the challenging world of framing is quite what you're looking for." Lucia shifted her dreamy focus to the quiescent ceiling fan. "Let's talk more about our friend Trevarr. Tell me how that leather looked in daylight. Talk about his eyes again."

"Silvery. Spooky," Garrie said shortly. "Come on, Lucia. Don't tell me you don't feel it, too. Things have been quiet around here for years. It's all about unsettled human spirits. Big whoop. We haven't seen anything from darkside for over a year, and even then it was just a small pack of glooms."

"This is a *good* thing," Lucia pointed out. Denied the opportunity to revel in the qualities of their mystery visitor, she sat up straight, crossing her legs and pulling a pillow into her lap. Her pink fleece shorts and cap-sleeved, belly-baring matching top disappeared behind it, leaving her looking alarmingly naked.

Juicy Couture. Not a designer about which Garrie would have known five years earlier, when she first met Lucia. Rebellious Latina princess, swamped with relief to have met someone who understood her inexplicable perception of emotions; the only member of the current team to have met Rhonda Rose just before she departed. Now she looked at Garrie with all her five years of experience and repeated, "A *good* thing, Garrie. A nice happy Sim City, no big evils. Maybe we just took care of them all."

Garrie slanted her a disbelieving gaze. "You really believe that?"

Lucia gave it a moment and suggested, "Maybe they all went somewhere else?"

Garrie made a face. "I suppose I could go on the road."

"Road trip!" Lucia practically squealed, and the pillow went flying. "We can track down the bad vibes and play pied piper! Let's start with New York City. I've always wanted to shop in New York City."

"Or," Garrie said, "we could start in San Jose. Where we know there's a problem."

Lucia turned her sternest look upon her. "Garrie," she said, long-suffering. "Who just said he's *not safe*? Much better to talk about his butt and drive off in the opposite direction."

Garrie shrugged. "Can't have it both ways," she said. "Here I am, whining about boredom and potential—I can't turn away from the most interesting thing to happen in ages just because it comes with a little potential sting. None of the reckoning comes with a guarantee— you know that."

"Yeah?" Lucia said. "Well, this one comes with a warning label."

Garrie knew he was there as soon as she pushed out the condo's back exit, black and bulging Hefty sack in hand, dressed in her scantiest of running outfits. She knew because she saw the cat, slipping shadowlike from stairwell to the trash bin.

She didn't get the cat thing, but she accepted it. They had a connection, those two. It wasn't the strangest thing she'd seen, even if she would have thought to find this particular man with a sleek Doberman or staunch Rottweiler.

"Wow," she said, flinging the trash into the cinderblock-enclosed bin and not even bothering to look for him. "This is so sexy. Waiting for me by the Dumpster."

"Yes or no?" he said, offering no more preamble than she. He stood in the shadows, of course, just around the corner of the building. The top of his head just barely made its own shadow, protruding into the sunshine.

"Jeez, you never heard of foreplay?"

And he said nothing, so she sighed dramatically and went to lean on her own corner, the one in the sunshine. Close enough to touch, close enough to smell the leather, but out of sight. Dramatic, yeah. "I have to talk to my people."

"I don't need your people. I need you."

"So charming," she muttered. "You might not need them, but I want them. We're a team. That's how I work."

"Not always."

How the hell—? "We're talking now, not then," she said sharply. "I've already got Lucia." *Play your cards right, and* you've *got Lucia, too.* "I want to talk to the others. We're talking road trip here. It's not a small decision for them."

"We'll fly," he said.

"No kidding. You gonna sprout wings and take us all away?"

In the silence that followed, Garrie had a momentary and horrible premonition that he would say yes. But then, that's why she was a reckoner and not a precog, because he actually said, patience grinding his voice a little lower, "Airline tickets. For all of you, if that's what it takes."

"Fine." She made her voice so cheery that he couldn't possibly believe that she'd bought his patience act. "I'll get answers before the day's out. Can you live with that?"

He hesitated so long that she suddenly remembered what he'd said over not-eating ice cream. *I owe someone.* Just *how much* did he owe someone?

And what would he pay if he didn't come through?

The cat, still tucked away somewhere, made a querulous noise. Trevarr straightened—she heard the brush of leather against stucco, saw the shift in his exposed shadow—and said, "I'll be back."

She opened her mouth to say something smart, but he'd somehow already gone. So she just muttered,

"Wrong accent," and amused herself by practicing the classic Schwarzenegger line all the way to her condo.

In the wrong accent.

Sklayne knew the others would come. They'd come for the Garrie person—and he'd heard it in her voice, felt it in her very presence . . . she'd be there. She hungered for it, thirsted for it . . . needed it. A small person wrapped around much power.

As was Sklayne himself.

She wouldn't even know what she wasn't seeing at that besieged house, immersed as it was in roiling spirits. She might sense it, but she wouldn't identify it. Wouldn't focus on it. Would never know the real stakes, the true action occurring in layers just out of her reach. She'd do her part, leaving Trevarr free to do his.

And then Sklayne and Trevarr could go home. Not in disgrace, not in trouble, not denied the chance to fulfill Blood Honor.

Home.

5

Ascertain your ethereal destination before embarkation.
— **Rhonda Rose**

Maps are your friends.
—**Lisa McGarrity**

Garrie shifted in the airline seat, wishing it reclined just another degree or even that her feet reached the ground. Finally she kicked off her low-heeled Sketchers and pulled her knees to her chest, sighing as the plane straightened out to level flight, darkness pressing in against the windows. *Wow. Zero to sixty in no seconds flat.* And she wasn't thinking about the plane.

Beside her in the middle seat, Trevarr didn't appear to notice. With his ever-present sunglasses still in place, he'd closed his eyes at takeoff, reclined the seat, and now appeared to sleep, buffered all around by the muted roar of the plane's engines and his own personal assumption of space.

Looking at him, at the tension in his face and the faint flair of naturally defined nostrils, Garrie quite suddenly realized that her new client didn't like to fly. She wouldn't go so far as to use the word *afraid,* but only because it didn't apply to the man who'd so suddenly tempted her with reckoner excitement.

In fact, to judge by his careful assessment of minor air travel details—the overhead compartments, the seatback trays, the seat-reclining controls, the various exit doors and furnishings of the plane—she was tempted to think he'd never flown before at all.

But that didn't make any sense.

Still, when she shifted again, she was careful not to disturb him. The businessman in the window seat had taken much the same tack; although he worked a diminutive EeePC minilaptop, he'd still managed to squish himself into the corner away from Trevarr. Garrie caught him eyeing Trevarr, from tonight's neatly clipped-back hair to the black duster to the high, worn boots. The man perceived her regard. Rather than look away, he shared an expression that meant *Can you believe this guy?*

He hadn't noticed they were together. Not surprising, given the utter absence of casual conversation once they'd boarded. Garrie gave the man the faintest of shrugs, the faintest of smiles. *Yeah. Go figure.* She amused herself with the thought that under other circumstances, the businessman wouldn't have given the young woman with the blue-streaked hair a second glance.

Her thigh cramped; she stretched it out and then tucked her foot beneath her, yoga in an airplane seat. And she knew in her heart that her restlessness didn't come from sitting in an uncomfortable seat beside an uncomfortable-making man, but because two rows behind her, in the only other adjoining seats available on the flight, sat only two of her reckoners.

She didn't even have to look to see Lucia, happily planning her shopping goals, headphones attached and no doubt filling her head with Enrique Iglesias. Years of dealing with undirected, unrecognized talents had defined those coping mechanisms, that perfect facade of a shallow young woman. And Drew beside her, his daily stubble shaved except for a spot that this evening looked suspiciously like an incipient soul patch. *Yuck. Not on my watch.* He'd had a rolled-up *Archaeology* in his back pocket when they boarded; no doubt he was already deeply engrossed.

But not Quinn. Quinn, with whom she'd once had an early, brief affair and now counted as a friend—and perhaps on whom she now counted more deeply than she'd thought. Brilliant mind for detail as long as it wasn't anything mundane; the one who usually provided the crucial piece that pulled a case together.

The team felt unaccountably incomplete without him. And playing the moment over again in her mind, Garrie felt both completely taken by surprise—and as if she should have known all along.

"Can you do the job without him?" Trevarr asked her, not turning his head or so much as twitching in his seat. Not so asleep after all. The businessman startled at that deep voice with its faint accent, giving Garrie a look of faint betrayal. She met it without qualms; he had made the assumptions, not she. And she didn't pretend she didn't know what Trevarr meant.

"He's right," she said. "He can't run out on the store now."

This time he did look at her, tipping his head just enough so she knew it, sunglasses notwithstanding. "Not what I asked." But his voice held little in the way of challenge, and more understanding than she'd expected.

Instead of returning his gaze, she looked at the bouffant hair of the older lady across the aisle and one row ahead of them. Not a color found in nature. "He's right," she repeated—more like admitted, and a little sad about it at that. "He can probably do this better by phone than on site. As long as we can be his eyes . . ." But who knew what Quinn saw when he looked at something—what he noticed? What he took back to his books?

Trevarr's hand rested beside hers on the armrest, startling her; she stared at it, finding nothing more than long fingers and blunt hard nails, a certain amount of long-term hard living written across the knuckles.

"I need this," he said, words lacking their previous demand now that he had the *this*.

"You've said."

He tipped his head down slightly. "You need this, too."

"You don't know us." Garrie's troubled response lacked fervency; she searched him out behind those sunglasses and found only herself. "You just met us." But his words had gotten to her anyway, deeper than she'd wanted them to—deeper than she'd expected them to. "I just wish . . ."

He lowered his voice, as if before he hadn't cared that their neighbor might overhear and now he did. "It's not easy," he said. "The leaving. But sometimes necessary."

She hunted for equilibrium. Hard enough on the ground, but in midair? *Hah.* "You're an expert?"

His face hardened a little . . . but only a little, there

and gone again, as if he fought to keep something from the surface. His hand tightened beside hers. "An amateur."

Oh-ho. But she didn't push. Kindness, she thought, deserved kindness. And so together they sank back into their thoughts, regrets both separate and yet now somehow shared.

I just wish . . .

Because it had not gone as she'd expected.

Drew greeted Garrie outside the early evening Albu-querque airline ticket counter lines, hauling a framed hiking backpack stuffed to capacity. "Come to the airport?" He said, repeating the words of her short phone call. "Pack for a couple of days of easy San Jose weather and come to the airport? That's A-B, Garrie. Way A-B."

Garrie shifted her secondhand overnighter tote on her shoulder and looked at Lucia, eyebrow raised.

"Ass backward," Lucia murmured, busy with her BlackBerry. Her expression lit up, Lucia-the-beautiful on shopping endorphins. "Union Square in San Francisco!" she said. "Coach, Gucci, Prada . . . and street performers on the side. What's not to like?" She looked up just in time to catch Garrie eyeing her bag, a giant black, sleek Andiamo made from ballistic nylon and leather. "Get real," she said. "There's barely more than a change of undies in there. That's for what I bring *back*."

"There's Quinn," Drew said, nodding at the travelers trickling in through the revolving main departures door. Quinn was easy to spot, tall and blond and moving without hurry.

Without luggage, too.

"Not going," he said without preamble as he approached the group. Lucia frowned, as if unable to comprehend the words, and Drew's mouth opened—but he glanced at Garrie and closed it.

For the words landed hard on Garrie, hard enough to rock her. "Quinn . . ." Gahh, pathetic. She cleared her throat, and said more brusquely, "You're sure? We'll need you."

"I'll finish up the patio house job," he said, not meeting her eyes. Not hard; he just didn't look down. He and Trevarr were the same height, but Quinn had nothing of Trevarr's faint menace—none of the *whatever it takes* about him. The oldest of them at twenty-seven, an easygoing guy who liked to keep his brain, extraordinary repository of reckoner trivia, as busy as possible. He finally looked at her. "Besides, my library doesn't exactly travel lightly . . . none of that stuff is on e-book yet. I can be of more help here." He held up his cell, waggling it slightly.

He was right, of course. And yet . . .

Garrie looked over her shoulder, found Trevarr in line at the ticket counter, his impatience palpable as he inched closer to the Southwest counter, watching them—waiting for conclusions. The travelers lined up in front and behind had left a noticeable buffer zone around him.

She didn't blame them.

"Look, chicalet," Lucia said, voice quiet. "You know I'm in. The shopping, right?" As if she hadn't been with Garrie before the others had come on board, and as if she wouldn't have gone on regardless. "But it's maybe time to spill, yes?"

"Right," Drew said. "Let's hear the four-one-one."

Garrie thought about asking him if he knew he was actually a nerdy white college student, and then she thought about borrowing Lucia's makeup mirror to *show* him he was a nerdy white college student, and then—as she had so many other times—she just let it alone. She'd get over it. Again. And it was really just her mood, her ongoing discovery that the status quo was possibly no longer the status quo.

"San Jose," she said. "Winchester House. Our friend from last night was for real. He's willing to pay our way."

"Winchester Mystery House?" Quinn said, and not as though it was a good thing.

Garrie spoke quickly, overriding his pending reaction. "Look," she said, "I know what you're thinking. It's a big fat hairy tourist trap. But what've we got to lose? It's a free trip. There's shopping for Lucia. And whether or not the reckoning pans out, Drew, you *know* there's gonna be history behind the place." Oh my God, she sounded desperate.

She *was* desperate.

There was a pause as they all made silent note of the *desperate.*

Garrie gritted her teeth and fought the impulse to walk to the nearest wall and bang her head against it.

Then Quinn cleared his throat. "Winchester Mystery House," he said, taking on his recitation voice. "Thirty-eight years in construction, completed in September 1922. Seven stories until the 1906 earthquake; four remaining. Two basements, forty bedrooms, forty staircases, nine hundred fifty doors—"

"Too bad you can't remember your mother's birthday," Garrie said. Good old Quinn, giving her a chance to fall into old patterns . . . old equilibrium. But—

"You're sure?"

He shrugged, not looking at her again. "I had to ask for extra hours at the bookstore. I can't just walk away from that."

"And I'm gonna miss some classes," Drew said. Part-time student since their work had slacked off, he nurtured dreams of morphing into Indiana Jones, applying his extra sense of history to great archaeological discoveries—even if he struggled to restrain his talents in a setting that didn't acknowledge them. "So details would be good."

"The house works," Garrie said simply. "Just as Mrs.

Winchester wanted. The ghosts are really there. But something's gone wrong and they're turning dark—and it's about to get out of control." She suppressed a little frisson of excitement, the guilty wish that Trevarr had truly assessed the situation correctly.

Quinn eyed Trevarr, and his genial gaze went harder than Garrie had ever seen it. "Says the guy who stalked you into coming with him?" As if he could hear from that distance, Trevarr stiffened, turned his head to look directly at Quinn, sunglasses barely cutting the force of his regard. Garrie squelched an astonishing impulse to throw herself between them, blocking direct line of sight—except she would have had to grow a foot or so to do it.

"Hey," she said sharply, startling Quinn into glancing her way. "If it's for real, then we're stopping disaster. If it's not, we've got a free ride to San Jose."

"I've always wanted to see the Winchester House," Lucia said, her voice somewhat smaller than usual.

"Dude," Drew said, earnestly, "the *history* in that place."

Quinn looked at them all a moment, glanced at Trevarr again, and shook his head slightly. "Yeah," he said. "Just make sure they're round-trip tickets."

And Garrie turned to Trevarr, briefly displaying three fingers. He gave the slightest of nods and moved ahead to the ticket counter. She had no doubt he'd somehow acquire three last-flight tickets to San Jose.

She turned back to her reckoners, and found herself looking at Quinn's back as he walked away.

And she could still see it. Standing in the baggage claim area with night covering the plate glass windows along the exterior wall, waiting for Lucia to grab her suitcase and Drew to find his backpack, she could still see Quinn walking away.

It makes sense. Of course he stayed. And still . . .

"What happened to the cat?" she asked Trevarr. As if it was truly the most important thing about the moment.

It drew his attention from where he stood by the exterior wall, somehow all but blending into a support column while he eyed the room from that vantage point, his sunglasses back in place. Something akin to humor lurked in a face much more relaxed—if no less alert—than it had been on the plane. "Not my cat."

"Oh, please. It followed you across town."

The humor remained, but he only lifted one shoulder in a shrug by way of an answer. By way of a *not*-answer. And Garrie wanted to call him on it, to draw the line—that if they were to work together, she'd need answers.

But she couldn't bring herself to do it over a cat.

Trevarr shifted slightly, the faint humor gone; Garrie followed his apparent gaze—hard to be sure behind those dark lenses—and discovered Lucia smartly trundling her suitcase along on its little wheels and already heading for the door and the nighttime car lane chaos of dodging taxis and bright overhead lights. They joined as a group, their first real chance to talk since the rush to make the flight.

"We'll be at the Moorpark," Garrie told them. "We've got adjoining rooms. Club Queen."

Lucia gave Trevarr a quick, assessing glance. "On his nickel?"

Garrie heard Lucia's unspoken words well enough. *On the hottie's nickel?* She turned to her friend and mouthed, *Not safe,* complete with exaggerated frown. Never mind that her face still bore the imprint of his shoulder where she'd fallen asleep on the plane.

"Hey," Lucia said, understanding perfectly. She flipped sleek black hair over her shoulder. "You're the one who brought us here."

Drew, recovering from the jostle of someone moving

through the pedestrian flow, sent them both a baffled look. "What . . . ?"

"Secret girl stuff," Lucia said easily.

"Never mind, then." Drew adjusted his backpack, hastily uninterested just in case the word *tampon* should be involved. Lucia rolled her eyes at Garrie, a *men are so easy* signal, and aimed herself at the curb.

And then Trevarr, stalking along slightly in front of them . . .

Trevarr *moved*.

In fact, as a young man slid past them, shouldering sideways to skim through the crowd, Trevarr quite suddenly turned predator. Lightning fast, his hand clamped down on the tender spot where the young man's neck joined his shoulder, stopping him so suddenly that his feet took several steps to get the message and so nearly went out from under him.

Garrie instantly opened herself to complete ethereal awareness, hunting additional threats. A hazy gloom of a darkside presence clung to the back of a man headed across the street for the parking garage; skittering movement in the carefully landscaped bushes at the edge of the parking structure itself caught her eye. But nothing hovered around this young man in particular, and she came off ethereal alert to find herself merely curious— not to mention in the way, their little group disrupting pedestrian flow. Tired evening travelers moved around them, muttering imprecations; Garrie shuffled them forward slightly, a little closer to their untamed escort.

Trevarr pulled his sunglasses off, hooking them through the second buttonhole with one hand. He stared hard at his captive—looking down at him, looking quite suddenly larger than him in every way. The young man glared up into Trevarr's gaze and started visibly, and he seemed all but pinned there as Trevarr—expectantly, implacably—held out his hand.

"Garrie," Drew muttered in her ear—okay, above

her ear, but she heard him. Garric gave her head the slightest shake—*Let him play this out.* Less muss, less fuss . . .

And more to feed her hungry curiosity.

The young man's original indignance wilted. Damn, no . . . *melted.* Pulling his hand from his pocket, he held out a . . . Garrie frowned. A necklace? Strung on a braided cord that gleamed scaly black in the mercury lighting, a heavy metal disk dangled out in the open— but only for an instant. Trevarr scooped it up and deposited it in the pocket of his duster with the ease of long practice. He tipped his head toward Drew, offering his first staccato words of the encounter. "His, too."

Behind Garrie, Drew stiffened and began patting his pockets—a search aborted when the young man meekly held out a battered brown wallet. The moment Drew took it, the thwarted pickpocket glanced at Trevarr—an instant of indecision—and then made a break for it, sprinting wildly across to the roadway to the blast of blaring horns and the squeal of brakes.

"How—" Drew said.

"Wow," Lucia said.

"Show-off," Garrie muttered, not meant to be heard. But she felt again the faint wash of power she'd discerned at the Albuquerque ice cream parlor, and Trevarr turned to meet her gaze head on, holding it.

She could have sworn she saw that faint spark of humor, returned to the silver of his eyes.

But he only nodded at the curb and the flow of traffic and said, "I've found that taxi drivers rarely stop for me."

"Oh, I'll do that," Lucia said, and rolled her suitcase out of the disturbed pedestrian flow, leaving it in Drew's care as she stepped up to the curb, skinny jeans and baby-doll top, Albuquerque girl already gone California dreamin'.

And Trevarr looked at Garrie and she was sure of it.

Somewhere inside that intimidating exterior, a smile lurked.

Sklayne waited.

And waited.

He thought *cat,* and took that form through dry desert hillsides north of the city where Trevarr had left him. He met with a skinny doglike creature on long legs with a hungry gleam in its eye.

He thought *big* and watched the creature skitter away.

But not very far away. Sklayne, too, was hungry.

::Silty alkaline soil, dark thin night, crunch of bone:: Doglike creature no more.

In the darkness, a human giggle, feminine and beguiling. A deeper voice, beguiled. Coming into Sklayne's waiting place, this private area beside the big homes that thought much of themselves.

Sklayne consulted his stomach. Full enough.

And Trevarr wouldn't approve. Trevarr would say *hide.*

Sklayne, being contrary, hid by not hiding. He let himself go from the *cat,* a quick push of being everything abruptly condensed into the energy that was only Sklayne, invisibly hovering right where he'd been. Unnoticed.

The male human dropped a blanket to the ground with careless distraction, sweeping the female up in his arms to the sound of that throaty giggle.

More interesting than the crunch of bone, oh, yes. Sklayne extended himself to hover beside them, tasting, so startled by those flying human feelings and sensations that he snapped back as if overstretched, fizzy-feeling bubbles popping inside his head, his favorite internalized cat self going *yow!*

Oh, tasty! Why had Trevarr not told him of this adventure? The giggles, the soft lip and body noises, the happy groans . . . Prepared this time, Sklayne expanded himself and hovered closer, still entirely undetected by these preoccupied humans who had no sight to see him anyway.

Tug.

No! Sklayne hissed faintly, a sizzle of grounding electricity that the humans might have noticed if they weren't so full of *oh!* and *yes!* and *now, baby, now!*

Tug.

Sklayne made a mouth, enough of a mouth to go, "Mow!" in protest.

But Trevarr was his. His being, and his responsibility. *Sklayne's,* and no others.

Tug.

"Mow!" said the mouth, and Sklayne went. He found the nearest power line, the anchor around which he'd confined his meanderings, a stark tower rising out of parched scrubby desert. Already distracted from his human diversion, already homing in the lines that would lead him to a subtle but familiar call from Trevarr. So convenient, these contained highways of power. They fed him even as they transported him.

He subsumed himself in the correct line, the best line, and the sensations of a New Mexico night went flat and distant; happy fizz sparkled at the edges of his awareness. ::Shiny!:: He gamboled along the way, moving faster than thought and yet tumbling within himself, snagging at the fizz. Catching the fizz, eating it. A fine refreshing dessert after the doglike creature.

Far too soon, he emerged before Trevarr, popping out of the wall socket into an unfamiliar room. Trevarr's room, already marked by tiny amulets in the corners. Sklayne perceived them without distinct effort; perceived the others nearby. The small person of great power and the companions of smaller, quieter presence.

"What by Kehar were you doing?" Trevarr asked, crouched by the wall, his finger still lightly touching the socket where he'd extended his call. He stood, shaking his head. "No. I don't want to know. The cat, please."

Sklayne thought *cat*. Much with the ears.

"Better," Trevarr said, and went so far as to run his knuckles from the cat head to the cat tail. Sklayne was horrified as the cat spine, of its own accord, arched to the touch.

Trevarr failed to notice, however. Trevarr was already looking at the door between the two rooms, the door beyond which the small person sat. Sklayne felt it again, felt it stronger—the tension. The guilt. And now, regret. And what by Kehar's tiny little man-parts— *what*—

Guilt and regret and the strange tight taste of fizzy—

::No. No, no, *no*.::

Sklayne wanted to go home. Sklayne wanted the guilt gone and the tension restored to the fierce focus of the hunt. Not things that would happen if Trevarr diverted himself here, if he liked what he tasted—if he even *realized* what he tasted. And Sklayne said, ::She is what you need.::

Trevarr looked down at him, a little surprised and a little resistant.

Sklayne wound between his ankles with a commanding, upright tail. ::*Use* herrrr.::

6

Know your spiritual boundaries.
—Rhonda Rose

Good fences make good neighbors.
—Lisa McGarrity

The sudden gust of ethereal breeze, close and unexpected, jarred Garrie out of her meditative state and brought her back to the here and now, eyes still closed. She sat cross-legged on the overstuffed chair in the corner of the classy, mahogany-appointed room, leaving Lucia sprawled across one bed looking at the room service menu and Drew's lanky body testing just how much of the other queen bed he could take up—though not for long, to judge by the sound of it now. His voice seemed suddenly to come from the roomy bathroom, echoing against the stone floor and countertop.

"Check it out! Dryer, coffeemaker . . . on top of the DVD player! Way phat! And a robe—there's a robe in here!"

"You can't say *way phat,*" Lucia told him. "You're totally mixing cultures. Eras, even. And there'd *better* be a robe, because I didn't pack one. But this *is* nice—their free breakfast is white rice, miso soup, and tofu. Más guay!"

"We got takeout," Drew objected, his voice louder as he emerged from the bathroom; he threw himself back down on the bed and commenced to rustle among crumpled bags. "I bet we could kind of warm it up on the coffeemaker plate, too."

"Oh. My. *Dios,*" Lucia muttered. "We will *not.* And while we're at it, there will be no crude man stuff while we're sharing this room. No freeform burping, farting, armpit noises, snoring, or failing to brush your teeth in the morning. You got something outstandingly smelly to do? Clench your cheeks and find the public bathroom."

"Jeez," Drew muttered, subdued. "Maybe I should stay next door with Trevarr."

Dead silence followed that statement.

"Good," Lucia finally said, deadpan. "Let's just knock on that door and ask him, yes?"

"Um." Drew's voice shrank. "Clenching."

Good choice, Drew. Not that it was fair to put him in a room with Lucia in princess mode. Garrie dealt with it after years of long practice, but Drew . . . Drew had no defenses.

And not, she was beginning to see, that there was only one side to Trevarr. She'd seen that humor at the airport, she was sure of it—even if it had come after a serious moment of full scary mode. But then as they'd hunted down food, scary Trevarr had been the one who thought to include the tired driver in the drive-through order. He'd been the one to—

This isn't getting the job done.

She'd been running a wide sweep before that unexpected smack of breeze had knocked her out of it. Spreading herself thin, casting out over the entire San Jose area. But now the breeze was gone, and she should go back to work.

She knew the lay of the land in New Mexico—the *ethereal* lay of the land. The bright spots, the dark spots . . . the sticky places and the unpredictable ones— she knew them all, in a permanent internal map. It was a job made considerably easier by the fact that she strictly respected the reservation boundaries. The ethereal world felt much different within Native American lands, and she wasn't uppity enough to pretend otherwise. *Know your spiritual boundaries,* Rhonda Rose had told her . . . advice with many layers of meaning, all of which Garrie took to heart. For it was her job, in the big picture, to rebuild weak fences in the ethereal map, as well as usher trespassers away.

And that meant that here, in this new place, her first order of business was to get a sense of the ethereal map. So she settled herself, allowing the conversation between Lucia and Drew to fall away into the background, and she opened herself to the breezes—cautiously at first, until she confirmed that the gusty little activity nearby had settled. She was tempted to hunt for it, to identify it—but patterns were the important thing at the moment. Patterns, and not individual blips and breezes. So she pulled herself back to wide focus, let herself sink away from analytical thought . . . thought of herself as a giant spy satellite over San Jose, assessing the big picture of the ethereal activity.

She found the frenetic and obvious—downtown, as it often was, and following the ridges of the dry brown ranges surrounding the city. She found pools of silence, and, toward the south where the ground turned fertile and green, bright happiness. Little green smiley faces for the southern area, yeah.

San Jose in general proved to be a happy ethereal place. The blots of darkness were hazy, the deep darkness confined to individual spots that made Garrie long to investigate . . . to *fix*.

But she was here for a reason, and she'd found it. There, in central San Jose: a roiling haze of not darkness, but colors—colors so thoroughly mixed as to be mud, with intense bubbles of purity popping up only long enough for a glimpse before the mud consumed them. *Trevarr was right.* Whatever it was . . . it wasn't good. Wasn't good *at all*.

Unwittingly, she drifted closer, drawn in by the riptide breeze of it. Unwittingly, she focused in, until it was no longer just the sight of it, but the smell of it and the sound of it. Fetid swamp breezes cut by slices of sharp citrus, a dank pressure against her awareness, a low grind of protest.

The screams, when they came, clamped onto her like a leg-hold trap. Deep moans spiraled rapidly upward over a demanding rumble, tangling furiously within her—stealing her thought, stealing her calm. Stealing even the *run away, fool!* The muttered cacophony built, snarling, and then burst into a sudden shriek of sound, a chorus made of voices below bass and beyond ultrasonic and everything in between, buzzing and twining and reverberating into complete incomprehensibility—

—And she couldn't think or move or even flee, and still the sound climbed and spiraled and battered away until she joined it, screaming into her own head, entangled in the chorus—

"Garrie!"

The sound cut off. Cut off flat, the only remnants of it the strangled noise she made in her own throat.

She filled her lungs, ignoring the leftover whimper she made on the way. And then she smelled the leather, realized she no longer sat in the chair but on the hard floor and against hard muscle. She would have stiffened, had she the energy. Instead she opened her eyes and tried for a scowl.

She found Lucia, crowding close, precise features charged with worry. Beside her, Drew, his lank hair askew and eyes all puppy-dog big and by God that *was* a soul patch.

"Garrie." The voice, again, was Trevarr's—rumbling both in her ear and against her back. He held her with care, with consideration; one hand supported her head. She looked up at him in surprise—at being there, at what she'd experienced . . . that she'd been caught up in it at all.

His concern, writ so clear, quickly shuttered away. "You're all right."

"I'm back," she agreed, not quite answering the question, because she wasn't all right—she was mad. Mad at Lisa McGarrity, reckoner extraordinaire. Damned careless reckoner, that's what. Arrogant, Rhonda Rose would have called it. Mad, and . . . and . . .

Yeah. And scared.

She barely felt his hands tighten—at the back of her head, around her shoulders, and maybe she only just imagined it—before his hold lightened considerably. Carefully, not wanting to put her hands anywhere she *really* didn't want to put her hands, she disentangled herself, ending up on her knees not far away even as he straightened himself out beside her.

Her gaze went inward a moment . . . the echo of the screams, bouncing around in her mind until they somehow, all on their own, resolved into a faint clarity. No words, still too distorted for that, but . . . a plea for help, a demand for surcease, a roar of fury . . .

"Garrie?" Lucia asked, voice as worried as her face. "Are you okay? What happened, chicalet?"

Garrie pulled herself together, applied some firmness to her voice, and knew before she spoke that it hadn't taken. "He's right," she said, still wavering—speaking to Lucia and Drew, although it was Trevarr's silver gaze she met head-on. "He's totally farkin' right."

"Define *right*," Lucia said, a wary look in her eyes.

The Winchester House loomed large before them, with only the charming little ticket booth between them and the landscaped front grounds. Lush trees, lawn, flower beds and bushes, standing out as a green island in the middle of brown, brown summer San Jose.

And Garrie felt no alarm. No darkness. No roiling swamp of muddy color, no thought-shattering chorus of resentment.

Then again, she was hardly putting herself out there. *Shields up, Mr. Scott!* She tugged at the hair just behind her ear. *Chicken.*

"Garrie?" Lucia hovered beside her, clutching her satin Louis Vuitton Love tote. The violet color set off her skin perfectly, of course, and matched the sunglasses perched at the top of her head. "Because I brought some Baggies, but I don't have enough for Armageddon, you know?"

"Lu, we've been through this." Garrie couldn't keep the irritation out of her voice—not quite. If Lucia remained anxious about the events of the evening before, Garrie wasn't the one with comfort to give. Not after the night she'd spent *not* sleeping in the wake of her unexpected contact. "Last night, I went knocking. Today, we're tourists."

"Quinn!" Drew said behind them, using the kind of cell phone voice that made everyone else part of the conversation whether they wanted it or not. "Yeah, we're here. We're about to go in."

At the head of the line, decked out in that leather duster and somehow not discomfited by the rising heat of San Jose's summer morning any more than he'd been by Albuquerque's dry desert afternoon, Trevarr turned to look at him. Hidden behind the sunglasses, shadowed by the booth's extended roof . . .

He, too, seemed to be thinking of the evening before.

"It's quiet," Garrie told him. She took another look around—bright green landscaping, gathered splashes of living color and stone sculpture and wrought iron, the tired, grayed asphalt parking lot behind them, the massive café-au-lait house with its striking red roof and ocher and brown trim—all washed out by the morning sun, all looking oddly veiled to Garrie's eyes. She dared to ease open her vision and yet saw nothing else. She looked back at Trevarr, found him attentive, shook her head slightly. "I mean . . . it's *really* quiet. I would have expected . . ."

"There's no one here?" Lucia whispered, looking around them.

"Yeah, the hotel is great!" Drew said loudly. "You should've come, maybe we could have had a room to ourselves, and then I wouldn't have to worry so much about—"

Lucia, swift to shift gears, discreetly kicked him with her pointy-toed flat. The shoe's cute little braided metal details jingled slightly; Drew's jaw dropped. Trevarr took two long strides and acquired the cell phone. "He will talk to you later," he told Quinn, and snapped the phone shut.

Behind them, the short tail of the line offered a smattering of applause as Trevarr held the phone out. Lucia took it and tucked it into Drew's front shirt pocket. "They didn't want to hear it, either," she informed him sweetly.

The ticket booth associate, perhaps sensing restlessness among the visitors, slid into place a few moments early. He processed Trevarr's payment with undue speed, and the reckoners plus one moved into the tiny courtyard between the booth and the gift shop with its attached café.

"I'm gonna check out the gift shop," Drew said, giving Trevarr wide berth. "Might be able to, um—" he glanced at the family coming through from the booth— "pick something up."

"I'm gonna hang," Garrie said. "Come get me when they're going to start the tour, will you?"

"I'll get you," Lucia said, noting Drew's already retreating back. "I'm going to see if the café has anything that can be called coffee. *Y tú?*"

"Don't think they'll let us take anything in," Garrie said absently, eyeing a flicker of darkness easing through a heavily trimmed juniper. "I'll wait."

Unexpectedly, Trevarr added, "See if they have Dr Pepper." He pulled a wad of bills from his pocket, tugged one free, and would have handed it to Lucia if she hadn't laughed.

"This'll do," she said, and plucked another from his hand. "Be back in a mo." She turned crisply on her heel, threading her way past the two families that also negotiated their tour-waiting time outside the gift shop.

Garrie targeted the rejected money. "A hundred? You were going to give her a hundred for a soda?"

He returned the money to his front pants pocket in pointed silence. Then, "Is it truly quiet?"

They'd drifted into the shade of a tree already, but Garrie kept her sunglasses on—polarization was a reckoner's friend. Her gaze caught the two families lingering in the area. They knew each other, she realized—that had given them the boldness to offer their smatter of applause. But now the two fathers stood together, and while the mothers wrangled the kids—juice boxes, a last smear of sunblock, an admonition to stay together on the tour—the fathers eyed Trevarr, muttering in a disgruntled manner. Sensing the not-safe.

Smart dads.

Both looked to be in their early thirties; Silicon Valley types who hadn't seen a gym in a while, but who probably didn't quite yet realize that it made a difference. One actually put himself between them and the children, protectiveness written all over his office-pale face. The other hesitated, looking over his shoulder as if he thought maybe, just maybe, he should strike up a conversation.

Ohh, let's not go there. So many ways that could go wrong.

She could step between them . . . but as with Quinn, her height would render such a move ineffective. She could draw him off into the shade. She could pretend to faint.

"I see them," Trevarr said. "They are not why I'm here."

And what, exactly, did that mean?

"Tell me what you see," Trevarr said, no less a demand than if his voice hadn't been low and downright pleasant.

It raised her hackles. "You," she informed him, "are *not* the boss of me."

It was the wrong thing to say—she knew it was and she did it anyway, helplessly watching herself in the process. Wrong not because of Trevarr's reaction, but because the dads noticed, their concern escalating, finding in her upset response an excuse to approach Trevarr, to remind him this was a family event. To draw lines that he shouldn't step over.

And then Trevarr laughed.

Laughed.

It was a low sound, easy and truly amused. He reached out to the side of her face, smoothed a spiky piece of her hair, and somehow turned the movement into a touch that glided along her jaw.

Garrie couldn't have moved if she'd been told that hair was on fire. If she'd been shoved. If she'd been *propelled*. No. She was rooted to the spot with astonishment.

And even as his hand withdrew, as she kicked herself for not recovering fast enough to slap it aside, she felt the tension from the family group dissolve. A glance showed her that the dads had relaxed and turned back to their families.

"*You*," she said, in barely more than an outraged whisper, "you did that *on purpose*."

He regarded her evenly from behind those dark lenses. "I did it for many reasons."

"Yeah?" She found herself shaking. That was stupid. This wasn't worth shaking over. What happened the evening before, yes. Here in the bright daytime with no darkside creatures in evidence and all ghosts quiet . . . no. With great effort, she kept her body language neutral, her voice low. No point in stirring the dads up again. "Well, *don't*. Again, I mean. *Ever*, I mean."

He tipped his head infinitesimally; she had absolutely no idea what it meant. But the humor was back, and that couldn't be good. "Tell me," he said. "Is it truly quiet?"

Yes, it was quiet. Good and truly quiet. Way too . . . farking . . . quiet.

"There should be a spirit or two." Garrie opened herself a little more, lifting her face to receive the faintest of ethereal breezes.

Nothing.

On sudden impulse, she gathered power from within herself, aimed a soft shove at Trevarr. He took a startled step back, stiffening with surprise. His reaction flickered across his face so quickly that Garrie couldn't read him, not at all. He closed his eyes—she saw it faintly, behind the sweep of those dark lenses—his mouth tightened, nostrils flaring, jaw clenching.

And then it was gone, and he said flatly, "Don't."

But she'd seen it, and whatever mix of distrust and resentment and intrigue he'd offered, she hadn't meant to hurt him. Quick guilt washed over her, the same honest guilt she'd felt that day Rhonda Rose swooped down upon her and told her she'd been causing pain in the ethereal realm with her childhood games.

"I'm sorry," she said. "I was only testing. There aren't any breezes . . . there aren't any ghosts. Never mind what this place is supposed to be, pretty much anywhere has a ghost or two hanging around, and everywhere has its own currents. I just wanted to—"

She stopped herself from babbling. "I didn't mean to hurt you. I won't do it again."

"You didn't hurt me," he said shortly, but he wasn't looking at her. "What about last night? Do you feel that?"

Garrie made a face. "I'm not that deep," she said. "And I don't want to be. Not here. I'll go through the house, assess it at this level. If I go deep again, it'll be from the hotel—and this time, we'll be prepared."

As if anyone could be prepared for *that*.

Sklayne prowled the hotel room.

::Bored.::

Far too small, this room. Sklayne himself was not a large entity, but he was an entity of large and restless curiosity. The vast desert suited him better. And so leaping from lightbulb to lightbulb quickly grew monotonous; employing the precise kinetic energy to burn neatly scripted words into the half-finished newspaper crossword puzzle on the Drew person's bed took far too little time.

Trevarr would be displeased with him for that. But Trevarr shouldn't have left him here. Trevarr should have known the one room was too small. That the *two* rooms were too small.

Here. The bathroom. Most entertaining. Scents and colors in a copious pile, all belonging to the empathic one. Slopped at the edge of the sink, sitting in the torn wrapper, the hard little hotel soap used by the Drew person. Off in the corner, a neat kit with oooh softly scented soap. ::Soft, soft, tan with speckles, tickle-scented, purr-making oh soap hug::

Soap no more. Oh.

Maybe the small person wrapped around much power wouldn't notice.

It was Trevarr's fault. Trevarr should have known the one room was too small.

Trevarr should have allowed Sklayne to go hunting, too.

He'd said there'd be no hunting for any of them this day. Just looking. But Sklayne knew better. And Sklayne should have been there. Helping with the hunt.

Protecting.

He'd been here the night before, hadn't he? Felt the

cries of the small person wrapped around power? The surge of Trevarr's alarm-concern-guilt?

Stupid, the guilt. The small person proved only that Trevarr was right to be here. That he had the right trail. That if he followed it, they could go home.

Stupid, to follow that trail without Sklayne.

But the smaller person would detect him. Trevarr said so; Sklayne knew so. As cat, he could come . . . but *not* as cat, because the cat had not been seen to travel.

::Different cat!::

How to pass the time, yes. Thinking *different cat.*

Sklayne pushed himself out, encompassed the world, shrunk back to himself as cat.

Reddish tawny cat, big with the eyes, long with the legs. Much with the ears. *The same cat!*

::!!:: A rapid twist, turning inside out of self, and he was Sklayne, invisible to those not Trevarr and those not wrapped around power.

Think. Different. Cat.

Sklayne pushed himself out . . .

Again! The same cat! How could he protect? How could he hunt?

"Mow!"

Again . . .

For Sklayne *would* protect his hunter.

Oh yes.

7

Two families with their total of five children, three reckoners, and . . . Trevarr.

No one else showed up for their tour group, the first run of a midweek morning. At the rising level of child restlessness, the guide—a remarkably compact, early-elderly woman of utter competence—did not delay their departure. With brusque efficiency and not even a second glance at Trevarr's dark leather-clad appearance, she gathered them at the juncture of the café and gift shop and launched into her welcome speech.

Garrie paid more attention to the Winchester House servant's entrance across the groomed courtyard than to the guide, so she was caught by surprise when they began to move—and at the anticipation jolting down her spine. Apparently she'd only *thought* she was being cool about their impending engulfment by the house of ethereal mud and color.

But just outside the gift shop door, they piled to a halt beside a garbage bin. "Juice boxes and drinks here," the guide told them, eyeing Trevarr's brimming soda, size large. "Cell phones off, please." Lucia dropped her insulated coffee cup from between two fingers as the families deposited their accumulation of juice boxes and Drew fumbled with his phone, no doubt trying to recall the last time he'd actually turned it off.

Unhurried, Trevarr downed his entire large Dr Pepper in a series of deep gulps. The oldest boy—all of six, perhaps—watched open-mouthed, drawn forward in his awe. "Mondo!" he said. "Now are you going to burp?"

His father hastily tugged him back into the family group. Trevarr appeared not to notice, although by now Garrie knew better. He gave the question a moment of thought, the slightest shake of his head. "Perhaps later."

"I should mention," their guide said, deadpan, "that few of the thirteen bathrooms in the home are currently functional."

"Ai Dios," Lucia muttered, for Garrie's ears only. "I could be shopping. I could be *anywhere*."

"Everyone ready?" the guide said, as dryly as only a woman who's seen everything can be.

Who thinks she's seen everything. But Garrie didn't say it out loud. And she didn't blurt, "Yes! Let's *go*!" because the kids were doing that for her.

Across the courtyard they went, an area all full of green with the house looming so big and tall, all striking brick red shingles and scaled siding, turrets erupting from rooms erupting from towers—and there, suddenly, was the servant's entrance before them. The guide stopped for her patter about Sarah Winchester's background and her need to gather friendly spirits, to appease those killed by the Winchester repeating rifle, and to confuse and evade those bent on malice, all as advised by that nameless Boston medium after the death of her husband. She moved on to the anecdote about Teddy Roosevelt—

"Expect to go in through the servant's entrance," Quinn had told them on the phone the night before, last-minute research bearing fruit in a late phone call; everyone tired and gritty-eyed, Garrie still wrapped in the extra blanket she'd taken from the closet after her encounter with the Winchester House spirits. "No one used the front entrance even when Mrs. Winchester was alive. Not even before she had it boarded up after the

1906 earthquake, which she took as a sign. Frankly, she took everything as a sign. Anyway, even President Roosevelt was told to go around to the side."

"Did he?" Drew had asked, the closest to the tinny speaker of his cell phone. It sat in the center of the desk and they sat around it, aside from Trevarr, who lingered in the doorway between their rooms but apparently had no trouble hearing from that distance.

"Not according to the story. Who knows, really. Point is, Sarah Winchester ruled that house with her whims while she was alive and she rules it with them now that she's dead. Everything I've heard tells me that her name, her story, is treated with the utmost respect. If you get to asking questions, pretend she's the queen and you might just strike the right note."

Drew laughed.

"All right then," Quinn said, "pretend she's Trevarr's mother."

No one laughed.

—and then the guide opened the narrow, glass-paned door straight into turn-of-the-twentieth-century opulence, holding it for the family and Drew and Lucia and Garrie and finally Trevarr, and then—

The door closed behind them.

Instantly, the breezes buffeted around Garrie; instantly voices assailed her ears, and barely discernible forms distorted the entrance area. Lucia whimpered, freezing up before her; Drew made a squeaking noise. *Danger, danger,* said a mildly hysterical voice in Garrie's head while the families burbled on ahead in oblivious excitement.

Trevarr's hand landed on her shoulder. The guide tsked at them. "Sensitives. Of course. Take a breath, young people. It will pass." And off she went, discussing stairs that led straight to ceilings and cupboards that opened into walls and doors that opened into thin air.

Take a breath. Not nearly enough. These weren't the

half-expected aggressive, angry spirits from the night before. No, these were distressed, beseeching spirits, battering against her with their pleas for relief. *Relief from what, exactly?* Already her reckoner mind-set clicked into play. The spirits here weren't just vengeful, they were in need of help. Under attack? Trapped?

She couldn't tell.

She'd never felt anything quite like this and she couldn't—

"Lisa McGarrity." Trevarr's hand tightened on her shoulder; his voice rumbled in her ear, the breath of it stirring her hair. Goose bumps shot down along her arms and she anchored on them—on the reality of them. She brought her buffers back up to full, layers of protection closing in around her.

"I'm fine," she said, too brusque to be truly convincing, but she knocked his hand off her shoulder firmly enough so that he straightened, stepping back to give her space. Who said that whole scent of leather was supposed to be a good thing, anyway? Garrie went over to Lucia and reached into her tote to pull out the small pack of tissues that always came with Lucia, she tucked one into her friend's hand, patting a tear-stained cheek until Lucia blinked. "Wakey-wakey," she said. "Close it off, Lu. We can do this."

Lucia blinked. She looked at Garrie; she looked at the tissue. "Ah, *caray*," she said. "Am I good?"

Garrie gave her an obvious, squinting once-over. "It's good," she pronounced, finding Lucia's makeup largely unaffected by the neat tear trails. "Do the dabbing thing. No one will notice."

And as Lucia dabbed, Garrie gave Drew a poke. "Hey, history boy. Come on out and play with the rest of us."

Drew started back into awareness. "Garrie! Oh my God! This place is stupendous! This is amazing! Do you *know* how well preserved it is? How many layers of history? How—"

"Easy, big fella," Garrie said, but grinned. While she and Lucia fought the grimmer effects of the house's current situation, Drew had been reveling in the best of it. "If you start bouncing off the walls, they're gonna kick you out. And if we don't catch up, they're gonna kick us out."

"Or worse," Lucia said, and shuddered. "That woman will scold us."

As a group, they hurried to reach the others, who had been through some discussion about imported materials and now stood in front of a board made of little glass windows, some of which held paper numbers.

"—and because Mrs. Winchester slept in any one of her forty bedrooms each night, the servants only knew where to find her by this annunciator. These cards would drop, identifying Mrs. Winchester's location and letting the servants know she was ready for their attention." The guide smiled knowingly at their arrival, but didn't acknowledge them out loud. Garrie breathed a sigh of relief as the woman moved down the hallway. "Now, let's talk about the number thirteen. Thirteen bathrooms, thirteen panes in many of these windows, thirteen ceiling panels in many of the rooms, thirteen fixtures in a custom chandelier, thirteen cupolas, thirteen palms lining the drive. No one really knows what significance Mrs. Winchester found in the number thirteen, but it's obvious that she did. Keep your eyes open and see if you can spot the thirteens before I point them out . . ."

She'd keep her eyes open, all right. It was all she had to work with right now. With Trevarr breathing down her back, his impatience palpable . . .

Goose bumps. She shivered slightly, closed her eyes, and murmured words that sounded childishly petty even as she spoke them: "I don't trust you, you know that." She just barely moved her lips, and yet she knew . . .

He'd hear her. And he did. He leaned in behind her, close enough for her to hear his equally quiet response. "I know," he said. Right in her ear, *right there*. And the humor in his voice too damned obvious.

She turned on him, keeping her voice down only with great dint of effort. "You're laughing at me."

But suddenly he was quite serious. "No," he said. "I'm *understanding* you." And he looked at her, eyes exposed in this dim light, the sunglasses again tucked away and leaving her vulnerable to that silver gaze. It was enough to hold her there, and for that moment, she had the strangest feeling that he was about to—no, that he *had*—fingers touching her jaw and cheek and smoothing her wayward hair—

Except he didn't. Hadn't. Not with his hand. Not with—

Confused, she turned away from him. *She'd told him not to. Ever.* Then what—?

Garrie drew a ragged breath, hunting composure— and realized they'd fallen behind again. She cleared her throat, moving forward in steps that at first came from a trance state, then steadied. Back to business.

Yeah, right. Business.

"Reality check," she said, her voice as wobbly as her steps had been until it, too, steadied. In the corner of her eye, Trevarr smiled—but not in amusement, no. Understanding. Dark and private understanding. *Great.* "I'm gonna need to come back here." Up ahead, the guide opened a door that led directly into a wall while the children exclaimed *how stoopit* it was. "At least once more. I'll try to take a better look around, but if I'm half blinded by the activity in this place, it's going to take awhile to figure out what's going on. Unless you care to share some clues?"

He didn't respond, and after a moment she thought he wasn't going to. Finally he said, "Later."

Later, what? Later he'd share clues? Later he'd complain that she couldn't suss things out in one fell swoop?

Later she'd find out, apparently.

They saw the storeroom, with its rolls of expensive sculpted English wallpaper, uninstalled art glass collection, parquet wood pieces, tiles and mosaics . . . Victorian times, all piled up in a room. In the gleaming ballroom, she again tried to look at the ethereal layers around her—and closed back up with an audible gasp that echoed so loudly against parquet floors and wood walls that both families stopped their fidgeting and turned to fix her with a single look. "Hiccups," she said, and faked another one. "Excuse me." And of course the children laughed, but the guide fixed her with a wise eye.

As far as Garrie could tell, she was completely mobbed by spirits at all times. Totally and completely surrounded. They cried for her and pled for her and clung to her and begged at her. Benign spirits, in distress, desperately in need. They'd recognized her for what she was the moment she'd set foot in that servant's door, and now they had no intention of letting her go.

Not that they'd have much choice.

Lucia was in no better shape, strained and overly bright-eyed in the dim original lighting of the house, her smiles growing trembly around the edges.

Lucia would not be coming back.

Drew, on the other hand . . .

They'd be lucky to keep him away. Kid in a candy store. Kid in a candy store at Disneyland. Kid in a candy store at Disneyland *with a pony*. Oh, yeah.

They navigated an endless set of broad stairs that rose a scant inch or two for each riser, the hallway as short and narrow as all of them. Garrie felt perfectly well at home; behind her, Trevarr walked in a constant hunch. Sarah Winchester, it seemed, had been a very small lady, and had built her house to suit.

Fireplaces, chandeliers, bedrooms . . . all appointed with exquisite taste and the finest of materials, and all a blur as Garrie eased herself open to the thinnest veil of awareness and finally, finally, got some sense of the twisted pain gathering in this house, the unnatural ethereal vortices, the dead spots and the quicksand she couldn't help but walk around even when it caused the guide to raise an eyebrow. The guide cast her a meaningful look as they entered a final gloomy room and closed the door behind them. "You might enjoy this. Only one way into this room, but three ways out—this was Mrs. Winchester's séance room."

Dark, low ceilings, no windows, cloak closets with thirteen hooks, an ominous lowering in the air . . . even the guide abruptly stopped smiling, her expression tipping over into uncertainty.

The lights went out.

Of *course* the lights went out.

"Mommy!" A handful of thin, scared little voices cried out in chorus.

"This isn't funny," said one of the Silicon Valley dads, his voice set to firm-on-the-edge-of-annoyed.

"Ay, *mierda*!" and "Garrie—" and a deeper rumble that might have been a noise of discontent from Trevarr.

Garrie's hair stirred slightly. "Oh, crap," she said, barely audible.

And the guide, her voice firm and confident. "I assure you, this isn't part of the tour. It's an old house; I'm sure we've just blown a fuse. Someone will fix it within moments."

"Does this sort of thing happen often?" a dad demanded.

No, Garrie wanted to say. *It happens never.* She didn't dare open herself any further than the buffeting breezes she was already taking, but she felt the sharp edge to them . . . she knew the cause.

We're almost done. We're about to leave. They can't let that happen, benign or not—

"They're too desperate," she whispered, not knowing if Lucia was close enough to hear, if Trevarr would understand. And louder, she said, "Get us out of here! Get us out now!" Too many years of séances in this room, too much focus . . . too much power. She couldn't let them have their way, whatever it took. Dignity was for those clever enough not to walk into the Winchester séance room. "I'm claustrophobic! I swear I'm going to—"

Silicon Dad had the answer for that one. "Young lady, get a hold of yourself—"

And then the children screamed, and the mothers screamed, and the guide screamed, and Drew shouted *"Garrie!",* and Lucia cried out and Trevarr grunted in surprise, and a deep roar filled the room, a rush of wind through nonexistent trees and a storm funnel without the storm. *Oh, crap, crap, crap,* crap.

Around and around, herding them, feeling them out, sorting them, tightening down until they huddled together in the center, tightly enough to know the parents had gathered their wailing children, clutching them near; close enough to know Lucia was protecting the guide as best she could, that Drew and Trevarr fought to give Garrie space as Garrie struggled against the spiraling cyclone of power and *what if I don't* want *space?*

Because that's just what those enraged, desperate spirits had needed. They'd separated Garrie like dogs on unwitting sheep, and the roar skipped a beat and came back tenfold—but now it circled Garrie and only Garrie. The power twisted from wind into threads into twine into braided rope and, there in the darkness, it clamped down—no moving, no twitching, no thinking, no *breathing*—

If you won't stay and help us . . . then stay and join us.

8

As the skills are yours, so is the responsibility.
—Rhonda Rose

One is a lonely number.
—Lisa McGarrity

Breathing. It suddenly seemed so important. Garrie made a mighty effort, struggling against the stunning power brought to bear by so many distressed and confused spirits at once—all her focus on that one thing: on winning enough freedom to take in air.

She managed a tremulous squeak.

Lisa McGarrity, reckoner extraordinaire: *hear her squeak.*

She would have smacked her forehead, if she could have moved at all.

But that squeak of indrawn air . . . it wasn't enough. Nor was the next. And her lungs burned and the spirit storm raged around them and panic edged at her thoughts along with the roar of wind and the overlapping, twisted voices of pain and fury and blame. It struck her hard and sudden, then—*no one even knows*. They hadn't heard her painful squeak in the chaotic darkness, not with the spiritual storm and the kids crying and the fathers demanding explanations and the mothers shushing and the guide . . . the poor guide . . . "Fuse!" the woman said,

for the first time at an apparent loss for words. "Mainte
nance plant malfunction! Stay calm!"

Even her reckoners, who well knew what was going
on, thought Garrie could handle it. *Was* handling it. Not
squeaking for air, with the sounds fading around her
and her vision going a weird lighter gray all speckled
with dappled red spots . . .

As the skills are yours . . . Rhonda Rose used to say
so often, pausing so young Lisa could dutifully finish,
so is the responsibility.

Right. Meaning no one else would step in. Wouldn't
they just be surprised when the lights came on and Garrie didn't?

You don't want to do this, she tried to tell the spirits.
I can't help you this way—

But of course she had no voice, and she had no more
energy to reach them as they held her upright in their
braided wind and power while the storm battered her,
trying hard to whip her hair around and failing.

At last, her defiant hair prevailed.

As an epitaph, it sucks. Panic sparked through her
thoughts, scattering them, leaving her only with the im-
mobilized will to *live* . . .

Alone in a crowded dark room.

A presence invaded the space the spirits had
carved out around her. Large at her back, unfamiliar;
the last of her breath squeaked out. A hand landed on
her stomach—spanned it, fingers splayed and assuming. Strong hand, long fingers, rough against the paper-
thin fabric of her layered shirts and suddenly an
anchor to her world.

Trevarr.

The pressure of his hand pulled her firmly back to
him. The wall of Trevarr. His other hand brushed the
side of her head, hovered . . . made itself at home, fingers resting in her hair and on her temple and just below
the curve of her jaw where her pulse beat so wildly. He

ducked his head along her other ear, his cheek alongside hers, and above all else she heard—or felt—the
strong, solid thump of his heart at her back. Warmth,
counteracting the chill. And the low rumble of a voice
in her ear, or maybe in her mind, or maybe in her own
throat. *"Use me."*

You must be kidding.

Or not. Because he gave her a sudden hard jerk,
pulling her in closer, legs threatening to tangle. His
voice went deeper, more gravely. "The skills are yours.
Do it."

Only then did she feel more than his hand against
the straining muscle and tender skin of her lower belly,
with cold metal warming fast between them, an imprint
pushing home through shirts that suddenly seemed *what
was I thinking* negligible. For an instant, the sensations
swamped her, taking her away from the chaotic attack
and lifting her to a place of heat, of conflicting danger
and security. Never mind the storm raging in the room
when this new storm raged more tightly around her,
wrapped in leather and feral grace.

Or maybe she'd just been without adequate oxygen for
too long, choking her way from one breath to the next.

"Garrie."

As the skills are yours . . .

And wasn't this what she'd come here for?

Garrie quit flailing. She quit fighting the invisible
restraints. She knew better than that. And she should
have known better than to be taken so unaware, just because this house had greeted her so quietly. She'd seen
what lurked below the surface the night before. Knew it
was big.

But not bigger than I am.

She hoped.

She reached for her own winds, her own power. Ex-
isting only on shallow gasps of air, she slipped power

around herself—spinning, moving . . . a layer of spiritual WD-40. As thin as a sheet of thought. And then she doubled it, and doubled it again . . .

Breathing again. What a concept.

But that was enough to get their attention. To turn the storm up past force five. Even the guide shrieked, unable to hold to her impressive composure any longer. A pane of glass broke somewhere, sending shards whirling past; Trevarr ducked around her, shoulders a living shield, his hair suddenly free to blow in her face as her own could not. The muscles of his jaw corded and flexed, a startlingly intimate sensation beside her ear. At her belly . . . metal burned cold.

And the cold burned deep. Her own efforts faltered, barely buying breathing room after fighting so hard just to survive those crucial moments of orientation after their attack. Out of practice, that's what.

Use me, he'd said.

She was about to find out what that meant. It was instinct that reached for that cold burn, and desperation that let her do it. Completely unfamiliar, that cold-heat energy. Poison cloaked in power, for all she knew.

And yet she felt the measured strength of his hands clasped around her, his body curled to protect her . . . and she thought not.

"Better not be wrong," she muttered out loud, her voice a ragged imitation of itself. Cold power flushed in through her belly, sending intrusive tendrils toward her groin. "That's *mine,*" she snarled, and pulled hard, redirecting the cold burn into her torso and chest, wrapping it around her heart and lungs until her teeth quite suddenly chattered, her body full of chill electricity hunting for retribution. *No,* she whispered to it. *Boundaries.* She warmed the power, absorbed it to herself . . . felt it slide home. She took a breath, free and easy and grounded; the presence at her ear rumbled with satisfaction. She grinned, a fierce expression in the darkness, defined at the spot where her cheek met his.

Garrie shaped a breeze. A gust, strong enough to smack through the anger-fed storm, the spiritual tantrum of the myriad ghosts of Winchester House. She held it to herself, letting it mature . . . and then at the right moment sent it away with a flick of her fingers. *A warning shot.*

The storm stuttered, tumbling from cohesive winds to momentarily fractured strands of power.

Behind her, Trevarr jerked. A kicked-by-a-mule jerk, a pained grunt in her ear, the harsh struggle against it.

She winced. Dammit. She should have thought. But . . .

Freedom.

Enough to move her arms as well as her hands—even as the spirits regrouped, surging back at her . . . giving her no choice. "I'm sorry," she whispered, not expecting to be heard.

"Do it," he growled, words that vibrated down the side of her neck, the hard edge of his accent curling around those two spare words.

Yeah. She took a deep breath—oh, yeah, damned fine, that air—and she shaped another gust, this time with the resources to do what she did best—using what she had within to gather and shape what was without. Using their own battering power against them. No more warnings, not with this bunch. Time to get their respect. "If you want help," she said, low words riding the energy she sent out to those raging spirits, "then *be nice.*" And *flick,* a sharp double-handed gesture, a starburst of ethereal power with a Garrie epicenter, hard and strong and *make no bones.* Their shock bounced back at her; their vehement ferocity tumbled in on itself.

Trevarr's fingers spasmed at her belly; his hand dropped to her shoulder, where suddenly she held him up and not the other way around, his grip bruising hard.

His breath gusted in a curse and damned if his knees didn't just plain buckle—

"What?" Garric whirled into him, leather and the incongruous hint of wood smoke, grabbing a fistful of that duster, losing it, grabbing at his shirt, finally going for his belt where it wrapped sharply around lean hips, all by feel in the darkness, a jumble of mismatching movements while her own personal shockwave shattered the ghost storm around them.

The unnatural storm fluttered into silence, a few errant grasps of power shaking the shuttered closet doors before the howl of wind gave way to the howl of children. With utter darkness still around them, parental demands joined in loud accompaniment. Lucia called out, "Garrie?"

"Not—" *Yet.* Not yet, she would have said, if she hadn't seen the faintest gleam of burnished silver, just a glimpse and then gone hooded—the way a man's eyes would disappear in the darkness if he turned his head away. "I see you," she said, not meaning to. *I see you,* and suddenly so aware of his arm over her shoulder, his wood-fire-and-ash scent now around her, their utter entanglement. She stiffened.

"It's dark," Trevarr said, his words far too casual for the moment, if low enough to go unheard by anyone else under siege of the family chorus. He couldn't hide the rasp of his breath, not with darkness, or the tiny spasms of his body—little aftershocks of . . . of whatever she'd done to him.

Unaccountably, that casual dismissal of what had just passed between them . . . it peeved her. "I *saw*—"

"The ghosts," he reminded her.

Lucia's concerned voice cut through the vocal volume of the tourist families. "Garrie?"

"Hang on, Lu . . . running some clean-up."

"I don't have—"

Containment. The Baggies. Or, when things got

tough, the giant zipper bags that could double as sleeping bags if they ever needed one. "Don't need anything. Just hang on."

"Ay-yi, chicalet, you sure?" Doubt crept into Lucia's voice, obscured as it was by the guide and parents, the *we've got to get out of here* versus *the lights will be back on in a moment and then it'll be safe* versus *just get us away from this cruel trick, you've terrified my kids* and then the expected throwaway words about lawyers and court and *sue the hell out of you*.

"Excellent priorities," Trevarr muttered dryly, and then hissed between clenched teeth, bending over his knees so Garrie had to follow.

Dignified. At least the lights were still out. "Are you—"

"The *ghosts*," he said through still-clenched teeth.

Okay, dammit. She couldn't do everything at once. Not quite.

"Fine," she said out loud, and she stirred the power around just enough so the sullen lingering spirits would know she spoke to them. "You wanted my attention? You got it. You had it all along, if you want to know."

"Who *is* she talking to?" one of the mothers asked, breaking off from her attempts to soothe her still-crying children and sounding just a little bit brittle herself.

Hard to blame her, really. Best haunted house *evahr*!

Trevarr wouldn't think so. Trevarr, trembling now against this new fluctuation of breezes through the room.

Why had he even come with them? What was he doing even *near* this job, this business, if he had some weird peanut-type allergy to what she did?

Sklayne stretched—so luxurious, every cat muscle extended, paws spread, claws extruding oh so slightly. He turned it into a belly-exposing roll, twisting atop the pillow.

Her pillow.

There, he slowly relaxed. Still absurd. Reveling in it. Replete from the soapy snack, soaking up the scent of the lingering energy here. Gingie root from his home forest, damp sharp leaves after rain. ::Yesss.::

He rolled his shoulders into the pillow. Just so.

As well he deserved to, whether Trevarr expected it of him or not. Left here, waiting, while nothing happened. Nothing out there—because yes, a familiar would know. Bound familiar at that. No choice but to know, if the important things happened. And so definitely nothing happening in here.

Not with the soap gone. And the housecleaning person, come and gone and no clue about Sklayne hovering at the ceiling and tumbling down to nip at the ends of her hair, knowing Trevarr would disapprove.

::Should have taken me.:: The disgruntled thought took some of the satisfaction out of his victory over the pillow. He'd eaten the mint, too. He'd hovered around it just before returning to *cat,* absorbing it without disturbing the paper. Let the small person of much power figure *that* one out.

Unless Trevarr saw it first. Trevarr would know. Trevarr would throw the paper away in a tiny crumpled ball, and cast a scowl in Sklayne's direction. It wouldn't matter if Sklayne hovered in his unseeable self-form or not. Trevarr always knew where he was.

Bound familiar.

Sklayne comforted himself with the aftertaste of the mint and sprawled on the pillow in the sun, twitching, dreaming waking dreams. His forest. His forest before Trevarr. His forest before Sklayne had grown too curious, gotten too close . . .

A cold tingle burned his cat bones from the inside out. He made a startled cat noise, flipping right-side-up in one smooth, sudden motion. *Not right.* He tasted of the air, using the small pink nose smudged with black at the edges. *Krevata?* But no, he was alone here. The energies were quiet here.

Not *here* at all.

::Trevarrrr?::

Not so often, words over distance. Too hard, not worth it. More with the nudges and the impulses and the feelings. But Sklayne paced the length of the bed and back. He pulsed his claws in and out of the bedspread. He twitched his tail. ::Treyyy?::

Trevarr's presence hovered as it always hovered— touchable, tangible, familiar—but did not respond to him. Busy.

Not good. Not when he used the wheedle-voice. ::Treyyyy?:: The inner voice that sounded so much like this cat's very purr. The voice that made Trevarr stop what he was doing and roll his eyes and refuse to admit that it tickled his thoughts.

Not this time. The cold shot through Sklayne's bones, squeezing out a startled, protesting yowl. The scent of woodsmoke drifted past his mind. It was all the warning he got before the vice of crushing pain wrapped around him, compressing fur and skin and bones—and he saw it then, as the bond snapped wide open. Immensity of power, channeling through the small Garrie person. A gift from Kehar, given and unwittingly received, embraced and unknowingly used, churned into a bastardized mix of different powers that flowed smoothly through her control even as it scraped Trevarr—*Sklayne*—from the inside out.

Sklayne snarled imprecations; he snarled warning. ::Half-blood,:: he said, and ::Beware!:: he said, and ::Danger there!:: he said.

And Trevarr said nothing, but Trevarr knew, and Trevarr fought against what was within, what was always within but always so deeply buried . . . never allowed any freedom, for fear it could never be caged again. Never controlled.

Sklayne knew that fear. Lived beside it. Had seen it woken once on this world aready. Woken first with Garrie-power, clean and pure and simple, for a simple and earthy response. Controlled, then. Not even unpleasant.

Never farking mind that. If he turns into something for the Garrie person to kill, no going home for Sklayne. Ever.

From the outside in, he saw it. From the inside out, he saw it. The eyes . . . always the change showed first in the eyes. The skin patterns, tattoos inborn, trailing and growing from those vestiges present at birth. After that, few knew . . . because few had survived. Or been allowed to. The bastard-breeds . . . they were the worst. The strongest. The hardest to control. Too torn between what they were and what they weren't to live by the rules of any given being.

::Half-blood!:: he said, and ::Beware!:: and ::Danger there!:: but by then he knew the power had stirred and scraped and howled, stripping away carefully guarded layers with the shock that made this cat form writhe upon the bedspread these miles away. Trevarr, hurt. Trevarr, struggling. Trevarr surrounded by beings who did not know, who *could* not know.

Sklayne snarled a rudeness at the weak cat form and the feeble damage its claws had done to the bedding. *He* knew. *He* should be there.

Bound familiar.

::Take,:: he said, and gave what he could, across the miles. And knew he was heard when that gift was received, when Trevarr held ground against that which had been woken within. When he persisted, even as the Garrie person wielded her bastardized breezes, her terror turning to confidence and profound competence.

So Sklayne gave, until the moment was done. Until he felt the faintest of touches, a mental scritch along the fur of his spine. And he collapsed in on his corporeal aspect and let himself retreat back to this hotel room.

Oh, most disapproving.

::Cat-form, so very broken.::

Fark.

Sklayne set about fixing it.

9

Enjoin the spirits to remain calm, regardless of their plight.
—Rhonda Rose

Take a breath! Or whatever.
—Lisa McGarrity

"Listen up," Garrie told the lingering ghosts, keeping her voice low—Soccer Mom would hear her, but she'd have to guess at the words. "This house was made for you—to keep you sane, to keep you going in happy circles. Hot damn, you've had it good for years, haven't you? And now you're panicked because things aren't quite right. Well, grow up!"

Still bent, still trembling over the power she'd laced with her words, Trevarr made what might have been a twisted sound of amusement.

"Something's wrong here, I get it. But I do this my way. And that means not scaring the Fisher-Price Little People, right? It also means we're leaving, but we're *coming back*. So take a breath!" Okay, that probably wasn't feasible. "Or whatever," she added, not lamely at all.

If they'd been in the flesh, there'd have been a lot of toe digging and throat clearing and looking anywhere but at her. As it was, they eased away—their presence dissipating, their energies finding outlets through nooks and crannies and even straight through the walls. "Ohh, no," she said, and her voice suddenly sounded a little louder than anyone else's. *Oops.* Garrie went to silent running. Harder . . . it took more concentration, sending her thoughts out on energetic breezes. *I need better than that. You need to leave us alone, now. And I want to hear that you'll leave* all *the tourists alone.*

She should have known Trevarr would shudder at her use of the energy, that he'd slowly go down with that last straw—taking her with him, as it happened. She didn't have to see in the dark to know he fought it; she felt it in every quivering muscle. Could hardly avoid knowing it, trapped beneath a bent leg and a bowed shoulder.

Which didn't mean she released her hold on the spirits. Not now. It would be the same as . . . well, in second-grader speak, letting them win. "Sorry," she whispered. And asked them all, *Do we have an understanding?*

No direct answers here. Just a wash of anxiety, of wariness. Of concern. The translation was clear enough, after so many years of this: *then you'll help us?*

She clamped her thoughts down on impatience. *It's why I came.*

They didn't quite believe her. She wasn't sure she blamed them. Their distress was genuine, their need, great. It would be hard for them to watch her walk away. *I need time to figure this out,* she told them.

They didn't quite believe that, either. But she hadn't truly left them a choice. With the power she'd gathered from Trevarr, she was in a position to dissipate them, one by one—supposing that was something she ever did except as a last resort. But she let them believe it; she let them feel the pressure of it. And she felt their assent.

So she let them go.

They left swiftly and they left quietly—no special effects. As Garrie took a deep breath—all leather and inexplicable wood smoke at that—the lights flickered back on.

Being so close to him in the darkness, unseeing; being so close in the suddenly bright overhead light. *Two different things.* Yet she just sprawled, stunned, realizing anew the size of him. *Not safe.*

Hell, no.

And realizing, with the family cheering in the background and the "Mommy, I want to *go,*" clamoring in her ears, that even on the floor, he kept his head turned away; he'd closed his eyes. She used a low voice that she now trusted he'd hear even if no one else did. "I saw you."

His eyes flashed open; they fastened on her. Cold silver, just a little wild around the edges. Not glowing at all. He might even have fooled her if she couldn't still feel the tension in his limbs.

She'd give it to him. For now. Because here came Lucia, long legs crossing the room in a few quick strides, dark eyes full of worry. But not her voice, for Lucia knew the value of a public face as much as or more than any of them. "Up with you, chicalet," she said, reaching out a hand as if she hauled Garrie off the floor—and out from beneath leather and limbs—several days a week.

Behind her, the guide tried the door through which they'd come in. Her short gray hair stood up every which way and her face flushed ruddy red; her glasses sat askew on her nose. But she reached for that door knob with a determined confidence, ready to march them onward. Or at the very least, to keep them from bolting ahead so quickly that they got lost in their quest to leave.

Garrie had little such confidence in the door. Ghosts didn't always clean up after themselves when they left.

And then, since she was the only one who knew why Trevarr hadn't bounded back to his feet—and because she had the feeling he'd do anything to keep it that way—she turned to him in an imitation of Lucia and held out her hand. "Up with you then, chico-wuh."

Lucia snorted, adjusting her little designer tote at her shoulder as Drew came up uneasily beside her. "Chico. *Wuh*. Cute, Garrie."

Mission accomplished. None of them paid the least bit of attention to Trevarr as his gaze latched onto hers again. She couldn't read those metal-hard eyes—*still not glowing, Garrie*—and she couldn't imagine anyone ever would. She raised her eyebrows at him in a silent *yeah, or what?* and he reached up to grasp her hand.

She didn't let on, either, just how much of his fluid rise to his feet actually came from all that time she spent in her condo's workout room.

Distraction beat at them from behind. "What do you mean, it *won't open*?" Silicon Dad, at the limits of his patience, shouting at the guide. Not nice.

"Hey." Trevarr stood full height again, his voice at full depth. It got Dad's attention. And it was all he had to say.

The guide, truly shaken for the first time, looked at Trevarr with gratitude—or she might just have seen Dad Two, trying to save the day, slipping along the outside wall. "*Here's* a door," the man crowed, reaching for the knob of the crisply painted portal—not looking, particularly, at his destination so much as at his family behind him. The guide looked only faintly annoyed—until the knob turned in the man's hand, and then her expression flashed to the kind of horror even the ghosts hadn't evoked from her.

Drew, too, slouching behind Lucia, came to instant attention— Garric hadn't known he could move that fast, leaping across the intervening space to jam his lanky form between the dad and the door, the perfect hockey check. Dad Two turned on him with a snarl. "I've had just about enough of you weirdos—"

"Hey!" Garrie recoiled in offense . . . but Garrie held sway over spirits and ethereal storms and darkside creatures, not humankind.

Trevarr didn't hesitate, only one long step away from that confrontation and then suddenly a part of it. Lucia snagged Garrie's arm with anxiety—still influenced by the spirits, her fingers wrapping tight. And tighter, as a low rumble permeated the room. Too low to hear, low enough to feel—cut short, as though suddenly aware of itself. And then Trevarr cleared his throat, quite a normal sound after all. He tipped his head at the cluster of children and parents and guide at the unyielding doorway, his voice low. "You're scaring the small ones."

The man looked over, then away, just as Drew finished turning the knob and pushed open the door and said, so seriously, "And you should watch where you're going."

"That door should be locked," the guide said faintly.

"Whoa." Lucia took a step forward, bringing Garrie with her. "I can see why."

For a moment, they all looked at the open floor beyond the door, and the long drop to the room below. Directly below the opening sat a large gleaming kitchen sink, complete with fixtures. "That's gonna hurt," Drew said, mildly enough.

"You knew," the guide said, looking dazed. She took a startled-sounding breath, passed her hands over her hair, straightened her glasses, and regained some of her equilibrium. "You must have seen the DVD. Of course."

Drew squinted at her, his own hair still in complete disarray, his geek-squad striped polo shirt twisted. Lucia released Garrie to step smartly to him, tweaking his shirt and tugging his collar into place. She left the hair up to him. "The gift shop DVD," she said. "You know."

"Um," Drew said. "Right. Way cool DVD."

Smooth. That was Drew.

By then Trevarr had stepped back, suddenly unobtrusive—not that Garrie would have believed it possible. He scraped back hair to reveal angled features somehow more pensive than before. Lucia dipped into her bag and pulled out an elastic hair band, matter-of-factly offered. He took it with a flicker of surprise.

"Your hair," Garrie muttered at him. And she gave him an eyebrow, but let it pass. Especially with Dad Two retreating to the families, though she couldn't help but peer down into kitchen revealed by the open door, wondering about the clambering potential.

"Psst," Lucia said, taking hold of the door with the firm grip that meant she was going to close it. "Fine for *us,* maybe."

But not so much for the guide. Garrie glanced over her shoulder. Yeah, be fair. The woman had held up remarkably well, considering. She hadn't done or said any of the denial-based things people usually did. And she hadn't made things harder, either.

Then again, the Silicon Families were enough to keep anyone busy.

"I don't know why that door won't open," the guide said. "But the next group will be along shortly, and they'll find us."

At that, the youngest child broke into a loud wail, a sound verging on ultrasonic. Not the fear from moments earlier, but from something more urgent yet.

Lucia put her hands over her ears, perfectly manicured nails flashing pearly against her black hair. "Ay-yi, make it stop!"

"Holy shit," Drew muttered, which Garrie only knew because she'd seen his lips make those words before.

Even Trevarr looked faintly horrified, glancing at her

for guidance in a manner she might have found comical if her eardrums hadn't been bleeding. "Don't tell me," she said, and then didn't have to finish, because the little dance performed by the screaming child—hands twisted in his shirt at the level of his crotch, toe-stepping in place—made it perfectly clear she'd guessed right. "And here we were worried about *you*," she told Trevarr.

He spread his hands in silent indication of himself and his perfectly satisfactory status. Drew glared at Garrie as if somehow it was all her fault; he shouted, "I am *never* having kids!" and stalked over to the one of the double-door closets, pulling them open with a vigor that left the guide open-mouthed. Poor woman. He indicated the closet with the impatient flair of a doorman, and when the families gaped at him—except for the dancing child, who had switched to a bounce move that Garrie thought unwise under the circumstance—Drew repeated the gesture with emphasis.

"But I haven't been that way for years!" the guide said, loud enough to make most of the words heard over the din. "We'll get lost!"

"No, we won't." Garrie grabbed Lucia's hand, trusting in Drew . . . his sense of history. Once she got closer to the closet she could easily see what Drew had known all along—a step up, a few steps through, and they'd exit into a different room. But after her initial impulse to lead the way, she hesitated . . . in spite of spiritual promises, she'd couldn't risk the potential backlash. She nudged Lucia ahead and stood back, watching Drew lead the way, as Lucia followed without hesitation. The guide clearly intended to usher everyone out, so Garrie stabbed a decisive finger toward Wailing Boy. "Him," she said. "Get him out of here." With any luck, the next room was larger and would absorb the sound better. Or Wailing Boy would be satisfied with their forward progress and hush. Or the act of climbing through the closet would make him wet his pants, and the urgency would be resolved. Garrie was voting for either of the latter two.

Once the children headed for the closet, the parents quickly intermingled, guiding their families and resuming the reassuring tones that might have been more useful earlier in the adventure. *Be nice, self,* she said, and tugged the hair behind her ear. Everyone had weak spots.

"You go ahead," the guide was saying to her. "You don't look all that well, if you don't mind me saying so."

Really? Huh. So that tingly numbness in her fingers and lips, that wasn't just her imagination. But she said, "If you don't mind . . . I'd better close the door behind us."

The guide regarded her a long moment, disheveled but again completely composed. Then she shook her head once, firmly, and carefully, the woman entered the closet.

Trevarr should have been next—should have been ready to go. But when Garrie turned back to him, she found him with a gleaming metal disk in his hand. The same one from the airport; the same one that had been pressed against her belly. And ooh, she *wanted*.

"What is that?" she breathed, taking a step toward him, hand reaching of its own wistful accord. The memory of that cold burn of power raised the hair on her arms; an echo of the disk's imprint flushed cold-hot beneath her navel. Her other hand crept to cover that spot.

He looked up at her. He made no attempt to hide the thing; he might have smiled—just a little, there, on the side of his mouth where the tiny scar resided, and his eyes . . . She wasn't entirely sure if he'd actually shaken his head, or whether she just knew it anyway.

"Another time," she allowed. Meant it, too. But not

with the dancing-bladder child still waiting, and not when she wanted to get this door closed behind them. She gestured at their unusual egress.

He closed his hand around the disk, an abrupt, snatching-it-out-of-the-air motion, and tucked it away inside his duster. He stepped through the closet, ducking and stepping up at the same time, and no longer with any hesitation; she certainly couldn't attribute his stealthy grace to any assistance on her part. Whatever had happened—whatever she'd done to him when she'd wrangled the spirits into line—it was done and gone. Trevarr was at full power.

She just wasn't sure if that was a good thing.

"This isn't on the DVD," the guide said, a frown in her voice. "And even if it was, you'd have to be quite the remarkable young man to have memorized it."

"Oh, he's quite the remarkable young man," Lucia said. "Just don't ask his sister about—"

"Hey!" Drew said sharply, although he'd appeared to have been paying no attention at all, his head slightly cocked, his eyes half closed—not even looking at the rooms through which he led them. Closed-up rooms with sheet-covered furniture; some of it partially finished, some of it showing damage from the 1906 earthquake, all of it just as obviously opulent . . . simply not spit-shined for the public eye.

"Oh, right," Lucia said. And then, in a stage whisper to the guide, "We don't talk about that."

"Who *are* you people?" she asked. "Please tell me you're not a plant from the board. Not on my watch. Not *today*."

Garrie had instant mercy. "I don't even think the most devious board of directors could come up with us."

Drew hesitated at an oddly angled hallway with one hand lightly touching the wall. The jittery child had infected his brother; both commenced to whine at the delay. Without looking at them or raising his voice, Drew said, "If I can't concentrate, we don't move."

The whining stuttered away; the children checked with their mother, seeking confirmation; she gave them a look. The families clustered in the hallway, subtly yet perceptibly apart from Garrie and her reckoners. Garrie grinned to herself, as grim as the situation was. Like the man on the airplane, they'd made some assumptions about her when this group had first begun its loose association. That she needed protection from Trevarr. That she was his in the first place. That she was not a person of consequence—petite young woman dressed in her thin stretchy layers, a batiqued off-the-shoulder, long-sleeved shirt over a tank top, no bra straps in evidence, crop cargos riding low and loose.

No one, she thought, should be assumed to be a person of no consequence. Not even if she was short and funky and kept her personal energy well withdrawn. It didn't matter what they didn't know—that all that wiry strength came from working out, trying to run her energy-washed body to ground. That electric-blue streaks in nut-brown hair, a tendency to go goth with eye makeup, and an idiosyncratic touch with her wardrobe didn't mean there wasn't more to her than airhead faux-goth chick.

Drew lifted his head; his tense shoulders relaxed and he let out a deep breath. "Left, right, right," he said. "That gets us right in front of the séance room again. Not that I think we should go in or anything, but—"

"But I can take it from there," the guide said. She struck off to lead the way, her pace more urgent now.

No, this was a forced march of rapid retreat, and now that Drew was no longer needed to lead, he let the families scoot ahead while the reckoners drifted toward the back. When they reached the exit—the same way they'd come in—the guide turned to them. The Silicons were long gone, bolting across the little courtyard for the restrooms by the snack and gift shops, parents sending wary looks back over their shoulders and children unabashedly holding their crotches in a universal signal that all but cleared the way for them.

Garrie wanted to be long gone, too. Oh, boy, did she. The faint buzzing in her lips had moved to her teeth; her fingers tingled nonstop. She wanted to ask Trevarr what he'd done to her. She wanted to drink three or four gallons of sarsaparilla soda. She wanted . . . she wanted . . .

Something.

But the entrance area remained crowded, and hardly any of them were tourists. Lots of red-vested staff, neat and groomed and worried, bearing walkie-talkies. They'd perceived the problem from outside; they'd cleared the house as best they could. And now they'd want answers. So when she realized that the guide was about to delay them, giving the others a chance to close in, she went preemptive. "I *really* need to sit down," she told Lucia.

"You look it." Lucia glanced at the red-vested group, pensive. Several more officious staff members in red jackets arrived, their voices annoyed and peremptory.

Garrie snagged Drew just as one of the guides tried to draw him away from the group. A charming young woman, and he'd fallen for it. Big surprise. "Drew! We need to stick together right now. Let's go."

"I think my supervisors would like to talk to you," their guide said, apology in her tired features.

Garrie snorted. "I don't *think* so. What happened in there happened *to* us, just like it happened to the Silicons." Oops, she'd said that out loud. Oh, well. No point in pretending she hadn't. "Ask *them* what they saw." She rubbed the tips of her fingers over her numb, tingling lips. "I deserve a nice sit-down. And I'm going to go have one."

Lucia tucked her tote over her shoulder, behind her upper arm. Back straight and elegant, expression determined . . . too formidable for casual opposition. "We'll grab something at that café. Trevarr's paying, so the tourist prices are no obstacle, and the uncomfortable seating—"

"Is at least *sitting*." And Garrie let Lucia lead the way, formidable mode turned to high. Across the courtyard, back to the gift shop and café building. Garrie glanced behind to make sure the staff members weren't planning an end run and discovered that Trevarr was already on it, scanning behind them, alongside them . . . watching every possible approach. And then she lost all interest in boring, living Winchester House staff, because halfway between the house and their little group, she saw the being who *was* following them. Bold and determined and frightened, extremely well realized— not just any monochrome spirit, but in full color detail. "Yo," she said to her crew. Trevarr had moved ahead to the first spot of shade; now he lingered there, waiting. "We didn't leave everyone behind."

Trevarr's gaze sharpened; his hand went to his duster and she thought *really don't want to know what else you might have in there*—except she did. The other two didn't catch the gesture, too busy scanning for red vests. "A young woman," Garrie said. "Awfully skinny, but I think it's reflective." Reflective of how she'd been when she died, that is—as opposed to representative, which could be highly metaphorical. Get a ghost in a representative state, and things got a whole lot trickier all around. "A little older than me, and not recent." They sure didn't make bell-bottoms like that anymore. "Flower child. She looks upset." And coming straight for her, too, in a determined march. Although for all of that, the spirit wasn't making much progress toward them.

"She means no harm," Lucia said, lifting her chin in

the funny little way she had when she was tuning in.
"She . . . she's like all the others. She's desperate about
something."

Garrie crossed her arms, watching. The staff, still in
conference, looked back at her—frowning, thinking
themselves the object of her interest; she ignored them.
And the spirit suddenly began to look a little thin and
fuzzy.

"Oh!" Lucia said, and took a step back. "Now that's
just panic. I don't need to listen to that."

The spirit glanced over her shoulder . . . and broke
into a startling sprint. Her flared bell-bottom pants
flapped and floundered around her legs; her arms
pumped. But she gained only a few more yards—and
then, quite abruptly, she snapped away.

"No shit," Garrie said, unable to hide her astonishment.

"She's gone!" Lucia said, a startled half-question;
she looked wildly around even though she couldn't see
anything.

"Slingshotted right back into the house," Garrie told
her.

"Whoa," Drew said. "That's gotta hurt. Have we even
seen that before?"

"We," said Lucia, "have never seen it." She didn't
like it when Drew made himself at home with their history, given his short tenure with them.

Garrie threaded an arm through hers—silent communication. *Let it be, Lu. He's a dork, but he's our dork.*
Out loud, she said, "Nothing quite like that, no. I've seen
restricted spirits before, though. And you know what?"
she added. "Food. Sitting down. Nonnegotiable."

"The café," Lucia repeated with assurance. "Now."
And Trevarr slid along the shadows to lead the way, always with a glance behind him.

The café. Burgers and fries and chili dogs. The Sili-

cons lingered by the bathrooms—children still subdued, parents a mix between wild-eyed and resentful.
They cast no few looks at Garrie and Trevarr. "As if it's
my fault," Garrie grumbled, throwing herself at a hard-
seated chair while Drew went right to the fast-food-
style serving counter.

"Well, chicalet," Lucia said gently, "unless you
mean to say that the ghosts *weren't* trying to get your
attention . . . but color me a hard sell. I felt their desperation." She plucked several napkins from the table
dispenser and spread them on the table before setting
her tote down.

"I'm surprised you managed to deal with what they
were putting out." Garrie said. "Damned intense."

Trevarr glanced at her. He hadn't yet taken a seat, but
assessed the room with a personal energy she could
only call ready for . . . *I did* not *just think the word* battle. He said, "Best if one of you orders." He reached inside his duster and pulled out his money clip.

"God," Lucia burst out, finally noticing just how many
things went in and out of that coat, "you're a walking
man-purse!"

Garrie clapped both hands over her mouth, muffling
an amazingly loud guffaw. Trevarr squinted at Lucia—
baffled and trying to decide if he was offended, and trying to hide both.

"Hey," Drew said across the long, narrow room from
them and lounging at one of the turnstile rope stan-
chions. "We gotta fill my grill before we talk about the
fact that two of us know a whole lot more than the other
two of us."

"There are," Garrie said firmly, "only three of *us*
here. Quinn stayed behind."

"Whatever. What do you want to eat?"

"Fill my grill," Trevarr muttered, repeating the words
as though they left a lingering odor in the air.

"He's hungry," Lucia said shortly. "Don't worry about it. We don't understand him half the time, either. The fruit salad, Drew. And iced tea."

Garrie told him, "Carbs, fat, and high-test carbonation. Do I need to translate that?"

Drew snorted. "Fries, burger, cola, supersized. Trevarr?"

Trevarr looked over at the counter, where the young woman behind the cash register had been about to put on an air of impatience but suddenly changed her mind. "Hamburger," he muttered, "grows old."

"Have a chili dog," Drew said. "They're spicy, though. Um, not that I scarfed one down earlier or anything."

"I have yet to encounter food here that I consider spicy," Trevarr said.

"He wants a chili dog," Drew told the counter girl.

Lucia, however, had crossed her arms, taking his comment as a challenge. "When we get back to New Mexico—" She stopped, tipped her head slightly, almond eyes regarding him from beneath a sweep of lashes. "Or did you mean *here,* San Jose?"

"Here," Trevarr said, and made a vague gesture that didn't answer the question one bit.

"Are you going to sit?" Garrie asked him abruptly. "Because you standing there, looming . . . it's not working for me right now."

Trevarr pulled a bill from the money clip, handed it to Drew, and returned to take the chair Garrie had left between her seat and the wall. Lucia said, "Don't give him that hundred. You didn't, did you?"

Trevarr slouched back in the chair, arms folded over his chest. "It was not a hundred."

"Money," Garrie said to Lucia, pushing it just a bit, "doesn't seem to be a big deal."

"Fixing this situation," Trevarr said, "is the *big deal.*"

"Why?" Garrie asked, blunt with frustration. "Why *you*? Why *me*?"

Lucia looked at the table top. "Too, too late for that, chicalet."

But Trevarr only caught her gaze, silver eyes so much colder than she'd remembered. No yield in those eyes. No acknowledgment of what they'd been through in that séance room not so very long ago. Still with the leather; still with that cool untouchable aura. The wood smoke had, somehow, faded. Something in her ached for all of it. Or resented all of it. Or both. She tugged the hair behind her right ear, hard enough to hurt.

Quite abruptly, he straightened in the chair. Lucia gasped ever so faintly as he reached out to that tugging hand, firmly but gently, and untangled Garrie's fingers from the short locks, closing his hand over them to fold them into quiescence. "I," he said, catching her eyes with a much different look, a searching look, "*owe someone.*"

"So you said." She sat back, crossed her arms again— most defiantly, this time—and let out a huff. "You won't mind if I keep asking, though, seeing what's at stake."

"Ay-yi," Lucia muttered, and fanned herself. She nudged her tote until it rested *just so* on the table, sat more primly upright, and speared Garrie with her own meaningful stare. "You're not the only one who wants answers, chica. I hope you have your stories straight, because the moment Drew gets here with that food, the *grilling* won't have anything to do with his mouth."

"Grill," Trevarr mused, albeit pretty obviously to himself. "*Mouth.*" He shook his head slightly in wonderment.

"Incoming!" Drew called, swooping in with an overload of oversized drinks. "No dehydration for us!"

Garrie and Lucia grabbed at the unstable configuration of sloshing cardboard cups, playing a quick shell game to get them properly assigned. Drew said, "Got you a Dr Pepper, Trevarr. But you can trade for my 7UP if you want. I don't really care. Be right back."

"Get ready," Garrie said, and Lucia responded with a determined nod. Trevarr stood.

"Oh, no worries," Lucia told him. "He likes this. Controlled chaos. It's his favorite."

"Controlled chaos with *food*," Garrie added. And indeed, here it came, all their food piled into precarious balance on one tray when it should have been two or even three. Garrie caught her fries as they hit critical balance; Lucia spun a burger plate into place and snatched her own bowl of fruit. Garrie grabbed the chili dog when Trevarr didn't reach for it, sliding it in front of him; he gave it the briefest of double-takes before he seemed to realize he'd ordered it. The next few moments were full of crinkling and salting and munching, as Drew finally sat down to his own towering concoction of a hamburger, carelessly pushing change across the table at Trevarr.

Lucia, the only one of them using a fork, poked through the chunks of melon and apple and pineapple to spear a grape and then held it aloft while she similarly speared Garrie with a look. "You," she said. "Talk."

Garrie made an incredulous noise through a mixed mouthful of hamburger and fries, only belatedly remembering that she was a civilized being. A glance at Trevarr revealed him to be eating as he always had—neatly, efficiently, and boy she wouldn't want to be that chili dog. A swift gulp of soda gave her enough mouth room to protest—under the cover of her hand—"Grill! Full!"

Lucia pressed her lips together, trying not to smirk at that. "Swallow, then. And delay your gratification long enough to give us a clue!"

Okay, that was only fair. Not Lucia's fault that Garrie's fingers still felt numb and her stomach rang hollow and something behind her eyes felt . . . inverted. Skipping breakfast . . . not such a great idea. Besides, the rate at which she'd been eating . . . she glanced down at the heavily chomped burger. The ol' stomach could probably stand a moment to adjust. She managed to clear her throat and said, "They're mad."

Lucia rolled her eyes and threw her hands up in the air, fork and grape notwithstanding.

"We had that particular clue," Drew said helpfully, in case Garrie couldn't interpret.

"I mean *really* mad," Garrie said. "I mean, come on, these aren't naive ghosts here; they haven't lost touch. They're not confused and they're not stupid. But they couldn't wait until I had a moment to duck the Silico—" She glanced up at movement beyond their table, discovered the families in question descending upon the food counter, the youngest boy still hitching his pants around to some comfortable configuration. She closed her mouth, raised her eyes heavenward.

"Not a private table," Trevarr noted. The chili dog was almost gone. If it had been spicy, he hadn't appeared to notice.

All Garrie had been thinking about had been getting the food, as fast as possible. "You could have said something."

"The next time you choose the least defensible seating in the room, I will."

She stared at him. "You just said that like it was perfectly normal."

No, not perfectly normal. Trevarr-normal, indefinable accent and all. And now he just looked at her, and picked up one of his curly fries to look at *it*.

"Eat it, don't stare it to death," Lucia said calmly. And to Garrie, "You've forgotten to make this about us. *Me*. Drew. Telling us what happened."

"Snapshot," Garrie said. "They aren't in a reasonable mood." She eyed the middle child, who hung off the queue rail to cross his eyes at her. Too damned bad the only one her ethereal push had ever worked against was Trevarr. She swallowed a sudden surge of crankiness. "They went for me in the—" a glance, and there was Soccer Mom, disapproving of her. Maybe her hair, maybe her clothes. Maybe just Garrie feeling cranky. "They pretty nearly got me, too. I wasn't expecting that kind of trouble, not after all the penny-ante whining."

"And did they say," Trevarr asked, depositing the fry back in the little cardboard basket, "what had upset them?"

She made a face. "Vague allusions to doom." She took another bite of the burger, but . . .

Food, it seemed, was not helping.

She sighed, put the thing back on its paper plate. "Truth is, we need to go back in there. And isn't there a tour of the grounds? And some behind-the-scenes thing? Because we really don't know much more than we did."

"We know they were willing to go for you last night," Lucia pointed out, picking out the lone strawberry from her fruit bowl. "And they did it again today. So I think we know they'll do it again. Too desperate to be smart."

Drew spoke around a mouthful of . . . something. "Yeah, but Garrie put the whup-ass on 'em, so we're covered."

Garrie said nothing. Garrie thought of the cold, burning energy; her hand crept to her belly. She thought of the way it had warmed; she thought of the way it had warmed her in return.

Drew cleared his throat. "Yeah," he said, just a little louder, "but *Garrie put the whup-ass on 'em, so we're covered.*"

Trevarr watched her, elbow casually askew on the table, chair angled so its back was to the wall. Watched her, but also scanned the rest of the room as several additional families arrived and staked out their turf. Still, she knew what he was waiting for—worried about, even. How much she'd reveal, that's what.

"Garrie?" Lucia said, putting the strawberry back down.

"Garrie?" Drew echoed, shuffling stray bits and pieces of his burger into one spot.

"Garrie," she told them, "got slammed."

Lucia took in a deep breath, held it a moment, and bit her lip as she let it all out. "I thought maybe," she admitted. "But I couldn't figure out—"

"Down for the count," Garrie said. "Tied up in a nice ethereal bow."

Drew squinted at her. Swallowed his current mouthful. "But you came back. You dealt with it."

She glanced at Trevarr; he returned it with a steady gaze, and she couldn't read him at all. It didn't seem right. After all that? She should be able to tell at a glance. Uneasily, she looked away. She said, "It was a close thing, Drew. It was a really, *really* close thing."

Trevarr shifted slightly. Barely perceptible . . . a release of tension. Maybe not impossible to read after all.

"But you're ready for them now," Drew said, still that hopeful tone in his voice.

She pushed her food away. Not only no longer hungry, but sorry for what she'd eaten. "I hope so," she said. She pushed the heels of her hands against her cheekbones, up high. The pressure seemed to help. "Well, I was looking for some action. Don't ask for what you don't want, right? Too bad Rhonda Rose moved on. I have the feeling she would have liked this one." She glanced at Trevarr, thought briefly about explaining the whole Rhonda Rose thing . . . but he didn't look all that curious and she didn't feel like sanitizing the conversation for curious eavesdropping ears.

"Chic, you need to eat." Lucia frowned at her. *Cheek,* she said it. "You know how you get after things are . . . intense. We don't need to be scraping you up off the floor."

Trevarr shot her a hard look, but Garrie just snorted. "Been there, done that already today."

Drew, scowl and all, disappeared behind the large soda cup to take a noisy gulp. When he emerged, his expression had shifted. Drew, eternal optimist. "Hey," he said. "At least there wasn't any poop."

Garrie covered her face again. "As mad as they were? We'd have been chin deep. And there'd have been no explaining *that* away."

"Failure of the maintenance plant," Lucia said dryly. "Unauthorized emissions." Drew snickered, Garrie giggled, and Lucia smiled at her strawberry.

But only for a moment.

For after that moment, the café entrance filled with a gaggle of red-jacketed official-looking people—a good number of them, really, more than seemed reasonable for any normal shift. Not completely oblivious, then, to what happened within the walls of their idiosyncratic mansion. Now they hesitated, and their eyes lit with recognition when they saw not Garrie and her reckoners, but Trevarr, sitting against the wall.

"Inconspicuous," Garrie muttered. "Not."

Trevarr might have growled. It might have been Garrie's imagination. Hard to tell.

But the squeal from the counter girl, that wasn't her imagination.

And neither was that sudden . . . *smell* . . .

"I didn't do it!" Drew said immediately.

Lucia waved him off. "Garrie, are you—?"

"I don't—" Garrie started. The food plate swam before her; she clamped a hand over her mouth and swallowed hard.

Her reaction didn't go unnoticed, not with the Silicons taking up so much room at the counter. "Mommy, look, that lady's gonna puke from the stink!"

Not from the stink. From the energies, a weird unfamiliar swish and sway that made the world move around her and within her. Not the ethereal breezes with which she was so familiar; not the cold, burning energy Trevarr had fed her not long ago. *Rhonda Rose, how much did you not tell me?* Shocking, the notion that Rhonda Rose had kept things from her. That maybe Rhonda Rose hadn't *known*.

That, too, was enough to shift her world.

"Good Lord," said Silicon Dad. "What the hell is that? Don't you *clean* those soda machines?" And the children shrieked in horrified delight, exclaiming over the grossness and hopping to see over the counter, while Soccer Mom glared at Garrie as if it must somehow all be her fault. The red-jacket people, originally focused on Garrie's table, hesitated where they were, uncertain.

A vast belching noise shook the cafe, rattling windows and eliciting screams and shrieks and instinctive ducking.

"I don't—" Garrie started again through the fingers of the hand still over her mouth.

"No," Lucia said firmly. *"Don't."*

Trevarr reached inside his duster—no nonsense, no hesitation—withdrew the disk, glanced at it, and tucked it away before Garrie could so much as give it a covetous glance.

Probably just as well. Touching that disk right now . . . likely not the smartest idea.

Lucia assessed the situation in a series of quick glances. Quite decisively, she stood—pushing her fruit bowl away, popping that strawberry into her mouth, and plucking up her tote. "We're outta here."

Drew pulled his curly fries in closer. "But I'm not—"

"Yes," she said, "you are. We'll get some real food at Safeway—it's just down the block. Or we'll get room service; they had some very fine things on that menu."

"Room service!" Drew said, shoving back his chair as he got to his feet. "Okay, we're outta here."

"I don't feel very good," Garrie finally finished saying. Past that first flush of potential barfing and into the first flush of potential passing out.

"Exactly," Lucia said. "Come, people. Up with you, Garrie. Fresh air, chicalet."

Trevarr, too, had come to his feet—no chair scraping, no untoward extra movement. Just . . . there. Another hollow, echoing belch rattled the room, eliciting a new round of shrieks—as well as the sudden exodus of the most recently arrived tourists, right through the red-jacketed clump of managerial types.

"There," Lucia said, satisfied—as if she hadn't grabbed for a steadying chair just like everyone else. "They've broken a path for us."

"I'm up," Garrie said. And then, "Am I up?"

Quite suddenly, she was. On her feet, a steadying hand curved around her ribs. Snug up against that long leather coat, tucked so neatly beneath arm and shoulder.

"You're up," Lucia said. "Let's go."

Garrie moved her feet and left the rest to everyone else. In fact, she just plain closed her eyes, and at some point she was aware that the air had turned fresh on her face, that bright sunshine hit her closed eyelids but quickly gave way to dappled shade. City noise filled the distant background with rumbling trucks and tires humming against asphalt, but also the discordant twitter-chirp of birds quarreling over tourist scraps and tree turf. The energies out here rippled more shallowly, with less mingling and interference. The weakness receded; her feet began to feel as though they might just be attached to her body after all.

And by then they stopped moving, her feet on grass and her body in shade. Trevarr lowered her to the ground with so little effort she might as well be a sack of feathers.

Come to think of it, she felt like a sack of feathers. Pretty much the same amount of brain.

"Good?" Trevarr said, but she got stuck answering simply because she had no idea.

"Come, chic," Lucia said, crouching down so her voice was level with Garrie's ear. "Time to open your eyes, yes?"

"What *was* that?" Drew asked, facing the other way, looking back at the house. "I guess it could have been spirits, but . . . aren't they tied to the house? And . . . something about it just didn't seem . . ."

"Ghostish," Garrie said.

"Ah, so you *are* there," Lucia said. "I thought so. Our friend the walking wall isn't talking. Your turn, Garrie. Open your eyes, rejoin us. Speak."

Garrie assayed a cautious squint. Bright midday sun splashed off the cars in the parking lot and heated up the asphalt, but she found herself in a little shade island—thick, cultivated grass populated with several well-tended trees. She found Trevarr, too—he'd come down to a crouch, hunkering down in such a way that made her think he could simply hang out for days, waiting, if he had to. He wore the sunglasses again, but it wasn't like those eyes gave anything away anyway.

She shook her head carefully. "I've never felt anything quite like this. It . . . doesn't agree with me."

Lucia snorted. In a princess way, of course.

"I already said I think we need to come back." She squinted at Lucia. "I did say that out loud, before—didn't I?"

"Yes," Lucia confirmed, but she looked doubtful. "You want to go on another tour?"

Drew made a dismissive noise, plumping himself down in the grass behind Garrie—sitting cross-legged, leaning back on his arms, his face tipped up like a sun geek. "Waste of time," he said. "No wonder Garrie got slammed. Those people . . . too strange. Totally in the way."

Garrie laughed, as unconvincing as it was. "You can

be darned sure they're saying the same about us right now."

"I think right now they're looking for the fastest way to hose themselves off. They really should have gotten out of that café faster," Lucia suggested, tipping her head in the direction of the building. "But Drew has a point, yes? What do we gain by doing *that* again?"

"We don't," Trevarr said, a deep growl of counterpoint.

But he still intended to come again; Garrie could hear that much. She opened her eyes all the way. "You want to come back after hours. To break in."

He lifted his chin slightly in affirmation.

"Oh, surely not," Lucia said. "There will be guards, and locks, and alarm systems . . ."

"It's not a bank, Lu." Drew's amusement stated his position pretty clearly: *all for it.* He wanted to play in the candy-land allure of this place; that was obvious enough.

"Still," she said, sounding stubborn—the only one of them still standing. No grass stains for Lucia.

"The inner grounds might be useful," Trevarr said.

"Private tour," Garrie suggested. "They do them, for groups. I don't know how much notice they need."

"Wow, you've been reading the brochure," Drew said. "Almost like Quinn was here."

Nothing like if Quinn was here.

"I need to call him," Garrie murmured. "Maybe he can find something about this activity. And besides, I just need to—"

"Call him," Lucia finished for her, and then offered a bittersweet little smile. "I miss him, too. We totally need someone spouting off irrelevant facts at the worst possible moment."

Maybe we do.

"So, okay," Drew said, without opening his eyes or turning his face away from the sun. Garrie, still feeling the cold burn, full of flush and goose bumps at the same time, was glad enough to stay in the shade. "We'll come back tonight, then. Late. *Way* late. But what do we do between now and then?"

"You must be kidding," Lucia said. "Did you not see my places-to-shop list?"

"Not on purpo—ow! What's that for? Reading over your shoulder, or not caring?"

"Both." Lucia retracted her precision toe and crossed her arms. "The point is, I'm covered. Don't tell me you didn't bring classwork, if nothing else. And Garrie, I think . . . she sleeps."

"Hey!" Garrie said. "What if I want to see the Tech Museum?"

Lucia raised her naturally arched eyebrows. "Then do that. If you think it's best."

Garrie scowled; she prepared to argue. But Trevarr alerted to someone approaching from the house and gift shop, and fairly vibrated with unspoken warn-off.

Not that it deterred the young woman in question. She hesitated at the edge of the parking lot and then came on, her chin stuck at an unconvincing angle and her steps a little too close to *forced march*. Lanky, her red tour guide vest and button-down shirt over a narrow torso and hips flared wide by nature and not padding, she headed straight for them. As she grew closer, her features came clear—just as lean as the rest of her and not much flattered by long, sandy-red hair drawn back in a complicated twist and secured with sticks. She crossed the sparsely populated parking lot and marched straight to their little oasis, stopping on the edge of Garrie's shade, one foot on the high curb. "I need to talk to you," she said, her voice high and tense. He gaze drifted upward, her head unconsciously tilting up to follow, as she found Trevarr's face and obscured eyes.

Garrie made a grumbling noise. "What do you think?" she asked the others. "*Go ahead and talk* and then we don't listen, or *you can try,* or just pretend we don't hear her?"

"You can try," Drew said immediately.

"We use that too often," Lucia protested.

He sat up straighter. "Because it's so rad, man."

"Not sure that means what you think it means, these days," Lucia muttered. "I vote for pretending we don't see her. Then we can go."

"Hey!" The young woman scowled. "How is that supposed to work? I'm right *here.* I can hear you discussing the whole thing."

Trevarr looked down at her; his rough-edged baritone came as a complete surprise to her, to judge by her briefly widened eyes. "They are wiley beyond imagining," he said, deadpan. Garrie made a choking noise.

"Look," the young woman said, not without exasperation. "My name is Beth. And I know what you're seeing. In the house, I mean. I've been coming to tours here since I was old enough to bike in. I used to see . . . I *still* sometimes see . . ." She took a deep breath. "I can always hear them."

"And we care . . . why?" Not that Garrie wasn't willing to believe her. What she *wanted* . . . that was the crux of it.

Trevarr, she could tell, didn't care at all. The way he drew himself up—as if he needed to be any taller— the way he held himself, as though he might go for some I-mean-business weapon at any moment. Something with a blade.

Garrie closed her eyes, briefly hid her face in her hands. *What am I even thinking?*

But when she looked at him again, she was no less convinced.

Neither was Beth, who faltered. "Look," she said, again. "I heard what Carolyn was saying. How you reacted to the house. How things happened in the séance room. It's a dead giveaway if you don't scream your lungs out like everyone else, you know. And you—" she pointed at Drew, gaining confidence. "You knew things about the house that even Carolyn doesn't know, and she's been here longer than any of us!"

"Hey," Drew said, with extreme and completely false modesty. "I have a great sense of direction."

"Cool," Beth said. "That totally explains how you knew which doors went where. Oh, wait. Gee, it *doesn't.*"

"But," Drew said, startled. "The DVD—"

"Gives you a deliberately unstable view with no context at all. From that, you reacted faster than Carolyn? Or did you not hear the part where I mentioned how long she's been doing this?"

Garrie couldn't keep the amusement from her voice as she straightened her back and crossed her legs, perking up into this conversation. "Maybe he's been here before."

Beth made a noise. *Pfft.* "Too late for that one."

"What *do* you want?" Lucia asked, one hand on her hip, head gently cocked—like Garrie, mildly amused.

Trevarr . . . still not amused. Beth wisely inched away from him. *"You,"* she said. "Look at you. Hiding in the shadows, wearing *leather* on a day when most of us are peeling off as many layers as we can."

Garrie thought it was the first time she'd seen him startled. *"Hiding?"* She climbed to her feet, still a little unsteady, but . . . definitely finding herself again.

"You're the one who feels it most, aren't you?" Beth asked her.

Garrie shrugged. She tugged her shirts down, found her pants askew and straightened those out, too, giving herself a reassuring pat-down. *There, there. Everything's where it was. Belly button and all.* She resisted the urge to lift her shirts and see if the disk had left an imprint on her skin . . . or even a tattoo.

Beth took a step closer. A little too earnest, but Garrie stood her ground. The young woman might be pushy, yes, but she hadn't yet given off any *be wary* vibes. Drew apparently thought the same; he, too, had come to his feet, moving up behind Garrie. Beth looked at him; her gaze lingered there. If she thought he was calling the shots . . .

No. More likely she found him the least intimidating of all of them. In any event, it was enough to get her started. "Can you tell me what's wrong here? Why they're so unhappy? Because things haven't been right for the past month."

Garrie wasn't ready to tip her hand to this tour guide, not yet. "How so?" *Turnabout . . . fair play.*

But Beth hesitated, and Garrie shook her head. "You know, the red-vest people were pretty eager to talk to us. After we got by them twice, you don't suppose they might have sent out a nice person of our own age to find us . . . to *relate* to us? Who are you reporting to, Beth?"

"Oh," Beth said, and she blushed furiously. She had the kind of thin skin that showed it, too, all the way down her throat. Drew made a noise of protest, and Garrie took a step back . . . just enough to step on his toes, aim unerring. When Beth spoke again the words tumbled out. "They're always murmuring," she said. Not an answer, not yet. "Just to themselves, as they wander. But in the last month, they've been gathering in clusters— more and more. And now they're talking to one another. It's loud and it's unpleasant. It's like all they know how to say is *we need help* and they say it to each other because they don't have anyone else to talk to."

"Until today," Lucia said, musing to Garrie as if Beth weren't even there.

"Yeah," Garrie muttered. "Too bad they couldn't come up with something I can work with."

"I'm right!" Beth wrapped her arms around her waist in a self-hug that might have been restraint, might have been reassurance. "I knew it! Finally!"

"Finally?" Drew said, taken aback.

"Oh, come on. We get people through here all the time, talking in stage whispers about how they see ghosts. Looking for attention, trying to impress us with Aunt Lulu's pantry ghost and the things they think they see here. Trying to be more special than thou."

Hmm. Garrie could come to like this woman.

"That's what you *didn't* do," Beth said. Briefly, she hugged herself a little tighter. "That's when I knew, I think."

And Garrie looked at her in the silence that followed, and realized suddenly that Beth probably wasn't more than a year or two younger than Garrie herself, and yet Garrie felt . . .

Whoa.

Seasoned. Older.

Jaded, even. Yet right there in Beth's eyes she saw the excitement that Garrie, too, had once followed to adventures beyond the ken of Beth's Winchester House Wannabes.

What Beth saw on her face, she didn't know . . . except that the silence stretched longer, and no one really seemed to know where to go from there, and the longer it stretched the worse it got.

Drew of all people saved the day. "You know," he said, his *casual* failing miserably, "it might really help me to have a talk with Beth. Draw out some rooms, learn some of the things she knows about the house. It could come in handy when we . . . later."

Saved the day and nearly gave the game away, all in one breath. "Sure," Garrie said through teeth that were only mildly clenched. "If you think you can keep yourself to Rhonda Rose Rules."

Beth blinked. "Rhonda Rose Rules?" she said, perhaps just a wee bit wary. "What are those?"

"Friend of mine," Garrie said. "A very discreet individual." She shot Drew a look over her shoulder.

Beth pulled back slightly. "In other words, you want to suck me dry for information, but you don't want to give it up."

"That," said Garrie cheerfully, "is it exactly." Because she worked by word of mouth, just as Trevarr had found her. Personal recommendation. And she checked out her new clients, generally a whole lot better than she'd ever checked out Trevarr. He'd gained a lot of leeway when he'd handed off Amanda Myers' name.

Not to mention when he'd promised her real ghostie action.

She had to admit, she couldn't complain on that front. She'd had more action in the past day than in the past six months. And now that she was getting over the startle factor of it all . . .

It felt familiar. It felt *good*—a challenge, her blood stirring, her conclusions not foregone.

But Beth . . . she had nothing. And Garrie wasn't about to let her in on the good stuff, not that fast. Not with so much already at stake. "Truth is, you haven't told us anything we don't already know. You might want in on this, but we can easily go without *sucking you dry* if that's what it takes."

Beth scowled at her. "I'm not going to stop trying," she said. "But I won't be sneaky about it."

"Hey," Drew said, and cleared his throat. "That seems fair, doesn't it?"

"It's not about *fair*," Garrie shot at him, mainly because he should know better. And yet . . . it did seem fair. She glanced at the others, took Trevarr's cold disapproval in stride, and turned back to Beth. "I'm Lisa, but you're going to hear them call me Garrie. This is Lucia, Drew, and Mr. Friendly there is Trevarr. If you want to talk to Drew on those terms, then go for it."

"I can meet you," Drew said, destroying any illusions of *how-casual-are-we*. Garrie glanced at Lucia and rolled her eyes, but only a little—Lucia's eyebrows were already climbing skyward.

"I—" Beth started, as if suddenly she wasn't sure.

"Here," Drew said. "Or at the hotel—the lobby, I mean. Or somewhere else if that's what you want."

"Public, then," she said, glancing at Trevarr.

"Sure. And I'm pretty sure Trevarr is busy. Doing something . . . *else*."

Trevarr relaxed just the slightest bit; maybe he'd decided she was harmless—or that Drew was harmless, one or the other or even both. "I am certain of it."

"Well, okay then," she said. "I have a car. I can come to your hotel—" She broke off, stiffening as though poked.

And Garrie, too, stiffened, crouching slightly as the ground seemed to jerk beneath her—except that no one else seemed to notice at all.

"*Qué?*" Lucia murmured.

But Garrie's feet stayed steady; she had no sudden urge to lose what little she'd eaten of lunch and no inclination to faint. Nothing but the slight, contradictory cold heat of that disk-shaped spot on her lower belly. "I can't do anything with it," she told Lucia, not hiding the annoyance in her voice. "We have *got* to get a handle on this before we go back in there. Quinn—"

"Hey!" Beth whirled with righteous vehemence turned to utter bafflement, her hand flying to cover her ribs. "Ow!" She whirled back in the other direction, slapping at some invisible encroachment.

"Ohh-*kay*." Lucia said. "That's not particularly ghostish. I mean, usually if we're going to get direct contact, we get some sort of ethereal manifestation. Darkside?"

"I'd feel it," Garrie said, frowning.

Beth squeaked; both her decorative hair sticks clattered to the ground, hair itself tumbling thick and free.

Her voice rose in pitch. "Can't you—*hey!*—stop talking and *do* something?"

But if it wasn't ethereal energies and it wasn't darkside energies, both of which she could wrangle, then . . . She stepped out of the shade to close the distance between them, looking hard . . . blind in broad daylight.

Drew did more than that; he stepped off the curb to join Beth, standing at her back with his arms slightly spread—defensive. Garrie opened her mouth to say it wouldn't do any good—once spirits targeted an individual, they weren't easy to deter or distract. But where Drew now covered Beth's back, she no longer reacted to the poking and prodding and pinching she'd evidently been receiving. And Drew had clearly become a target, both of them now slapping at air until Beth cried out, "Oh! It's in my *hair*—!" and started beating at her head with the kind of frantic mindless panic that meant her personal freak-out buttons had been pushed—with Garrie still standing there, mouth dropped, at a loss.

Not so Drew. Drew turned to Beth as though she were an old friend and pulled her in, tucking her head down and wrapping himself around her as best he could. He flinched as a bright red mark appeared on his cheek, but he didn't give up his charge. He glared at Garrie. "*Do* something!"

"Like *what*?" she shot back, just as frustrated. She pushed at the energies, physically mirroring her ethereal efforts, but couldn't get any kind of grasp on them. Trevarr moved up behind her, fumbling at something— that damned duster—but she paid him no mind as another red mark bloomed on Drew's face. Beth jerked within his protectively circling arms, her cries muffled, as her vest yanked away from her and then tore.

"Ohh," Lucia breathed, edging off to the side. "I think we should leave. *Escapamos!*"

Trevarr cursed under his breath; Garrie heard a snick

and clatter of cold metal against metal, a gun sort of noise. She stiffened, and as a high piercing whine shivered through the air around Drew and Beth, he snapped at her, "Don't move—"

As if. Draw a freaking gun *behind my back—*

She stepped back with one foot, setting her weight, *Action Figure Reckoner*, whirling to—

Whirling to—

Not whirling at all.

Because the whining escalated to a piercing shriek, vibrating until the air shimmied, and Garrie's elbow hit unyielding flesh—ribs and muscle wrapped tight and closer than she'd thought—and Trevarr's arm instantly clamped around her in inexorable shoulder belt mode. She struggled only for an instant, subsiding to watch, wide-eyed, as all of Beth's very long hair stood on end, drawn up into a vortex of energy. The shrieking escalated, air shimmied faster, the hair rose higher, and Lucia said, "No, really. I'll just go, and there won't be so many of us to worry about—" as she inched away, and then abruptly couldn't stand it and shouted, "What part of *run away* do you *not* understand? Ai! *Estúpido! Cerebro de calamar!*"

Garrie doubted that Trevarr listened, squid brains or no. Not while fumbling one-handed to deal with whatever he held off to the side. She glimpsed the flick of his wrist, the way his thumb worked, and the responding metallic slide of sound. Whatever it was, it had a flat, wide strap, braided hair that could have been horse hair had it not been darkly iridescent. Garrie caught a flash of color and burnished silver and sleek curves, and nothing more.

She managed to meet Lucia's torn and anxious gaze—and to think, in midst of it all, *she's not reacting*. These spirits— whatever they were—they were angry. *Furious.* Emotions ramped up full force, yet Lucia hadn't as much as blinked. Hadn't shed a tear, snarled an out-of-character curse, or otherwise lost her head. "You *should* go," Garrie said, words that neatly ceased to exist beneath the wail of the razor-edged tones. Behind her, Trevarr made a sudden move—

"Whoa!" Drew cried out, staggering sideways and taking Beth with him. The whining sound stopped; Beth's hair fell thick and heavy and tangled, engulfing them both.

Trevarr staggered quite suddenly backward, as though someone had let go the other end of a tug-of-war rope. He dragged Garrie with him, and they might even have stayed on their feet if Lucia hadn't rushed in to help and then waited an instant too long in a little *should I touch him* dithering dance and down they all went, awash in conflicting momentum. The only ones still standing were Beth and Drew; they clung to each other, tangible reassurance in the wake of intangible insanity.

Not to mention that they could hardly separate cleanly at the moment, not with Beth's hair tangled around them.

"It's gone," Garrie said, as wondering and dazed as the rest of them. "Whatever it was . . ." She took a deep breath, clean and free of any taint of the weird shimmering energy that had been so focused on Beth. "It's gone."

And there she was, leaning against corded muscle that turned out to be a thigh, with a long leg crossing between hers and Lucia, tangled at her ankles. She turned to Trevarr with a scowl. "How long have I known you? Thirty-six hours? And how many times have I ended up on the ground like this? That's not a great record, Trevarr."

He barely glanced at her, lost in some struggle—it showed, just barely, in the play of muscle at the back of his jaw and the strain at his mouth, just enough so Garrie's annoyance somehow got stuck in her throat and died there, and she wanted instead to reach out and . . . yeah, and help. Somehow. As if he really ever needed help, this man.

He does. That's exactly why he came for you.

Isn't it?

Crap. If a reckoner couldn't trust her gut instinct, it didn't leave her with much. And still, her hand ended up on his knee—tentative, fingers light on worn leather pants where they met with those idiosyncratic boots—just in case, somehow, he needed not to be quite so alone in the crowd this time.

Beth scraped hair from her face and tugged it free—rather wildly—from the button at the top of Drew's polo shirt. "What did you *do*?" she asked, also rather wildly. "What did they want from you?"

"Chica," Lucia said, climbing to her feet to regard the green grass stain on her perfectly rounded bottom with some disdain, "if they wanted something from Garrie, they would have been messing with *Garrie*. You follow?"

"They . . ." Beth said. "Me?"

Drew put his hands over hers, stilling them, and then took over the task of freeing her from him. Hair caught on the button, hair tangled over his shoulder . . . he petted it as if it were a living thing, returning it to her. His care with the windblown strands didn't blunt the look he threw at Garrie. His face still bloomed with welts, bright enough so Garrie thought they might even scab. "I can't believe it," he told her. "You couldn't do a thing with them!"

"Hey!" She disengaged from Trevarr, pushing off the knee where her hand had been resting. "It's not like I didn't *tell* you. I've *been* telling you. There's something here that doesn't give horny-toad spit about me or what I do."

Beth was finally free, if in a state of complete disarray; Drew stepped away from her, waiting for her to realize it. "But *why*?" she said. "What have I done, other than what I've always done here?" Mindless fingers smoothed her vest and the shirt beneath it. What wasn't torn was totally disheveled.

"Come out here," Lucia said, as if that explained everything. And when, to judge by the baffled look on Beth's emotion-flushed face, it explained nothing, she acquired a patient look and said, "*You* can tell us about the house. And I don't think I'd go back there for the rest of your shift. Not today."

Beth didn't get it. She bent to retrieve her hair sticks, and she made quick, sloppy work of gathering her disarrayed hair and twisting it around at the back of her head, stabbing the sticks into place. But her face . . . still in shock, still blank in response to Lucia's words. "My next group leaves any minute now—"

Drew took her by the shoulders, pulling in what focus she had. "They came for you because *you* came out here to us," he said, and Garrie had never seen his indeterminately murky eyes look more serious. "You can't go back there now. It's not safe."

"But . . ." she said. "My shift—"

Mutely, Lucia held out her BlackBerry.

Garrie wasn't as silent, especially as Beth just stared at it. "Call them," she said. "Tell them you ate something off from the café right before that mess started. Stick a finger down your throat if you need convincing sound effects."

"I—" Beth said. "I couldn't."

Drew took the phone. "What's the number?" he asked. "I mean, we've got the public number, but I bet you've got a direct line."

She looked from Garrie to Lucia to Drew to Trevarr. Her gaze lingered on Trevarr—who'd gotten to his feet and again stood apart from them in the shade, once more a country unto himself—and returned to Drew. Finally, she muttered the number.

Drew punched it in without hesitation, and within moments he said, with just the right mix of concern and regret, "Hi, I'm calling for Beth . . . yeah, she can't come to the phone right now." Not a single misappropriated, misapplied or outdated slang word. "Oh, really? I'll let her know. Yeah, thanks. I'm sure she'll be okay. That café just got a little gnarly there, she said—bad timing on that snack."

Okay, he'd made it until the very end, anyway. And Garrie barely waited until he cut the connection before the exclamation burst out of her. "I had no idea you were such a good liar!"

"Huh," he said, looking at the phone before he handed it back to Lucia. "Me, either. But it doesn't look like it's any big deal. They're closing down the house for the rest of the day while they check things out. Grounds are still open, though."

"They what?" Beth looked more shocked at this news than she had been at the attacking entities. "They *closed*?"

"You're free and clear," Drew said. "So let me take you to lunch. We'll talk."

She looked down at herself. Torn and disheveled and pale; what a mercy there was no mirror to reflect the state of her hair.

"You'll feel better," Drew said.

"Okay," Lucia said. "*I* am going shopping. No more lingering here." But she dug into her tote, pulled a brush from its petite depths, and motioned Beth over. "Garrie is going back to the hotel to rest and order some real food from room service. And Trevarr?"

He merely looked at her, probably wondering where this particular organizational frenzy was coming from.

Garrie knew. As Lucia gestured to Beth again, impatience evident, Garrie knew. For Lucia was ready to shop. Ready enough that she threw her hands up and went over to the tour guide, plucked out her hair sticks, and began tackling the tangles with swift but gentle efficiency, the tote dangling at her elbow. Beth froze, a deer in the headlights, while Lucia made tsking noises at the mess.

"Let me see the phone," Garrie told Drew. "I left mine at the hotel, and I'm thinking it's time to get out of here. I'll call that taxi."

"Oh," Beth said. She had a funny look on her face, as though she wasn't sure why she was speaking up at all—but said it anyway. "No need for that. I've got my car."

10

Look askance at what lures you.
—Rhonda Rose

Parlor, fly.
—Lisa McGarrity

Lucia squeezed out of the backseat first, her posterior poised in the doorway, complete with the brush of green over one ass cheek. Trevarr glanced that way; how he'd ended up in the middle seat of the subcompact car, Garrie wasn't sure. In fact, she'd been sure they wouldn't squeeze into the vehicle in the first place. Back at the Winchester Mystery House parking lot, they'd all stopped short at the sight of the hunkered down little Honda Fit, exchanged equally dubious glances, and started pasting on various polite expressions as a prelude to backing slowly away.

But Beth showed the first signs of regaining her quiet

determination. She beeped the doors unlocked, stuck the upper half of her body into the back of the car, and began rearranging seat sections with a vengeance. "Sorry, I was hauling costume gear. There's this con—" She stopped, shook her newly coiffed head. "Never mind." She finished flipping seats, reemerged. "There. This is Bill the Pony."

"This is a car," Trevarr said warily.

"Psst," Garrie said, with no attempt to lower her voice. "It's a name. She named the car. Bill the Pony."

"Oh, come *on*." Drew eyed Trevarr in disbelief. "There's no way you dress like that and haven't read Tolkien."

And that's when Garrie, acting on some impulse, had climbed into the vehicle and pulled Trevarr in behind her, so he ended up in the narrow little spot between the two main backseats of Bill the Pony, and Lucia dropped in beside him and pulled the door closed.

Garrie suspected that Drew had been aiming for that front passenger seat all along. He certainly made no effort to disembark from it, not while Lucia's derriere now hovered there in the exit, gave a peculiar little wiggle, and then moved out with such abrupt alacrity that Garrie knew exactly what had happened—Lucia had hailed a cab before she'd even left the car. Garrie barely saw her trailing wave, too distracted by the briefly stunned look on Trevarr's face. "I swear," she told him, "she didn't do that on purpose. She just doesn't . . . think."

"She thinks, all right," Drew said, barely audible from the front seat. "About *shopping*."

How Trevarr then got himself out of the small, low car so easily, Garrie wasn't sure. He just . . . did it. Out the door and suddenly turned around, offering her his hand. She wanted to wave him off, levitating out into the bright afternoon just as he'd somehow done. But she was tired now and coming on cranky; whatever energies had washed through her body this day had left her wrung out and twisted around. So she took his hand and in spite of the strength in the roughened fingers that closed around hers, she still stumbled as she got out.

"Door!" Drew reminded her, before her second foot even hit pavement. She closed it a little harder than necessary and the Honda Fit made a little hiccough as Beth shifted it into first and drove off.

For a moment, Garrie simply stood there, absorbing the fact that although they were planning a haunted house break-in that evening, although they'd just returned from not one but two significantly inexplicable ethereal encounters there, and although they had a wealth of debriefing to do, her team had nonetheless scattered here at the hotel entrance, leaving her here to . . . what, *nap*? Was she seventy? She gave a haughty sniff, turned on her heel, and promptly tripped over her own feet.

Trevarr righted her, of course. Without comment.

Not safe, indeed. "If Quinn was here," she said, very small, "he would have stayed."

"Quinn. The boyfriend."

She shot him a quick incredulous look. "I—no! Hey, maybe once. Okay, maybe twice. It was a fling! And, oh—" because he'd shown no reaction at all, "You didn't really want to know that, did you."

He slanted her a look. Hard to tell with those sunglasses on, but she was getting adept at reading the nuances he granted her.

Just not so sure that's a good *thing.*

He said, "I was not soliciting."

"Well, fark that," Garrie muttered to herself. A weird warping moan vibrated through the air; it fit the moment so perfectly that she barely noticed it as she stalked into the hotel to jam her thumb on the elevator call button. A good nap, that's what she needed, all right. And food. Just as Lucia had said. And then she'd call Quinn and she'd take a shower and she'd see what Drew had learned, other than just how fast one socially inexpe rienced ghost geek could infatuate himself with a starstruck tour guide. Or more precisely, a reckoner-struck tour guide. *Aiiee.* She dragged her hands down her face, pulling on cheeks and lids and mouth and ignoring Trevarr's somewhat startled regard.

Yeah. A nap. Because if she knew one thing for sure, it was that her recently complacent life had not pre-pared her for any of this.

But heaven help her . . . it still called to her. Past her tumbling mind and her jarred nerves and her whirled-up internal energies. This, finally, was a job to do Rhonda Rose proud.

Of course, she wasn't expecting to leave Trevarr at his own door, dig the card key from her thigh pocket, push it in and out of the lock with quick efficiency, and stride in to stop startled at the sight of her bed.

Okay, the maid had been here, that was clear enough. Both beds made. Mints all around. Drapes perfectly set to half open, new plastic cups on top of the minifridge, and the instant coffee packets resupplied. But—

"Hey," she said, indignant. "Who's been lying in *my* bed?"

For her side of the bed was a mess.

More than a mess. The bedspread had been pulled back from the pillow; the pillow was sideways. Garrie tugged it carelessly straight, discovered the mint—

No, wait. The outer wrapping of the mint. The *empty* outer wrapping of the mint. How weird was that? And when she ran her hand over the rumpled spread, her fin-gers caught in the holes that hadn't been there that morn-ing. "No way!" She dropped down beside it, pulling it straight . . . running her hands over the several areas that had been . . .

Wow. Shredded.

"That's just not right," she murmured.

Besides which, it made no sense. Not in the ghostly context—because sure, a determined ghost with a dark-side partner might figure out how to inflict this kind of damage, but there hadn't been any ghosts here. And not in the housekeeping context.

Garrie splayed her fingers out over the bedspread. She'd have to call the front desk and report it. She narrowed her eyes at the damage, felt her chin get annoyed and determined. Fine. That wasn't going to go well, but fine.

It could wait.

She grabbed her pillow, squinted at the many inexplicable fine hairs drifting to the floor, and marched over to Lucia's side of the bed, kicking off her shoes. There she lay down, rolled the bedspread around her body like a cocoon, and plumped her pillow over her head instead of under it. And there, within the darkness, her thoughts drifted away.

Cold wash of heat and a deep startled grunt and a hard, heavy body dragging her down and far, far too many unanswered questions . . .

They lingered there, at the forefront of her mind, poking and prodding at exhaustion she shouldn't have felt from one simple visit to even the most wildly haunted house. As she finally drifted to sleep, she felt only the faint physical memory of a hand on her belly, cold-hot metal pressed up against her through thin shirts, and the addictive rush of energy reaching for every inner corner of her being. And just on the verge of sleep, she suddenly wasn't sure if the energy had come from the disk she hadn't yet truly seen . . . or from the man himself.

Sklayne sat quiet, so quiet. Pulled unto himself, invisible in every sense.

If he made no movement, no breezes for this small person of much power to discern, she would have no idea he sat tucked away at the back corner of the massive red mahogany stand holding the delightfully chaotic *television* and the drawers stuffed with clothes and half the copious pocket contents of the lanky person who listened to the past.

Sklayne didn't think the lanky person would miss those hard candies with the linty outer layer. *Crunchy.*

But now he sat quiet, so quiet. He heard Trevarr moving around in the adjoining room, as silent as Trevarr liked to think he was. Soon, time to return there, to understand better what had happened during the away. But here, now, he waited. The small person's breathing grew deeper, more regular . . . occasionally included a muffled little purr of a snore.

Sklayne stood. Cat body, Sklayne energy . . . the in-between form, barely visible. Cat of purest glass transparency, tinted faintest indigo blue. He moved a tidy paw . . . waited. Went unnoticed. A flip of ear, a flick of tail, and he bounded quite suddenly across the room and up onto the bed, making little dimples of progress across the puffy bedspread.

Shredded.

Regret at that. He stopped, delicately sniffing the damage. Trevarr had questions to answer, oh, yes. But first . . .

The scent of her drew him. Just as he'd found her pillow so irresistible, he now found her. He padded up to the curve of her hip beneath the rolled-up bedspread, more shape than he'd expected for the otherwise scant nature of her. She'd turned over to her side, clutching the end of the bedspread around her, her head beneath the pillow.

Odd person.

He touched her chin with his whiskers, sniffing

delicately; scent filled his nostrils and threatened to wring a sneeze from him; he butted his head into the puffy quilted covering and muffled the sound of it.

So strong. So intense. So unique.

So tainted.

Sklayne's tail lashed; he glared at the adjoining door. *Answers, Trevarr . . .*

But he couldn't bring himself to do the smart thing, to tear himself away from this sleeping one and go brace his *atreyvo*. His bonded. No, he drew in close, pulling in the scents, luxuriating in what she was . . . and analyzing what she wasn't supposed to be.

No wonder she had been tired, walking through the door to fail to notice him. No wonder the very essence of her tasted wrong now. What had Trevarr done?

Sklayne moved around her, precise paw placement stitching an outline of her body. He shaped the breezes around her . . . made them soothing, made them cleansing. And then, when she stirred slightly, he repaired to the end of the bed to pay fastidious attention to one already spotless—still transparent—paw, grooming assiduously between the toes. Just observing.

On impulse, he slid awareness to the room next door—to the man who sat slumped, staring off through half-opened curtains, sunglasses tossed aside and eyes neither covered nor disguised. Elbow on the little fake desk thing, legs sprawled out to take up more than their fair share of space . . . and tired. Just as tired as Garrie.

What happened?

What did you keep from me?

He eased back up to Garrie, inhaled deeply.

All the hair on his cat tail puffed out to twice its normal size; all the hair along his back stood on end and his bony, unremarkable bottom jutted up in the air to join it, making him all fierce at nothing in spite of his best attempts at control. *All fierce at some*thing*. At the* deeply buried hum of Trevarr making dissonance in the small person. Interfering with her inner breezes, invading her inner spaces.

But it was fading . . . Sklayne thought he saw the signs that the incursion ebbed.

He hoped he saw the signs.

He patted her, so gently, transparent claws carefully sheathed . . . she made a snuffling little noise and fell more deeply into sleep.

Fine. Good. *What have you done?* Still sitting right there, the beige bedspread quilt pattern rippling slightly beneath his transparent self, Sklayne stared at the adjoining door . . . slid his awareness back over to the one who had bound him. Slid in deep, as he rarely did—rarely welcome, either. Found the lingering pain there, deep and aching, and followed it to memories and feelings and *what*—

"Mow!" and *Get out!* overlapped in startlement and fury, sending Sklayne tumbling off the bed with a hiss and a spit.

Get in here!

::Your mind,:: Sklayne sent back at him, prickly and claws digging into carpet. ::Make it up!::

In. Here. Now.

And with that last, Trevarr gave a jerk of the command tone he seldom used, the one with real physical consequences; the one Sklayne couldn't defy or ease his way around or even drag his heels over. "Mow!"

Garrie stirred.

But it didn't matter. By the time she shoved the pillow off her head and squinted her eyes open, Sklayne would be long gone, a quick *pow* of energy, a literal explosion into his pure form and beneath the door.

Heat assailed her. It made her twitch, startled, with the impulse to find cool earth, to go to ground. But darkness already swirled around her, along with sharp, astringent scents and the faint patter of something wind-borne against her skin. Insects, pollen, random debris . . . she knew only that it stung.

Something wild howled in the night, an arching, ulu-lating cry that seemed to come from all directions at once . . . seemed to surround her. The air landed thick on her throat and tongue, settled in the corners of her lungs. *Not the right air.*

Spt-spt-spt-spt! The cry broke off into rapid-fire hiss-spitting just to her side; she whirled and found eyes, only eyes, big night-creature orbs wide and un-blinking in that swirl of darkness that was, she realized, literally billows of inky fog, so thick as to obscure what must have been daylight. It puffed at her and cleared, long enough for her to see huge tufted ears and a sinu-ous furred body and childlike paw-hands and a long flick of a tail. It yowled—not to her—and *spt-spt-spt,* definitely at her, and then it bounded away, pushing off thick bangs of darkness as easily as climbing solid ground.

Yowled, but not to her . . . *There are others.* She in-stantly drew on the breezes, pushing at the fog, trying to clear her path and clear her mind, but the moment she reached for familiar energy, the unfamiliar poured in, cold and harsh, a dam break of frothing, churning flow, filling her from the core outward. Turned burning, somehow familiar. She gasped on it, floundering in the sensation—reveling in it and panicking all at once. But gasping only brought in that thick, sharp air—*not the right air*—and as she struggled with it, she found more eyes in the darkness, silvered cat's eyes, full of glow and meaning. Something shifted through the dark-ness . . . a man's torso, muscled and lean . . . but not. Tattoos, blooming to the surface . . . but not.

Air, filling her lungs . . . *but not.*

Not the right air . . .

Not the right energy . . .
Not the right life . . .

Sklayne rolled into the room, a roiling bundle of energy, and expanded—faster than his wont, encompassing the world, pulling himself back together to *cat*. To chastise. "Mow!"

"Don't," Trevarr said, before Sklayne had even stopped moving, before his feline protest had died away. Sklayne's whiskers pulled back on a hiss of protest—but it was a scolding kept silent. Trevarr grim, Trevarr battered at the edges. Not the right time.

::What?:: he demanded, in spite of it. ::How?::

Trevarr rubbed hands down his face, made the expression that meant annoyed reluctance. But Sklayne had been bound too long . . . he knew the annoyance was not for him.

At least not all of it.

Trevarr reached to an inner pocket of the coat that held everything. Sklayne should know. Sometimes it held him. He pulled out the Gatherer—sleek thing, fitting in Trevarr's hand when it should, but holding so much more. He pulled out the Tracker. Both clattered onto the minimalistic work desk. But when Sklayne leapt lightly to that surface to inspect them—a sniff, a touch, all so catlike but using senses no creature from this world had ever possessed—Trevarr's hand slapped over them both, startling Sklayne away.

Hiss-spit!

Trevarr ignored that, pinning Sklayne with a gaze the bound one knew well to avoid. Dark-edged silver, sometimes wilder than others. This was not a time to dare a glimpse. "Mind yourself," Trevarr said, and his voice confirmed it. *Not a time to dare.*

Except that it had to be done. Sklayne had duties. Obligations. And he'd never make it back home if Trevarr didn't do this right. Fur ruffled up; he smoothed it.

Tail puffed out. He sat, licked a paw, rubbed it over his face. Convenient cat habit, covering so much. Uncertainty. Embarrassment. Or even fear of one's own temerity. ::Felt you. Felt *it*.::

"It's not a problem," Trevarr said. Definitely a growl.

Sklayne hesitated in his wash, paw held poised for the next lick. Clear in his skepticism.

"It surprised me," Trevarr said. "This place . . ." He stopped, looked over to the closed door between the rooms. "*Her*. It won't happen again."

::Hurt her,:: Sklayne said. Observation, not accusation. He gave up on the paw, put it beside the other to sit primly on the table. Out of reach. Sitting beside Trevarr's travel satchel with its spilled sundries—the memory stone, the blood token, the *kirkhirrra* with its complexity of knots and history.

Trevarr's expression tightened; he looked away. Sklayne licked furiously at his back, hiding confusion. Not an expression he'd seen often. Trevarr said, so quietly, "I hope that won't happen again."

Hope.

But now . . . no, not the time to dare. So well he knew this bond-partner of his. So many runaways brought back together since he'd taken those steps away from his trees.

None quite like this.

He put a paw on top of Trevarr's hand, claws ever so slightly extruded. Trevarr scowled; his fingers tightened around metal; his eyes—safer now—narrowed. "Not much in the way of readings. Rebound presence, echo presence. The Krevata are entrenched; there will be no direct trail."

::The dead ones?::

"Tormented," Trevarr said grimly. He closed his eyes, tipped his head back . . . fumbled at the nape of his neck, and pulled away the fastening. He dropped a black hand on the table and scraped his hair back, a luxury for a being who allowed himself none.

Not that Sklayne noticed. Not really. Not with that black band sitting there. *Taunting.* He reached a tentative paw . . . batted at it. It flipped across the smooth wooden surface; he slapped his paw down on it. *O victory!*

Trevarr made a noise without looking. Deep in his chest, it was. Sklayne quickly straightened himself, *not seeing* the band. Not feeling the flex of it or the way his claws had caught its rubbery nature or the deep satisfaction it would bring to snatch it up and sink his teeth into it. No, no, no. Sat up straight, didn't look. Attentive. ::And?::

"The Krevata are riling the dead ones. Restricting them . . . preying on them. They didn't expect the dead ones to react to Garrie. It panicked them. Made them stupid."

::*Are* stupid,:: Sklayne pointed out, quite primly.

The faintest of smiles quirked Trevarr's mouth. "So they are," he murmured. He opened his eyes, glanced at Sklayne, tipped his head just so. An invitation.

Sklayne knew it. Knew unspoken the parameters of it. *Take a look, but don't go any farther.*

He did just that, sliding along the connection that always hung between them, slipping in deeper—invited, this time, and strictly observing. Through the eyes of Trevarr's memory, he saw the café interior—there was the Garrie person, gone pale and small as unfamiliar energies left their mark inside her. The Drew person, so disorganized on the exterior. The Lucia person, so very organized. Not so far away, the small young people, bouncing around, staring, being nosy and noisy . . .

::Crunchy snack::

He said it to hear Trevarr's warning noise, the quiet but unmistakable snort. To push Trevarr a little.

He was not disappointed.

And then in the memory, the world belched. Sklayne couldn't feel the warning energies—not from Trevarr's memories, not when Trevarr could not sense such things.

But he could feel Trevarr's unusual awareness of the Garrie person, the touching without touching. The *fizzzz*. He wanted to follow *that* memory, to feel more of it. Maybe to purr. But Trevarr shifted in the chair when he tried. *Too close.* Too raw to touch without creating reaction.

At least, not without getting caught.

So Sklayne watched the café belch, watched the people react, watched the Garrie person fade—knew the Krevata to be at the root of it all. Knew things would only get worse. But his paws kneaded wood as Trevarr pulled her to her feet and took the weight of her, touching *with* touching, and even in the chaos of the café, the need to leave, the worry for the Garrie person . . .

::Purrrrr.::

He stopped himself. *Not right.* He did not care about the Garrie person. He did not care if lonely Trevarr got to touch the Garrie person.

Pay attention. So he did. He watched the exodus to the paved area with scattered cars; he fast-forwarded through their dazed recovery there. And then came the new person, nervous and brave and so much with the hair. Then came again the Krevata.

Sklayne stiffened. He quivered. He crouched. His tail lashed. He couldn't see them, since Trevarr couldn't see them. But he knew they were there, oh, yes.

Prey.

But Trevarr failed to gather them, so exposed there where no one would understand. Sklayne felt the frustration of it—Trevarr's, building in the moment. His own, building in the aftermath, as the rampaging Krevata recognized danger and fled. Garrie had not known why; none of them had known why. Just as they hadn't truly understood why the attack occurred. They'd come close; they'd known Beth was a target. They'd known it was because she'd come to speak to them.

They hadn't known it had nothing to do with Garrie, and everything to do with Trevarr.

And they had no idea what was truly at stake.

Air, filling her lungs . . . *but not.*
Not the right air . . .
Not the right energy . . .
Not the right life . . .
"*Garrie—*"

A touch on her arm. Garrie shrieked into motion, flailing around inside the bedspread, pillow flying. A hiss, a spit, a retreating *mraowh!* and she hit the floor, thinking of hot scented air and tattoos blooming to stark intensity and glowing eyes—inspired, then, to scrabble away until she could gain distance and her feet.

If only she hadn't run into legs.

"Cat," she said faintly, as if that was the most important thing about this moment. "I heard—"

Large hands found her upper arms, pulled her to her feet. She didn't fail to notice bare toes on the way up, loose leather pants neatly creased where they'd once been folded inside high boots. Trevarr said, "There is no cat." And she could have sworn she heard amusement there.

It made her want to kick his shin. But not, on second thought, with her bare feet. That still left her with plenty of scowl.

He took her head between his hands. Warm, those hands. Warm and dry and cradling her jaw. She tried to turn away; his hands didn't yield. A kick to the shin suddenly seemed more likely.

"Sah, little one," he said, as if it ought to have made sense. "I want only to see that you are well."

She found his eyes tarnished dark at the edges, pupils tight even in this modestly dim light. That gaze caught at her, as it always had. So visceral, her response. *Hey, bay*-bee.

She wrenched herself away. "I did *too* hear a cat. Did you see my bedspread? And I thought that door was *locked*. You know. From *this* side."

He lifted one shoulder, barely. "You . . . made noise. I was concerned." A tip of his head, thick hair shifting. Tiny braids glimmered silver from within darkest brown, freed from the binding to briefly appear.

She snorted. "Sure. After this day? Surprise, weirdest dreams *ever* bashing around inside my head." She grinned suddenly—surprised herself, and then laughed. "It's just what you said, isn't it? *Something*. I got what I came for. I've got a job where I don't *know* the ending. I don't even know the next piece!" She shook her head, smiling wryly at herself. "The question is, did *you* get what you wanted?"

He gave the slightest shake of his head—shifted back, pulling away.

As if she'd let that happen.

She snatched his wrists, wrapping her hand around stillness—strength in muscle and bone, shifting ever so slightly beneath her fingers. "Don't," she said. "You're holding back. You *know* something."

For a long moment, he looked at her, cold silver up close. For that long moment, she wondered if she'd made the biggest mistake of her life. *Not safe.* And then he shook his head again, barely perceptible. It was enough. He freed himself from her grip with no effort at all, turning away.

As if that would stop her, just because there was a bed now in the way. Instantly she jumped up on it, teetering on the unsteady footing. He took hold of her waist, which seemed to surprise him as much as it did her. From the other room came a strange little sound, a hissy little spit to which she might well have paid more attention had she not been so preoccupied. Big hands, warm and low on her waist, thumbs cupping her hip bones. Damned personal. *Don't get distracted.*

Oh, so not safe. Pushing him, when she knew better. Doing it anyway, because the stakes meant she had to. "That's not good enough," she said. "The strong, silent thing, I mean." He frowned, bafflement behind it. "Don't even pretend you don't know what I'm talking about."

"Not answering," he said carefully, as if feeling the way through the words, "is not the same as not knowing. Or *pretending* a not-knowing." Up close, the nature of his accent drew attention all over again; she couldn't help but watch his mouth, as if it would give her clues. This close, the little scar off center under his lip looked less like an old piercing and more like a healing cut, the center deep and still pink, the ends already silvered and nearly invisible. This close, she could see that the significance of it hid in the shadow of his lip, and that the wound had once probably gone all the way through.

"Oh, as if that's even good enough." She put her hands on her hips, fisting them right on top of his. "What was that metal thing in the parking lot, Trevarr? What was the disk you had in the séance room? What did it *do* to me? I thought maybe an energy focus of some sort, but . . . but you know, I trusted you—I took that energy, and now I'm not so sure it was a good idea."

His hands tightened around her—painfully so, until he seemed to realize it and made a deliberate effort to relax his grip.

"Tell me," she said, lowering her voice but not her intensity. "What did you do to me? What did you put in my body?"

"You *took*," he said, grinding the words out.

"Because I *trusted*," she snapped back at him.

"Because you *needed*," he shot back at her. "You *used*. You farking played those spirits with it."

"Because I'm *good*." She was, suddenly, not very damned far away from his face. Bending over him some, intimidating him not at all. "But I need to know what I'm working with, and it's *really* clear you're keeping all the good stuff to yourself!" She glared at him from that close quarter, glared her hardest. He didn't return it so much as he went broody, anger coming at her from beneath a lowered brow. "Maybe I should just see if you can make good on those return tickets after all."

"You can't," he said instantly.

She laughed. "Because why? Because I'm so desperate for this work?" Okay, truth there. And he knew it. "Yeah, walking away would mean that when I'm eighty, I look back on this moment and wonder what my life would have been like if I'd stayed. But I'm not stupid and I'm not working blind. I can live with wondering."

"Can you live with what happens here if you don't stop it?"

"Get real." She jabbed a finger in the vague direction of Winchester House. "In twenty-four hours, that place will be inundated with wannabes and pros alike. They'll deal with the unsettled spirits and then they'll see who can be the first to write a book about it."

"No," he said. "They won't. They can't. They don't have—" His accent grew hard and strong, and then the words cut off.

"What?" Garrie snorted. "*You?* Tell me that's not what you were going to say."

"It is." He frowned. "Today should have shown you that."

"Gosh, no," Garrie said, ever so sweetly. "Why don't you explain it to me. Use small words, so I can keep up."

He snarled something under his breath. She didn't see

it coming when he grabbed her, hands closing around her upper arms and jerking her in—steadying her when she lost her balance on the shifting mattress.

Panic fluttered through her. *Get a grip* and yet *you must be kidding* with those gleaming eyes so very close, all burnished at the edges and looking directly at her, so much tension in him she could all but feel the vibration of it. Panic with very good reason, because *there he was,* his breath warm on her chin, his lips close enough to brush hers if he so much as spoke, and Garrie knew, bone deep, that if it went beyond that there would be no—

She would be—

Everything would be—

Changed.

There was only one thing to do, hovering there, treading panic as if it were water. *Way, way over her head.*

Go on the attack.

"Still waiting," she said, and now it was her lips that nearly brushed his. "Still wondering what you did in that house. Still wondering how you did it. And mainly wondering what else you haven't told me." She narrowed her eyes, lowered her voice. "And how much it's going to matter."

For an instant, he held her tighter yet. Then he closed his eyes, and something in him seemed to shudder, barely perceptible. "Don't," he said, his voice a deep rumble. "Don't push. You have no idea—"

"Who do you owe, Trevarr?" she asked, pushing. "What do you owe him? And why *me*?"

He looked at her and she could have sworn that was a smile, wry as it was, just tipping the corners of his mouth. Then again, she would have sworn that when he lifted his head slightly and took that deep breath, he was doing more than breathing. He was inhaling. *Her.* Those well-defined nostrils flared slightly; his pupils, nearly always cranked down against the light, dilated visibly. His voice, when he finally responded, sounded much more normal . . . and completely distracted. "I told you that. A friend recommended you. She spoke of you with much regard, and still . . . there was much she did not anticipate."

That last bit didn't make perfect sense; she let it go for now. "Right. Amanda." Her own voice was less than steady. Two people carrying on an absurdly normal conversation under absurdly far-from-normal circumstances. She was going to be so sorry for skipping the background check, relying on the reference rather than on research, so very sorry.

She realized she'd closed her hands around his arms, a grip not nearly as careful as his—steadying herself, grounding herself. She realized that if she reached for it, she could feel the same energy that had filled her in the séance room. Nothing she'd ever felt before, that. It wasn't as though she hadn't on occasion reached for something through Lucia. Or through Quinn. Clear, defined crystal breezes from anyone she'd ever touched that deeply.

Not so what she'd felt in that house. A mix of flavors there, a mix of sensations. Multidimensional. She wondered suddenly just how rude it would be to reach for that feeling again. Lucia had never discerned it; Quinn had never discerned it. No one had ever been able to feel her touch. And how different was it, really, than standing here and . . . *inhaling*?

Almost without conscious decision, she allowed herself that little trickle—not taking anything, because that wasn't what she did. She pushed breezes around; she rounded up spirits and darksiders and on occasion she pushed them *out*. Rhonda Rose had taught her that but no more. *"Be content with not knowing more than you should,"* she'd said, words that Garrie had taken to memory but not to heart.

Right now, she wanted to know more. More than Trevarr was saying, and quite obviously more than he intended to say. The little trickle . . . it was a start.

Except even as she got that hint of him—unfiltered by any mysterious metal disk, undiluted by the chaos of attacking spirits and screaming tourists, full and rich and marbled in layers—he stiffened, and his eyes went wide and more dilated yet, and she took in the rising scent of ash, bitter at the edges. He shook her, quick and hard; she yelped a protest.

"Mind yourself," he said, his voice full of hoarse smoke.

Garrie's reality spun around the axis of Trevarr—the ethereal taste, the very physical presence. The wild howl in the darkness, the hissing-spit of warning, the black fog . . . the scents of him, the absurd strength of the arms that held her, a thin, tight braid gleaming among burnt-sienna-brown and pewter-edged eyes and suddenly she blurted, "Do you have tattoos?"

Tattoos, blooming to the surface, but . . . not.

"Tattoos," he repeated, so blankly she knew he'd been taken by surprise.

"Scales. Feathers. Though . . . not either, really."

"Not," he said, "that I know of." They were no longer quite so close; he'd managed a step back, even as he kept her steady on the bed. But there was still something tight left in his voice . . . something familiar. She'd heard it in the séance room, too.

He reached for her waist, about to hoist her off the bed and back to the floor—to turn away, and become just as impenetrable as ever. Her words tumbled out a little more quickly than she'd planned. "You said before that I didn't hurt you . . . but—" Okay, deep breath here. "At the house . . ."

He went momentarily distant . . . completely still. She thought he wouldn't answer at all—that he'd just swing her off the bed and turn away. But his gaze returned to her from whatever inner place he'd gone to. "That," he said. "Yes. That hurt."

"I'm sorry, "she said, very small once more. "I wish . . . I wish I couldn't say I wouldn't do it again. But they would have killed me."

"Yes," he said again, and hesitated, searching her gaze . . . looking for what, she didn't know. Finding what . . . no clue. "So you see. That which I did, I would also do again. If necessary."

That which he wouldn't talk about. Great. "I get that," she said. "The difference is, you know what happened to you. You know what happened to me. I don't know either." And she jumped off the bed her own damned self, ignoring the trailing feel of his hand at her waist.

Pretending to ignore.

Over to the phone, which she picked up, stabbing the numbers for housekeeping. She briefly explained the need for a new comforter, listened to the *blah blah blah,* told them, "I have no idea what happened to it. I returned to the room and found it this way," and must have had enough edge in her voice to put an end to the questions, for she received a promise of a new bedspread. Eventually.

She half expected to find Trevarr gone when she turned back to him—in her mind's eye, employing ninja stealth to disappear and reappear back in his own room, the door neatly closed behind him—but no, there he was. Watching her. She tipped her head back, gave in to her *aurgh* impulse, and scrubbed at her hair—*hide the mirrors!*—with both hands. "Aurgh," she said, to complete the ritual. "That was *not* enough sleep. That was only tease sleep."

"You should get more," Trevarr told her. "It will help the dissonance."

"No telling when housekeeping will drop by." Garrie reached for the minifridge, pulled out a soda, and popped the top. Dehydrating, that ghost wrangling. As an after-thought, she went digging in her claimed drawer for a granola bar. "Want one?" she asked. "It's got little marsh-mallows and everything."

"This is the *real food* your Lucia spoke of."

"No, this is the food we don't tell her about. I'll get around to the *real food*. Want one?" She scrutinized him—the angles of his face looked harder, and fatigue had settled around his eyes. The morning had left its mark. "You look like you could use it."

"The . . . local fare . . . isn't entirely harmonious."

She laughed, a spurt of sound. "Isn't *what*?"

He frowned slightly.

She laughed again. "And here you were all macho on Drew over how the spicy didn't bother you."

The frown looked a little frustrated. "There is no *bother*. It leaves me . . . wanting."

Ahh. "Doesn't stick to your ribs?" Hard muscle, he was. A little *too* lean, maybe. "I don't know what you're used to, but surely we can find it here." A noise filtered out from his room, as if someone had turned on the sink faucet and gotten spitting air. "Did you hear—"

"The coffeemaker, perhaps." But he was a little *too* relaxed as he said it, eyes half slitted—pretty much a predator, ready to strike.

Garrie scrubbed her hands through her hair again. "Oh, *fine*." But it wasn't. And she hadn't given up, not on any of her questions. She just knew when to retreat. She grabbed the room service menu from the top of the television stand, stretching to her tiptoes to reach it. Drew had put it there, no doubt. "Look," she said, flipping pages. "Big honkin' steak. Comes with fries, which you've had, but I didn't get to eat mine. Comes with veggies. Tell me you eat your veggies?"

"I eat," Trevarr said, "whatever it takes to survive."

She shot him a slanted look, returned to the menu. *Questions, more questions.* "We'll skip the grubs and

grasshoppers this time around. Whoa, check it out—
here's a dessert called Whipped by Chocolate. Gotta
have that. You want one? No, never mind. I'll just order. If you don't eat it, I'm sure someone else will." He
just looked at her, so Whipped by Chocolate it was.
And two of the big honkin' steaks.

And a whole lot of dismay. "Forty minutes," she told
him, and looked at the granola not-health-food bar she
hadn't quite opened yet. "That is approximately *forever*."

"Put your not-food away," he said. "Leave this room
to the hotel for their repairs. Come over and sleep."

"In your room," Garrie said, deadpan.

"Yes."

She looked at him. She looked at the doorway. She
looked at the beds, which she could glimpse through
the doorway. "Parlor, fly," she muttered.

Impatience crossed his features and left them impas-
sive. "Come and sleep," he said. "Or lie here waiting for
a knock on the door. Whichever you prefer." And he
strode through the door, leaving it open.

"Shoot," Garrie said, still muttering. "When you put
it that way, it makes me kinda sound like a jerk." She
dumped the granola bar back in the dresser drawer,
emptied her various cargo pockets while she was at it,
and shoved the drawer closed with a little more force
than was strictly necessary. Then she went to the connecting doorway and hovered.

One bed, king size, with an imposing padded head-
board. The same giant TV stand and dresser; the same
little work desk with overstuffed chairs—the only area
to show signs of Trevarr's occupation, with the duster
thrown over the chair and Winchester House pamphlets
littering the table. Instead of the brick-red chair in the
corner, this room held a couch, and at the moment, the
couch held Trevarr. Not completely, as he didn't recline

fully at one end and his feet stuck off at the other. Or would have, had he kept both of them on the couch. As it was, one foot rested flat on the floor, and Garrie had the impression—one she didn't doubt—that he could be up in an instant.

He gestured at the bed, then folded his hands over his stomach and closed his eyes. Garrie stepped into the room—*no turning back*—and realized instantly that it was warmer in here, warm enough to verge on uncomfortable. Warm enough so he must—

Sure enough, he had the window open. Distant city noise made its way up from the street, just a few stories below but some distance from the hotel setback. Okay, his room, his choice. But she stood there a moment longer, hovering between uncertain and awkward, until a huge yawn caught her unaware and made up her mind for her. She knew better than to go into a reckoning unrested. Ghost fodder.

Not that she assumed they'd be able to resolve this one tonight. Always dicey, trying to handle ghosts while worrying about the whole *getting caught* detail. But she'd have a better idea after she spoke to Quinn. Which she could do now . . .

If she thought she'd be even close to sentient. And somehow, it felt very important to sound in control when she spoke to Quinn. Casual, even.

So she headed for the bed. The bedspread, she noted, was pristine, unscathed by mystery marks. She had the sudden impression that he hadn't slept there at all, and glanced at the couch. He lay with eyes closed, chest gently moving, convincingly asleep. "Sleep," he told her without opening his eyes, catching her entirely off-guard. She somehow managed to refrain from squeaking in surprise.

"Fine," she muttered, closing the door except for the merest crack to hear room service. "This is such a bad idea." She climbed onto the bed, instantly succumbing to the comfort of it. His scent on the air around her . . . yeah, he'd used the bed. "*Such* a bad idea." A mere mumble that time; if he heard, he gave no sign of it. She sighed, pulled the extra pillow over to wrap her arms around it and half roll over on it, and realized: not awkward. Perfectly content. Safe. Not worried about drifting back into that nightmare. Glad for the warmth tucked up against her bare feet.

And if that last somehow didn't make sense, she didn't stay awake long enough to figure out why.

11

Keep to your center against influences of chaos.
—Rhonda Rose

Give me the soft, fuzzy, blue security blanket anytime.
—Lisa McGarrity

Sklayne didn't bother with words. Sklayne sent pure annoyance at Trevarr. To bring the Garrie *here*, in Sklayne's room! It meant hiding. It meant not being himself in any fashion.

It meant not pestering Trevarr while he tried to sleep.

Not a bad strategy after all.

He rubbed his whiskered cheek against the Garrie's toes; opened his mouth and briefly pondered nipping. A glance at Trevarr and he decided against it.

::Find the others?:: he asked, somewhat plaintively, knowing Trevarr would ignore him if he'd dozed.

Not that Sklayne truly blamed him. Here where the

light shone so bright but the sun shone so cold; here where the food was filling but not fulfilling. Here where Trevarr had already been forced to absorb energies that stirred things neither of them could afford to have stirred.

They would have been better off without the Garrie after all. Even if her energies *were* delicious. He hesitated, again, over a nibble on her toes. They twitched in her sleep, as if anticipating needle-sharp little canines. But she slept deeply, hugging the extra pillow, and did not otherwise stir.

Because I keep the nightmares away.

Good enough reason to stay, perhaps. But if he was going to be working with this pack of humans who called themselves *reckoners,* Sklayne wanted to know of them. More of them than Trevarr's informant had told Trevarr, conversations to which Sklayne had not even been privy and that had included only information on the Garrie.

Not enough. Not enough to assure success, to acquire their quarry and end the sanctions imposed by the rites of Blood Honor.

::I want home,:: he told Trevarr, quiet and plaintive. ::Tonight, finish this. Take us.::

But Trevarr did not stir. Sleeping on the couch as he'd done half the night, because it had a view of the doorway and the bed had none.

The half of the night he'd been sleeping at all, that was. Because the first half of it, he'd left the room—with his reckoner people none the wiser—and walked the hotel perimeter. Learning the grounds with Sklayne, because that's what they always did. Out in the dark, navigating the night as easily as day, assuring themselves that they knew all the traffic patterns and hiding places and escape trails. Sklayne explored the trees, declared them officially insufficient—as were they all, if not of his home forest—and then they walked the streets, learning those. Learning this area as a whole—the taste of it, the smell of it, the sounds. So they would know when something was subtly amiss.

Like the smell coming in on the breeze through the window . . . faint, that odor, but Sklayne recognized it from Trevarr's memories nonetheless. *The café* . . . He sat up, wrapped a prim tail around his legs, and dared to chirp, "Mrrp!" for attention.

Trevarr ignored him. Sklayne knew it was not Trevarr *not hearing* him. Trevarr heard far too much. No, he'd just decided to stay in his sleep place.

Sklayne never did more than doze. A sip of rare pure sunlight gave restoration enough. Here, sucking on a wall socket did the same. Or a ride on the lines themselves. Not this sun; not enough. But so many wall sockets to choose from . . . almost an embarrassment. His own kind would never believe it—unwarded energy, free for the taking! Better than drinking out of a toilet!

If he ever made it home to tell them of it.

Fresh breeze, fresh stench. What was going on out there? He flicked an ear. Was that a subsonic rumble he heard? A glance at the Garrie . . . sleeping. A glance at Trevarr . . . sleeping. He could reach Trevarr beyond any ignoring, but it took focus, going that deep without invitation. And it took facing the ire if Trevarr took the intrusion amiss.

Any wall socket.

He did not need Trevarr to find out what was going on out there. He had two from Garrie's pack to target, tastes he could seek out and reach. Not going deep, but going long.

Sklayne jumped lightly to the floor—this time leaving no mark on the bedspread to betray his existence. With half an eye on Trevarr, he strolled to the light socket near the door. Meandering slightly, as cats were wont to do . . . as Sklayne was wont to do, far too curious. So he'd been told.

Many times.

The Garrie slept, her breathing muffled in the pillow. Trevarr slept, as much as he ever did.

And Sklayne drew breath and exploded himself, expanding to encompass the world, shrinking down again to brush past and through it all until he was as compact as he came, a density of air complete with whiskers and twitches and claws. He hesitated another moment to see if Trevarr would stop him—and when it didn't happen, hesitated yet again. Not safe, perhaps, to leave this room unwatched.

But in the end, the lure of the light socket, the pop and fizzle of the snacks awaiting him, and yes, his curiosity, they all drew him on.

After all, his curiosity had once gotten him into this.

Original Joe's was the name on the restaurant. Sklayne picked it out of the Drew person's head, going deep.

So much effort, going even that shallow layer into someone not Trevarr, but there, in the séance room . . .

Connections forged, even so faint . . . allowed him access. Through his presence with Trevarr, through the chain of energy to the Garrie. And so he found the feel of the Drew person, and followed the tug, and emerged from the power stream with a nearly silent *pmpf!* of sound, extruding Velcro-hook claws everywhere in an effort to—

Slow down! Legs amok! Tables and chairs everywhere! Ow—dodge—yow! A last desperate hiss-spit and Sklayne finally snagged flowing material that turned out to be a tablecloth. Static sparked everyone at the table, prompting a startled outcry and then somewhat nervous laughter. By then Sklayne had moved on, under control and coalescing in glass cat form—easier, here, to manage himself that way. He dodged ankles and shoes and skirts, sniffed up a few stray crumbs, and absorbed the thick, heady odors of garlic and pasta and sauce—the names of which he snatched from the Drew person's head as he spotted that table and shifted to full speed, blink-of-an-eye-and-there-he-was.

A full half-circle booth, two familiar people sitting across from one another. He made himself at home in the empty gap at the end. Off the floor, curled up under the table . . . glass cat, hidden behind a drooping table-cloth. Invisible enough.

Even as he settled there, the waiter person arrived with the food, and conversation came to nothing more than murmurs of thanks and "oh, that looks good." And then silverware clinking, and fresh bread breaking open—Sklayne breathed deeply of those yeasty mole-cules, resisting the urge to sample unseen.

The Drew person was not like the Garrie; his skills sat quiet and receptive. But he might still have some special sight to him. Sklayne tucked his tail around his front feet and let his eyes close to patience.

"How's your fettuccine?" the Drew person asked, most politely.

"I love their Alfredo sauce," the new Beth person said, equally polite. "And your prawns?"

"Don't get 'em like this in Albuquerque," the Drew person said. "They're way pha— I mean, they're really good."

Sklayne yawned. Rudely. It would have been loudly, if he'd had his say. Oh, ho hum. Boring people. Enough of this. He made the connection, slipping into the Drew person's thoughts. And he learned that this restaurant was called *Original Joe's* and that the food was *Italian* and that the Drew person was desperately nervous. That at least, had some amusement value. Sklayne settled in.

Never should have done this lunch thing. Panic sweated Drew's palms. Dammit! Would she notice if he wiped them on his pants? But the easy and very natural interaction from the Winchester grounds had grown strained and awkward. *Big mistake. Should have stayed with the others. It wouldn't have been obvious if we stayed with the others.*

"Sorry about foisting myself off on you," he heard himself saying, "But I really think Garrie needed to get some rest. I've never seen her so whipped after—well, you know."

Beth peeked up at him from over her glass—one of the clear sodas, he couldn't remember which. No caffeine, she'd joked, but her laugh had been nervous; she'd meant it and he didn't blame her. She really didn't need to be any more wired. Her cheeks had taken on a high flush, and he'd already realized she was one of those women who, although not a classic redhead, had subtle coppery redhead undertones in her freckles and hair and whose pale, thin skin showed every flush of emotion.

Damned cute.

He cleared his throat and pushed a prawn around his plate. "How about you? That was pretty intense. You okay now?"

"Better," she said. "I'd be better if I wasn't here." But even as he dropped his fork, she looked up in horror. "Oh, no! I meant, *not here* as in still working. You know. Busy. Not having any time to think about it."

Be chill, man. Pick the fork out of the ravioli that had come with the prawns, wipe down the handle. "Sure," he said, and his voice squeaked a little. He took a sip of his tea and tried again. "I mean, yeah. I get that. But you must be used to this sort of thing. You said you'd been seeing them all your life."

"Hearing them," she said. "I rarely see them any longer. And today—that was different. They've never come after me before. Don't tell me you're *used* to that?"

"Sure," Drew said again, trying for casual. Except then he had to add, "Maybe not quite like that. Usually Garrie can see them, or she knows what's going on. And usually—" He would have said that usually, Trevarr wasn't there. And that Garrie was much more in control, herding spirits around as necessary. Not wrung out like some old dishrag, practically carried out of the café. He *would* have said. But he remembered Garrie's warning. And he remembered the reporter who'd tried to make them look like fools, dogging them worse than any disturbed spirit, and he remembered hearing about the whacko who'd gone after them with antique surgical instruments. Garrie still kept several of those as mementos, and he definitely remembered the impact of handling them for the first time. So he stuffed a prawn into his mouth instead of saying more.

Beth got it. She might still be a little shocky and a whole lot overwhelmed, but she still got it. "Ah," she said. "Rhonda Rose Rules."

"Hey, yeah!" His admiration that she'd held onto that factoid in spite of the circumstances confused her, so he waved his hand to dismiss his words. Erasing them. "Right, I mean. Y'know, Garrie's the boss. She's the real deal. The rest of us . . . we do our thing. Maybe we argue with her. But bottom line . . . she's the one with the goods."

She forked up some fettucine, chewed thoughtfully. "Okay," she said after she'd swallowed. "I mean . . . I want more. I don't want to be in the dark. This is my house, if you follow. This is a place you're visiting, but it's a place I love."

"Hey, I get that." He couldn't help a smile, a big one. He realized suddenly that it was his goofy smile, the one Quinn aped back at him, and he quickly went for the napkin cover-up, as if he'd somehow gotten sauce on his chin.

Well, probably that, too.

"Surely you can at least tell me more about yourself," Beth said. Her flush seemed to deepen just a little. "Where you're from—not from around here, I guess?" Hope lilted her tone.

"New Mexico," Drew said, glad to see the disappointment on her face. "Well, I don't know about Trevarr. I haven't asked."

"I can see why," Beth muttered. "He's just a little bit . . . imposing."

"Is he?" Drew did his very best to sound surprised at that notion. "Mostly I haven't had the time." Oops. Dammit. Rhonda Rose Rules. Beth was no dummy— the opposite, in fact. She'd catch on that Trevarr was new to them.

But if Beth was stuck on Trevarr, it didn't show. She took a few careful bites of her lunch, washing them down with equally careful sips of her soda. She tucked a long—very long—stray hair back around the hair sticks; she'd never really gotten her hair back under control after the parking lot incident. Then she said, "What is it you do, then?"

"Do?" Drew echoed, and then winced, suppressing the urge to smack his palm against his forehead. *Could not possibly sound more stupid . . .*

She gave him a quick smile. She had a dab of sauce on her chin, and it made him feel better. Maybe it was okay if he wasn't perfect. She said, "Garrie is your big talent, right? You all looked straight at her today when things got wild. Even she expected herself to be able to do something . . . and no one else even tried. But you must do something? You and Lucia and Trevarr?"

"Oh, *that*. Sure. Hey, um . . ." He mimed wiping off his own chin and her blush flared to life; she quickly dabbed at her face with her napkin, shooting him a quick visual query to see if she'd gotten the spot. A little seed of pleased warmth surprised him—just that small gesture of trust. Wow. *Ignition* . . . He swallowed and said, maybe a little hastily, "I can get the history of a place. That's how I knew about the trick door in the séance room, when that dad guy was about to charge through where there was no floor."

Understanding lit her face. "You're the one," she said, her fork sagging down to her plate, forgotten, as her face lit up. "Carolyn said that one of the tourists had an uncanny knowledge of the house. I think that's one of the reasons the office wigs were so hot to talk to you all. And that's how you led everyone back to the séance room, even though you were in a section of the house that's been closed off for who knows how long—"

"Office wigs?" Drew put down his fork. Her eyes were such a blue . . . they caught the light when she widened them, so expressive.

Hello. Drew, dude. Lives in San Jose. You don't. Dump some icewater down your pants.

Okay, just the thought of that was some help.

Fortunately, Beth was oblivious—or pretty good at pretending she was, but he thought it would show on her face. She had that kind of face. But all it did at the moment was make a little dismissive nose-wrinkle. "Management. Big wigs. Office wigs. I know, I know . . . it works for me, though. So you can really do that?"

"Either that or I had the world's best luck today. And so did dad guy. Because man, he wasn't looking where his feet were going, that's for sure." But he could see from her attention, her curiosity, that she wanted to see him in action. For a moment, he was the one who blushed. No one ever paid attention to what he did. It wasn't flashy, not like Garrie. Anytime she introduced the team to a client, he could see their eyes drift over him, barely acknowledging him. They wanted the flash. They wanted to know what *she* could do for them.

She'd always said not to mind it. She'd said it made them stronger, because they could work without so much scrutiny. She'd said it let them exceed everyone's expectations. But this once . . .

There were those clean, clear blue eyes, looking right at him. And it felt good.

Icewater, dude. Seriously.

"Nineteen fifty-six is when this place opened," he said, easily slipping into reading mode. This place was proud of its history, nearly sang of it. "Things didn't go so well in the seventies, but they hung in and now it's generally packed. Lots of family business, definitely family run—there's pride all over the place. The Hideout upstairs is new with the remodel in late 2007 . . . these tables and booths are new, too, but the layout is basically the same. New bathrooms, if that matters."

"Trust me," she said. "That always matters." But she had that wide-eyed look . . . the one he usually saw reserved for Garrie.

"You didn't think I'd get it?"

She didn't hesitate; she shook her head and added, "I just didn't think you'd have that kind of detail." She returned to her dinner for a bite or two, and then asked, "What about the others? Or does that come under Rhonda Rose Rules? And just who is Rhonda Rose?"

Okay, that definitely came under Rhonda Rose Rules. "A friend of Garrie's," Drew said. "Her mentor. But she . . . moved on." He'd never understood that. Rhonda Rose had been a ghost. A seriously together ghost, what Garrie called a cohesive spirit. One of a kind, really. And she'd stayed with Garrie for years, until one day . . . she hadn't. Moved on, was all Garrie ever said. But Drew didn't get the feeling that Rhonda Rose had dissipated or been dissipated or even just gone beyond, though Garrie couldn't bring herself to offer an opinion. He had the feeling she'd decided to go around the world in eighty days. *Or something.* He only knew that Garrie still missed her terribly, and that she wouldn't talk about it.

Quinn had always thought that Rhonda Rose considered her work done, and that her time had simply come. That she'd been around for a century or so and had gotten tired and simply let herself go. But Drew always felt like kicking him when he said it, because he watched Garrie's face and saw the grief there. Through all of Garrie's strained, atypical childhood, Rhonda Rose had been the one she could talk to. The only one who understood. And the one who channeled her amazing abilities, keeping her on the good side of the Force.

Drew didn't even want to imagine a Garrie aligned with some of the darkside creatures they'd encountered. Things that ought to *stay* dark, that's for sure.

Finally, he realized that Beth was watching him. Not impatiently, but as if she appreciated his pondering. As if it, too, told her something. "Lucia," he said, and it came out in an unmanly croak. He pretended to have food stuck in his throat, taking a healthy gulp of tea—and then dabbing up what he'd dribbled down his chin. *Cool, man. Too cool.* He started tearing a piece of warm, crusty bread into tiny little pieces. "She *feels* things about a site. She feels what the spirits are feeling, or the echoes of what someone felt, if it was strong enough. What some people feel, too, if they're emoters."

Beth's eyes widened. "It must be very hard for her."

"You gotta understand—" he had quite a pile of crumbs by now—"She acts all abrupt and shallow sometimes, but she's really not. She just has to do that, to deal with the rest of it."

She smiled quite suddenly. "You must be a good friend."

"Ha," he said, but oh, that warm pleased spot was happy. "Ask Lucia about that. And don't even bother asking Quinn." Quinn hadn't quite accepted him yet . . . felt some encroachment on his know-it-all turf, that's what Drew thought. At the look on her face, he added,

"Quinn stayed in Albuquerque. He's kind of our research guru. He wanted to be by the books." He hadn't wanted to leap to Garrie's beck and call, proving his independence after a fling that had been over for a year, that's what Drew thought. *Get over it already.*

But it turned out that Beth's expression hadn't been a query over Quinn. She frowned; she said, "What are you . . . ?"

He looked at the crumbs, piled there by the edge of the table. He looked at his hand, about to brush the entire pile off onto the unoccupied booth seat that curved around between them. "Oh," he said. "I, uh . . ." He withdrew his hand, fighting the impulse to just do it anyway. "I wasn't thinking. Er. Sorry."

"Looks like it got to you, too," she said, understanding on her face. Not a pretty face, not really . . . just somehow exactly as it should have been. "That stuff in the parking lot. I bet you're not used to seeing Garrie come up empty like that. It sure surprised *her.*"

He thought of the look on Garrie's face—the frustration, the instant of helplessness . . . and then, of course, the renewed determination, because that was Garrie. And he thought of the rest of that day, with the spirits coming on them like a ton of bricks, and the way she'd gone down in the café, and the unexplained things that had so obviously passed between her and Trevarr in the darkness of the séance room. "It was a pretty big day already."

Her eyes widened—at first he thought he'd done something bizarre, like dump the crumbs anyway or accidentally hit his fork to flip food onto someone else's table. But he double-checked himself—hand on drink, if closed around the glass a little more tightly than was probably wise. Fork quietly on plate. Nothing else amiss that he could see. And by then he'd gotten a glimpse, too.

. . . *scuttle* . . .

"What—?" she said.

"Did you see—?" he asked.

. . . scuttle . . .

"Tell me that's not a roach, right out here in the dining room." But she lowered her voice to say it, barely audible alto.

He searched the floor; he found nothing. But his peripheral vision registered another scuttling movement, and he did what he'd learned to do with Garrie when darkside entities were present—he didn't try to look directly at it. He kept a soft focus, and let his awareness slide to the outer edges of his vision.

Yup. Definitely something moving. Something rare, because even with darksiders, he couldn't see them all. Garrie could—well, until this morning, Garrie could see them all. Suddenly Drew wasn't making assumptions any longer. "Don't try to look at it," he told Beth. "Look beside it."

"Like trying to find something in the dark?"

"Bingo," Drew said, trying not to look too puppy-dog-eyes-impressed.

"I see it," she breathed, stiffening slightly. "I . . . I think I'm done with lunch. My appetite seems to have deserted me . . ."

Drew's stomach was made of sterner stuff. Besides . . . *prawns . . .* He grabbed one without looking, his gaze still roaming the room. *Yup, there's another one.*

He and Beth weren't the only ones to notice, either—a gasp rose up from a nearby table, and several people pointed. Okay, *that* triggered his uh-oh alarm. It didn't surprise him that Beth had seen it—she'd established herself as a sensitive. But your average out-to-luncher?

"Drew," Beth whispered, her flush fading to paleness, "they're *everywhere.*"

And suddenly they were, no need for vision games

any longer. An explosion of them, bursting forth from the seams of the room, scuttling every which way—a veritable carpet of wiggly, many-legged, thumb-size entities, hinged carapaces over squat bodies.

And they smelled. Of *course* they smelled.

Inevitably, someone screamed.

Here we go. Drew snagged another prawn and sucked down the meat, buttery garlic, watching as the first of the diners leaped to his feet, the second not far behind. Roach-things poured across the carpet; the first man up tried to stomp the closest ones and stopped in horror at the utter futility of it. A woman snatched her purse and fled—and another followed, and another, and soon the restaurant was full of stampeding, screaming—

Drew lifted his feet. Beth did likewise, sitting sideways in the booth. "What—?" she said. Or he thought she said—the noise level had shot through the roof, swallowing her words.

He shook his head and shouted back an answer. "I don't know." Quinn might know, but even that was doubtful. He might be a wizard with trivia and at putting seemingly unrelated pieces together to provide insight, but there was no such thing as a field guide for darksiders. Drew reached for another prawn, chewing it faster than such blissfully good scampi deserved. It didn't stop him from scowling mightily. From wondering what this had to do with the Winchester House and just how bad it was. *Don't panic.* Observe. Be ready to report.

Beth had no such intentions. "Let's get out of here!" She mimed fingers walking to the exit in case he couldn't hear her shout; her nose wrinkled from the rising stench of them. Rancid butter. Rancid *moldy* butter. Drew nodded, but indicated the crammed exit. They'd go, for sure, but . . . might as well wait here, with its better vantage point.

Scuttlers, so thick the floor appeared to writhe. Scuttlers, still pouring out from cracks and crannies, climbing over one another in their hurry to get . . . wherever. An enraged shout rose from behind the bar, followed by the explosive sound of a discharging fire extinguisher.

"It can't be related," Drew said, even though she couldn't hear him. "We're too far away from the mansion. There's no way . . ." And yet . . . coincidence? Pretty intense. And too weird. Their black bodies had an oily gleam, their legs were too numerous, their tiny little heads were nearly hidden in the overhang of the carapace. Bright lime-green spots speckled their back ends; a brushy cluster of eyestalks dotted each little head. He grabbed another prawn, fingers groping, gaze riveted to the panicked and ear-splitting crowd—and then jumped as something made a strange, barely audible hiss-spit noise, and as Beth let out a little shriek— but not quite in time.

His fingers closed over not warm, firm prawn but slick, wiggling darksider.

Drew yelped like a girl. As fast as he flung the thing away, his fingers blazed into a fiery pain, the dip of flesh into a living fire. "Yeow! Ow! Ow ow *ow*!" He flapped his wounded fingers in the air. Beth twisted over the table, grabbing his hand and grabbing his ice water, plunging the one into the other. Drew managed an inarticulate noise and forced himself not to snatch his hand back and cradle it, whimpering.

If this was darksider stuff, it wasn't like anything he'd seen before. A whole heck of a lot more substantial. More . . . "Ow," he muttered, and withdrew his hand to look, and to find blisters already forming. Beth recaptured it—more carefully this time—and turned it over so she, too, could see. Her breath hissed through her teeth.

At least, that's what it looked like she did, in this

clamor. But definitely she looked at him with trepidation; definitely she said, "We need to get out of here."

Drew snatched up his fork and slammed the tines into another scuttler as it headed for Beth's side of the table. For sure, *run away*. But doing it didn't seem so easy. Not with the floor covered and the entryway still packed, the people at the back of the crowd doing a scuttler-flamenco dance on the encroaching bugs as one of the busboys ran up with fire extinguisher and blasted away at them. Drew flipped one off the toe of his shoe and zeroed in on the emergency exit at the other end of the restaurant. Not close . . . but not crowded, either.

He nodded his head at it, saw her understanding, and shouted, "Run for it?" even as he lifted the fork and stabbed another scuttler.

Beth made a face—fear and disgust and determination, all rolled into one. She stood up on the booth seat as Drew did the same, and then, as she hesitated, held her hand out over the table. She didn't have to say *hold my hand*. Drew knew just the feeling. Wiggling his blistered fingers in a self-test, he gingerly took her hand, found it soft and warm and careful with its touch.

"Okay," he said, getting ready, voice raised but not bothering to shout. She could read his lips on this one, he was pretty sure. "One, two . . ."

Sklayne disengaged then, pulling away from the Drew person in whom he'd been immersed so long—the one he'd tried to warn, a vocalization he shouldn't have allowed. Because unlike his unwitting host, he knew exactly what the scuttlers were, and he knew they didn't belong here.

He knew exactly where they did belong.

And that it wasn't good.

Before the Drew person could move, Sklayne pulled in breath and held it, expanding himself. Out of glass cat shape, into self-shape. Condensed self-shape, little

Velcro claws everywhere. Faster than the Drew person could even think, he scrolled under the table, clearing his own path. He scrolled himself across the floor.

Crunchy. Infinitely crunchy. Small snacks. Can't have just one!

And so whether they noticed it or not, Sklayne cleared the way.

Heat assailed her.
   Not the right air . . .
   Not the right energy . . .
   Not the right life . . .
And somehow so familiar. She knew to be frightened. She knew to be *terrified.*

So of course she planted herself in the middle of it and she shouted, "Come and face me, you big bully!"

The darkness only swirled around her. The rustle of feathers . . . or maybe it was the faint rasp of scales. Close by . . . brushing past her back. When she whirled, she saw only the black fog, disturbed by passage. Over the pungent scent of foliage, peppery hot, she thought she detected something else. A quick pattering of droplets on leaves whirled her around again; something small and lightweight rustled along the ground, a skittery insect sort of noise. The heat suffocated her senses. *Wood smoke?*

She thought she heard something whisper her name. She thought it held longing. She ought to run, she knew that—but run *where,* in this black fog? She fisted her hands and threw her head back and cried, "Show yourself, then!"

Nothing did, of course. So she muttered, "Oh, *fine,*" and she reached out for the breezes, so cautiously, not having anything to push against but needing the reassurance of it, the familiarity.

Face it. The soft fuzzy blue security blanket of her own inner strength.

Except the instant she reached, the instant she grasped, she opened the doors to another kind of energy, a tsunami of it. It splashed through her and around her, burning her cold, it tingled through her arms and legs and ran streaks of fiery bold lightning through her fingers and breasts and legs. She thrashed and batted at it, suddenly without any reference for *up* or *down* or *ground.* The black fog carried her; the lightning stroked her. She whimpered; she turned it into a fierce curse.

A whisper in her ear. A solid presence at her side. A touch at her face, the wood smoke gone strong and mingled with leather. A hand on her shoulder. And words, soothing words that came in a familiar voice and familiar accent, but made no sense as they settled in her mind.

Didn't matter. She leaned into the solidity. She gave a little sob of relief at the fingers smoothing her hair. The darkness receded; she found gravity again, and the soft luxury of the bed beneath her. And then she fell back asleep, dreamless and no longer alone.

Power crackled and popped around Sklayne. He hovered in the lines, hesitating on choice.

Trevarr needs to know now. Or go learn more.

Hovering. Thinking of Trevarr on the couch. Trevarr asleep. Trevarr worn. Trevarr with the Garrie, growing that possessive look Sklayne had seen over blood family but never over another.

He'd known too much of her before he got here. He'd come to want more of her before even meeting her. Sklayne thought *mistake,* and then quickly decided it would never be said out loud.

Ever.

But the Garrie slept now, too. And Trevarr wanted it that way.

Decision. Sklayne wouldn't interrupt. No, he'd follow the faint tug of the Lucia person. He'd learn more.

He'd bring information back to Trevarr, enough information so Trevarr could make decisions of his own without becoming tangled in the Garrie.

He chose his power conduit and raced forward, gathering speed and wicked glee in equal measure until he squirted out of a light fixture from high overhead, black iron and glass dangling on an iron chain. The light blew with a noisy sputter; Sklayne extruded a lightning-fast claw and hooked himself into the chain, swinging wildly around the fixture until he bled off his speed.

Here. Somewhere. The Lucia person.

A massive collection of store fronts spread out before him—brightly painted brick rowhouses filling each block and towering high, leaving room for this arching entryway with its formerly functioning lights. People ambled the sidewalk below, pointing and peering and leaning up to windows, paying no attention to the light fixture with a life of its own.

Sklayne descended—controlled descent, balancing energies just so, an amorphous cloud of self invisible to those with their human eyes and their round human pupils. He hunkered in and got a good read on the Lucia person, and he poured into speed. Following the edge of the buildings, not varying his path for such things as tubs of flowering plants or temporary sidewalk displays. Right over one startled dog; right through a rack of clothes. Around the curving glass corner of one remarkably color-uncoordinated building—and quite suddenly his sense of the Lucia person grew stronger.

The tug of it drew him onward, squeezing small through the closed crack of a door and big again to find himself *utterly surrounded by disembodied feet*. A spit, a hiss—Sklayne blew up to encompass the interior, innumerable paws and claws scrambling in every direction. He snatched at composure, pulled himself inward—had to pull very hard. There, suddenly, he was *cat*. That same cat. There in the middle of an open carpeted space and still *surrounded by disembodied feet.*

A spit, a hiss, a very feline noise of offense; his tail puffed to twice its normal size and followed him as he scooted for cover, slinking close to the ground. A shadowed nook beneath steplike displays of *farking disembodied feet* and he hunkered in a tight crouch, panting neatly through his tidy cat mouth.

"Did you hear that—?" asked a light and unfamiliar female voice, not completing her sentence.

"Must have been something on the store music," responded another. "Look, I think we've got a live one."

Farking disembodied live *feet!*

The Lucia person was here. The Lucia person would know about the feet. They weren't part of the Winchester House effect; they couldn't be. No one else seemed to notice them at all. Unless no one else even saw them . . .

Just not right.

He curled up tightly in the corner beneath the hollow steps, hidden behind a tidy stack of boxes with tissue paper peeking out. Empty boxes. Brushing up against them shifted the whole stack, and he froze, easing away. But nothing to worry about. The talking people had moved away; he heard their firm footsteps on the floor, the swish of skirt and leg. He heard their words of greeting—and he heard the Lucia person's voice in response. And so he settled in, tucked his paws under, and reached for her.

Shallow at first—cautious. Uncertain he would have fine control in the presence of the feet—and someone as sensitive as the Lucia person would feel such reactions. He slipped into place with his inner eyes closed, unwilling to see the room—and its contents—just yet.

Oh . . . they're gorgeous!

That, then, was unexpected. Sklayne stretched one

paw out to knead the carpet, absorbing the Lucia person's delight and enthusiasm. He let her quick inner calculations—a mix of *allowance* and *budget* and *low income right now,* contrasting with *opportunity* and *savings* and *wantwantwant*—ripple past.

This was a puzzling place.

But he found nothing of fear in her and everything of pleased anticipation. She had no concern over the people approaching her in this place of feet—she even had expectations of their behavior. That they would be modestly deferential. That they would respond to her requests.

He was here to do a job. He was here to gather information, to report to his *atreyvo.* And he'd come because he knew what no one else yet knew—that the Winchester House effect was far more profound, far more devastating, than anyone else suspected.

He sunk his claws into the carpet. Deeply. He squeezed his eyes closed. *Do not fear the feet.*

He settled in.

Lucia sighed most happily. The airy, soaring space of the Taryn Rose store made the perfect setting for the beautifully arranged shoes, some of them perched on little stands, and some of them on model feet. She frowned at the odd little stutter of her heart as she gazed around the store, but it smoothed away and left her to admire the shoes. Craftsmanship, beauty . . . comfort. *¡Alegría!* And one of these lovelies would be in her hands, possibly on her feet, before she left this store.

The two sales associates knew a ready-made sale when they saw one. They listened with just the right amount of interest when she told them she was in from the Southwest and had only the afternoon to shop, so of course she'd come right to Santana Row. No doubt they recognized her designer tote; they were fools if they didn't see she'd already been in Burberry and now wore a sleek little number with a check-etched band to replace the lovely watch she'd carelessly worn on a recent reckoning job. Nothing a petty little angry ghost liked more than to wreck the delicate workings of a finely crafted watch.

And then there was the formidable Rhonda Rose. That woman was sharp. Lucia couldn't even bring herself to think of Rhonda Rose as a ghost. Garrie had certainly mourned her when she'd left, even if she'd been already dead in the first place. Always properly dressed in mid-Edwardian style, her hair worn in a modest twist, and no apparent makeup—although Lucia didn't believe it. She concluded early in her short acquaintance that the living woman had perfected the subtle natural tones used in her era, and certainly wouldn't let herself go just because she found herself in an extended and complicated afterlife.

Lucia could appreciate that attitude. She hoped she would have a similar attitude, especially if she died as young as Rhonda Rose—although maybe in her day, going on forty hadn't been all that young after all. Going on forty, spinster aunt living with her brother's family, taking care of her brother's children . . .

No wonder she'd stuck around. She'd had a lot of living left to do.

"The Cheval in gray accent?" she asked the sales associates. An older woman and a younger one, both impeccably dressed and coiffed, one quite robust and the other in need of calories. "And the Kegan wedge in chocolate. Size seven. I'll be choosing." Heels or practical wedge . . . not that there was anything *not* gorgeous about the suede wedges with their ribbonlike patent accents. Then again, the Cheval . . . gorgeous vintage style, Victorian boots with cutouts and contrasting panels, done in suede . . .

Lucia found herself one of their very comfortable chairs and commenced making up her mind. Both shoes, oh so comfortable. Both shoes, oh so stylish. But . . . "These," she said, caressing the Chevals as though they would purr back at her. "These can be made to suit classy or funky." The sales associates—both of them, hovering most helpfully—gave her equally doubtful looks. Ah, yes. She was dressed in Daddy's Princess mode today, wasn't she? They probably didn't believe her capable of the other styles. She smiled gently at them. "Yes, the Cheval will do, thank you."

She slipped back into her own comfortable flats— Barefoot Tess Classics, acquired online for half their retail price because now and then she liked to prove she could—and retired to the register to consult her shopping wish list. *Burberry, watch.* Check. *Taryn Rose, shoes.* Check. *Joseph Schmidt Confections, truffles for all.* Next. And maybe they'd have one of Joseph Schmidt's exquisite chocolate sculptures on display. She pulled out her AmEx, tapping it idly on the counter while she waited, and resisted the sudden inexplicable impulse to taste the eggplant-colored tissue paper the sales associate put on the counter in preparation for making up her purchase bag. She frowned and twined her fingers together in a posture of quiet patience, making it impossible to reach for the paper.

And otherwise, all so normal. Pleasingly so. Lucia, shopping in the afternoon. Choosing purchases with taste and forethought, moving briskly through her plans for the day so she could return in time for a nice dinner and then go out and break into one of San Jose's historical landmarks to help rid it of spirits gone twisted and harmful. Situation normal.

Situation so suddenly *not.*

The floor made a squishing sound beneath her feet. She glanced down without thinking and did a double-take. The tasteful carpet oozed a big blotchy spot of oily darkness. "Gross," she said. "One of your customers left a calling card."

"How's that?" the sales associate said absently, engrossed in processing the sale while her partner created a smartly pleasing arrangement out of the shoe box, tissue paper, and the store's slick designer shopping bag.

Lucia eased to the side of the dark blotch. "There's a huge stain on the carpet." She finished off her electronic signature with a flourish and replaced the pen. "It's nasty. Someone's shoes could get ruined."

That got their attention, all right, here in a store where the least expensive shoe cost several hundred dollars. Leaving the bag on the counter for Lucia to collect, they came around to look at the spot—and to gasp.

"Actually," Lucia said, frowning at it, "I think . . . it's bigger than it was."

"Just now?" one of the women responded, squinching her nose at this impossibility.

The dark, oily stain exhaled a bubble and briefly extruded a visible skim of liquid. All three women gasped, stepping back—and Lucia's heel went *squoodge* and she froze, statuelike except for the merest turn and tip of her head to look down behind her.

"There's another one," she said, and her voice somehow didn't make it above a whisper. For while the other two women were still merely baffled, she knew too much—and simultaneously not enough. She knew enough to drop what defenses she had, to search for any feel of disgruntled spirits—but not, when she found nothing, to understand what was going on around her.

For there, several yards away, another dark spot bloomed. More quickly now, growing before her eyes—going from a damp darkness to a corruscating puddle of deepest, light-sucking black.

There might not be any spirits hanging around to give her a clue, but Lucia had seen enough. "We need to get out of here," she told the other two, reaching over the spreading stain to snatch up her bag of shoe goodness.

"I'll call security," said the older of the two women decisively. She stretched to scoop up the counter phone. "This has got to be some sort of environmental problem."

Oh, you must be kidding. "Right," Lucia said, perfectly willing to go for the explanation they would swallow. "And it's probably toxic, don't you think? I mean, just *look* at it—"

"Look," the younger woman interrupted, pointing a trembling finger off to the side. "What does *that*?"

Lucia really didn't want to look. She really, really didn't want to. But she clutched her tote and her new purchase, and she slowly turned her head.

Fingers of oily darkness crept *up* a nearby display box. Not the way water might soak up into fabric, but gravity-defying fingers. Probing, searching fingers. And when they found a shoe, the shoe quivered, and it tumbled from its perch to splat down into the thick puddle.

"Oh!" gasped the younger woman, impulsively lurching forward to rescue the footwear.

Lucia just barely got a grip on the back of her blouse, pulling her up short—albeit not without a little ripping sound. "Don't!" she said, her voice shooting straight to alarm mode. High alarm, because she'd seen what she'd seen and she knew what she knew, and while these women were still thinking in terms of *distasteful* and *disgusting,* Lucia thought of ghost poop gone atomic. The older woman let the phone sag to give Lucia an incredulous look and the younger woman turned back in offense, straightening her blouse—too bad about that button—and Lucia realized they had no *idea,* that they thought she'd gone hysterical.

She stabbed a finger at the shoe . . . or at what remained of it.

Which wasn't a whole lot.

The darkness burbled happily around it, tiny little bubbles as though something had put it to low boil and left it to simmer, and the younger woman let out a little shriek and stumbled back into Lucia. Lucia steadied her. "Make your call from next door, yes?"

From the petite little Nanoo children's store beside them, someone screamed.

"Make your call from the pay phone on the corner!" Lucia said desperately. The older woman fumbled to hang up the phone without looking—missed the cradle in her haste, and let the handset fall to the counter unchecked. She took her associate by the elbow. "Let's go."

"But my purse—"

The older woman shook her. "*Leave* it. We'll come back for our things when we can."

But Lucia was looking at the entry, gleaming glass doors beyond a wide moat of spreading blackness. "Or not . . ."

"Up on the counter!" the woman said, but that, too, was covered in streaming tendrils of black. From next door, a new spate of screaming erupted, and the younger woman suddenly clutched at them both, staring wildly all around them, because—

"Ay, *caray!*" Lucia muttered. Surrounded. Surrounded and losing ground to the viscous substance now moving vigorously enough so she could hear it, swampy sucking noises and gloppy plopping and even the *ooze* made a sound, creeping over conquered surfaces . . .

Hiss-spit! and Sklayne tore free of the Lucia person, no time for finesse or niceties. *Hiss-spit!* and here he was, trapped in the back corner behind empty boxes melting into the black *eatsll,* blackness coming up to nibble at his toes, *should have come out to look sooner—*

But unlike the Lucia person, unlike the other women, Sklayne had seen it before. And Sklayne knew how to deal with it. The problem was, whether the women could deal with *him*.

12

That way lies madness.
—Rhonda Rose

Stay on your own side of the car.
—Lisa McGarrity

Garrie knew she wasn't alone before she even opened her eyes. Never mind the scent of the place; she'd fallen asleep to that, bolstered by someone else's pillow. No, it was the slight dip to the bed and the simple sense of *presence* pressing against her skin. She opened her eyes, and yeah.

Right there on the bed beside her, one hand stretched toward her head, almost touching it; The rest of him sprawly, loose-limbed and lost in sleep.

How had that happened, again? She closed her eyes, searching to find murky hints of terrifying nightmares— just enough clarity remaining to know they hadn't really tasted like nightmares at all. More like memories that hadn't truly felt like hers.

One way or another, Winchester House had gotten to her. She only knew for sure that these nightmares had come from outside her, and not from within. That had been one of her first lessons, the most important one—that difference between what was hers, and what was thrust upon her. For what was hers, she had to work through, just like anyone. But what came from without . . . that needed boundaries. She had to be ever careful not to absorb or own it. *That way lies madness,* Rhonda Rose had explained.

Stay on your own side of the car, Garrie reminded the intrusive lingering feel of those nightmares. She focused instead on the buffered peacefulness clouding around her . . . the sense that she hadn't been left to it alone.

And then her eyes flew open again. How had he even known?

And just exactly how long had he been—okay, say it—*in bed with her*?

If she was quiet enough, smooth enough, could she slide right off the bed and slink back into the other room, where air-conditioning would cool the sudden flush over her neck and arms and cheeks? Probably not. She probably didn't dare to move. In fact, she found herself vaguely surprised that her regard alone hadn't roused him.

She watched him, then, waiting for signs that he was about to wake. A flicker of eyelid, a change of tension . . . she realized, suddenly, she hadn't ever seen his mouth fully relaxed before now.

Well, at least he wasn't drooling.

At that moment, he opened his eyes.

Please tell me I didn't say that out loud.

But when she shifted, ready to slip off the bed now that waking him wasn't an issue, something in his expression stopped her. An instant of baffled vulnerability. His gaze fell on her, lingering; she could all but see the thought balloon over his head: *Wha . . . ?*

Just for an instant. And then there he was. He rolled smoothly off the other side of the bed and onto his feet before she could even open her mouth, and one look at his face told her he wasn't going to talk about this moment—not now, possibly not ever.

Not the waking up in bed with her. A man like that . . . she thought he'd shared his bed with plenty of willing women.

No, it was the being vulnerable . . . never being mind caught at it.

She slipped off the bed in a more leisurely fashion, stretching, and looked at the garish red numbers on the alarm clock, instantly dropping her thoughts to make a strangled noise. "What happened to room service?"

"I postponed it," Trevarr said. He probably had no idea that his shirt lacings had loosened so the garment hung askew on his shoulders, or that his hair was as rumpled as the shirt. Very . . . nicely . . . rumpled.

"Did you?" Garrie asked, and thought she sounded just a little bit like Minnie Mouse. *Get a grip.* And then, *No, get a farking grip.*

That helped. "Okay," she said. "I'll call them." But when she did, she was utterly unprepared for their verbal wrangling. Oh, they were happy enough to provide room service, but then the hotel restaurant turned the phone over to the front desk, where that person asked about the cat in her room. "I think," she told the woman, so surprised at such an accusation that she floundered for composure, "that I would know if I'd brought a cat along. On the *plane.* From my house where there is *no cat.*"

Trevarr came to attention from where he was scraping his hair back, losing half of it from his grip as he applied the band Lucia had given him. Garrie made a face at the phone for his benefit. "Well, look," she told the woman. "Maybe I should just talk to the manager. Because I really hate to think someone else somehow got into my room. You know, I was just figuring that housekeeping replaced the bedspread and didn't realize the clean one had been damaged in the wash, but if you're saying there's no way, then that means someone was in my room, and there should be an investigation into that, don't you think?"

Uh-huh. She thought not. "Dinner's coming," she said a moment later, hanging up the phone. She bounced up on the bed and took Trevarr by the shoulders, ignoring his startled expression as she stripped the band from his hair. "Like this," she told him, and had enough experience with Lucia and her younger sisters to efficiently finger-comb his hair—thick, strong, and yes, there were little braids hidden throughout—and wind the band around it in three quick flips. She resisted the urge to twitch his shirt straight—*just leave it alone*—and bounced back off the bed. "They decided the bedspread must have been laundry damaged after all. Still . . ." She slanted a questioning look at him. He returned it, evenly; said nothing. She gave up. "Okay, then, I'm gonna wash the sleep off my face before the food gets here. And Lucia and Drew ought to be back any time now." *Oh please.*

At least, that's what part of her said. And the other part wanted to ask questions until she found the right one to get her some answers. Oh, he wanted things resolved at Winchester House, all right . . . but it was much, much more than that. She wasn't—hadn't ever been—naive enough to think otherwise.

Just naive enough to think she had a chance to figure out the full story.

But not before dinner. So she slipped into the artificial coolness of her own room, noticed that the bedspread had indeed been replaced and the bed remade, that the weirdly empty little mint wrapping was gone, and headed for the sink with its fancy stone counter and gleaming fixtures and—

Where was her soap?

Gone, that's where. Totally gone. What, housekeeping had a hankering for handmade coconut-almond? Retribution for the bedspread? As if they could know which soap was hers in the first place . . .

Serves you right for packing it, she told herself, and unwrapped a new minibar of the hotel soap, making do. She ran a wet fine-toothed comb through her hair to get rid of the day's effects, then scrunched it up to make it more interesting. Those blue streaks would need touchup soon . . . nothing more pathetic than fading punk.

She heard their voices before they reached the door—tumbling out of the elevator and down the hall, talking over one another and bubbling in a faintly manic way. They burst into the room after only the briefest hesitation at the door, a subtle snick of the key card and here they came, only belatedly realizing, "Oh, wait—Garrie—nap—" though she couldn't have said just who burbled what.

She waved at them, there in front of the mirror at the exterior sink. "Yo," she said. "Not napping. Lucky for you, I might add."

"Garrie!" Lucia cried. "You'll never believe—" She dumped her upscale shopping bag on the bed with its recently refreshed bedspread. *Taryn Rose.* Meant nothing to Garrie. Lucia never hesitated, upending her silk mini–tote bag on the bed, spilling its contents everywhere and then leaving them behind as she headed straight for the big television stand/dresser.

"Seriously!" Drew threw himself down on his own bed, and only managed to stay there for an instant before popping up again. "I bet it's on the news—what station is the news?" He didn't wait for an answer, but grabbed the list of stations from the television stand, turned on the set, and began flipping channels without consulting the guide—or turning the volume down. By then Lucia had laid out a new bag and quickly, efficiently plucked up items from the jumble on the bed.

"Is that a *fanny pack*?" Garrie asked, incredulous. The television blared: *removes stains! The majestic lion— make my day- -this just in—*

Lucia shot her a look full of scorn. "Puh-leeze, chi-calet. This is a *waist bag*. And it's a Roots. That makes it urban chic."

Oxy-blast!—in two short weeks—I've got a bad feeling about this—natural hair!

Garrie snatched the remote from Drew's hands, turned off the television, and tossed the remote beside Lucia's things, knowing he'd never trespass there.

"Hey!" He contrived to look wounded.

"Put your neurons in order," Garrie snapped at him. "You, too, Lucia. What's going on? You weren't even in the same place this afternoon. And where's Beth?"

"At her apartment," Drew said, and appeared to be relieved to have an easy answer at hand. He backed away from her a step or two, and Garrie dialed down the fierce. Maybe those dreams had left their mark on her after all.

Or maybe he deserved a smack upside the head and was actually getting off lightly.

"She's going to meet us at the house tonight," Drew added helpfully.

Garrie gave him a wary squint. "She knows our plans?"

"She's down with it," Drew said. He'd gotten some of that puppy-dog look back. "I think it's great, the way she's willing to help—"

"And you don't think she's not going to *warn* them? Drew, that house is her life! *Working* there is her life— how she identifies herself. How could you—"

She broke off; she knew the instant before she heard his voice that Trevarr stood in the doorway behind her. It wasn't the sudden apprehension on Drew's face; he was a beat late to notice. It wasn't the way Lucia's expression shifted to something slightly more formal, so subtle only someone who knew her would notice at all. Lucia, struggling with the overlay of outside emotions all her life, knew how to hide herself from casual observation.

It was just . . . knowing.

Even before he said, quite flatly in that edged accent of his, "You told the guide."

"Beth," Drew said, and Garrie could see it took all of his courage to hold his ground—but she had to hand it to him, he even pulled himself up a lanky inch or two. "I trust her. After what we went through . . . she knows it's got to be done."

Lucia snapped the flap on the larger of the two square, side-by-side pouches. "Garrie, you really need to hear this."

"I've been *trying* to hear it!" Garrie sputtered. She glanced back at Trevarr—found droplets of water still glistening at his hairline and his shirt front neatened, even if the back half still hung out. She hadn't been the only one freshening up. "I just need for someone to spit it out!"

"Bugs!" said Drew.

"Goo!" said Lucia.

Garrie covered her face with her hands. After a moment, she peeked out into the silence. A meaningful peek.

Drew pulled in a deep breath and said, "We went to eat at Original Joe's downtown and halfway through the meal, beetles started crawling out of the woodwork, and I mean literally, and there were a *lot* of them. I thought darksiders because sometimes I see those, but *everyone* saw them, and not only that, they—well, look!" He thrust his hand out toward her. "We had to run for it, and I mean literally. I'm still not sure how we made it through. The front doors were packed and we had to sprint over this *carpet* of beetles—only trust me, these weren't any beetles you've ever seen before."

"What did they look like?" The sharp interest in Trevarr's voice startled Garrie, but not enough to take her gaze from Drew's hand. Thumb and first two fingers were profoundly reddened, blisters already weeping. She stepped forward, grabbing up the hand— carefully—and pulling it in for a closer look.

"Watch it!" Drew said unnecessarily.

"Ay, *caray!*" Garrie muttered. "We need some serious Band-Aid action here."

"Got 'em," Drew told her. "Beth and I picked some up on the way back here. But she said I should wash off first. In case some of the acid or whatever is still on my skin."

"Yes," Trevarr said. "Do that. Do it well."

Garrie dropped Drew's hand. "Do it now," she said. And to Trevarr, "You know what did this?"

Drew snorted on the way to the sink. "No way, homie." Not that badly hurting, then, if he could still whip out misplaced colloquialisms. "Seriously. These little dudes were like the Hummers of armored stink beetles, that's what. With fluorescent freckles on their asses and a weird little cluster of fiber-optic eyes up front."

Garrie frowned at him. He looked back over his shoulder as if sensing her regard. "You know. Eyes on stalks."

Fine. Back to Trevarr. Who said nothing, but she would have bet anything he knew exactly what Drew meant. "Okay," she said. "It's another question for Quinn. It's not anything I've ever seen, but that doesn't mean it's not rare darkside. If the Winchester situation has things torqued around that badly . . ." She glanced at Trevarr, but he didn't seem inclined to correct or confirm. And meanwhile Lucia was all but vibrating with the need to share her own adventures.

"Goo!" Lucia burst out again.

Oh, right. The goo.

Lucia hovered on the edge of exclamation, unable to pull the words together, her expression growing more frustrated and her eyes getting wider. Finally she gestured wildly and blurted, "Everywhere!"

"Whoa, Lu. Take a breath." Not often one saw Lucia at a loss for words. Garrie gave her a starting place. "Where?"

"Santana Row." Relief cleared Lucia's expression. "The most *amazing* collection of stores. And I was right there in the shoe store and suddenly there was *goo* everywhere. Black, icky, oozing goo."

Garrie just looked at her.

"*Climbing* goo," Lucia said. "And it *ate the shoes*." She gave the store bag on the bed a proprietary glance. "Not mine."

"Ate?" Garrie could imagine goo doing a lot of things. Dissolving items, for instance. Sucking them in. But eating . . . that implied a whole separate set of facts about the goo in question.

Lucia straightened. Beauty pageant posture. She wasn't kidding around. She lifted her chin and announced, "It *belched*."

"Ohh-kay." Garrie took herself over to the chair in the corner and carelessly fell back into it, pulling one leg up to keep her company. "Goo everywhere, and it ate things."

"It was in the store beside us, too, a cute little children's store. I think someone there was injured. Hard to tell, what with the firefighters and all hosing down the goo. They called it an environmental spill." Lucia made a face. "They wanted me to stick around. Witness and all that. I thought it would be better if I didn't. That cat sure saved the day. Again. I don't think we'd have gotten out of that store at all if it hadn't been for the *gato*."

Garrie felt herself stiffen. "What do you mean, *cat*? There was a cat? What did it do?"

Trevarr, standing in the doorway in his partly reassembled state, feet still bare, fooled her at first glance. Remarkably calm, only modestly curious. But when she looked at his toes, she found them clenching the carpet.

He must have felt her regard; the toes relaxed. They stayed that way as Lucia explained about the handsome cat with the somewhat overlarge ears, and how it had come out of nowhere and how the goo had literally seemed to give way before it. "I'm not kidding, chicalet. We were trapped. The cat came out and stood and *stared* with squinty cat eyes, and the goo just . . . *parted.*" Drew nodded enthusiastically; he'd obviously heard this already.

"And was the cat's name Moses?" At Lucia's offended expression, Garrie waved the comment away. "No, no, never mind. The cat parted the goo. I get it. You didn't bring it back here with you?"

"The goo?" Lucia asked, confused.

"The cat," Garrie told her dryly. "Since we don't have a beetle and we don't have the goo that eats things, even the cat would be helpful."

"The cat," Trevarr said, as if aware no one would truly listen, "might have been a coincidence."

Lucia sat on the edge of the bed—not listening, but looking at Garrie—disappointment drawing her brows together. "You really don't know, do you? What's going on?"

"Other than not believing in coincidences and therefore thinking this is tied into Winchester House?" Garrie shook her head. "Not a clue. It isn't the spirits—but I bet it's part of what's driving them."

"Then we'd better figure out what it is," Drew said, quite seriously. He, too, sat on his bed, a towel cradling his injured hand. "Because this isn't small potatoes, Garrie. This is the big bling. And it's really, really public."

"The big bling," Garrie murmured. But she couldn't argue with Drew's sentiment. Reckoning was best done silently. Things started to go really wrong really fast once people did take particular note—too much fuss to do the job properly, too many people trying to prove that she and the team must be full of crap or that they must have a screw loose—or worse, that they must need help to get the job done. Garrie shuddered.

"I think Drew's right," Lucia said. "I think it'll probably make the news. But that's not what I'm most worried about." Garrie looked at her. Lucia made an impatient gesture. "Drew got burned. The goo ate shoes. Who's to say it wouldn't have eaten *us*? Or that the next time out . . . it won't?"

"Enough is enough," Garrie said. "I need a cell phone." Didn't have to be hers; just had to have Quinn's number programmed in. Lucia instantly proffered her Black-Berry; Drew lay back on the bed to grope around in his baggy front pocket until he came up with his own cut-rate version of a phone—one of the sturdy ones, marketed for people who chronically sat on their phones.

Trevarr didn't so much as move. Garrie wondered if he had a cell phone at all, and then couldn't quite picture it. She took Lucia's phone just because she liked talking into a phone not shaped like a phone, and fumbled through the barely familiar menu system to find Quinn's number. She glanced at her watch, realized she had no idea whether he'd be at work anyway, and activated the call.

The phone rang . . . rang . . .

Rang.

Just as she got ready to talk to his voice mail, he picked up—snatched up, by the sound of it, and all breathless at that.

"Whoa," she said. "Did I interrupt a little afternoon delight?"

He hung up.

Garrie thunked her forehead with her hand several times and passed the phone back to Lucia, who tossed her hair back, pushed a few efficient buttons, and dialed again. She waited a shorter time. "Quinnie," she said. "It's me this time. Don't hang up, no?" A nod, another nod . . . she crossed her legs over the knee and idly rotated her foot around. "Yes, yes. She was rude. Takes you for granted?" She glanced at Garrie, who made a face of horror and mouthed *no, no.* "Could be some of that, you think? Yes, of course she's right here. Will you, then?"

She took the phone away from her face. She gave Garrie a look. She held out the phone.

Garrie took it. She didn't glance Trevarr's way. Embarrassing to have her mouth sometimes. Especially when things were coming at her fast and it went on the offensive without her. She cleared her throat and said in a cheerful voice, "Oh, hey, Quinn, how's it going?"

"Miss me?" he asked dryly. No longer breathless.

"Yes," she told him, without reservation. "I wish you were here. We *all* wish you were here. Can you come? We're doing B and E at the estate in a couple hours. Bet you can be here by then. Charter a flight. We need you."

There was a pause. A long one. Garrie winced, looking at Lucia to see if that, too, had somehow come out wrong, but Lucia gave her a thumbs-up and returned to her fanny pack chores. Drew rolled dramatic eyes and threw himself back on the bed.

Trevarr disappeared back into his room, and his back looked tall and tense.

"Seriously," Garrie said into the phone. "Lucia has a fanny pack. That's worth seeing, isn't it?"

"It's a *designer waist bag,*" Lucia said, voice raised.

Quinn let out a funny huffing sound. "Okay," he said. "I mean, not *okay, I'm coming.* But okay, you made up some points with that little episode of begging."

"I was *not*—" Garrie stopped herself. "Yeah, I was."

"You've done a damned good job of convincing me

you don't really need me lately," he said. "Are you finding out that you're wrong, or were you just trying to convince yourself? Because you said you could handle it when we—"

"Room service is coming," Trevarr announced from the next room.

Garrie squinted in his direction. Drew said, "No way, man, how can you tell—" And of course that's when the knock came. Drew bounded to his feet, a believer. "Food!"

"*My* food!" Garrie cried.

She needn't have worried; by the time Drew returned with the room service tray, Trevarr was back, too, and Drew quickly took the tray to the little work desk and left it, conceding the entire corner of the room. "I've already had two lunches, anyway."

"Sorry," Garrie told Quinn. "Chaotic moment here."

"Good timing for you," he said.

"I didn't know you felt that way." No problem with picking up where they left off. Definitely no problem with feeling the chagrin. She wasn't sure if she'd truly given him reason to feel shoved out or if he was the one having trouble dealing, but either way . . . "But it's not true. It was never true. Things have been a little slow lately—"

"And here you had such a nice start."

She could readily picture his expression, all wry and dry and borderline annoyed. Telling him to get over it . . . probably not the best choice right now, no matter how tempting. Besides, she got the message. *Don't duck the issue.* "I *can* handle it," she said, pretending privacy. "What we did, that we aren't still doing it." She ignored the fact that Trevarr was barely five feet away, his shirt now completely tucked in, his hair now held back in the silvery clip with the sheen that wasn't quite silver and a pattern stamped into it—or woven into it, or burned into it, or some other unfamiliar artistry—that made her eyes go slightly dizzy with following it. He stacked the lid from his dinner atop hers and pulled out a sharp, tidy little knife that had been . . . where, at his waist?—in lieu of using the perfectly serviceable hotel steak knife. Garrie tore her attention away from how it just plain melted its way through the meat, and from wondering if the steak was that tender or the knife just that sharp. She said to Quinn, "I *am* handling it."

He made a noise. "You're not sorry we—"

"You should eat," Trevarr said, barely glancing away from his plate.

She gave him another squinty look. A hard one. How did he know just when to interrupt?

"Tell him about the beetles!" Drew urged her.

"The goo," Lucia said firmly.

Garrie tugged the hair behind her ear. "Chaotic," she said, rather desperately. "And no, I'm *not* sorry. If there's . . . if you've . . . Quinn, this is what we've been waiting for! *Real* work! A job no one but us can handle—and I'm not sure we're going to get it done without you."

She could just about hear him shaking his head. "It's not going to happen, Garrie. I'm here. I'm dealing with my life here. Maybe once this work *was* my whole life, but the way things have gone since—"

"Ask him about the book," Trevarr said, giving a vegetable a suspicious sniff and setting it aside.

"Eat that," she told him, not hiding the annoyance in her voice or the return of the squint in her eye. *Timing.* "It's good for you. And *stop interrupting*."

"The book," Trevarr said, unmoved—although he gave the strange lanky yellow vegetable another look.

"The beetle!"

"The goo!"

"I'm supposed to ask you about a book," Garrie said,

giving up. "And to see if you know about these beetles. And the goo. And while we're at it, spirits or darksiders who might remain invisible even to me. Not to mention the belching stench from the café."

"You *have* been busy." Quinn stretched. Probably on purpose, too, knowing she would hear it and how she'd associate it, because Quinn clearly wasn't through talking about what they hadn't ever talked about. But he paused, and he grew more thoughtful. "I thought *you'd* sent this book, though I couldn't figure out . . ." He shuffled papers, and she heard the sound of a heavy object being shifted—weighty pages being flipped. She knew where he was now. At home, in the office half of the small apartment's living room. "I've never seen anything like this, Garrie. From the type of leather binding it to the scrollwork in the leather to the construction . . . where did you get it?"

"Take a step back," she said. "To the part where you *thought* I was the one to send the book. Because I'm just now learning about it. What is it? Resource stuff?"

"Like you wouldn't believe." The awe in his voice couldn't have been feigned. "This is information I haven't even seen hinted of—it's beyond your notes from Rhonda Rose, way beyond."

Garrie made a sniffy *huh* kind of noise.

"I'm not kidding. Problem is . . ." and there was a frown in his voice, "there's no context. It reads like a batch of notes taken in the middle of a conference where everyone else knows the main subject matter and you don't. Knowledge, but not wisdom."

"Philosophical," Garrie said dryly. "How about I pass the phone around, and you can hear about the beetle and the goo." *While I eat my dinner before it gets too much colder.* "By then it'll pretty much be like you're here, anyway."

"Except not really," Quinn said, not buying it.

Well, okay. "No," she admitted. "Not really." And

she gave the phone to Lucia. She didn't know if she'd done it—satisfied whatever thing had been chewing at Quinn—but under these circumstances, it was as good as it was going to get. It had never occurred to her that any of the others would take her self-doubts and career examination as anything other than what it was—and as far as she knew, Lucia and Drew didn't.

Then again, Lucia had the benefit of long conversations over horchata and a glimpse into Garrie's struggle with the diminishing engagement of their work. And Drew just plain hadn't appeared to notice. And Quinn . . .

Quinn was the only one who'd slept with her. She should have known; even a guy as generally sensible as Quinn couldn't quite stop filtering things through the conquering caveman framework, not even all these months later. She should have realized it when she saw him drawing up at the airport, bristling just a little more than the others at Trevarr's presence. Not because of the logistics or the sudden turn of events, but because a guy like Quinn looked at a guy like Trevarr and knew he was no longer the alpha of the group.

Great.

Listening to Lucia chatter in the background, she slid into the chair opposite Trevarr and picked up her napkin and silverware. He took the lids from her plate and set them off to the side, and there it was: big honkin' steak. Veggies. Fries. More food than she'd get down in one sitting. She glanced at Trevarr's plate; half the food was already gone, including the oddball string-sliced veggies. Squash, lightly cooked?

Maybe he'd split her meal. He looked as though he could still use it. She hadn't imagined things earlier; for all the substance he carried, he showed too lean in places—she'd felt it, too, in the séance room tangle. "I'm only going to eat half of this," she said. "If you—"

"Yeah!" Drew's eyes lit up from across the room.

Garrie didn't so much as glance his way. "—Want this," she finished, cutting her steak in half while she was at it, and stabbing it with her fork to lift it slightly, waiting.

Something in his eyes flickered; she shifted the steak over to his plate and wondered that she'd ever found those eyes hard to read—and in the next moment, didn't have a clue what hid behind them. She spent a few moments eating—chewing slowly, her thoughts getting in the way—and by then Drew had taken over the phone, and Lucia had moved to sit beside him on his bed, close enough to hear Quinn's responses if Drew held the phone tipped—which, after a poke, he did.

The steak was stupendous, filling every lurking carnivorous craving. The weird veggies were crunchy-tasty, with enough seasoning to keep them interesting. The fries were just how she liked them, crisp on the outside and tender on the inside. And still she had to remind herself to taste them at all.

"Is it more than you expected?" Trevarr asked her suddenly, keeping his voice low.

She gave him a startled look. "Don't you even try to second-guess me. If you think anyone else could have handled that ambush today—"

He shook his head—only the slightest of movements, but it silenced her. "I came to you for a reason."

"Why?" She put her fork down. "Why, *exactly*? Because you certainly don't seem to trust me."

He lifted his head, a rare direct gaze—startled more than anything, though he hid it quickly enough.

She leaned closer. "There's something going on here—something you know about and I don't. *We* don't. So you arrange for Quinn to get a book, but you won't tell me outright? You warn Drew about his hand, but you won't tell us what you know about the beetle? Why even ask for our help—why *insist* on it, and pay our way here, and go through the motions, if you're going to leave us out of half of what you know? You think working blind makes it *safer*?"

"Yes. That's exactly what I think. You do what you know, Lisa McGarrity. It's what I need. It's what your—" An infinitesimal hesitation there; she wasn't sure why. "—This city needs."

She muttered under her breath, and considered taking her steak back.

"Do what you know," Trevarr said, more firmly this time—as if he was convincing himself, which she didn't actually find heartening at all.

"You're not going to tell me anything, are you?" She licked steak sauce off her thumb and sat back to regard him. "You're not going to tell me about the devices I'm supposed to pretend I didn't notice. Or why it affects you so unexpectedly when I push the breezes around, or what you did to me—"

"For you," he corrected her, with no heat to his voice.

"To *and* for me in the séance room. When you—" she stopped, realized she was about to say right out loud how that cold heat had warmed every part of her, how it had invigorated her. *Woken* her.

Yeah, maybe not. Not with her little audience, pretending not to pay attention—as if the phone call utterly absorbed them. She rubbed her palms down her thighs, a soothing gesture—didn't expect to find the little quiver in the muscle there. Worse yet, when she gave Trevarr a quick glance . . . she knew he'd seen. Double-worse, she was pretty sure that was understanding in his expression. So subtle, around pewtered eyes and strong angled lines and beneath shadows from the careless hair framing his brows. She pulled herself together, picking up her fork to drag it along the side of the dessert. *Whipped by Chocolate.* What had she been thinking, to order a dessert full of innuendo in front of this man?

Then again, given his occasional cultural drop-outs, he'd probably missed that.

She licked the fork, deliberately focusing on the thick, creamy texture of the torte and mousse, the sharp, bittersweet chocolate mingled with a milder layer. She found every molecule of flavor before she swallowed. Focused on the mingled swirls of energy still riling her body.

Trevarr hadn't grown bored; hadn't lost interest. Far from it. The knuckles of his hand, resting by his dinner tray, had gone a little white. She used her empty fork to point at him, restrained as it was. "And you don't make sense, either. Not the way you talk, not the way commonplace things aren't quite what you expect, not how you perceive the things you do. None of it. Am I right? We're on some strange need-to-know basis, except you're not even telling us that much."

Those knuckles turned whiter. "It doesn't matter," he said. His voice came through strained, a rumble at the bottom edge of it. *"Do what you know."*

"Holy cow," she said, eyes widening—realizing it. She'd cornered him. Somehow—she wasn't sure just how. But suddenly and obviously, he was struggling for composure.

He leaned over then. Far too quickly for her to do anything but blink, and just as quickly he had her by the wrist—but mostly he had her with his gaze, penetrating and sharp. For an instant, only an instant, the dark pewter rims of his irises seemed to blur; breezes pushed at Garrie like a gulp of cold air. But she blinked and they were gone, and there were only his fingers tightening around her wrist. "This is no game," he told her. "This home of yours depends on what we do here today. *Tonight.*"

"I'm not playing a *game.*" Garrie jerked her wrist away, but it didn't move an inch. She frowned fiercely at him, wiggling her arm against the grip— which, really, ought to have been clear enough.

But apparently not. Evidently he waited for something else. She had a wild impulse, a completely insane and entirely irresistible impulse, to throw herself across the desk at him. She'd already dipped her elbow in steak sauce, knocked veggies off the tray, and come perilously close to the chocolate.

Not, she told herself, *the chocolate.* It was a sudden note of sanity, and it cleared her thoughts.

The moment she relaxed, quit her quiet struggle to pull away, Trevarr released her—looked at her wrist, in fact, as though he wasn't sure why he'd had hold of it in the first place. Something primal going on there—something she'd triggered.

Garrie realized suddenly that the entire room had fallen silent. If the phone call was still in play, no one was talking—not even the murmur of Quinn's voice from the BlackBerry. And then—classic Lucia—the sound of a long yawn filled the silence. "Get a room," she said, patently bored. She rose from the bed—clear of its scattered items, now holding only the flaccid silk tote and the neatly packed *waist bag*—and wandered over to the window, her hand lingering along the frame as she pushed the curtains aside to look out. "I wonder if this thing opens," she murmured.

"Go over into Trevarr's room and see," Garrie said, picking up her fork again. If they were going to pretend all was Mayberry-normal, then she was damned well going to eat this chocolatey goodness. *Farking* well, if that fit the scene better.

Lucia gave her a look that simultaneously meant *No way am I going over there* and *you were* in *his room?* and then she wondered aloud, "Which way is Winchester house from here, then? Close enough to see?"

Trevarr nodded briefly in a direction that sent Lucia's gaze out to the oblique left. "Not quite that close."

Lucia stiffened; she leaned forward. Something in her posture caught Garrie's attention, and she left Trevarr and his lingering tension to join Lucia at the window. "What?"

Lucia glanced briefly her direction, then at the desk. "Best keep an eye on that chocolate." She gave Drew a meaningful eye. Garrie snorted, and gave Trevarr an equally meaningful eye. Lucia raised her eyebrows in thoughtful acquiescence. "Ah, right. But he won't be there all evening." Another glance at Garrie. "*Will* he?"

"None of us will," Garrie said. She didn't bother to keep her voice low; she'd gotten the firm impression that Trevarr's better-than-average hearing would have picked out this particular conversation from the lobby of the hotel, and they were currently less than ten feet away, the subject of the conversation not in the least distracted by any other thing. "B and E, remember?"

"There!" Lucia said, giving the window glass a sudden stab. "See?"

"Give me a hint—oh. Wow. Damn." She caught it, just out of the corner of her eye, but she was looking right there in the next moment when it happened again. A fiery disk of flame, spurting into place above the city—spitting giant tongues of white-hot gold and yellow into the faded afternoon sky and then winking out again like some giant godly eye. "*Hot* damn."

"You saw it, too," Lucia said, her voice muted now. "I thought maybe . . ."

Garrie gave her a concerned look. "Aw, Lu—this place getting to you?"

"This is crazy," Lucia said. "Drew's beetles, my goo . . . the way things went down at the house today . . . the café and the parking lot . . . and you know, the feelings tied to that house . . ." She leaned closer to Garrie, who knew it wouldn't begin to create privacy from the man who was just now finishing his half of her steak. But she completed the circuit by leaning forward into Lucia's confidence. "You know how it was, when you found me."

"Hey," Garrie said. "It's been a long, long time since anything like that happened. And you're a whole lot better now at controlling how you take this stuff in. You know where it's coming from, and you know how to let it roll off."

"That's the thing," Lucia said. "I *don't* know where this is coming from. It all feels different. What if it's getting through my veils? What if it's screwing with my head, and triggering . . . you know, the unreal things?" She didn't quite shudder, but Garrie thought it was close.

"It's been a long time, Lu," Garrie repeated firmly. "You'd know. Even if it happened, you'd know. And in this case, it *isn't,* so that's a good . . ." But she trailed off, realizing what she was saying.

"A good thing? *This?*" Lucia finished for her, and laughed, if darkly. But not for very long, because Trevarr had finished with his second helping and pushed back the chair and come to stand behind them—close behind them. In a moment of complete cognitive dissonance, Garrie realized that while Lucia had inched away, shifting perceptibly toward the window, she herself stood completely unperturbed at Trevarr's inclination to crowd her.

"What's going on?" Drew asked, still working on his hand; a glance showed first-aid detritus spread out over the bed while he fumbled to affix a final Band-Aid to the afflicted hand.

"Nothing much," she said. "Fire in the sky, blah blah blah."

"Is it *close?*" He looked up in panic, his fingers tangled in adhesive strip.

"Nah. Mile or so."

"Well, that's okay then." He pulled the wrecked bandage away, stopped, and gave her a squint. "Isn't it?"

"You know," she said, "I suspect not so much." And then she realized that Trevarr still stood poised behind her in searching mode, and when she looked she found the faintest frown, his eyes narrowed—the pupils constricted to pinpoints.

The sky . . . too bright for him. What seemed obvious to her had so far escaped him. She angled her body slightly to point straight at the suspect spot of sky, lifting her chin just slightly, and an instant later—

There. Lucia sucked in a breath; Garrie couldn't help but do the same, forgetting to let it out again. "I take it back," she said, when she finally ran out of air and had to give up what she had in her lungs and start anew, breathing again. "That just can't be good."

"No," Trevarr agreed, suspiciously little emotion behind the word. But he should have been surprised. He should have gone *oh shit,* or something close to it. But no. He'd seen this before, she was pretty sure.

"Tell me," she asked him. "Just what else are we in for?"

"What?" said Lucia, startled and turning to look at them, from Garrie to Trevarr and back again. "What does he know?"

"You talk of me," he growled, "as though I'm not here."

"Do we?" Garrie asked, at the same time Lucia said, "We do not." And then Lucia stood taller and she looked down her nose at Trevarr even though she had to look up to do it, and she said, "We know you're there. We just don't care. Get used to it."

"Seriously, dude," Drew said, the resigned voice of experience, close to victory with the current Band-Aid. "Just get used to it."

"Also," Garrie said, "we notice that you do a lot of

that. Avoiding the question. Like just then. As in, 'what else are we in for?' "

He crossed his arms. She should have seen it coming. "I do," he said. "Get used to it."

Lucia scowled at him. "Okay, chico-wuh, but that's not funny." She stabbed a finger at the window. "*That's* not funny."

Drew drifted up to the side as the sky lit up again—a little closer, Garrie thought. A little more fiery. "Oh, snap," he said, even though he wasn't a sixteen-year-old girl. "That *isn't.*" He turned serious, looking at Garrie. "Can you even imagine the panic out there right now? And when word gets out to the people who already know about the beetles that there was goo, and the other way around, and now when the people who see the fire hear about any of it—"

"It's not going to be pretty," Garrie agreed.

"The question," Lucia said softly, looking out the window, "is how long people pretend things are normal, if maybe a little bit on the *Where the Wild Things Are* side. And when do they start packing up their cars, battening down the hatches, and shooting their neighbors by mistake?"

Trevarr looked at her in surprise. "I didn't know you'd been through this before."

"We haven't," Garrie told him. "But we've talked about it. What if things got really out of hand . . . went everybody-sees-it. It generally doesn't happen because most people are in so much denial, they can see one outrageous thing and find some justification for it."

"Outside the restaurant," Drew said. "They were talking about global warming and seventeen-year cicadas."

"At the store," Lucia said. "Environmental incident. Investigation already under way."

"But no one sees all of this without running scared," Garrie said.

"Except us," Drew pointed out.

A low rumble filled the air. Loud enough to instantly cut off all conversation, brief enough so they had no time to kick into gear and hunt for the stairwell. *Earthquake.* Earth shake, anyway. As though someone had turned on a vibrating sander with loose parts.

"Maybe they'd just better pack up and start running at that," Garrie said grimly.

Trevarr looked out the window, his reactive eyes staring straight into the hot blue. "They can't run fast enough," he said. "They can't run far enough."

Oh, snap.

13

Heed the observations of those around you.
—Rhonda Rose

I'm doing it anyway.
—Lisa McGarrity

The world growled around them.

Sklayne let himself dip into being Trevarr . . . to feel Trevarr's relief in the darkness, to tip his head back and take in the scents of the arid climate, intensified by the faint excuse of a dew. Only a slight remnant of a headache from the day, his hunger as sated as it ever got in this place, his constant awareness of the Garrie person minimized by the distance.

Sklayne had known she would be trouble. The hours spent hearing about her, what she had accomplished in this place of limited resources and knowledge . . . even Sklayne had been enthralled, curled up in his corner as that which was not quite cat. Not knowing then what it would come to mean to them, the teaching and the sharing and the direct gifting of knowledge—that one day they would use it in an attempt to restore their lives to what they had once been. To restore Trevarr's blood to what it had been.

It should have worked. It should have *worked.*

"Mow," he said, winding between Trevarr's legs. Not affection, no. Just to see if Trevarr was nimble enough, with those lengthy legs, to avoid crashing down. In the dark night sky above them, tiny eye fires bloomed and faded like so many insects. Not the crunchy kind.

Nor were they as big as the one the Lucia person had first spotted, her tension radiating from the one room to the other, to Sklayne sprawling under the bed. Now they scattered far and wide, spitting sparks over a dry desert. None of them coming close to ground, but the panic . . . it scoured the city as much as any fire. People fleeing, people panicking . . . vulnerable people dying. Sklayne felt that, too—distantly, because these were not his people. Only felt at all because of the numbers of them.

The Garrie did not know, which was just as well.

Here, the ground still rumbled on occasion, but there was not much talk about that. Ground rumbles were familiar to these people, and these were not rumbles to cause alarm.

Yet.

Not everyone panicked. Not everyone fled. Some hunkered in. And many—most of them—believed the talking person on the television. *A rare and wonderful manifestation of the aurora borealis,* he had said. *Enjoy this amazing sight!* the talking head woman had said. *I'm going to head home and sit in the dark with my camera, what about you, Stan?* And the talking head man had gone *hearty ho ho, yes indeed!* And then Sklayne, unable to resist any longer, had investigated the television from the inside out, and there had been no more talking head people in the Garrie's room. Just the Drew person, frowning as he stabbed unresponsive buttons on the remote. ::Aurora borealis,:: Sklayne observed out loud. ::Stupid people.::

"Because they believed?" Trevarr hunkered down to regard the sky, a pose he could maintain for hours. Sklayne knew this better than he wanted to, *o interesting Trevarr hunkered down in the sweet woods, but why?* until Sklayne's curiosity had taken him too close and he found out why.

::Stupid people,:: Sklayne repeated.

"They had no other choice," Trevarr told him. "Nothing in their lives ever prepared them for this."

Sweet dark woods, deeply scented, fire eyes blooming overhead in reflective energy of stalkers down below.

But the stupid people had not yet realized the stalkers. ::Stalkers will show them to believe otherwise.::

"They may be reflecting from home, not here," Trevarr said. But he looked away from the sky, looked down to Sklayne, and added reluctant words. "For now."

::We go to the house, then,:: Sklayne said, barely the question it should have been. ::We finish this, while the Garrie keeps her dead ones away. We stop the Krevata. We go home.::

"This place rubs off on you," Trevarr said. "So many words."

::Talking heads. Blah blah blah, Stan.::

"You ate them," Trevarr observed dryly, if not literally.

::No no no. Coincidence. Accident.::

Trevarr made no response, and Sklayne didn't have to dip into being Trevarr to know he didn't believe such excuses for a moment—but that he wouldn't push. Because Trevarr had other things on his mind, hunkered here in the darkness. Eventually he voiced them, though

Sklayne could have gone to get them if he'd felt bold enough. "Was it as they told?"

::As they told.:: Sklayne thought a moment. There was no need to explain that he had been at both restaurant and store; no need to explain that he had interceded for both the Drew person and the Lucia person. Trevarr had picked out his presence in those stories. But . . . . ::Worse than they said.::

"They couldn't know," Trevarr murmured. Not that the beetles ran in notorious swarms, stripping all life before them. Not that the goo was called *eatsll* and moved underground on the hunt, easing up to surround unwary victims. Not that there was very good reason neither entity appeared in the Garrie's notes or collected resources.

Not just how dire circumstances had so suddenly become, if the crossover had expanded so quickly, so significantly. How badly the fabric of this place had begun to warp at the hands of the Krevata.

::We should go,:: Sklayne said suddenly.

"We will," Trevarr said. "The tours reopened after we left. We wait for the house to close."

::We should go *now*.:: Sklayne used their connection to push that meaning over. Just the two of them, to go in while the house was still open. To assess things. To do what they could to slow the Krevata progress. ::They saw us. They fear us. They escalate. Waiting, too late.::

Trevarr said nothing. He didn't have to. Sklayne felt his understanding.

Except when Trevarr did speak, they were the wrong words. Sklayne's ears flattened even before his bond-prime had finished. "Not we. Me."

::*We!*::

"Curiosity," Trevarr murmured, "will get you killed." Not that Sklayne could argue the point. It had, after all, gotten him bonded. "Sklayne, little friend—"

Indignance burst out all over Sklayne in the physical manifestation of violet spikes tufting out from his cat-furred self. *"Mighty."* Trevarr looked away, rubbed his chin in a way that contrived to cover his mouth. As if Sklayne didn't know there was a smile there. "The better word is mighty, of course." But then he went and shook his head. "They will feel your energy before you cross the threshold of their claim."

Sklayne radiated sullen refusal to acknowledge this truth.

His role, it was, to help. To keep Trevarr safer than Trevarr alone could keep himself.

"I won't linger," Trevarr said. "As much as it needs to be done. But I need the readings I couldn't get this morning."

Sklayne looked away, into the night. *Not seeing* Trevarr. But Trevarr reached over and ran a finger just behind his cat ear. "You can listen."

Sklayne would have done it anyway. But having an invitation . . .

He leaned his cat ear into the touch. Just a little.

Garrie put the room service tray in the hall by the door and pondered a shower—at least until she saw Lucia gathering her things. Drew, too, saw the signs—he dashed into the bathroom, and then dashed out again just as quickly, getting out of the way.

"We've got an hour or so, then?" he asked, grabbing the remote for some futile clicking at the expired television set. "Before we leave?"

"At least," Garrie said. "Beth said they were running some special late tours tonight, right? We can't go in until they're done with that and shut down and gone."

Drew smacked the remote against his palm. "I wonder if they left the café open . . . still serving people. That'd be mad phat!"

Garrie just stared at him. "I don't know which horrifies me more," she said. "*Mad phat* or the fact that you think it'd be anywhere near cool to have people eat out of that café after what happened there today."

Drew just grinned. "Yeahhh," he said. "My work here is done." He smacked the remote again.

Garrie snatched it from him, all of a sudden run over with grouch. "It's dead, Jim. Didn't you see it die right in front of your eyes?"

He returned her grouch with baffled hurt. "Well, yeah, but . . . you won't let me call for a replacement—"

"No!" She reacted to the very notion, then took a deep breath. "We can't. Not after the bedspread thing."

He looked at his empty hands. "Then what's the harm if I play with it? It's not like I'm going in to get Trevarr's set . . ." Though he cast a longing glance at the adjoining room.

Garrie flushed and looked away. After a moment of inner turmoil—*jeez, could he be any more right?*—she tossed the remote down on his bed. "Trevarr's outside. If the set's not bolted down, I think you should go for it. He doesn't seem like the TV-watching type to me."

"Can't exactly see him sitting in front of *Two and a Half Men*." Drew jumped to his feet, any resentment forgotten. "Want to give me a hand?"

Garrie shook her head. "I think I'll check on him. It's not a good time for any of us to wander off."

"He's not *us*," Drew pointed out, lingering in the doorway between the two rooms. He gave her an unusually perceptive look. "Better be careful, Garrie. Things might have been kinda dull, but that guy . . . he goes a little too far in the other direction."

"You might be right," Garrie said, wryly enough. "But I'm going to see if I can find him anyway." She left Drew's doubt lingering in the doorway with him and headed out of the room, choosing the quiet stairs over the ding and clatter of the elevator. They spilled her out into the far edge of the lobby; she headed out to the well-lit front entrance, hesitated there, and then followed instinct around the end of the building where darkness pooled. A single dimly lit entrance beckoned to her on the way past.

This end of the grounds held overflow parking; the landscaping started plush and faded off into low arid scrub. Not quite as tidy as the rest of the grounds, with lighting that had gone by the wayside. If she used her imagination, she could see a figure there, crouched down where the landscaping made its transition to unruliness. But she waited a long moment, looking out at the parking lot—someone had slunk in with a camper-topped pickup—and then up at the sky. No moon yet tonight. Without it, the deep and infinite black of life, the universe, and everything looked even darker against the sporadic disk-shaped flares that spurted to life here, sputtered toward extinction there.

Strange manifestation of aurora borealis. Yeah, right. That they made no sound seemed somehow wrong. There should be a low roar through the night, swelling louder each time one of the flares appeared, but no . . . utter silence. And it unsettled Garrie that as much as she could see the things, she still couldn't feel them. There's no way they were popping around up there without disturbing the ethereal breezes, and yet . . .

They were.

Quite suddenly, she didn't want to be here in her aloneness any longer. Letting her feet follow the unfamiliar ground, she circled slightly to keep the faint dark shape in her peripheral vision. A faint ethereal breeze stirred between them . . . no telling what entities roamed this restless night. It moved off slightly and went silent.

Close enough, she lost her doubt—even in the darkness, recognizing the set of Trevarr's shoulders. He hunkered there in perfect ease, his forearms resting lightly on his knees, the lower half of the duster piled up on the ground. A dream memory fluttered through, heat and darkness and thick, spicy air; her hand went to her belly, pressing there where the disk had been, where the cold heat had started.

She swore she could still feel it, surprisingly intimate. "That's mine," she muttered, reminding it— reminding, perhaps, herself.

"Garrie," he said, as if he'd known she was there all along. As if he'd known it was *her* all along.

"I know you probably came out here to get away from us," she said, without much apology in her voice. "But since we're going back there tonight, I thought I'd see . . . I thought I'd try one more time."

"I still have no answers for you," he said, not turning to look at her.

She tried another way. "Why give Quinn the book, and then not talk to me?"

He shifted slightly, one knee going down to prop against the ground. "The book does not hold what you want *now*. It offers insight on what might be left behind."

"Because that was supposed to make sense, too."

"It will," he said, and he didn't seem the least tempted to add to those words.

She scowled at him through the darkness, crossing her arms. Wait a minute. *Left behind?* Suddenly it didn't seem so warm out here after all. "Hey," she said. "Left behind, when?"

She wasn't really expecting an answer. Good thing, too. Trevarr only tipped his head slightly, listening to something she couldn't hear; he rose fluidly to his feet.

"Why give Quinn the book, when he's not here?" she said slowly. "Why give it to anyone, when you *are*?" She didn't have his length of leg, but she made it over there in three quick strides anyway. "What are you planning?"

Because she'd seen the intensity settled in hard on his features in the darkness, fairly vibrating along the lines of his body. It told her plenty . . . starting with the fact that he had something up his sleeve. "No," she told him. "Whatever it is, just . . . *no.*"

His eyes had a sheen in the darkness, enough to show her that his pupils were, for the first time ever, mildly dilated. It softened his expression beyond expectation; she almost missed his words. "It was good to finally meet you, Lisa McGarrity."

"Finally?" she said.

And at that he smiled. Fleeting, it was. "Finally," he repeated. The smile gave way before intensity, and only an instant of warning at that, the utter certainty—*he's going to—oh, no—oh, yes—* In that instant, he'd stepped up and cupped the sides of her head, and in that split second she mustered only a quick inner babble of startled shock.

By then he was kissing her. Thoroughly and completely. No question about it, kissing the hell out of her, deep and confident and *who even has lips like this?* Her hands betrayed her, creeping up to grab at him—arms, shoulders, the front of his shirt. Nowhere was enough. Her feet betrayed her, tipping up on her toes to give her extra inches, as if somehow *taller* would translate to *closer*. Her leg betrayed her, hooking an ankle around his calf and the supple leather of his boot.

Her mouth betrayed her, kissing back. Not delicate or retiring, this mouth of hers. Apparently not.

His hands moved from the back of her head to the side of her face, thumbs following the lines of her features—tracing her cheeks, the corners of her eyes, the wings of her eyebrows. A faint sizzling trail of hot-cold power, trickling in through her skin and swirling around until she gasped, breaking off the world's best kiss ever. Not that he shifted away, or even had the grace to look abashed, not even chagrined. No, that was his predator's face up close, pupils gone truly huge in tarnished silver, lips still brushing hers where their panting breath mingled. "Finally," he said, breathing it.

Her voice came out as a horrified whisper, a hoarse thing that sounded afraid to let the words out. "I don't even know you."

"Don't you?" he asked her in that rumble, not so much deeper but simply how it came from his throat.

"Not like I should."

He frowned, a mere compression of brow. "By whose rules?"

"Mine. Everyone's. No one's . . ." She trailed off as she realized the question had been a serious one. As if she came from some tight-knit little religious cult and had to wear two-point-five layers of skirts and a padlock on her underwear.

On the other hand, the way she felt this moment, maybe she could use a padlock on her underwear. Zinging energy playing her from the inside, staging an invasion of crucial areas . . . hard to ignore.

He shifted back far enough so he could frown down at her, eyes still set to *stun*. "You could have stopped this, if you'd wanted."

"Because you *didn't* just make that decision for both of us—?" But she stopped at the offended look on his face.

"Did I?" he asked. She realized he'd gone still, restraining even his predatorial energy, hands just skimming her arms instead of holding them, his fingers spread open in a quiet gesture of release.

Now, she realized, a thought pushing toward wild. *Now is when I say no*—or turn away, or run back to the hotel to hit the lock on that door between their rooms and crawl under the covers to hide her head beneath the pillow, possibly never to emerge again.

And then *now* was over. Point made. She could have walked away right then, turned her back and simply pretended it hadn't happened and it hadn't mattered. Probably *should* have.

Too late for that now. He took her mouth; he took her shoulders and pulled her in, reconnecting with a vengeance. *Okay, no . . . this one . . . best kiss . . . ever . . .* Her hands returned to his shirt as if they belonged there, and then just got in the way as she pressed herself up against him, feeling every curve of bone and muscle, every lean response of his body, all tension and intensity and unverbalized growl. It was the body that gave him away—not only the obvious response to her, but the depth of it; he trembled.

It was quick; it ran through him like a shudder. She absorbed it with a surprised gasp, momentarily overwhelmed, her hands tightening on his—

Wow. When had her hands ended up there? She brought them up, fingers stroking the flex and play of his back, finding the wing of his shoulder blade and the line of ribs, feeling the frisson of reaction and then running down his spine.

He broke away from her, holding her head between his hands, touching his forehead to hers. Not only breathing heavily, an occasional tremor still rippling through to reverberate in her, but with a funny hitch she felt clearly under her hands. And there, again.

Garrie, her head spinning and her toes tingling and all clenched up beneath her, leaning into his hands with an urgency quite out of her control, suddenly understood. Garrie, her thoughts fractured by the absurd insanity of her response to this *not safe* barely known definitely not comprehended predator of a man, stiffened in indignation. "You are *not* laughing," she said, and the words came out with a peculiar squeak she couldn't quite recall hearing in her voice before. "You are *not*."

"Garrie," he said, still right there, pressing his cheek to her brow in a touch that felt as meaningful as his kiss, stroking her hair back with an endearing lack of finesse—not a smooth, calculated thing, that touch.

She resisted it. "Because you damned well better know there's nothing funny about this." For he still held her. Her arms still wrapped around low at his hips, her hands still clinging, still pulling. What they'd done to one another still roiled between them, low and hot and alive. "It would so totally suck if you think this is funny." Oh, humiliation—behind that voice squeak hid a waver.

"Garrie," he said again, more quietly this time. He kissed the spot against which he'd been pressing his cheek. "I laugh at myself, *atreya.*"

She chose more wisely this time. She let her silence speak her lack of understanding. She stood immersed in the energies they'd brought to life, a subtle dance of lilting breezes and deep-noted pulsations and aching physical need, all words temporarily suspended.

"Garrie," he said once more, down in his throat where it turned into a caress for her ears, his accent brushing hard on the words. "I laugh at . . . the unexpectedness. The way this is not . . . *me.*"

Her words came back in a rush. "Oh, really? Because guess what, this isn't exactly *me,* either." It didn't escape her that in spite of her flush of anger, neither of them moved; neither broke the contact between them. If anything, her hands tightened against him; if anything, held her a little closer, his head beside hers now as he took the deepest of breaths . . . inhaling her, another faint tremor running through his frame. "I'm a fun date, I'll have you know. I'm casual. Miniature golf with stupid fake cactus, a tromp around the Sandias. Meet a guy one day, go animal on him the next . . . that's not *me,* either."

Where her initial anger hadn't gotten through to him, where her initial babbling hadn't stopped him from— oh, my *God,* what was he doing to her earlobe?—her final words seemed to make an impact. He exhaled a final time on that earlobe, but it was only a sigh, even if it did raise a lingering wistful round of goose bumps down her arms. He lifted his head and he released her arms; he gave her hair a last caress . . . but it was a gesture that held regret.

"I'm sorry," he murmured. "It was not the thing to have done."

"Oh, don't even go there," Garrie snapped, just as irritated by the apology as by the explanation, so unsettled overall that she barely knew what was about to come out of her mouth. "You were right. I could have stopped this. Don't go making it all worse by being *sorry*."

He stiffened, straightening—startling her into a little spurt of uncertainty, enough to remind her that she truly didn't know this man after all. Her hands finally dropped from where they still lingered lightly over the thick leather of his belt; she would have stepped back, if his hands hadn't tightened on her shoulders. Nothing gentle about those hands, now—not a lover's touch.

Garrie scowled into the darkness, quite sure he could see it perfectly. "Hey—"

He cut her off, a quick, hard squeeze and even quicker shake. Astonishment silenced her and she chambered up a no-nonsense kick—but by then she'd realized he no longer looked at her but out into the darkness, and she aborted it. He must have perceived it anyway; he gave her shoulder the briefest of touches, his attention still entirely elsewhere. After a moment he shifted to scan over her shoulder in a way that made her spine tingle—an entirely different and not nearly as pleasant sensation as only moments earlier. She recalled what she'd seen of the area now behind her—the battered parking lot with its single squatting occupant, the landscaped trees growing scraggly around the edges, struggling waste scrub between here and the gas station on the nearest adjoining lot. The tingle down her spine turned to a crawl. The night sky moaned around them, a dissonance of warping air, there and gone again.

She opened her mouth to ask. His fingers landed on her lips before any sound came out—but not peremptorily this time, and he let them trail briefly across her lips as he removed them.

Garrie wasn't sure if it was apology for words already said, or apology for deeds about to be to be done.

"We need to be inside," Trevarr murmured, barely making sound at all.

Garrie glanced over her shoulder. *Inside* suddenly seemed very far away. She opened her mouth on *why?* and closed it again without prompting; he nodded ever so slightly in acknowledgment of her silence, and her understanding.

They weren't alone out here, that was why. And whoever had joined them was a threat.

Garrie wasn't sure who Trevarr would consider a threat, but she was pretty damned certain she didn't want to tangle with them. Especially not given how the day had gone for Lucia and Drew and the now-spotty fires still blooming and fading to life above them.

With that thought, she reached out on the breezes—turning her back to Trevarr, protecting him. She directed the breeze away with the faintest of pushes, pinging out to see what would reflect back on that radar. He felt it anyway—it came through in his sudden tension, every muscle quite suddenly tightly strung. But he didn't move away from her and he didn't jerk or make that little gut-wrenching noise, so Garrie set herself to listening . . . to hunting.

But she couldn't interpret the muddle that came back to her. No clear, hard edges; no obvious feel. No return ping.

"Inside," Trevarr murmured, although in truth she wasn't sure that he actually did make sound that time, or if she just felt it in her bones. But she felt his urgency for certain, and she took a cautious sideways step toward the hotel.

Mistake!

The darkness exploded into motion around them, slamming into Garrie—except somehow Trevarr had moved faster, snatching her up and swinging her out of the way so she took only the glancing force of it. She took brief flight through the darkness—*stay loose, stay loose*—oof! Whatever it was hit Trevarr full force, slavering wildly and barely pausing in spite of the profound impact and then the second impact when they hit the ground.

And Garrie still couldn't see a thing. She scrambled wildly, blindly, finding her feet and a whole fistful of thorns in the process. "Trevarr!" she cried—a stupid, helpless reaction from the one not used to being helpless at all. *Lisa McGarrity, Reckoner,* the one who handles the hard stuff, the scary stuff, the things no one else could do but not this time— *"Trevarr!"* But there came only that inhuman snarl, a grunt of pain, the wrenching sound of effort.

She slung blood off her hand; she squinted into the darkness. Dimly visible forms rolled around on the ground. Cloth tore and Trevarr snarled something unrecognizable except for the *"Fark!"* in the middle and then a startling moonlight glow cast the area into silvered blue light, painting a confusion of deep shadows and dark lines and flashing movement. A flashlight at a distance, help on the way—but she didn't look, didn't take her eyes from the confusion.

Confusion she just couldn't sort out. She couldn't help it—hovering there, unable to discern who was what, dizzied by the sudden rush of light and lively ethereal breezes all around her—she swore in loud frustration.

And then she realized. She'd expected Trevarr to be on top, and he wasn't. She'd expected him to be the bigger one, and he wasn't. Just like that, the visual pieces fell into place—the massive attacker sprawled over Trevarr, their legs wound together and twisting, Trevarr straining for leverage while one hand pried a ham-handed grip away from his throat and the other batted away persistent blows. Just when Garrie saw the glint of metal, Trevarr fumbled and the metal flashed down and there it came again, that same grunt of pain. Horror struck hard as Garrie realized *knife* and that this wasn't the first time it had gotten through.

She shrieked a wordless sound of fury and launched herself onto the giant, clinging like a burr at his shoulders and making about as much impact—until she latched onto his ears and dug her fingers in and clawed and yanked and *tore*.

The man yowled, an inhuman sound, rearing back and slapping air but too muscle-bound to reach her. Garrie caught a glimpse of Trevarr's face—a fierce, feral grin—and it was all the warning she had. Freed of the need to guard the knife, he gave a sudden twist and did something Garrie couldn't see—except suddenly both she and the giant were flying through the air and this time she could see the ground coming but it didn't make the impact any less jarring or the thorns any less sharp. "Shit!" she hissed, rolling to an abrupt stop against a giant land-scaping rock with her senses whirling. And the light was suddenly *right there*, and when she looked up . . .

She looked away. She looked again.

It was a baby blanket of glowing air.

With claws.

"*Move,* Garrie!" Heavily accented, as Trevarr came to his feet, braced in a staggered sort of way, hand reaching to his boot top. It was his alarm that warned her, sent her attention reeling to the fallen attacker—because, *oh, crap,* he'd fallen, rolled, and lumbered up again, his gaze fixed entirely on her.

For the first time, she saw his expression. Animalistic, just like the gutteral snarling sound he made. Blood poured down both sides of his head, blood smeared beneath his nose and across his mouth. And now he'd locked onto her, definitely not at all sane and definitely wanting to tear her apart.

"Shit!" she cried explosively, and scrabbled away without bothering to get to her feet, all of her attention on that savagely distorted inhuman human face.

"Move, atreya!" Trevarr shouted again, and the thread of fear in his voice lent new speed to her limbs with the startled realization that her attacker had gone from lumbering to lightning swift. She bolted up and away—but her half-heeled Sketchers skidded on the sparse natural gravel and she went nowhere really damned fast, one leg shooting out from beneath her entirely. That's when Trevarr finally lurched upright, arm slung back in a stance that she couldn't quite understand—not until his hand flashed forward and the man gave a sudden surprised grunt. Just as quickly Trevarr did it again—and again—and that third time Garrie heard the knife hit, an amazingly hollow, meaty sound.

The man toppled over on right on top of her, heavy as an old sleeper sofa and just as dead.

Or at least well on his way, for as Garrie struggled to breathe under his weight, he gurgled slightly and drooled blood down her neck, which was right when she lost it. "Get off off *off*!" she cried, her voice rising exponentially with each word and amazed at just how much breath she could get after all. Enough for another round of panicked, *"Off off* off!" before it degenerated to a wordless shriek of demand while his heavy limbs draped over her and his huge body trapped her, sweaty and hot.

But even in that mindless panic, the breezes unfamiliar and disorienting around her, she realized that the brute had suddenly become less of one, his mass shrinking, his size going from tremendous to merely large.

"Ease, Garrie," Trevarr said, strain in his voice, words not quite right but the meaning clear enough. "Hold ease." Metal snicked: a powerful hum filled her from the inside out and gave her a whole new reason to panic, except that it was over just about as soon as it started and *damn,* she whimpered like a little wussy girl, pushing ineffectively at her burden.

"Ease, *atreya,*" Trevarr said, hoarse and low, and then he was right there. The man's weight shifted, hesitated . . . rolled away. Garrie shot upward, colliding with Trevarr—oh, damn, pretty much clutching desperately at him, only then remembering the sick feel in her stomach at the flash of the man's knife and the *sound* Trevarr had made.

"He had a knife," she told him, as if he didn't know. "Did he get you? I thought he got you. We have to get inside . . . we have to get help . . . we have to call someone . . ." Which was when she realized that the blood on her hands wasn't from her paltry thorn slashes or from the dead man, but that it was warm and fresh and freely painted. "Oh, fark," she said. "He got you. Oh, farking fark, whatever it means."

"Not something," Trevarr told her distantly, "that nice girls say."

"Are you—?"

No. Apparently not. Because he made another unusual noise and suddenly she was taking his weight, just slowly enough to brace herself and avoid going down under him—just slowly enough so she staggered back and kept it controlled as he folded to the ground. And of course she said, "Trevarr!" for all the silly good it did.

Garrie flung herself down beside him, and the light—the inexplicable light with claws—moved closer, shone brighter. "Shit," she muttered, thus proving the versatility of that single word. She shrank slightly from it, unable to help herself, and its sparkling breezes turned gentler—but she didn't miss the anxiety beneath, the speeded whirl of the motion. "Okay," she muttered. She drew the deepest breath. She needed light; she had it. And Trevarr . . .

Trevarr needed help. She gave his shoulder a tentative touch; his head lolled. Ohh, that was bad, bad, bad. She had to get someone—

But if she ran to the hotel while he spurted arterial blood . . . also totally bad. She bit her lip, forced herself to be practical—and if she couldn't stop her hands from shaking, she could at least pretend not to notice. "Closer, please," she told the light, and damned if it didn't respond. *Practical, now.* She pushed Trevarr's duster over his shoulder, found blood welling along the swell of his biceps. Ugly, but not bad, bad, bad. With growing urgency, she tugged his shirt up, free of the solid leather belt riding his hips.

Dark blood obscured his ribs, smeared across skin and pooled in the faint hollows of muscle and bone. Oddly dark blood. *Later.* Enough to think about the short stab wound tucked away at the edge of his ribs, blood leaking steadily outward from between unexpectedly neat edges . . . nearly obscuring the faint tattoo tracings there, a pattern along his spine and flanks. She thought about what she'd seen, the motion of the man's hand, the twist of Trevarr's body as he fought to free himself. *Not the only one.* She rolled Trevarr toward her and pulled the shirt out from along the strong muscles of his back.

And oh, look at that. Blood, pulsing freely from the depressed lips of a wound. She gave it a long, horrified look; she turned her glistening palm over and looked at that, shifting it back and forth in the light, amazed at so much blood, so little time.

Shock, Garrie. It's called shock. And you're in it. With her teeth suddenly chattering, Garrie tore herself out of her daze and fumbled at her shirts, peeling off the top layer to wad up and press against that worst of the wounds. Deep breath. *Pressure first.* She tugged at his belt, struggling with the unfamiliar prong and half-cinch knot fastening, and finally got it loose, threading it back under his body—warm solid flesh beneath her hands, hard work but she did that, too, panting, swiping at her hair and remembering too late that she'd painted herself with blood.

Well. That was one way to get attention at the front desk.

She snugged the belt up tightly over her makeshift pressure bandage, wiped her hands down her remaining shirt, and considered the sports bra beneath.

Another way to get their attention at the front desk.

She skimmed out of that second shirt and tied it around his arm, ignoring the ripping sound as she pulled it tight. "Be right back," she told him. "Don't let the coyotes eat you."

But when she stood and stepped away, the evening air cold on her exposed skin and the dark sky flickering with diminishing fire wheels, the light pulsed at her; Trevarr made a noise and Garrie instantly wheeled back to him. "Hey," she said. "Can you hear me—?"

Clearly he couldn't. Not with his eyes rolled back behind half-closed lids, his jaw clenching shut and his head tipping back, the muscles of his neck gone to cords and his back slightly arched, his body trembling. Garrie grabbed his arm, as if that would do any good at all. "Hey!" she said again. "No!" The light flared at her, pushing . . . wanting something. Pushing too close, too hard—she flung a sharp, wary gust at it; the light flickered in surprise and backed considerably away.

Dismay flooded her as blood trickled from the corner of Trevarr's mouth; he choked a cough and it came with red-black foam. "What?" she said. "No!" She looked more closely at the cut angling up under his ribs, smooth skin covering defined form . . . found the blood frothy there, too. "No, no, no!" And she turned on the dead man. "What did you even do to him? *Why?*" She had no handy clothes left to rip off, so she scrambled to the dead man and yanked a knife from his body, using it to slash off a broad strip of his flannel shirt. "He hadn't done anything to you!"

"I didn't mean to do anything to *him*," the dead man said, a regretful sound. "Or you. Whoa, that dope was intense. Damn, man, I should have stuck with Motel 6."

"But you *didn't*," Garrie said furiously, hardly skipping a beat as she ran back to Trevarr and plastered the material to his side. Not good enough. "Why the hell did you come after us? And dammit, do you have anything plastic on you? A Baggie?"

"I came after *you*," he corrected her. He wasn't at all a formed spirit yet, just a collection of energies hovering over the body. He said, voice carefully expressionless, "Why would I have a Baggie?"

"Oh, stop it," she snapped. "If there's dope in one of those pockets, tell me. It's not like I'm going to snitch on you!" Trevarr choked, spilling blood from the corners of his mouth; he stiffened again, his hands curling into themselves, his body arching— "Tell me!" Garrie demanded. "Or I'll strip your body naked looking!"

"Hey, no!" The man's energies roiled with offense. "Hey, come on! I'm not a bad guy, give me a little respect! That wasn't *me*, I swear!"

"Plastic bag," Garrie said between clenched teeth, her hand on Trevarr's arm and feeling bundled wire-tension. "Do. Not. Care. About. The. Pot."

The man muttered and grumbled and finally said, "Right front pocket." But when Garrie dug into it, finding nothing, temper ignited—she gave the man a glimpse of her power, a quick, hard burst of air.

"Hey, hey! *Left* front. You'd be confused, too, looking at yourself this way."

She grabbed material to dip her hand in, bringing out all sorts of pocket lint and nastiness clinging to the tacky blood on her hands—and a sandwich bag nipped between two fingers. She fumbled with it, turning it inside out and ignoring the dead man's cry of dismay as dried leaf scattered across the ground. Unmoved, she blew the dust out of the bag. "Hey, it's too late for you to use it." She knee-walked back to Trevarr, slapping the bag over the bubbling wound and leaving it there.

"But *you*—!" he said. "Someone might have—! That was good stuff! And how do you even . . . ?"

"I know a lot about how people die," Garrie told him, more grimly than she meant to. "What's your name?" And then she only half listened to a long explanation of his name, and how it fit into his family's history—no, take it back. Really didn't listen at all, not with Trevarr's body strung up tight in constant tremors, his eyes eerily only half closed. The hovering light with claws crowded close, a reverberation no happier than hers. "Bob," she interrupted, and again when the dead man didn't quite get that she meant him with her random name assignment. "*Bob*. What did you *do* to him?"

"Eh? Oh. Er. Butter knife."

She turned on him, one hand still on Trevarr's chest. "Say *what*?"

He'd coalesced to some extent, reflecting his scruffy former self with some accuracy if yet without detail. It made her wary. Most spirits idealized themselves, or forgot themselves, or sometimes even decided to look like someone else. When she ran across a spirit who looked in death as the person had looked in life—never mind one who could string coherent sentences together—she knew to listen, to give the words credence.

And this time, she didn't like what she was hearing.

"Sad, huh? My grandma's silver butter knife. That . . . thing got into me, *whatever,* turned me into the Incredible Hulk, and next thing you know, I'm sharpening up my grandma's silver butter knife. Because it was there, I guess." He sounded quite matter of fact about it. Garrie began to suspect his *good stuff* had left its effect on him.

But the light with claws . . . it reacted to Bob with fluttery alarm, sending waves of that unfamiliar energy in her direction. *Nudging* her, she thought. Panicking, she thought. She looked at Trevarr and felt some of that panic herself. The plastic held, but blood glistened at the corners of his mouth. His breath came panting and shallow when his body's tremors allowed him to breathe at all. *Get help,* she told herself, not even sure she could bring herself to walk away from him at all.

The light flared in alarm and shoved, knocking her off balance so she sprawled back on splayed ankles. She snapped at it, "There's nothing I can do! I'm a reckoner, not a doctor!"

"I'm dead, Jim," Bob observed somberly.

"I—what?" Garrie spared him a glance, enough to see him looking down at his ethereal representation of himself. Trevarr made a gritty noise between clenched teeth and his fingers dug into the ground, and she thought *Oh God, yes, he's awake,* and the light with claws pushed at her.

"*You* do something!" she cried, absurd or not. "Or let me get help!"

"Hey," said Bob. "You can help *me.* I mean, you can, right?"

But the light, flickering in its uncertainty, moved toward Trevarr. Hesitated, curling all its impossible claws at once . . . afraid of something. "Do it!" Garrie urged, and then fervently hoped that was the right thing. "Whatever you're afraid of, do it anyway!"

The light . . . *pounced*. Garrie startled; even Bob made a noise of surprise. The light wrapped itself around Trevarr, enveloping him; it wrapped tight, expanding to cover him from head to midthigh. Silvery-pale illumination swelled to bright intensity; Garrie flinched, shielding her eyes. *Please, let this* not *be a mistake*. She could see nothing of him beneath that blanket of light, just his legs emerging from a rim of claws, thighs tight, boot heels digging into the ground.

"Are you sure . . . ?" she started, only to be interrupted by a chilling cry from within the blanket. Pain, protest, confusion, all wrapped up within that sound. The legs went slack; the blanket went dim. After a moment in which Garrie could barely stop from throwing herself over to pull the blanket off—supposing she even could—it became light with claws again and floated away—very little purpose there, and no direction at all. Just limply riding the breeze.

Garrie didn't need an invitation. She plunged forward, a hand on Trevarr's chest, the other tentatively poking at the makeshift bandages, belt, and shirts, and then finally, when she couldn't believe what she was seeing, the plastic bag.

No more bleeding.

No more bleeding.

"Rhonda Rose," she murmured out loud this time, "what have you *not* told me?" Until now, Garrie would have said *nothing*. Rhonda Rose had prepared her for this work, had given Garrie everything she'd needed to carry on.

Until now.

Under her hand, Trevarr's chest rose, an abrupt deep breath. She turned to him in this dimmer illumination, the light with claws drifting nearby. She found Trevarr's eyes opening, and after an instant, they went wide—not in annoyance, not in realization . . . not in anger. Not any of the things she expected of him. No, they widened in confusion and alarm, a wild-eyed thing—at least until he fell back with her hand pushing at his chest.

"Ease, Trevarr," she murmured, using his own word. She swiped at the cut beneath the belt. Definitely no more welling blood; definitely . . . healing started. "Rhonda Rose, you got some 'splainin' to do," she murmured.

Trevarr frowned ferociously, started to form a word and stopped, then tried again. "What?" he demanded, as much as it could ever be called a demand at all.

But Garrie heard what it was meant to be. "Bob here hulked out and came after me," she said. "And then you got in the way, and guess what, he'd been sharpening up Granny's good silver butter knife—"

Wild again, just a bit, as he looked around the barely lit area. "Bob?"

"Dead," she told him, plucking her sodden shirts away from his skin. His own was a ruin, but not coming off just now. And as for the rest of it . . . she turned away from her reeling thoughts. It would almost be easier, she thought, if she knew nothing of reckoning, nothing of Rhonda Rose and the years of learning her craft. Then, at least, everything here would have fit in the same *you must be kidding* mold. Then she wouldn't have known that while some things were improbable, others were impossible. "He says something took him over. I don't suppose you can tell me—?" She slanted him a quick if pointed look, unbuckling the belt to tug it free and coil up, carefully placing it beside him.

He wasn't quite ready to push her hands away, there where she checked the nearest wound again. But soon enough he'd have all his hard edges back in place and he'd not give her any answers at all. For now . . . more than usual showed on his face, hard enough to see in the dimmed light.

"When Bob was on top of me," she said, taking advantage. "He was still huge. You did something to change that."

He closed his eyes, let out a slow breath. "You weren't supposed to notice."

More than she'd expected . . . and all she was going to get. He simply lay there, residual tremors passing through his body, a hitch in his breathing. Healing. Pretty much as she watched.

"Hey," Bob said. "What about me? My turn, eh? I could use some help, here. You can, right?"

"Depends," Garrie said, distracted. "You don't really seem to need my help, if you want to know. Looks to me like your . . . state of mind helped with your transition." Then again, maybe it had made it easier for whatever had invaded him to do that. To attack *them*.

Still kneeling there, she sat back on one heel, the opposing knee jutting into the air and providing a handy resting spot for her chin. "Look, Trevarr, I get it. You're not giving up your secrets and you don't want me to get help and maybe you don't even need it anymore. But you're cold, if you hadn't noticed– " and who knew if he had, goose bumps mixing with the tremors—"and I'm pretty much naked, if you hadn't noticed—"

His eyes opened sharply, finding her; widened ever so slightly when they did. Sports bra, decent enough . . . if a guy with leather pants, boots, and oddball hand-crafted shirts that belonged in a Renaissance fair was used to seeing such things at all. "I thought maybe you hadn't," she told him. "Well, feast your eyes, such as you can." Skinny like a stick, she'd heard often enough growing up. Recent years had helped; she had shape enough. Just . . . rationed. Not to mention kept spare by the never-ending drive to push through the conflicting sensations of her world. She might have great abs, exposed out here in the darkness with her shirts wadded up in their sodden balls of blood, but the whole combination didn't do much for curve and flow.

Trevarr, nonetheless, was still looking.

In fact . . .

She squinted at him, startled to notice that those dilated pupils of his weren't quite—*what*—?

He closed his eyes. Turned his head. A faint wash of unfamiliar breeze; he caught his breath on pain, his fist pressing into ribs. When she said, "Trevarr?" suddenly worried that she'd taken that healing too much for granted, he looked back and there it was, that distant cold edge of his back in place.

"You're right," he said. "We need to return. This is too exposed."

Not, she thought, to further attacks. But to discovery from those who might help.

Stupid Trevarr. Stubborn Trevarr.

Once, just *once* and long ago, Sklayne had been too eager.

Stupid and stubborn.

Yes, too eager . . . and then *wrong.*

An unfortunate combination.

And now, no longer could Sklayne step in to protect Trevarr when necessary.

Even though Sklayne had grown wiser, and understood that when Trevarr's kind came together for mindless pleasure, the noises were subtly different to those sometimes made when they came together for attacking. He would not make that mistake again, so surely there was no need for geas shackles. Right?

"No," Trevarr had said, and pinned Sklayne with the bond-link until shackles welded into place, leaving them both strained and exhausted and not speaking to one another.

And so now Sklayne was here, far away from home, watching Trevarr under attack and doing nothing but giving the Garrie light so that small person might act as best she could.

Sklayne hadn't anticipated the attack on the chakka's ears. He wished it had been his idea.

He hadn't anticipated the knife, either. Not *that* knife.

But Sklayne still had his chance to go home. Because the Garrie had acted, and given Trevarr the opening he needed, and Trevarr had channeled the chakka away, and then he had fallen to the ground like a cubling splayed out to die, letting his blood spurt out while poisons consumed him.

Stupid Trevarr. Stubborn Trevarr.

But Sklayne had fixed it. He might have purred for himself, had he any energy left. Barely enough to emit his signal-glow, and even that was fading.

Brave Sklayne. Noble Sklayne.

He hadn't wanted to give that energy. Too many things happening this night; with Trevarr down, both he and the Garrie to protect. But the Garrie hadn't understood, and even if she'd tried . . . her energies probably would have killed Trevarr before helping him. And so Sklayne had given everything he could, that Trevarr might recover quickly.

Brave, noble.

Hungry Sklayne.

"Come on," the Garrie said to Trevarr, and she was more shaken than she let show, her power tight in a roiling ball. A shame. Not long before, Sklayne had thought he would learn exactly which noises the Garrie made in mindless pleasure. "Can you get up? Can you make it back to the hotel? Maybe we can make it up the back stairs without being seen."

Sklayne. Trevarr's single-word directive came so indistinctly, Sklayne had the sudden impulse . . . *break away*. Maybe now it could be done. No more bond-mate. No more *do this, Sklayne* and *don't do that, Sklayne*. Just Sklayne on his own, doing his own Sklayne things.

But . . .

No getting home, either.

No more hunting together, no more with that wild gleam in Trevarr's eye, ineffable charge bouncing between them as their quarry ran to ground. No more *atreyvo*. No more of being with someone who knew Sklayne just that well.

Who rubbed his cat-shape ear.

Sklayne decided he was too weak to break away at this moment. Far too weak. Especially when Trevarr, with that single word, offered him a snack. Take the spilled blood, he'd meant. Sklayne was too drained to be precise—too likely to overstep the lines if he tried to get it all. But most of it, oh yes.

Tasty.

With the invitation, he swooped toward them, skimming over the Garrie and her gory hands. He wrapped himself around Trevarr, ignoring the Garrie's noises of dismay and alarm—busy, busy, with clothes and skin, with the outer edges of the healing wounds. That hurt, he knew—felt Trevarr flinch. But cleaner now, infused with what passed for Sklayne's saliva. He could have done the same for the Garrie and her torn hands, but . . . she wouldn't have understood. She would have been frightened. Or worse. As it was he felt her energy gather for an assault, but he was done, done, done, leaving a cleaner Trevarr behind as he peeled away.

"What the hell was *that*?" Garrie demanded. "And what *is* that thing?"

"Something that should not be here," Trevarr said distantly. Telling the truth, for what that was worth. But that contact had told Sklayne plenty, too. Why, then, were they not already heading for their claimed space in the hotel?

"Hey!" the dead man said. Trevarr saw him not, but Sklayne saw him plenty—vibrating layers of color that couldn't yet coalescence into anything sensible. The voice wasn't a voice at all, merely a set of energy vibrations more properly meant for Sklayne's kind. But the Garrie could hear it. It meant, he thought, that the Garrie would hear Sklayne, too, if he focused intently enough—bonded or not. "Hey!" the dead man said again. "What about me?"

That was the problem—the reason they were still here. This once-person body, lying here with Trevarr's knives jutting from its flesh, waiting to be found by people who wouldn't understand.

"Look, you can help me," the dead man told the Garrie. "I know you can."

"Another time," the Garrie said. "Though I'm *really* not sure what you think I can do for you. You're cohesive; you know what happened. If you have some unfinished business, you're better off hunting up a good medium. I do the ghost thing really well, but I don't always do the people thing so well. Or hadn't you noticed?"

"You were doing the people thing just *fine* with that man before I turned into the Hulk," the dead man said.

"Look, Bob, I might—"

"Oh, *good*," he interrupted, his colors vibrating out so hard with relief as to obscure his form altogether. "Put me back."

A silence.

"Put you back?" the Garrie said, and her voice held a particular tone of disbelief.

"Yes! Look, I haven't been dead long. And I'm *right there.* Look at you—look at the power you have. I can see it, you know. So you can't fool me. Just put me back."

"I think you overestimate me," the Garrie said faintly.

Sklayne perused the body again. Knives. Not quite everywhere, but enough of them. Damage. Not quite everywhere, but enough of it. Nothing to go back *to*.

"You can do it," the dead man said. "Seriously, I insist. And you know, I feel a pretty strong attachment to you."

"Sure," the Garrie said, suddenly sounding wary. "You would. That was pretty intense."

"Then you know I mean it when I say I can make your life a living—"

The Garrie bristled. "Do you have any idea how fast I can take you apart?"

But the dead man snorted. "You already helped kill me once—I think that was enough for you."

Sklayne felt the Garrie's quick floundering panic at this truth. And Trevarr beside her, wiping leftover blood from his mouth and, because he thought no one was looking, grimacing at the taste of it.

Sklayne, seeing it all.

Hungry Sklayne.

Fast, hungry Sklayne.

Oh, lovely snack. Crunchy inside bits, chewy shoes, juicy meat. Oh yes.

The Garrie paled. She recoiled—and then straightened, determination oozing from her energies. She glared at the dead man's shocked spirit. "If you want real help, I'll do my best. But if you think that threats are going to get anywhere with me, then," she said stiffly, "I think you *under*estimate me."

And, small person that she was, she nonetheless helped Trevarr to his feet, and bore most of his weight back to the hotel.

14

Prudence with ignorance.
—Rhonda Rose

You fake it, you break it.
—Lisa McGarrity

The body was gone, but plenty of evidence remained—
the truck with its camper, the signs of a scuffle. Garrie
had grabbed the sharpened butter knife, too aware of
the blood on it . . . too aware of how very easily she'd
crossed the line from reckoner to lawbreaker in that
moment. *So be it.* The hotel back entrance let them into
a quiet stairwell—just as well, for aside from their generally ragged appearance, Garrie was still without her
shirts; the light with claws had not been as careful
when consuming that blood. Damp and blotted and
stained, they shook out with a plethora of holes, small
and large.

Sports bra. The fashion look these days, right?

Trevarr's clothes had fared better. No obvious staining, no new blemishes. But his shirt hung loose and his
belt, though threaded through the crisscrossed loops of
his pants, flapped unbuckled. And his weight for sure
hung all over Garrie.

He stumbled at the top step at their floor; she
braced against the doorway, let him collect himself,
and pushed the handle to get them through, the key
card gripped tightly between her front teeth.

"I'm fine," he said, to which she could only snort,
teeth clamping down on the card so as not to lose it in
the process.

She was too tired, too precarious to do another balancing act while she plied the key card, so she plied her

foot, bouncing it gently off the door. "Lucia," she said, a stage whisper around the key card. "Drew! Someone let us in!"

Sounds of conversation from the other side, murmurs and a short argument, and then Drew opened the door a crack—only an instant before he threw it open to gape at them. "Shit!" he said. "Fierce shit!"

"Aiee, *Dios*, get it right," Lucia said, appearing from the bathroom wearing urban break-in chic, hair gleaming and freshly sleek, a makeup brush in her hand. "Fierce is fierce, it just stands on its—" she stopped, saw them. "¡*Mierda feroz!*" She glanced at Drew, who stood in the doorway gaping, and pulled him away, standing aside to hold the door open. "Get in here! Do you want someone to see you like that? Aiee, chicalet, where did you get that bra, at the Big Box?"

For a moment, Garrie couldn't move. "Wait. Let me get this straight. I show up at the hotel missing half my clothes and hauling along this cat-toy version of our client, and you're worried that my white-trash budget is showing?"

Lucia drew herself up. "You are *not* white trash," she said stiffly, clearly offended at the very implication that she would say such a thing. "But you know very well that your sense of style is deeply impaired."

"You think? *I* think we're all lucky I wore a bra tonight at all. Because sometimes—"

"No!" cried Drew, covering his ears and his eyes all at once, elbows and hands and whatever it took. "No, no, no! You're scarring me! Deeply!"

A hotel door down the hall opened; Lucia reached forward to haul Garrie into motion. "Just get in here—" But she stopped short, closing the door behind her, and gave them a suddenly doubtful look. "Is that . . . blood? Garrie, what? Talk to me!"

For by then Garrie was guiding Trevarr off into the

other room, where it was still warm from the open window of the day. She rolled him off her shoulder and onto the bed, where he sat stiff and precarious.

"We're not going tonight," she said, a general pronouncement. To Drew, who lurked in the doorway, "Call Beth, let her know."

"But . . . dire . . . blah . . . must act . . . blah . . . timing, blah blah . . ."

Garrie whirled on him, wobbling right on the sudden edge. She spread her hands wide. "Look at me!" she said, and his widened eyes told her he saw—bloodied hands, stains still etching her exposed torso, bruises and scrapes from the flinging and the sudden landings. She could feel every one of them, too. "Look at *him*! Do you really think this is something we should do tonight?"

Drew swallowed visibly as Lucia came up behind him, putting a steadying hand on his shoulder. She didn't push—but she didn't back down. "The beetles . . . the goo . . . the sky on fire . . ."

"Not to mention the people being possessed in a way I've never seen before," Garrie met her head on. "The man who did this to us? Not only taken over, but *changed*. Physically. Twice as big, who knows how many times as strong. He whipped Trevarr's butt."

Trevarr jerked to offended attention. "Because of the *blade*."

"He stabbed—?" Drew started, but didn't finish—because no, obviously Trevarr hadn't been stabbed. No gaping wounds anywhere. But Drew looked back at Garrie . . . looked at the blood. Leftover though it might be, no one had blood stuck in crevices unless there had been much of it to start with. No one had blood in her—she followed his gaze, looked down.

"Well, *crap*," she said. "In my *belly button*." And glared at Trevarr.

"It's yours, isn't it?" Lucia asked him, but he only looked steadily at Garrie.

Garrie let the question sit on silence for a heartbeat. Then she said, "Look. You're right. Whatever's going on at Winchester House, it's big. And it's bad, really bad. But if I go down tonight because I've been used as a soccer ball already this evening? *Then* what happens tomorrow?"

Lucia's eyes widened; they reddened around the edges, because Lucia was nothing if not transparent. Drew stared, floundering, and finally admitted, "I've never heard you talk like this before."

"You have." Garrie swiped at her belly button. Nope, crusted into place. "Just not on this scale."

"She's right," Lucia said, but she didn't relax any. "Plenty of times we've gone in slow, yes? Had Quinn check things out before we moved forward? It's just usually so smooth . . . I'm not sure we even notice."

We'll notice soon enough if Quinn breaks away. But Garrie stopped that thought short. Get through this first, then worry about losing her team. *Or what was left of it.*

She caught Lucia's eye . . . didn't have to say any of it. Lucia nodded, dabbing gently at the corner of one eye. "We need to call Quinn."

"Quinn," Drew echoed with relief. "He'll know what all this means. Or he'll find out."

Garrie favored Trevarr with a dark look, suspecting—*knowing*—that some of the answers sat here in this room with them. "He's probably already looking," she said. "He might not know about our oversized friend, but he's for sure heard about the *amazing aurora activity.*"

"I'll get my phone," Lucia said.

"I'll get a washcloth," Drew added helpfully—looking again at Garrie's midriff. "Man," he muttered as he retreated into the other room. "I didn't know you had *abs.*"

It gave Garrie a chance to move closer to Trevarr—to push aside the disarrayed strands of hair that fell past his eyes and somewhat over them, trail her thumb along his strong angled cheekbone, and lean in and say so quietly, "If anything happens to them . . . If I find out later that you could have done something to change it . . ."

He made no attempt to evade her tough front—bold of her, that, and yet after what they'd been through, after she'd had her hands practically inside his wounded body, it didn't seem like so much. "Nothing," he said. "It is what it is. Quinn's book . . . is for after." He smiled, barely perceptible. "And because you needed your friend to become part of this."

She pulled her hand back as if stung—not that it didn't, given the cuts and what she was certain was one big honkin' thorn still stuck in her palm somewhere—but more by herself than by Trevarr. Because she would never had said he was considerate enough, observant enough . . . bothered enough . . . to notice or act on the needs of her friends.

But he didn't let her go—not a physical thing, just a palpable one, sitting there and holding her with a deeply tired gaze still silver-bright—and she realized she'd been wrong again. Not for them. For *her.*

The phone rang.

It startled her; she jumped. She took a step back, squared her shoulders, lifted her chin, and made her own gaze just as cool as she could, simply because it was the only way to deal with the moment—or with the fact that he seemed to know her so well when he truly knew her so little.

"Hey," Drew said, popping his head back around the door frame as the phone rang again. "You gonna get—no, I guess not, not with your hands. Good thing I bought all those Band-Aids, huh?" And he tossed a wet washcloth at her, followed by her nightshirt, before grabbing the phone himself—if gingerly, with his blistered hand. Quite the pair, they were.

Only a moment or two later, he was grinning—dark amusement, but amusement. "Stay in the hotel this evening?" he asked, for her obvious benefit—and Lucia's, as she appeared with her cell. "Why? We were headed out to . . . well, of course I saw it. Pretty, wasn't it?" After another moment, he moved the phone away from his mouth just enough to inform them, "They're calling all the rooms. The *aurora* is way . . ." he paused for Lucia to wince, gave a little unconscious nod when she did, ". . . phat, but some people are taking it as an excuse to behave badly, so the hotel is advising us to spend the evening here. Free HBO! Free pastries in the lobby!"

"Is there a curfew?" Garrie asked, loudly enough for the phone to pick it up. Not that it mattered; she was so definitely in for the night. But it would be an indication of how serious things had gotten, city-wide.

Drew listened, and nodded, and thought he had a moment to break in but didn't, and nodded, and made blah-blah-blah talking motions with his hand, and finally had the chance to reassure the person on the phone that they'd be staying in for the evening and they might well come enjoy a pastry. "Wow," he said, hanging up the phone. "She's wired."

"Frightened," Lucia said.

"And she doesn't even know about Bob," Garrie muttered, wiping the wet washcloth over her stomach, down her arms.

"What about Bob?" Drew asked, and then looked horrified. "That wasn't fair! Quinn would have warned me!"

Garrie couldn't help but grin. True enough, Quinn would never have let Drew walk into that movie setup line. "Call him," she suggested. "I want to get his take on things from the outside of this—see what's being said, what information is leaking out. Not to mention he might be able to shed some light on the latest."

"And after that?" Drew looked at his watch again. "It's pretty early, on reckoner time."

"Then the reckoners sleep," Garrie said. "Because reckoner time also starts early tomorrow." Sleep, except for her. Too much going on this evening, too much roiling around inside of her—conflicting energies, conflicting emotions. The hotel had a workout room. She could run a couple of treadmill miles if nothing else. Something to put her mind into cruise mode, where it had half a chance of figuring out what was going on, and how much it would cost them.

Because right now . . . *I got nothin'*. She worked fiercely at her belly button.

"Easy, chicalet," Lucia said, arriving in the doorway with the BlackBerry, already at work in its menu. "You need that. You might want a piercing one of these days."

"Next on my list," Garrie muttered. She spread her arms in an *am I good?* gesture and got a moment of complete attention, and then Lucia's definitive nod. Garrie tossed the washcloth back to Drew and shrugged into her oversized *Ghost Riders in the Sky* T-shirt, crossing her arms over the ghostly hard-riding cowboys on the front. After a moment, she moved closer to the door, forming something of a huddle—for it hadn't escaped her notice that the others hadn't ever crossed that invisible line into this room. At least, not while Trevarr was here. A quick glance at the television revealed that Drew had at least staggered briefly through.

Lucia sent the call out and put the device on speakerphone just as Quinn picked up. "Do you know what time it is here?" he asked without preamble.

"Reckoner time!" Drew said, utterly without remorse. Silence, just for a moment—silence with a wary taste, even though the inadequate little speaker. "Is it all of you?"

"All of us," Garrie said, with emphasis on *all*. No mistaking Trevarr's presence.

"Okay, then," Quinn said. Something clattered in his sink; water splashed. Garrie instantly envisioned his small apartment and his even smaller kitchen. Serviceable, barely furnished . . . but with an amazing variety of thriving plants, the rustle of which made her think he was watering even as they spoke. She'd felt at home there, once. Quinn, however, wasn't thinking about then. As she should have been, he was thinking about *now,* and he said, "I almost hesitate to ask."

"You've been watching the news?"

"Reading between the lines." Definitely a rustling noise there. "Getting more from the Internet, actually—lots of little things the news isn't picking up on—but you know . . . no one's taken any good pictures, including pro photographers who theoretically knew what they were doing. Nothing but visual garbage. People really buying that aurora story?"

"I think they *need* to buy it," Garrie said. "You find anything on it?"

"In between looking for information on bugs and goo?"

"Oh, we're not done yet," Garrie told him, more grimly than she meant to. She looked down at her hand, flexing it; the drying slashes and punctures stretched painfully. "There's the Hulk to add to the mix."

Definitely a wary silence there. Not even any rustling of leaves. Then, "As in, the Incredible?"

"Well," Garrie allowed, "minus the green." And she explained . . . more or less. She left out the light with claws—just too much, that—and she still earned another silence when she was done. It sat hard on her with guilt, keeping things from them. Deceiving them.

Not just the light with claws, but every little thing she'd noticed about Trevarr and hadn't told them. Every detail kept to herself.

"Gonna have to get the phone charger," Lucia murmured into the silence.

"Everyone's okay?" Quinn asked finally.

"Kinda wishing you'd come along, now, aren't you?"

"Yes," Quinn said, clearly hating the admission. But then, more acerbically, "And no. These books aren't exactly in electronic editions, you know."

"But did you *find* anything?" Garrie asked him, giving Trevarr a quick glare for her certainty that he could solve all their mysteries in one fell swoop. Or at least most of them. Unconcerned, he bent to work on the buckles of one boot, stiff and pretending he wasn't.

"I know this for sure," Quinn said dryly. "We've got a good pattern going here."

"Which is that we don't know a thing about anything," Lucia said, arms crossed to prop the elbow of the hand holding the BlackBerry. "Am I right?"

"Points to you," Quinn said. "Though I haven't given up on this book. I'm thinking about taking it to the museum—you know, my friend there? Maybe if I can get some context on it—"

Trevarr froze, and then straightened with alacrity—too much so, to judge by the little grunt that slipped out, and the hand that went to his side. "Don't do that."

"I trust her," Quinn said mildly. "If it's contraband or something, it's not a big deal."

Trevarr stared at the phone in a way that made Garrie glad Quinn wasn't here to see it. "It would be," he said, "a very big deal."

The silence fell hard between them, until Garrie offered, "Maybe not right now, Quinn. Maybe when we have the time to be more discreet. The last thing we need is for you to end up in jail." Although she had the feeling that Quinn in jail was, somehow, not at all what Trevarr had in mind.

Quinn made a grumping noise that was as close to assent as they'd get. "It's damned hard to read. Weird handwritten script, tiny little notes . . . I'm taking so many notes that I might as well rewrite the book."

"Definitely not a searchable electronic version," Garrie muttered. "So, can't give us any more than that?"

"Sure," Quinn said, readily enough. "I can give you this: *prudence with ignorance.*"

As one, they chorused back what had once been Garrie's words alone, her response to Rhonda Rose's advice lo those many years ago. "You fake it, you break it!"

"Seriously," Quinn said, after Drew had finally muffled his resulting giggle-snort. "Be careful. Whatever's going on here, it's not like anything we've seen before."

Trevarr now worked on the second boot, but he paused long enough to look up at Garrie. "You have what you need," he said—again.

As if that was supposed to be reassuring.

"I think," she said, and not without a little glower, "that what you mean to say is that we'd better make do with what we have."

His gaze grew more direct. "I brought you here because I knew you could."

"Whoa," Lucia murmured. "That's practically a whole speech."

"And very pretty," Quinn said. "But it won't be particularly useful when you're in the middle of things." The blame in his voice went straight to Trevarr. "Listen, you. When this gets dicey—and it will—you'd better do your part. You'd better take care of them." *Take care of* her. Garrie heard those unspoken words and she was pretty sure everyone else did, too. Dammit.

"You can be here before morning," Trevarr said, not without annoyance.

"But *not the books*," Quinn said, clearly frustrated. "Without them, I'm just in the way. At least I know it."

Garrie wanted to argue with him, but the truth was, even with Quinn's amazing mind for trivia, he couldn't remember what he didn't know. And the things they'd seen . . .

They definitely didn't know about them.

Not yet.

"Garrie?"

She broke from that little reverie to discover that Quinn was signing off. She said her good-byes, tugging absently at her hair; by then Drew had ducked out to make his own quick call and returned to announce, "Beth is picking me up tomorrow morning on her way to work. I want to wander around, see what I can read on the recent stuff around there. Because this doesn't feel old to me—nothing I picked up inside the house itself gives me the impression this stuff has deep roots."

"You're just going to hang there until we get there in the afternoon?" She looked at the others. "Another recon, and then head back in the evening like we planned for tonight?"

"The extra day's information might serve us," Lucia noted.

"It's not the information I'm worried about," Garrie muttered. Not given the things happening in this city.

Beneath their feet, the hotel shivered with a faint seismic aftershock . . . and outside, a low moan filled the night. Low enough for whales and elephants to call it a song, but . . .

Garrie didn't think it was singing at all.

Talk, talk, talk. Sklayne wanted to snack. He wanted to top off his crunch and chew by sipping from the well-spring of power at the wall. He wanted to indulge in visual sparkles of delight. It would be a hard blow, losing this.

Home is better.

Yes. Home.

But there was no snacking, because of the *talk, talk, talk.* Talk about the next day. Talk about staying alert for darkside dangers. Talk about needing to work together. And then when the Lucia person and the Drew person left the connecting doorway to make busy with what remained of their toothpaste and soap and change into other wearables for sleeping, the Garrie lingered.

She could tell, Sklayne thought, that Trevarr was so badly hurt.

She could tell, too, that he was healing.

Sklayne thought she was equally bothered by both. A stupid person thing. How could healing not be good? *Go away now. Snack time.*

Now she looked at Trevarr and reached into one of her many pants pockets without looking, searching it gingerly. Her voice wasn't as tentative. She kept it low, with a glance at the open doorway, but . . . not tentative. "Bob didn't say a thing about putting stuff on the knife," she told him. "No poison. No nothing. He was pretty specific. Just a weird sharpened butter knife." And she dropped it on the bedside table.

Sklayne sucked himself into a smaller ball, scooting across to the couch. Trevarr . . . ah, he flinched. Shouldn't have done that. ::Shouldn't have done that,:: he said, risking the swift glare he farking well received.

Bob didn't help. He appeared, hands on his hips, petulance on his face. "That's *mine.*"

"I know," the Garrie said, not looking at him. "But we can't leave it out there. I can't put it in your camper truck, either. It's old; it's got gouges from the work you did on it. It's got blood all over it. It screams evidence, and there's nothing I can do to change that. I'm sorry."

"One would think you did this sort of thing all the time," Bob complained, and disappeared again.

Trevarr took the interruption in stride. Grateful for it, Sklayne could tell. And the Garrie seemed to realize she'd lost her moment. "We're not going to talk about this, are we?" she asked him. "You're not going to give me any answers. Again."

"No," Trevarr admitted.

She stared at him for another long moment, and then she scooped up the offensive knife. "Get some rest," she told him, and left—though at the doorway she turned back long enough to add, "I'm not going to stop asking."

"No," Trevarr murmured, but only after she was gone. "You wouldn't."

Sklayne darted back to him—a form Trevarr had learned to see, after a fashion, and could more certainly feel, just as he'd felt Sklayne in the sweet woods that day. Long ago day. He had been so young then. Now, suddenly feeling much older. ::Use her,:: he reminded Trevarr. ::Use her and leave her behind.::

Trevarr gave him a look Sklayne hadn't seen before. Something between resignation and a strange, muted hope. "Too late for that," he said, and stood, closing the door between the rooms and quickly pulling off his boots, his pants . . . draping them over the desk for Sklayne to clean more thoroughly. He pulled on the light drawstring linen pants for sleeping—an item he seldom bothered with, but that seemed to fit within prudent social norm for this place—and reached for the light. "Don't overeat. I don't want you bouncing off me during the night."

::I *never*,:: Sklayne said, with just the right amount of dignity. After all, it had been days.

He'd wanted to talk to Trevarr. He'd wanted the chance to assess his bond-partner's hurts, and his healing. He'd wanted to understand better this reaction to the Garrie, initiated long ago and snapped to life that very moment in the disgusting ghost poop exploding house.

But he could amuse himself with cleaning the clothes, if this was the way of it—Trevarr's breathing, already settling toward sleep.

Be sure. Sklayne drifted slowly closer, closer . . . hovering there, just above Trevarr's face, there where the breathing tickled and eyelashes rested against cheek. *Waiting.*

Trevarr didn't open his eyes. He barely opened his mouth. But the word was nonetheless implacable. *"No."*

Sure, now. This was the way of it.

Sklayne returned to the clothes. Amusement through analysis. This, blood. That, plant sap. This other, a small bug in the wrong place at the wrong time, Trevarr landing on his back in the dirt, even sliding a little. All the while, listening next door, and realizing suddenly that the Garrie was not there.

The Lucia person was there. She slept, and from her came soft waves of leftover emotional energy. A cleansing, a sloughing off of the emotions absorbed during the day. Clever body. Sklayne wondered if she even knew. He moved alongside her, spent some time studying her face in repose—every angle sleek and perfect, lashes long and sweeping over almond eyes, brows arched, touseled hair sleek. She lay on her side; the sheet draped over the curve of her hip, dipping to her waist.

Sklayne had spent enough time with Trevarr to know what he liked—to know *this* was what he liked. Not the Garrie, short and petite in all ways, boyish hips with many-pocket pants riding low. Short hair with its funny blue streaks, hazel-green eyes lacking any elegant slant, gamine face a little strong in the jaw and cheek.

Inconsistency from Trevarr . . . it alarmed him.

He paused by the Lucia person's eye and blotted

up the glimmer of a tear hovering there, artifact of the cleansing. The Lucia person slept with tissues by her pillow.

The Drew person simply slept. Sprawled over his two-person bed with careless abandon, his pajama bottoms riding low in a way that would catch much offended scolding from the Lucia person in the morning if he didn't notice before she did. Sklayne already knew them this well, even if they knew him not at all. Whatever the Drew person saw during the course of the day, whatever histories impressed themselves on him, they did not sink deeply into him.

Sklayne suspected that he dreamt of Beth. Strongly suspected. *Certain.* Yes.

And the Garrie . . .

Was not here.

Sklayne made himself *glass cat* and settled lightly on the bed where the Garric should be. Her nightshirt, here and scented of her, and of the blood and sweat she hadn't quite washed off before donning the shirt. Sklayne cleaned it for her, an absent chore in which he absorbed of her, just as he absorbed of Trevarr. He lingered a moment longer, the gentle energies of the Lucia person's cleansing lapping around his feet. But the Garrie did not return from wherever she'd gone, and he felt the lure of the energy outlet from Trevarr's room— here, too, but he knew better—and he decided he would see what it was like, being sparkly cat.

A replete, sparkly cat, an hour later. Two hours later. Trevarr's clothes cleaned, the worst of the damage mended on a molecular level. The sky watched; quicker than sight inspections of the hotel made, from foundation to roof.

Sklayne knew his part. Found comfort in it.

And so he was alert when the door to the Garrie's room opened, the quiet click of the electronic lock followed by the snick of the actual latch, and moments

later, the equally hushed sound of the latch reengaging
and the security chain sliding into place.

So much Sklayne had learned about this place, in
such a short time. He knew electric locks. He knew security chains. He knew the sound of the shower and the
even subtler sound when the water temperature warmed
in the pipes. Not a long shower, not like the Lucia person. Shampoo, a subdued rich scent. Soap, not the smell
it should have been. He suddenly regretted his earlier
dietary indiscretion with her soap. Surely he could have
left her half.

Or a quarter.

She hesitated when she came to the nightshirt—
noticing. Subtly different texture, faintly different
scent . . . material rustled as she put it on. Sklayne
crouched by the door, listening, not quite aware that
he'd crept away from the wall socket. And there, into
bed with her.

Within moments, he felt it . . . a disturbing burble in
the energy flow. Control giving way to fatigue. Trevarr
had done what he had to, helping her in the séance
room . . . but he had done her no favors. Not when she
didn't know. *Couldn't* know.

It didn't take long. The energy stirring up, riffling his
hair up on end . . . taking her away from herself, he
knew.

If Sklayne knew anything, it was energies.

She got out of bed, bare feet padding steadily for this
door. Sklayne crept away, even knowing she couldn't see
in this darkness as he could. As she hesitated there, just
the other side of the door, Trevarr's breathing changed.

::Yes,:: Sklayne told him. ::Already, it comes to her.::

Silence. From the Garrie, hesitating. From Trevarr,
waiting.

::Doesn't want to wake you,:: Sklayne said, and then
wished he hadn't. Trevarr might get the impression that
he cared.

Trevarr might as well have not heard him, for all the response he offered. But Sklayne knew he had, for he pitched his voice low and said, "Garrie."

On the other side of the door, she caught her breath. She pulled the door open, just enough of a gap to show one big dark eye, peeking through into the darkness. Not knowing that both Sklayne and Trevarr could see her perfectly well.

Trevarr swung out from the bed, already moving smoothly. Sklayne's healing at work . . . Trevarr's own natural healing at work. He pulled the blanket from the back of the couch and went to the door, pushing it another foot open. For a moment, she looked up at him—worried and hesitant, her pupils huge in the night and probably even able to see something of his face. A moment was all he gave her; he folded the blanket around her shoulders and gripped it to guide her into the room, pulling the door back to its barely ajar position.

She clutched the blanket and said, somewhat nonsensically, "It's just—" and couldn't even finish that.

Not that she had to. "I know," he said. "It will be quiet in here."

The Garrie knew what he meant. So did Sklayne. And there she went, following his light guidance—not to the bed, but to the couch. Sklayne retreated to a lighter contact—not out of respect, because he had already invaded Trevarr's mind at every imaginable moment, curiosity abounding. But because this time, he felt only strain. The peculiar hurt of wanting and not having. Of wanting and choosing not to have, because of how much worse it would be to then leave.

Sklayne hunched down tight. Not his decision. Not his pain. He told himself so.

He told himself repeatedly.

By then Trevarr sat aslant on the couch. The Garrie, so very tired, curled up in the blanket beside him, a small huddle of a person with her power still roiling around—but fast settling at that. She sighed against his shoulder; she let herself relax. Sklayne relaxed with her, his claws kneading in, out, in . . . his breath rolling over an unvoiced purr. Trevarr, too, slowly settled. He let his head tip back against the propped-up couch pillow, the one that had only the smallest nibble on the corner.

The Garrie sighed into sleep, just that fast, just that balanced; with Trevarr beside her, the invading energies within wouldn't roil up to seek their own. Her mouth fell slightly open; her hand fell from the blanket beneath her chin to rest on Trevarr's chest—there, where the faint signs of scales had almost been evident to her earlier in the evening.

A gentle, feathery touch, sliding over bare skin.

Trevarr's eyes flew open; he sucked in a breath. Sklayne's claws popped out, digging into the carpet.

Relaxed no more.

15

Beware the charlatan, for she diminishes what you do.
—Rhonda Rose

Woo-woo lives.
—Lisa McGarrity

Garrie woke stiff and cramped and paradoxically reluctant to move, tucked in under the weight of an arm, serenaded by the sound of quiet breathing, reassured by the steady rise and fall of the chest beneath her hand.

Then she woke just a little bit further and she thought

Trevarr! and suddenly she was quite damned awake, her eyes springing open to reveal an up-close-and-personal expanse of chest, contours smooth in the muted light behind thick privacy hotel curtains.

She didn't move. She forced herself to keep breathing—knowing instinctively that catching her breath would wake him if she hadn't already done so and her mind racing over *what was I thinking?*

That she'd needed to sleep, that's what. That the dreams had come on her just as hard as before, just as fast—even with miles of elliptical work behind her, the kind of exercise that usually settled her right down, centered her. That Trevarr had turned those dreams away with his touch once already, and could possibly do it again.

As he had.

She'd slept. She felt rested. She felt *right,* and ready to go.

So, quite obviously, did Trevarr. Awake or not. Thin pajama bottoms, style universal and material unfamiliar, hid nothing.

Oh, it was so time to leave.

She slipped out from beneath his arm, managing to drape the blanket over his lap in the process. There. That was better already. She lost an instant of escape time frowning at his torso, wondering whether those faint marks were bruising or weird tracings, if they were what she'd caught a glimpse of the night before when she'd been so intent on saving his life.

From what? Those wounds were nothing more than angry lines—thick, tender new scars.

It was too early in the morning to challenge reality. Too early to face the fact that she'd slept the night with him, in whatever fashion. So even as his gaze blinked into clarity—and possibly amusement—she clapped a hand over her mouth and muttered through the Band-Aids, "Gotta go. Morning mouth. Later." As she turned away she caught her reflection in the room's full-length mirror and squeaked in horror—bare legs, nightshirt just barely covering her ass, and her hair— oh, God, she'd gone to bed with her hair wet. She abandoned her mouth to clap her hands over her head. "Aiee! Morning hair!" and then almost tripped over his leather satchel and her own feet on her hasty way out.

Dignified retreat. So very not.

It wasn't hard to slip into the next room and out of her nightshirt—still feeling oddly crisp, not just washed and ever so lightly scented, but *new* somehow—and into a clean pair of crop cargos and a trim sleeveless hoodie over a thin, long-sleeved thermal with a bazillion or so tiny little flowers on it.

No doubt she'd be too warm within the hour. But for now, the early morning air was cool out there, and she'd already wet her hair with a quick finger-combing at the sink. Warm-blooded Trevarr, she thought, would be happy for his layers. *Put them on!* she thought in his direction. *Put them on now!* She eased out the door, coward that she was—key card, chapstick, cell phone . . . traveling light.

She hadn't really thought it through, heading for the parking lot—hadn't needed to. The need was too deep— another look at the arid scrub where Bob had died and where Trevarr had come so close. And where an ordinary man had somehow morphed into something so powerful and angry, there under the fiery blooms of a Northern California desert sky.

Garry had seen plenty. She'd seen invading dark-siders and possessing spirits both. She'd seen the rare darksider manifest into flesh, and ghosts with subtle, awesome control of both people and environment. But she'd never seen any entity that invaded a plain old human being and turned it into *something else*.

Yet somehow it had happened. Right here, on these boring, overlandscaped hotel grounds.

For now, the exterior of the hotel felt deserted. The sky, clean and blue and pale at the horizon, still looked washed out compared to Albuquerque blue. The grounds were neat and tidy and freshly damp from the watering system; the smell of it came strongly to a nose so used to *dry*. Garrie walked in silence, encountering no one. Somewhere between the close grounds and the overflow lot, desultory bits of trash emerged from the plantings—a bottle sticking out from the fancy tufted grass, a can perched against a parking curb. The fancy grasses changed to clumps of sage, scrub oak, and leathery-leaved bush.

Nothing to suggest that any great drama had happened here less than twelve hours earlier. Birdies singing, insects buzzing around . . . beautiful, peaceful morning. Ghost coyote playing pounce with an oblivious lizard, clearly puzzled by his lack of success and yet still enjoying the game. A distant haze that might have been a swarm of insects but was more likely a weak darksider *spive* incursion, soon to dissipate on its own. One spirit walking the edge of the distant road, a vague humanlike shape of energy without focus . . . had she been closer, she could have easily directed it toward either coherence or dissipation, whichever it needed.

Garrie stood at the junction of the two parking lots, where the main parking turned to overflow and the asphalt turned from black to weathered gray in a bumpy seam. At the far end, Bob's camper-topped truck sat abandoned but not yet rejected by management, sinking lower over its right springs, the tailgate patched with gray over dull red. She closed her eyes, remembering the darkness of the night before . . . orienting. When she opened them, she went straight across the back corner of the lot, straight to the spot where she'd met Trevarr.

A powerful spot, this one. It instantly caught her up with memory. Trembling legs and elusive breath and pounding heart and yes, even his damned laughter—

And she'd totally forgotten to sweep the area for disturbed breezes, and she'd forgotten to keep a lookout for unfamiliar trouble, and she'd clenched her hands and gone straight back to the moments *before* Bob . . .

"Gotcha, didn't he?" Bob's voice startled her so deeply she shied aside—and then turned on him with a scowl. He held up both hands, warding her off. "Hey, hey, not my fault. Blame your boyfriend."

"He's not my boyfriend." Garrie didn't turn the scowl off.

Bob snorted. "You should have seen the look on your face just now. I bet if you have a notebook, it has *Mrs. Garrie* . . . well, whatever his last name is . . . scribbled all over it."

Garrie didn't know Trevarr's last name, so she only scowled harder. Especially as that fact truly sunk in. It hadn't seemed to matter; he'd seemed complete enough without it. It wasn't as if she was going to mix him up with some other client named Trevarr.

Or *any* other client.

Bob just snorted again. "You're in denial, baby."

"I'm not," Garrie said. "I know exactly what happened here last night." Something beyond her experience, for sure. Something beyond any normal experience.

Something most people wait their whole lives to feel.

It didn't bear thinking about. Not with Bob, anyway. Bob, who was something else again altogether. She scowled at him and muttered, "Except for the part where I don't have a single damned idea what happened here last night." She brushed off the front of her hoodie— totally unnecessary—and looked around. Paved asphalt and scrubby untended growth everywhere, the gas station standing a lone watch an acre away. Behind her, the hotel no longer visible, lost in the cultivated live oaks closing in around the building. Oddly isolated, here in the overflow parking lot with memories and a reluctant ghost.

There—that area of crushed plant and disturbed dirt. That's where Trevarr had gone down; where he'd struggled with Bob. And over here—that's where she'd landed when Bob had thrown her, and then when Trevarr had thrown them both. Three feet of woody bush with leathery leaves and little red berries and *aiee!* look at those thorns. She was lucky it had only been her hands. She looked at them—sore and scratched, plastered with first-aid strips—and cautiously flexed them. Definitely sore.

"Spiny redberry," Bob said, matter of fact.

"You don't say." She reached out to run her finger over the tip of one of the thorns, wincing.

But there on the ground, there was no blood. Over where Trevarr had fallen and bled so badly, nothing. Where Bob had died . . . nothing. The mob would . . . well, *kill* for cleanup like this. "What was it?" she asked Bob suddenly. "Do you remember? When you were . . . *changed*. What was it that drew you to us? That made you so angry?"

"Nothing *made* me angry," Bob told her. In the daylight, he had a definite transient air—scruffy, hair that no longer bore any resemblance to its previous style, clothes frayed and mended beyond frugal and onward toward *or else do without.* "I pretty much came that way. I mean, once whatever it was got into me. That I came at you instead of running out toward the highway to get hit by a truck . . ." He cocked his head, gave her a thoughtful look. "It was the energy. Yours. Damn, I wanted it. Both of you stood out like big halogen lamps in the night, but his . . ." Bob made a dismissive gesture.

"Familiar. Yours . . . exotic." He stopped, frowning. "I can't believe I just said that. Any of it. Energies. Woo-woo!"

"Woo-woo lives," Garrie informed him solemnly. But then she, too, frowned, trying to understand the implications. Most of the entities she encountered recognized her energies immediately, although their reactions varied a great deal. Some of them ran, some of them pleaded, some of them greeted her with relief—and some of them tried to kill her. But they *knew* her. If not her personally, what she was.

Just do the job, Garrie. Quit getting diverted by things that aren't as they should be. Do what you can.

Starting with what she should have done in the first place—the area sweep. She let her eyes go to soft focus and extended from inside, first in hunting broad patterns. Not enough security here to go large, so she limited herself to the hotel grounds and a little more. She found nothing but quiet eddies and soft pools, energies not so much gathered as lacking any impulse to move. The playful coyote was a mere blip, and a pleasant one at that. The entity by the road carried disturbance, but nothing profound; it wouldn't do anyone harm and it would likely resolve by itself.

But here—right *here,* where everything had gone wrong the night before—ripples of red-black darkness spread from scattered points along the ground. When she looked more closely, they faded away. With a deep breath, schooling patience out of impatience, she went back to soft focus. Red-black ripples eased back into sight. Garrie moved into them, walking slowly . . . pushing a bit of breeze at them, and watching for reaction.

There wasn't one. Not to her personal energy and not to her deliberate breeze. Not real energy, then . . . only an energy echo. She'd seen them before . . . but seldom. This place still remembered what had happened here last night, but nothing of it truly remained.

Red-black energy. Just like Trevarr's blood, so dark in the strange illumination of the light with claws—and then it had been cleaned up and gone. Ingested, as far as she could tell. Too late to look closely now.

Maybe that had been the point all along.

"Whatcha doing?" Bob spoke right in her ear, nearly startling her back into that spiny porcupine bush or whatever he'd called it.

"Don't do that!" she snapped at him, driving him back a step. "Were you this rude when you were alive?"

"No," he said, without rancor. "But I'm experimenting with a newfound sense of freedom."

Garrie reached into her hoodie pocket and fished out her cell phone. "Don't experiment on *me*," she warned him, and gave him the slightest shove. "Fresh little ghosties like you? You are so *not* the big fish in this pond."

He stumbled backward, but recovered quickly enough, albeit with a frown. "Was that a horrible mixed metaphor, or did it just seem like one?"

"Just seemed like one," she informed him without remorse, and flipped the phone open. The most active energy was the push she'd just sent at Bob, so it *should* work. "It should work," she said out loud, encouraging the phone when it seemed to take a moment too long to respond to her dialing request. "Or," she added, "it could get drop-kicked."

"Man," Bob told her. "You need to chill out. Too bad you threw away my pocket stash last night. But hey, if you go in my truck—"

Garrie cut him off short. "Don't want to know," she said, singsong in her words. "Really." Ah, there. The phone. Finally. "Hey, Quinn."

"It's the Garrie-phone this time," he said. "Either the

others aren't with you, or you somehow convinced Lucia to use your clunky stone knives and bearskins tech."

"Got it the first time," she said. "Hey, we're an hour behind you . . . you really think anyone else is awake?"

"Did you really think *I* was awake?"

"Oh, damn! I'm sorry, I'm just—"

"Caught up in this one. Yeah. You think I couldn't tell? You're in deep, aren't you?"

"Maybe too deep," she muttered.

"Whoa," he said. Material rustled copiously—*sheets*—and she knew she really *had* woken him. "Since when do you talk like that?"

"You haven't seen this stuff, Quinn. It's . . . it's not right. It's not anything we've run into before. It's not even the right energy, and it doesn't respond to mine. How can I fight something that doesn't respond to what I *do*?"

"Shit," he said, sounding stunned. "Jeez, Garrie, when you talked this up in the airport, you were all 'it's onward we march, boys!' and 'into the fire, boys!' "

She gave him a suspicious squint, even if he couldn't see it. He'd hear it in her voice, along with the incredulous tone. "Are you seriously quoting *Scarlet Pimpernel* at me?"

"Unfair advantage," he said. "You've been into my ex-girlfriend's left-behind CDs." And only the shortest pause before he added, "And hey! I might be half asleep, but I can still see you dodging a question a mile away."

The disadvantage of being with a team who knew you just that well. But . . . she'd called *him*. So she said, "Yeah. Okay. You're right. I really thought this was what we all needed. I thought it could pull us out of this slump . . . pull us back together, you know? But this . . . I mean, what have I gotten them into?"

"Lucia and Drew?" He sounded more alert, now—a subtle difference, with more rustling, and she thought he'd sat up.

"Lucia and Drew," she confirmed. "I mean, how arrogant could I be, just assuming I could deal with this thing? I didn't know anything about it!"

Bob, it turned out, had already forgotten his lesson about boundaries. "You're assuming you can handle *me*, too," he pointed out, inviting himself into the conversation.

Garrie turned on him. "*You*," she said, employing a meaningful finger of doom, "I *can* handle. Right now. Want to see?"

"No, no no," Bob said, warding her off with a frantic waving motion. "No, ma'am. You just go right on assuming." He took a step back.

"Company?" Quinn asked.

"From last night," she said, tugging her hair. It's not like she could make it any worse. "A man died here. We haven't quite dealt with that."

Quinn made a noise of understanding. "Look, Garrie," he said, and she heard movement; her mind easily supplied the details of him swinging his legs over the edge of the bed. "If you weren't just a little bit arrogant, you wouldn't be able to do any of this. It's like being a surgeon. You've got to believe in yourself, to do what you do—and to head up the crew while you're at it. You think we'd follow you if we had any doubts?"

"I think you do have doubts," she said promptly. "Or you would have come along, books be damned."

Silence, filled with his breathing at the phone. "That's not about arrogance," he said finally. "I think you know that. It's just been . . . quiet. And . . . complicated."

Right. Taken for granted, he'd said.

"Are we good?" she asked him, a sudden impulse.

"What?" He'd been taken by surprise there, that was for sure.

"You and me. Between us. Friends. Are we good?" Because suddenly she didn't want to go into this day without knowing, and maybe this was why she'd called him all along. Well, that and hoping he'd managed a miracle overnight, completely absorbed the mystery book, and was packing to join them with a brand-new game plan in hand.

Not so likely.

More silence from Quinn, and then, rather warily, "Why do you ask?"

"Just because," Garrie said. So lame.

"Just *because*?" He blew out a gusty breath. *"Garrie."*

"Quinn. Does it matter why? Just tell me!"

"It's not a fair question. How am I supposed to say no?"

Her chest tightened. "Just like that. If you want to. Do you?"

Another deep breath, clearly audible against his phone pickup. She heard the scowl in it. "No," he said, finally, and just as scowly. "I just don't like the conversation."

The tightness melted away. Quinn, annoyed. But not saying *no*. "Get some coffee," she told him. "We'll let you know what's happening here."

"You woke me up for this," he said flatly, disbelief lacing his voice.

Garrie tipped her head back, examined the sky. "Looks that way."

"Garrie . . ." That was warning.

"Gotta go, Quinn. I think we're looking at a big day here."

"Garrie . . . " That was pleading.

Wish you were here, Quinn. But that wasn't going to help him. So she said, "Gotta go have a day, Quinn."

She thought she heard a growl as she was hanging up.

"Here comes company," Bob said from behind her, annoyance evident. "At what point do we get to me, I have to wonder?"

"When I'm done with this other thing," Garrie told him. She didn't have to ask who the company was. She felt it—deep within, the tug and movement of the cold burning energy that lingered within her. She closed her eyes—in some respects, giving in to it. In some . . . gathering strength.

"Pardon me," Bob said, "but I don't have a whole lot of confidence that you'll actually be around after you're done with this other thing that you don't even know what it is."

"Hey," she said sharply, scowling behind her closed eyes. "Keep in mind exactly how you got dead, will you? You know, the part where you tried really hard to kill us?"

"Wasn't my fault," Bob muttered. Garrie's sense of him faded; a retreat, then. She felt a moment's guilt.

"He was changed," Trevarr said, coming right up behind her as she'd known he would.

"I'm not turning around," she told him. "My hair is not to be seen. And who are you, the Amazing Kreskin? How did you even know I was talking to Bob?"

"I do not know *Kreskin*," Trevarr said, sounding oddly out of place—*more* out of place—than ever. As though for the moment, he simply wasn't bothering to pretend otherwise. "But *Bob* has been interfering with you since he died. He needs to take responsibility for his own fate."

"I heard that!" Bob cried, faint but clear.

"I don't think he agrees," Garrie said. She was half expecting it when Trevarr's hand just barely touched the back of her neck, smoothing down the fine hairs there. That he would touch her . . . seemed inevitable. That it would stir up those unruly energies . . .

Her heart pounded against it. Stupid schoolgirl heart. As if she hadn't been facing down the unknown since she was a girl.

Trevarr stroked the back of her head, barely touching. Conflicted, as was she. "Then he will be here for a long while," he said of Bob. "The chakka seldom invades a thinking being. It finds small predators and takes them, enhancing them—throwing them after prey they would never dare take on their own."

"Bob would have *eaten* us?" Garrie recoiled at the thought. Of course Trevarr had known. He'd known about the beetles and the goo, too. The book, he'd said, was for after.

After.

"Gross," Bob muttered distantly, still eavesdropping.

"Likely so," Trevarr said. His hand rested lightly at her nape, fingers closing reflexively. "But Bob was changed before the chakka took him, making himself weak to it. Do you follow?"

Changed *before* . . . She turned to look at him, eyes narrowed. "You mean the drugs? Because he altered his mind?"

"Does it not work that way with your spirits?"

"People *see* spirits more readily if they're stoned," Garrie murmured, remembering her hair then and stopping her impulse to clap her sore hands down on her head . . . hoping for the best. "But the whole takeover thing . . . it's just not as common as people seem to think." She looked directly at him for the first time— initially finding him as implacable as ever, but then suddenly once again able to read the very fine indications that he wasn't. A living visual illusion, one moment being one thing and in the next blink of the eye, suddenly becoming another. Then she saw uncertainty and concern, and the obvious lurking presence of words he didn't know how to say.

The words he *had* said hit home, then. "You mean, if Bob hadn't messed with his own mind, he might not be dead right now. That chakka might have gone into a lizard instead—and we'd have met up with a Komodo dragon, and not Bob the Hulk."

"Yes." But his face said there was more to it than that, with the worry hidden in those alternately torn and unreadable eyes, pupils back to pinpricks—sunglasses hanging in his duster's top toggle hole, and she knew he'd left them off because she preferred it that way. The short-cut hair at his off-center part softened features she'd once thought hard.

She took a step back, looked at the duster—found no signs of the harsh treatment it had endured last night. No crusted blood. His clothes, too, looked clean unto new, barely showing signs of wear. Even where he'd been stabbed—

She went to him without thinking, grasping at his shirt and pulling it up from beneath his belt—the feel of lean flesh absurdly familiar. His hands clamped down on hers; she would have said he was startled, if she wasn't inclined to believe that nothing startled him at all. But after a moment, he allowed it; he lifted his hands away while she finished that chore, tugging hard enough to shift his stance and finally freeing the shirt—looking at his back; looking high on his abdomen beneath the curve of his ribs.

Right here in the light of day . . . nothing but scars. Fresh, angry scars . . . but only scars. And there, what she hadn't quite been able to see in the hotel lighting—the faint tracery of old tattoos, incompletely removed, running along his sides and flank, disappearing beneath the flat belt leather. She touched them, feather light . . . following them. Feathers, she thought, or scales, or a little of both. His skin twitched away from her fingers. Unruly energy twitched in response.

His expression had gone stoic. Didn't want to talk about tattoos. Didn't want to talk about the healed wounds. She tried anyway. "You're still not going to answer any of my questions. Why *did* you come out?"

The morning sun beat down on them, warming Garrie

within the hoodie; she pushed her sleeves up and waited. He chose his words with obvious care. "I needed to see that you were all right."

She raised eyebrows at him.

"Much has happened. I needed—" He stopped, a frown at his eyes, hesitation at his mouth.

Suddenly Garrie got it—or she thought she did. "You mean because we kissed?" She snorted. "Forget about it. Seriously. Don't worry about it. Happens all the time." Except she couldn't go on. She briefly hid her face in her hands. "Okay. I'm lying. Obviously. I mean, *obviously*."

His expression cleared to brief amusement, and then she managed to startle him again as she took a step forward, standing so very close. And she realized again that no one else would have seen that startle at all, only the implacability that he so expertly showed the world. "How about you?"

He shook his head, a hint of bafflement there. "That doesn't matter. As long as you—"

"I'm all right," she said, but the conversation struck her as vaguely familiar. "And it *does* matter," she said. "And . . . wait a minute. What did you say? What are you saying? We're having this conversation *now,* why?" In her head she heard Quinn's voice, wary and right to be so, *Why do you ask?*

Trevarr wasn't likely to respond as she had to Quinn—not likely to say *Just because.*

But he'd come to her for a reason. He wanted to go into this day *knowing*.

And that scared the farking hell out of her.

But she didn't get any more answers from him, and they ended up back at the hotel and then they ended up, most mundanely, at breakfast. There, Lucia eyed Trevarr's heaping breakfast buffet plate with a wary eye. "Your arteries are going to explode."

Garrie looked up from her fruit plate, letting a chunk of pineapple settle in her mouth to suck out the juice. Second helping for Trevarr, to be sure, and just as much food as the first—the whole gamut from melon to sausage to eggs to hash browns. "She could be right. Ka-*boom*!"

Lucia frowned, cottage cheese on her poised fork. Her practiced gaze ran over Trevarr—all tucked back together, unusual style garnering the usual stares. Garrie could read her frown easily enough. *You don't look like a man who packs away several meals a sitting.* But Lucia didn't say it.

"Drew and Beth should have joined us here at the hotel," she said instead. "I don't like this, being separated. It's not our turf and there's too much going on. Besides, this is a great value."

Garrie didn't like it, either. But Drew was the one with the most to gain from time in Winchester House— absorbing information from the past. And once Garrie showed up there, the house was likely to roil up into action—the reckoners had better be ready to rumble. But Lucia already knew those things, so Garrie didn't repeat them. "Busy in here today," she observed, meaning the ghosts they couldn't see. "Busy out there, too." She nodded at the street-side wall of the diner, made mostly of windows.

"They're upset," Lucia said, looking at her fork. After a moment she seemed to realize she'd never eaten the cottage cheese, and lifted the fork to her mouth.

Garrie counted herself lucky . . . not feeling what Lucia felt. "They look upset," she agreed. "They're not all cohesive—some of them are old, and barely holding together—but they're riled enough to come out for this."

Barely holding together. *"I need to move on,"* Rhonda Rose had said. *"Before it's too late. Before I'm nothing but a nebulous ball of energies to be dissipated by a puff of breeze."*

"That'll never happen," scorned a younger Garrie, disbelieving her mentor would ever truly leave. Only five years ago, and yet half a lifetime. Leaving Garrie with her highly developed sense of obligation, of persistence. Her need to work on the reckoning.

A need grown desperate, and leading her here.

As the skills are yours . . .

Thanks a lot, Rhonda Rose.

Garrie brought herself back to the hotel diner. "Anyway," she said, "they're not happy, whatever their form. The thing that surprises me is that I'm not seeing more of the darksiders. Aside from the new entities and . . . well, effects . . . there's no more of them than average, really."

Trevarr glanced up from his meal. Here in this bright room of natural sunlight, he'd donned the sunglasses again, but Garrie caught that enigmatic glance all the same—knowing it held unvoiced answers. She kicked him under the table for it, too. Lucia pretended not to notice.

Somewhere in the high ceiling of this airy room, filled with early morning diners all chattering about the aurora borealis, something made a faint rattling cry. The kind of noise that could be expected to come out of a rain forest, not an air-conditioned San Jose hotel interior.

"So," Lucia said, spearing a grape with her fork and a quick, expert stab, "assuming I didn't just hear that, and that if I did, nothing significant comes of it, I'm guessing I *do* have enough time to do a little shopping this morning before we leave for the world's biggest haunted house?"

Garrie didn't try to hide her expression—the one that said, *But you just went shopping yesterday and you came back with expensive things and goo!*

Lucia made a quiet tsking noise. "Did you notice, chicalet? You used up the rest of the first-aid things this morning. And we need containment supplies—Baggies, and I'm low on sandalwood and horseradish. I'm guessing there's going to be as much dissipation as containment, but I know how you hate to do that."

"If we can contain them separately, they'll be more manageable," Garrie said. "I think many of them will be willing to move on. It seems to be what some of them want, but they feel trapped there now."

"That's the whole point of that house," Lucia said. "Lead them in, get them going in circles . . . that way Mrs. Winchester was safe. So yes, containment supplies. I didn't bring enough, I can tell you that. Fortunately, I've got the eleven secret herbs and spices."

"Eleven?" Trevarr asked, thus proving he was paying some attention.

"It's a joke," Garrie said, eyebrows raised . . . waiting for him to get it. He didn't. She sighed at him, gestured a *never mind*. "Take my word for it. It amuses us, and that's all that matters."

"Also," Lucia said, doggedly spearing another grape, "I'm going to get some Nair. And when Drew is asleep, that fuzzy malformed thing beneath his lip is going to go away."

Garrie pumped her fist. *"Yes!"*

Above them, the rattling cry sounded, a quick series of calls followed by a hollow, eerie hoot. Lucia's expression abruptly grew more determined. "In fact, I have a sudden urge to leave for this shopping immediately."

"Lu . . ."

Lucia threw her hands up, negligent of the fork she still held. "There's no point, Garrie. We have no idea what that is. There's nothing we can do to stop it. Did you even feel it coming?"

Garrie reached for it . . . felt it then, but only then. A small dark blot of differentness. It rattled out a new cry, adding several hoots to the riff. "No," she admitted. The other diners began to realize this was no deliberate charming special effect—that it wasn't, in fact, a bird at all. By then theirs was the only table around which people weren't looking up, craning their necks—their veneer of normalcy shattered by this small thing in a city where fires had burned in the sky and plagues of beetles, goo, and who knew what else had shattered the previous day.

"So I think, why stick around for it?" Lucia nevertheless picked up a sweet, ripe little strawberry, neatly biting off one side. "We should handle our errands, then deal with this house. Because handling the ghosts will fix this, isn't that the idea?"

They both looked at Trevarr. He pushed back his plate. "It is similar to the idea."

"You know," Garrie said, filled with a sudden angry heat that didn't keep her from shoving her leftover fruit plate in his direction just in case he might need a little variety on top of his he-man breakfast, "it would be really, *really* nice to get a straight answer from you. Just once."

He drank deeply of the milk he'd had waiting—still leaving a second, untouched glass beside it. "Garrie," he said, and somehow he *didn't* have a milk mustache, "if you do that which you know, the answers don't matter."

"Oh my God," Garrie said, while the unknown creature let off a truly rattling cry from above. "*Snatch the pebble from my hand, Grasshopper.* Could you be more profoundly obscure?"

"*Perfect wisdom is unplanned,*" Lucia intoned. She grabbed a napkin, dabbing at her mouth before digging into the waist pack draped over the back of the chair and coming up with some fancy colored lip protectant.

"You may mock it," Trevarr said. "But it is truth." He picked out one of the pineapple pieces and sniffed it.

"Did not see that," Lucia murmured, smoothly applying the lip stuff.

"I did," Garrie said, not taking her eyes off him. Pineapple . . . new and exciting. And to judge by his surprised expression when he bit it in half, unexpected.

The second half quickly followed the first.

"Much as I could sit around and watch the look on your face as you eat that," Garrie told him, "I think Lucia might just have a point."

"Thank you very much," Lucia said, *sotto*, replacing her makeup in the waist bag. More loudly then, as she pushed her chair back, "We're going?"

"We're going," Garrie agreed. "We'll wait for you in the lobby, Trevarr." For of course he was picking up the tab—and thanks to the cry of the mysterious ceiling dweller, they weren't the only diners leaving breakfast.

He stood, gathered up the duster, and scooped up another several pieces of pineapple, popping one freely into his mouth. He hesitated then—long enough to not say something, and to then come up with something else instead, after a long look at her through sunglasses that no longer completely hid his expression from her. And still, she couldn't truly interpret this one, only that it was deep and torn. "Be careful," he told her finally, and walked away.

"What?" asked Lucia in a whisper.

"I don't know," Garrie said, suddenly more sober than she'd been since this had started. Startled, yes; desperate, yes. But not this gripping certainty that things had just stepped finally, inexorably out of her control. "I really don't know."

16

Young spirits experiment.
—Rhonda Rose

Go *boo* yourself.
—Lisa McGarrity

But Trevarr didn't meet them in the lobby. Garrie walked circuits around the area, a poshly comfortable space with the same beige and mahogany theme as their rooms, and he didn't come.

"If you've got time on your hands," Bob said, quite suddenly at her ear and then walking beside her.

"Not talking to you here," Garrie said through her teeth, not even glancing his way.

From the other side of the lobby in a small seating array, Lucia gestured to her—and, having caught her attention, pointed at the muted television set tucked up into a niche in the wall.

Garrie wasn't sure she wanted to know, but she came over anyway. It was a San Francisco morning news show, chummy talking heads looking serious together. As Garrie approached, the screen flashed a blurry, un-recognizable photo, swirls of darkness and light over-laid with what looked like sunspots.

". . . *best shot of last night's aurora effect available,*" said the woman news-head's voice-over. She went on to express amazement at how the aurora had muddled every photo, and to promise that they would report the cause the moment anyone figured it out.

"*In related news,*" the male news-head said, looking as though he'd really rather not be reading this particu-lar report, "*San Jose residents also called emergency services for a variety of inexplicable events yesterday.*"

He went on to mention the goo, and several Bigfoot sightings, a pterodactyl, a rash of UFO calls, and numerous citizens gone amok. After all that, the constant trembling earthquakes—the origin of which couldn't be pinpointed—deserved only passing mention.

"He missed the beetles," Garrie said.

"You think the restaurant was going to call in someone official about a bug infestation?" Lucia asked her.

"Probably not." Garrie craned her neck to peer toward the restaurant, trying to spot the doorway around a large potted tree.

"But *Bigfoot*?" Lucia said. "We missed out on Bigfoot."

"Can't say as I'm sorry. Or about the pterodactyl thing, either." Unsuccessful with the craning, Garrie took a step to the side, and finally found the vantage point she needed.

"Never did see what made that noise in the restaurant," Lucia pointed out, even as the building shook in another shiver of aftershock. Or before-shock. "And you know what? I think we've been stood up."

"No," Garrie said, even as she knew Lucia was right.

"That's denial, chicalet. Wherever he's gone, it's without us. I'm not waiting any longer. This day has plans, and I want to get my hands on that Nair before anything new comes out to play. Then maybe we can head for the house and take care of this thing."

"Somehow," Garrie muttered.

"Have faith," Lucia said, a little too cheerfully, but it didn't last. "And you'd better, because we don't seem to have anything else to work with."

Maybe Drew would learn something from the house. Maybe the ghosts would talk to her when she got there today, instead of trying to kill her.

Maybe they'd have a chance.

"Go shop," Garrie said. "I'm going to check the rooms, and then hit the pool for a bazillion laps or so."

Lucia stood. "I'd tell you not to wear yourself out, but

I know it's pointless. Take a little nap if you can. We're not heading out until early afternoon, unless something changes."

"Right," Garrie muttered darkly. "Bigfoot, ptero-dactyls, goo . . . no chance anything'll go odd around here. No chance at all."

The rooms were empty. Not that she'd really expected Trevarr to have slipped past them and then waited here, but . . . she couldn't *not* check. She stood in the door-way of his room—here, where she'd spent the night—and on sudden impulse, she closed her eyes and inhaled, breathing in both the ethereal and the tangible. The en-tire room smelled faintly of him, mixed in the with fresh woody spice she'd found on her nightshirt. The window still stood open. Not a man who liked to be closed in, even when the air was too chill.

He *really* must have hated that plane.

She thought back to their conversation in the post-dawn hours, no one else awake, no one else around. *Except Bob.* She hadn't liked the sound of that conversation then, and she didn't like it now.

He'd needed it just as badly as she'd needed to know that Quinn had settled . . . that things were clearer be-tween them. Because she hadn't wanted it on her mind when she went to face off the Winchester House ghosts who'd almost killed her once already.

I wasn't paying attention. I won't make that mistake again.

And she wouldn't. But that wouldn't help a bit when it came to these new entities, these new incursions over which she seemed to have no impact whatsoever.

Beneath the hotel, the ground rumbled; her world tilted a little more than it might have. Garrie took one last deep breath, took her thoughts back to the unusual peace of the night. Not only the living dreams he'd kept away, but just . . . being there. Grounded. More grounded than anyone she'd ever known, and definitely more grounded than she ever was.

Like now. Now, with the cold yearning energy inside her starting to swell, the rest of her stirred up by the high background activity this morning. Swimming would settle her. The physical activity, the buffering nature of the water, the endorphins. She turned away from the room— but not without running her hand along the arm of the couch and hesitating there, giving it a final pat as if it were some living representative of the feelings she'd contemplated, the comfort and the unease and the yearning all.

Five minutes later, she had a one-piece on under a light pair of barely there boy-shorts, not bothering with a T-shirt over top. She didn't have enough clothes to use up, not after two of her shirts had sopped up Trevarr's blood and failed to recover as miraculously as he.

How could he even be walking today? How, even if the light with claws had done something to put him back together, could he come back from that blood loss?

The good thing about swimming was that it took concentration—enough so she didn't think about any of that. Staying in her lane even if she was the only one in the little pool; learning the length of the pool and when to take the turn. With the world distorted by goggles and her ears half covered by a swim cap—the chlorine did terrible things to her blue streaks—the rest of the world was muffled into splash and breathe and the occasional choke of misplaced water.

Until she submerged her face to stroke onward and found herself nose to nose with Bob.

Garrie churned straight up out of the water, flailing and choking and shouting, *"Bob!"* in startled admonishment. But of *course* there were sunbathers lounging around that end of the pool, and of course they gave her the *crazy chick* hairy eyeball with which she was so familiar. "Bug!" she cried, knowing even if they'd heard her clearly the first time, they'd grab at this more sensible explanation. "Great big—!" she snatched at empty water and scooped up an invisible bug, flinging it off to the side, and then sidestroked to the edge of the pool to collect herself.

"Boy," Bob said. "You should have seen your face!"

"Thought that was funny, did you?" Garrie smiled most sweetly at him, keeping her voice down low.

"Oh, yeah, this is great!" Oblivious to her ire, he sunk back into the water, his clothes and hair unaffected. "This is . . . I can just stay down here forever! The light reflections, the waves, everything bobbing . . ."

"No pesky need to breathe," Garrie muttered, swiping water from her face. She took her goggles off and dunked them, just to be doing something. "You're not stoned, Bob, you just think you are. Now get up here and talk to me before these nice people think I stayed under water too long."

His head emerged from the water, perfectly dry. That was a fifty-fifty thing . . . if a ghost expected to be affected, he was. Those who didn't think about it or who thought about it enough to form other expectations, weren't. Bob, she'd realized almost right away, was a particularly independent postliving individual. Now he looked at her and said, "Be nice. I just thought you'd want to know."

"And you're probably right." She forced her voice to remain pleasant, hanging on to the edge of the pool with one hand, her goggles in the other. She didn't say, *Want to know what? Is it Lucia? Is it Drew? Tell me!* and she didn't shove him around with the breezes so close to hand.

"About the yowling." But Bob didn't seem to be thinking about the yowling; when he frowned, it was at the water itself.

"Any *particular* yowling?" Garrie asked, through gritted teeth.

"Did you see that?" Bob asked, staring at the bottom of the pool.

Garrie quickly checked for breezes, felt nothing, and returned her attention—her glare—to Bob. "No. You want to give me a clue about the yowling? There's a lot going on in this city right now—"

"Yeah, but this was—are you *sure* you don't see—? Because things look a little different to me now and maybe, you know, it's just me, but—"

"Bob," Garrie said, grasping for thin patience, "I'm trying to get myself together here. I gotta tell you, this is *not* helping." But she felt a slight disturbance in the water, a weird series of bubbles rising against her leg. Warm bubbles.

Do bubbles even come *in warm?*

"Garrie," Bob said, frowning—and then disappearing, sliding beneath the water again to hover there, gaining a comfortable perspective Garrie's living self couldn't give her—even as another spray of bubbles brushed against her side and popped to the surface, releasing a fetid, tarry scent. Down at the other end of the pool, a huge roiling glop of air broke at the surface; the stench of it inspired cries of sunbather dismay. An oily substance spread out across the water.

Bob popped to the surface. "Out!" he cried. "Now, now, now! Out!"

Garrie's eyes widened; the water at her feet warmed perceptibly—from uncomfortable to painful in an instant, and she grabbed the side of the pool. "Ow!" and there were bubbles suddenly *everywhere,* the stench enough to gag her as she propelled herself *up,* heading for panic. Heading for deep panic, for just as she brought a leg over the edge, something grasped at her dangling ankle, winding around and around and yanking hard. She lurched; an elbow gave way and smacked against the concrete, numbing her whole arm.

Suddenly Bob was directly in front of her, leaning

over her and shouting at her. "Out out *out*!" he said, as if she wasn't trying. "Come *on,* Garrie!"

She lost track of him in that moment, thrashing in the water, crying out in fear that no one else seemed to notice because they were all busy gagging and tripping over chairs and stumbling away, eyes streaming against the sharp stench. The twining appendages wrapped around her ankle extruded sudden barbs that snagged her skin— Garrie shrieked, shoving off so strongly that she suddenly found herself free and sprawling on cement, fresh road rash stinging, her ankle throbbing madly, and the pool—its water no longer clear—boiling wildly behind her. She wiped at her tearing eyes, trying to orient—and Bob popped up in front of her.

"It wasn't expecting *me,* either," he said. "And oh, right. That yowling came from Trevarr's room."

Sklayne as cat, sipping up energy at the outlet and purring happily to himself, sparks rolling off his body from nape to tail tip in rhythm with his breath, one small piece of him traveling along with Trevarr's progress through the Winchester House—tracking the Krevata.

Sklayne in agony, twisting and rolling on the floor, his insides trying to be outsides, small powderless explosions dotting the air around him. Claws digging into carpet, body slamming into furniture. The bedside lamp fell over; a chair tipped into the work desk. The pain squeezed endless yowls from his cat body and when he tried to release the form, expanding himself to be everything and anything, it clamped around him like a vice.

::Trevarr!:: Sklayne yowled inwardly as well as outwardly, reaching to complete the bond-connection and finding only a blinding sheet of red-washed insanity. ::Trevarr!! *Atreyvo!*:: Reaching out any way he could, now, hunting any sign that Trevarr could hear him, feel him. Splayed and panting, half beneath the bed, drowning in panic and confusion and loss.

He barely saw the wet feet run into his field of view, strong slender ankles beaded with water that stopped short before him. "Ah," said the Garrie's voice, after a long and meaningful pause. "*You*. I knew it. I just knew it."

Garrie crouched down before the cat, thought twice, and went to shut the room door before returning. She didn't know where it had been all this time and she didn't know how Trevarr had gotten it here. She had no idea what had happened to it now, leaving it rumpled and wild-eyed, blood trickling from one ear and its small pink nostrils. It clung to the carpet as though the floor might try to dump it off the world altogether.

"Hey," she said softly, extending one cautious finger to touch its forehead.

"Mow." It was a weak reply, uncertain of itself. The cat pushed ever so slightly against her finger in acceptance of her greeting.

"What are you doing here?" she asked it, gently stroking a short path up its forehead. "Why did he even bring you?"

The cat looked directly at her, panting slightly. It flicked its ears back, forward . . . focusing in on her in a way that gave her just an instant's warning. And then a small, thin voice in her head said ::I brought myself.::

"Holy farking shit!" Garrie gasped, and fell back on her ass.

The cat flicked an ear again, pulling its whiskers into a brief expression of priss—but whatever caused its miserable state still clung to it, making its every move an obvious effort. ::One of *our* words.::

"Farking," Garrie said, if somewhat faintly. "Yes. I like it." *OhmyGod I'm talking to a cat and ohmyGod it's talking back oh shit oh shit ohshit.* She stared at it a long moment; it stared back, intelligence obvious in those deep green eyes. "What *are* you?" she finally managed, if only in a whisper.

::Sklayne,:: said the creature, straight to her head, its voice—or thoughts, or whatever it could be called—struggling to stay steady. ::I come with Trevarr.::

"Are you . . . *his*?"

Ears slanted back flat. ::I am mine.::

For all its dignified offense, its response felt out of true. "Really," Garrie said, before she'd quite thought it through.

The cat looked back at her, its expression briefly sour. ::Adjusted quickly, holy farking shit.::

She crossed her legs, opting for something slightly more dignified than the sprawled-back-on-ass posture. "Maybe I'm in shock." She thought about it. "Or this just isn't that different from talking to ghosts, and I've been doing that all my life."

The cat—Sklayne—gave her a slit-eyed look.

"Sorry," she told it, not terribly repentant but sympathetic to its disgruntled response. But in the next moment, it closed its eyes in obvious pain; its claws flexed into the carpet and its tail lashed briefly. "What's wrong?" she asked it, leaning forward, reaching out involuntarily, then pulling herself back. "Can I help? And where's Trevarr?" She tugged the hair behind her ear, spiky damp at the ends from the pool. No doubt she left a heart-shaped butt-print on the floor, too.

::Trevarr . . . :: it said, and the sorrow in that mindvoice got her instant attention. It yowled softly.

"What?" She leaned forward, elbows on knees. *"What?"* Then she covered her face with her hands. "Aiee, I'm making demands of a cat. What can I even be thinking? Cats are so *known* for their responsive nature. Even better than spirits."

::Not cat,:: the creature said, offended.

"No kidding." She gave it her driest look, decided the effort was wasted, and said, "Fine. Whatever. Where's

Trevarr, what's going on, and are you a boy not-cat or a girl not-cat?"

::Male am I!:: Sklayne's lips drew back for the faintest of hisses. But only until he added, ::Mostly.:: His tail twitched again; a shudder rippled down his back. ::Hard, to do this. Only with Trevarr, the talking. But he . . . you . . . :: He seemed to run out of words. Or voice, or possibly both.

"There's a connection," Garrie said for him, her voice softening to hesitation. "Since the séance room."

::Since before,:: Sklayne corrected, making no attempt to elucidate. The sound of him in her mind grew . . . not weaker, but less pure.

"Then tell me the important things," Garrie told him. "What's wrong? How can I help? *Where's Trevarr?*"

::Help him,:: Sklayne said, distantly enough so Garrie thought she would lose whatever rare thing held them together. She touched his forehead again, stroking gently, and he lifted his drooping head. ::This comes from Trevarr. At house. Help him.::

"He's doing this to you?" she blurted, horrified. He stiffened under her touch, a rejection of that thought— and then she truly understood, even more horrified, and it stole her voice and her breath away, leaving her with only a strained whisper. *"Someone's doing this to him."*

Krevata.

It was the only thing she could get from the cat. Not-cat. *Whatever.* The Krevata had Trevarr; the Krevata were hurting him in some profound fashion that went beyond Garrie's understanding or her imagination.

They had him at the Winchester House.

They weren't ghosts at all. And yet they were the reason Trevarr was even here. And if they weren't stopped, the destruction wouldn't limit itself to San Jose.

"The ghosts?" she'd demanded of Sklayne.

::For you to do,:: the little creature had told her, his voice only a thin thread. He'd then demanded to come with her, assuming she'd immediately charge off to Winchester House.

He'd been right, of course. "Meet me there," she'd told Lucia, a quick phone call even as she stripped off the wet bathing suit, flipping it into the sink and dashing around the room in the altogether—pulling the key card from the shorts she'd earlier tossed aside, snatching up underwear and bra and a paper-thin T-shirt of mottled purples, lacing up form-skimming bodice-vest over top and then, of course, the cargos. So many pockets, so very useful. Only then did she realize the cat—no, *not-cat,* whatever that was supposed to mean—had dragged itself to the doorway to watch.

"Oh, that's just sick," she snapped at him. He blinked in owlish innocence, a look not quite supported by his rumpled nature—she quite suddenly did what she should have done in the first place, had she not been so startled to find a cat under Trevarr's bed, never mind one that inserted thoughts into her head. She paused midstride as she reached for the little flip-fold jewelry case Lucia used to carry dried containment ingredients, and narrowed her eyes at the cat, bringing to bear all her ways of perceiving him.

Blue energies reverberated outside the cat, pleasant energies on the whole but not without distinct, random spikes, living sunspots. Energy lapped at his feet; his whiskers fizzed faintly like endless Fourth of July sparklers. So familiar, the look and feel of that energy.

"You," she said faintly, remembering the brief wash of unfamiliar breeze the evening they'd arrived here, the warmth against her feet as she'd napped in Trevarr's bed—and most recently of all, the blue moonlight that turned out to have claws. *"You!"*

::Holy farking shit!:: he told her, beyond smug even through their thin connection.

"Hey, two of those words were *already* mine." Garrie snatched up the bag, tucked it inside the small canvas backpack she hadn't bothered to cart around before now, and looked around the room for anything else Lucia might have left behind. Her gaze settled on the shoes; she gave Sklayne a sharp look. "That was you in the store. With the goo."

::With the goo,:: he agreed, and surprised her by adding, ::With the beetles.::

"Drew didn't say anything about a cat in the restaurant."

::Not-cat,:: he reminded her, and licked his foot in the most possible fastidious catlike way, holding it poised in midair as though he'd just barely stopped himself from wiping it over the top of his head before his gave it a nonchalant flick and returned it to the floor.

Garrie snorted. "Right," she said, and opened the backpack wide. "You coming?"

17

Discretion will serve you well.
—Rhonda Rose

I can't really explain. Yet. Or, you know. Ever.
—Lisa McGarrity

Sklayne in darkness, bundled into cloth and then into car, a strange driver whom the Garrie instructed to take them to the Winchester house. *Taxi,* uncomfortable and too abrupt with every turn and stop and start it made. He curled tighter, trapped as *cat,* flanks rippling with leftover pain he did well to hide from the Garrie. He'd felt it in her, the rising spike of panic and mindlessness when she'd realized what trouble Trevarr had found. The instant attempt to reach out to him, when even Sklayne could do no more than feel this oddly filtered, reflected pain.

She'd failed, of course. That which she and Trevarr had exchanged wasn't enough to surmount the distance between them, more than just miles right now.

Not yet.

So she'd thought the worst and she'd panicked, forgetting to breathe there in her bathing suit with her hair spiky and blue and her hazel eyes huge, goose bumps on her wet skin and her modest breasts pulling up tight. Much person in a small package, fully alarmed, heart open and vulnerable beyond her own realization.

And she didn't really even *know*. The Krevata, with their grudge. The Krevata, putting Trevarr's people into disgrace and exile with their conspired accusations. Waiting for Trevarr's absence to put weakened elders into impossible situations, fight-or-die or fight-and-die.

They had fought. And they had died, and they had been judged. And now those people, always on the fringes simply for having Trevarr among them, struggled to survive. And so Trevarr had been told upon return from the last hard bounty, "Find the Krevata and disprove them, or lose all."

Always this, for Trevarr, since Sklayne's bonding and since before. Not all of one thing, not all of the other. Not acceptable to either, except among these who had taken him in. Fine to be the one thing; fine to be the other. Not to be the both.

Sklayne had never understood. He still didn't. He knew that the both was strong; he knew it was fast. He knew it healed from wounds that killed the either even without Sklayne's help, that it had few weaknesses. He knew it was uniquely suited for hunting the bounties across all boundaries.

He knew it was lonely.

But the Garrie knew none of that. Sklayne touched her within, ever so shallowly—not daring more, not with Trevarr's pain and weakness drawing on him. She thought of Trevarr, hands tense around the backpack and yet kind when they touched Sklayne through the sturdy cloth. She thought of her friends, her city, her streets; the ground rumbling beneath the taxi wheels that made the driver volunteer some sardonic comment about the world coming to an end.

Oh, the Garrie had no idea.

Not yet.

"Garrie!" Beth said, spotting her in the gift shop with Lucia trailing. "We've been trying to call, but the phones—" She stopped, did something of a double-take. "Wait . . . we've got the place locked down . . . how—?"

Lucia swept past, appropriating a sales counter for her work and slapping down plastic bags, the many-pocketed jewelry holder, and a big squeeze tube of Vaseline. "You don't really think this is the first place to batten the hatches the wrong way out?"

"Wrong way . . . ?" Beth struggled to decode the comment, and took a surprised step back. "Did you . . . is that a *cat*?"

"Maybe," Garrie told her. "Where's Drew?"

"Hiding in the bathroom for now. Something went down in the house and they've been trying to clear it for an hour, but the last group keeps getting shut off, as if the . . . as if someone doesn't want them to leave."

"Well, of course they don't!" Lucia snapped, slapping a hand down on the storage bags. "How much more obvious can it be? Now quit wasting our time and get over here and help me do something more useful!"

"Lu," Garrie said gently, and plucked a tissue from the decorative box by the cash register, dropping it beside Lucia.

Lucia hid her face in her hands. "I'm so sorry," she said, misery seeping through her fingers with her muffled voice. "They caught me off-guard. They're very strong right now, and so very angry and frightened." She reached for the tissue without looking.

"I—" Beth said, quite at a loss. She finally took a deep breath, nodding; her hair bobbed only slightly, more secure today in a complex, clipped twist behind her head. The building shook almost imperceptibly around them, sending gift items rattling on shelves and the floor vibrating beneath their feet. "I'd like to help."

"Good." Lucia dropped her hands, tucking the tissue away in her watch band, her cheeks flushed and eyes bright, but all else under control. "Here, coat these bags—it's easiest just to put a glop of Vaseline inside and squish it around. But it's critical that you don't miss any spots. And I'll get the herbs and such mixed up, yes?"

"Sure," Beth said. "But I should warn you, there's no telling when my boss might return, or any of the others. And how come that cat isn't making me sneeze?"

::Not cat,:: Sklayne said in his pleased-with-self voice, piping into Garrie's head.

"Yes, yes," she told him, dumping the empty backpack beside Lucia at the counter, trying not to rush them straight through this small talk. They needed the small talk, especially Beth. "We'll handle what comes, bosses included. And Sklayne is . . . special, as cats go. Let's just say I'm still figuring him out. He belongs with Trevarr." She glanced at Sklayne, daring him to protest that careful wording.

Sklayne looked up at her with his tail wrapped around his feet, eyes slitted in feline inscrutability, apparently intent on pretending that the tail didn't twitch in time to the flickering spasm across his flanks. *Trevarr.*

At least he'd been good in the taxi. At least he'd stopped shooting off unexpected sparks.

Beth, squeezing petroleum jelly into a giant-size storage bag, said, "And Trevarr belongs . . . where?"

"Ooh," Lucia muttered. *"Zing."*

Garrie made a face. "Him . . . I can't really explain yet." Not the way he made her feel. Not the cold burning energy he'd shared with her and that now seemed to jerk and pulse within her, something wild and needing to be free. Not what he'd come to mean to her, this man she hardly knew.

"What's to explain?" Lucia said, too glibly, grabbing a storage bag as it threatened to slide off the counter with the vibrations of the building. "Tall, dark, totally hot, totally unexpected, and totally handy to have around if someone goes berserk on you. Who wouldn't want *that* around?"

"Stop it," Garrie said, taking a stiff half-step toward Lucia, her hands fisted at her side. "He's trapped in there with them, and he's been in agony for hours. He's not a *joke*. He's *real*."

Lucia looked at her with mouth half dropped, her poise not so much shattered as simply left behind. "Chicalet . . ." she said finally. "Is it like that? With him? *Not safe?*"

Garrie unclenched her fists, looking down at them. She realized that her breathing was distressed, her jaw clenched; she closed her eyes. "It's . . . complicated."

"Ohh, I don't think it's complicated at all." Lucia had her balance back now, and from the sound of it, worked swiftly with the secret herbs and spices.

Garrie managed a glare. "Don't be smug."

Hardly hesitating in her work, Lucia glanced up at her—and her eyes were big and Latin-tragic and sad. "Hardly that, chicalet. But first we save him, yes?"

Beth stared back and forth between them with no

little fascination. "About that. Do you know what's happening?"

Garrie transferred her ire to Sklayne. "I know I damned well don't have a clue. As near as I can tell, there's this whole thing with some party crashers called the Krevata—"

Lucia gave her a look. Beth gave her a look. Garrie clamped her mouth shut. After a moment, she said, "No. I don't know what's happening."

"Do you have a plan?" Lucia inquired sweetly. From the courtyard between gift shop and mansion, a rumbling, cavernous sucking belch sounded. Everyone pretended not to have heard it. "I had the impression, when you suggested we meet here, that you had a *plan*." She took the small bag of mixed herbs and shook it, perhaps a bit more thoroughly than truly necessary.

Sklayne preened, as much as any cat as rumpled as he was ever could. Garrie clenched her hands again, down next to her thighs. "I'm going to look around," she said. "And then we're going in."

Lucia froze in midmotion. "That's a plan?"

"I have *goals*," Garrie said, rather desperately. "Free the trapped tourists. That's gotta be good. Get the ghosts under control. Also good. That's all ghostie stuff—we can do it on the fly, especially with Drew to guide us in the house. They won't be expecting that—that we can't get lost."

"Okay," Lucia said. "I'll give you that much." She nodded to Beth. "Open the bags wide. I need to sprinkle the secret herbs and spices into the lining you just made. Yes, like that." And back to Garrie, "So then we have the house under control and the city stops falling apart around us and the strange darkside stops getting through?"

"I'm not so sure it's darkside," Garrie muttered. And

then, louder, "And then we find Trevarr and we help him . . . do whatever it is that he's trying to do. Our little friend here is being damned coy about the details."

Sklayne folded his whiskers back. ::Not mine to tell.::

"Which is exactly why you're going in there with us, Mr. Meow Mix."

Lucia exchanged a wary look with Beth. "Garrie. You talking to that cat?"

And Nero fiddles while the city burns . . . "Yes!" Garrie exclaimed. "Yes, I'm talking to the cat! No, I don't know what's going on, except . . . *I'm talking to a cat.* We're playing by new rules here, Lucia. Not Rhonda Rose Rules, not reckoner rules. Since when do ghosts do what we've seen these past few days? Since when do they cause *earthquakes*?"

"Or beetles or goo or eyes of fire in the sky . . ." Lucia murmured, resignation in the line of her shoulders. She didn't mention the recent cavernous sucking belch. She hardly had to. "You sure this is *our* thing to do?"

Garrie snorted. "Who else? The *I see dead people* kid is all grown up and making other movies now. John Edwards is off the air. I don't see anyone else standing in line."

::You,:: Sklayne said, suddenly alarmed and right there in her head, louder than he'd been in a while. He ignored her wince. ::You are the one. We came for you. The Krevata came *here* because of—:: and he stopped, ears flicking nervously, and abruptly blurted, "Mow!"

"You and Trevarr," Garrie muttered. "I *am* going to have answers from you before this is over."

"Mow," said Sklayne.

"Yeah, and guess what. I watch TV. I know that trick where the radio isn't *really* broken."

Sklayne fell silent on all counts. From the ceiling above them came the sound of skittery insect legs.

Lots of them.

"Oh, hurry," Beth implored them both. "If we can stop any of this—"

"Not you," Garrie said, hassled beyond diplomacy. "Sitting duck, you. Now give me a moment." She sat down on the spot, crossing her legs. Her hands seemed to expect it when Sklayne walked into her lap and curled up there as though he owned it; they rested lightly on his back, where she could feel his body's upset much more clearly than she could see it.

"What is she—?" Beth asked, impatient stage-whisper volume.

"She's hurrying," Lucia said. "Now hold that bag open."

Garrie started high and safe, looking down on the house, giant spy satellite mode in action. She kept herself veiled and the house dimmed.

She remembered the last time well enough. The foul swamp breezes, the weird slice of citrus cutting through it . . . and the noise, grinding and wailing and dissonant cries. Last time they had caught her up; this time she didn't let them close. She watched from afar, astonished at how quickly the disturbance here had intensified. The muddy colors shot through with vibrant, clashing colors that made her squint even though she'd protected herself, the scent enough to make her eyes water and her sinuses sting . . . the sounds . . . the *sounds* . . .

"What's going on here?"

Not exactly the sounds she'd expected. Intruding, too close . . . full of irritation and authority. But she wasn't quite ready to let go . . . not with the wildness waking inside her and fluttering high against the inside of her ribs—a thing of fear and portent, drawn to life by matching energies in the house. *Trevarr?* she thought, reaching out to it—and then stopped short, wary . . . instinct telling her *no*. Or at least . . . *not quite*. Slowly, she brought herself back to the present, her seat bones already aching on a floor too hard, warm Sklayne in her lap giving off tiny tingles of energy.

"Beth," said the voice, "I need an explanation." Hassled and unhappy and out of patience.

"I—" Beth said. And then, as Garrie lifted Sklayne and set him gently but firmly on his feet beside her, Abyssinian cat who wasn't, Beth found the determination Garrie had seen in her the day before. "They're here to help. You *know* there's something going on in the house, and it's getting worse."

"Not just the house," Lucia said, although her voice had that absent sound that meant she concentrated on the containment bags. Probably a mistake. Authority seldom liked to be given second place.

Ah, yes, here it came. "We're closed. You'll have to leave."

Garrie climbed to her feet, prepared for the surprise she discovered on the faces of the two red-jacketed people in the entry of the gift shop—they hadn't a clue she'd been sitting there. She suggested, "Think of us as pest control."

That didn't go over well, either. At this point, nothing would. As Garrie brushed her butt off, the two exchanged glances. One tall woman, designer glasses that just looked stern instead of trendy over hard features, blunt-cut bangs a complete mistake for her face. One shorter, plumper woman, older and no-nonsense. They had a radio; the taller woman held it tightly, almost like a scepter. They had sensible shoes, slacks with pleats, and blouses without personality—and they badly needed makeup tips. And then the shorter of them dropped her jaw in astonishment and said, "Do I see a *cat*? Beth Ann Carlington, did you bring a *cat* into this building?"

"Not really," Garrie said. "Look, we're here to help—don't even try to deny there's a problem—and we're probably the only ones who *can*. So . . . Any chance we can just skip this conversation? We'll track down your people, get them out of the house, and do our best to get this mess under control."

As if she hadn't even spoken, the tall one said, most inexorably, "You'll have to leave now."

"Well . . ." Garrie started, a bit apologetic and regretful and leaving them completely unprepared. "No."

"I beg your—"

"No." Garrie knew what she looked like in their eyes—scrawny intruder, funky clothes, punk hair. Standing in the backdrop of the gift shop with its display shelves and books and videos and incongruous candies, tourist trap attached to a ghost trap. "You've lost jurisdiction, I'm afraid. Or do you really think this mess has nothing to do with the way San Jose is falling apart around us? *Please* don't tell me you bought that aurora borealis business."

The tall one drew herself up. "That is entirely beside the point. I'm afraid you really need to go. Or we'll have to call—"

"Oh, go ahead." Garrie waved off the threat with a bored gesture. "I think they're plenty busy already." Not to mention they would never find her once she and the others entered the mansion. "You about done, Lu?"

"Just about," Lucia said, still distant with concentration.

"Good." Garrie went to the juncture of the gift shop with the café and raised her voice to a polite bellow. "Drew! Gearing up!" And then to the women, she said, "I'm afraid you can't stop us from helping. Not to mention, someone I care about very much is in that house, and he's in trouble."

"Understatement," Lucia muttered, efficiently rolling the bags together. "Seriously. These two in a room together? The air tries to combust." Garrie gave her an incredulous look, but Lucia shrugged it off. "Oh, *por fah-vor,* chicalet. I can only pretend to be oblivious for just so long."

Drew bounded into the room. "Garrie!" He said, and then came up short at the sight of the red vests, and even shorter at the sight of Sklayne. "Hey, that's the cat from the house in Albuquerque. You know, the one where we first saw Trevarr—"

"Trust me, I know," Garrie said. "And Sklayne's not a—" But she cut herself short, giving up on that one. He'd see for himself. "You ready? I hope you learned a lot today, because we're going to need it. Trevarr is trapped in that house somewhere, along with the last tour group. I need you to get me to them all."

"Point me in the general direction," Drew said promptly. "Been marinating here long enough." He gave the two women a doubtful eye. "We just going right past them?"

"No!" said the two women at once.

"Yep," Garrie said.

"You aren't going to get in," the taller woman said, her features particularly pinched and disapproving, though the shorter woman had fear hidden beneath her stern schoolteacher expression. "It's locked."

Garrie snorted. "You can't be serious."

That puzzled them. "Of course I'm serious. We locked down as soon as the trouble started."

"Ladies," Garrie said, somewhat gently, "healing places like this is what I *do*. How often do you think the doors are unlocked when I get there?"

Hold on, Trevarr. I'm coming.

Hold on, San Jose. I'm coming.

Hold on, world. I'm coming . . .

18

Knock gently upon those doors where welcome is uncertain.
—Rhonda Rose

Carry your picks and make your own welcome.
—Lisa McGarrity

Sklayne could have opened the door for them . . . but the Garrie didn't need that help, and Sklayne dove deep and fast to watch. The Drew person confirmed the age of the lock, but she'd already recognized the brand. She pulled a set of lock picks from the black backpack in which he'd traveled and quickly applied them . . . not without a touch of power, skimming along the precise metal surfaces to smooth the way.

"Bump it," the Drew person suggested. "Where's your bump key?"

"Medeco," the Garrie said. "Won't bump." She applied a little tension to the lock, located the fattest pin with its high resistance, and went to work, lifting it out of the way. Lift, repeat. Lift, repeat. Always that energy helping her to visualize and smoothing the way.

"What—?" The big loud red-jacket person with the hard energy and permanently compressed lips pushed up behind them. "What do you think—?"

Sklayne liked the sputtering. He hadn't seen this kind of sputtering before. He stood on his long springy back cat legs, front paws tipping lightly against the Garrie's leg, to get a closer look at the sputtering.

"If you've come to offer a key, don't bother," the Garrie said. "I've just about got—ah. There are." She gave the knob a gentle turn, looking back at the two women. "It's a good lock. Don't worry about it, generally speaking. Besides, it would have been a lot harder if we'd had to get in through the grates and gates and whatnot of the gift shop. Security system there, I'm assuming."

Sklayne noticed she didn't mention that she could fry a security system.

But the women had lost their defiance and replaced it with a different reluctance. They stood close together, not quite touching one another for comfort. The short one said, "Are you sure you want to go in there? There's no telling what's going on . . . We've been consulting with someone today—quite a respected medium—and now she's trapped in there with everyone else."

The Garrie gave the Beth person a swift, accusing glance. The Beth person stepped back, warding her off with both hands. "I'm just a drone!"

"Truth, Garrie," the Drew person said. "We figured there wasn't any point in calling you. And she seemed genuine . . . but she doesn't have a direct line, and she's definitely no reckoner."

The red jacket people looked taken aback. "What," asked the one whose features pinched together—eyes squinting, mouth pressed together at every opportunity, "is a *reckoner*?" She said the word like she might hold something disgusting as she discarded it.

"Come and see," said the Garrie, and led the way into the house.

But the women didn't come in. Garrie hadn't really expected it; she didn't give them a backward glance. Nor did she protest when Beth slipped through the door, face full of defiance. Fine. Drew's new best friend could be of help when it came to herding the trapped tour group out of the hot zone—and unlike even Drew or Lucia, she could at least hear and sometimes glimpse the ghosts.

Drew tried the door after it closed behind them— locked. Or just wouldn't open. "Leave it," Garrie told him, glancing just closely enough to see the energies twining around the jamb. "If we do this, it'll be fine by the time we return."

"Do what, exactly?" Beth said—the one who had no patterns to fall into, no established duties to fulfill.

"The plan?" Garrie righted herself as Sklayne wound between her feet, doing a damned fine impression of a totally real cat. "Making it up as we go, for now. Until I find Trevarr, we won't know the root of the trouble here."

"Did I miss that?" Drew wondered.

"You were keeping vigil in the bathroom," Lucia told him. She had the backpack now, full of containment bags; her glossy long hair stirred in a breeze that shouldn't have been there.

Garrie kept most of her awareness in the ethereal, watching for company and watching for trouble. "Beth can take us along the tour route until we find them. We'll wing it from there. Maybe we—" A breeze caught her attention—strong and angry, dark muddy color threading through it with streaks of lime. She stared after it.

"Garrie?" Beth had taken a few steps ahead; now she paused, frowning.

"Go ahead," Lucia said easily. "She's working. You'll get used to it. Just watch for that extraordinarily blank expression and you'll know what's up."

"I can still hear you," Garrie muttered, sending a shot of cranky Lucia's direction. It didn't help to find Drew smirking.

"This way," Beth said quickly, a display of quick wisdom as she took the lead and moved on out. Narrow shoulders, held straight; plenty of lanky hip, swaying with her determined strides.

She's scared, Garrie realized.

Another sign that she was, indeed, no dummy.

Not to mention how swiftly she rocked to a halt when Garrie said, "Oh, *ew*."

"What?" Beth said, her voice high and tight. *"What?"*

"Hey, it's chim," Drew said, whatever that meant. *"Ew* is not the code for *the monster's gonna eat you.*"

Beth cast him a skeptical glance, there in the warm wood-glow of the low hallway with the ambience of the meticulously kept house closing in around them. "What exactly would the code for that be?"

"Trust me, you'll know it when you hear it," Lucia advised her.

Garrie let their words wash over her, paying more attention to the collection of grimy unpleasantness lurking near the ceiling. "Anything?" she asked Lucia.

Lucia didn't hesitate. "Anger, resentment, blah blah blah."

Par for the course around here. But the ease with which Lucia handled the emotional aspect confirmed Garrie's assessment—not taking anything for granted in this place—and she used quiet breezes of her own to puff through the middle of it, gently dissipating it. Not any particular spirit, this stain . . . just the detritus of so many angry ghosts in one place. Ghost cobweb.

"It's safe now?" Beth asked, hesitating on forward gear.

"It was always safe enough," Garrie told her. "Just potentially unpleasant." But a step or two later, "Well, okay, *now* we have an audience." A trail of them, from women in Victorian clothing to a young boy in rough homesteader clothes that could have come from either side of 1900. Glowering, disapproving ghosts dogging their every step—but not crowding them. No indeed. Respecting Garrie, and stepping aside so she had plenty of room to work when she ran into cobwebs and ghost poop and dark pools of gleaming ethereal fear and sorrow. Lucia had a harder time, and pulled out the tissues.

"Huh," Garrie said, as Beth led them swiftly through the twisting halls, richly appointed rooms, earthquake damage, and bizarrely constructed stairs. "It's all classic ghostie stuff. Not even any darksider activity here."

"No chance of beetles, in other words," Drew said, scrubbing a finger down his soul-patch smudge.

"You are *so* reminding me of Shaggy on *Scooby-Doo*," Garrie told him. "And hey, here we are, hunting ghosts. With our new animal familiar. Not quite as big as a Great Dane."

::Mine,:: Sklayne told her, a startlement after padding along so silently for so long, simply watching her disperse ethereal artifacts. ::Not Trevarr's. Not *ours*. Mine.::

"It was a joke," she told him. He stared blankly back at her, inscrutable cat face.

Drew wasn't the least bit inscrutable, not with that scowl. "Shaggy had a *goatee*," he said.

"Right," Garrie told him. "What you've got is so much better."

"Nair," Lucia murmured, a singsong threat at odds with the gleam of tears on her cheek.

"God," Beth burst out. "Don't you people take anything seriously? Do you even *care* that we're surrounded by insanely mad ghosts? Who even knows what they'll do next!"

Lucia clutched the backpack. "Trust me, chica. We know. We care."

"Spit in the face of danger," Drew explained. "Bonding before battle."

Garrie drew back to look at him. "Maybe not so much with the spitting."

Beth threw her hands up and led them on, around a cramped corner and up to a set of double doors, where she stopped to frown. "These are usually open."

Garrie didn't have to look deeply, not with the wild

swirl of breezes building up beyond the door. "The tour group."

Beth reached for the doorknob . . . hesitated, and stepped aside.

"Shields up," Garrie said.

"Stick close," Drew translated for Beth. "That means we're covered, as long as we're within eight feet or so. Or unless she goes to extended shields—then we have about fifteen feet."

"It's not foolproof," Lucia murmured. "So, the usual rules, yes?"

Beth looked at them all, bewildered—probably wishing she'd stayed outside the house after all. "And those would be?"

"Easy," Drew said, and took her hand. "Don't get cocky."

Bewilderment turned to skepticism. "So when the going gets tough, the tough turn to *Star Wars* for guidance?"

"Works for us." Drew kept her hand, looking pleased about it.

"Going in," Garrie said, letting their words wash around her. "Stay sharp. They're going to react."

React they did, both the people and the spirits. Garrie staggered under the onslaught of breezes—gusty, gale-force winds *red-black murk slicing citrus shrieking dissonance* and there came Lucia's familiar hand on her arm, steadying her, Sklayne's less familiar form pressing against the side of her shin. "Got it," she said. Or maybe she said it. *Meant* to say it. Hard to tell sometimes.

"Sure?" Lucia asked her, through obviously gritted teeth. She, too, struggled for her equilibrium—and Beth, bless her, took a step out front, where Garrie saw her only vaguely, almost completely obscured by thick layers of ghosts.

"Hold off," Beth told the rush of tourists, her voice and posture changing. Tour Guide Beth, that's who she'd become. She commanded the huge room, all chandelier light and gleaming woods, parquet floors and walls, intricate crown moldings, ceiling panels and insets. "Be calm. We'll get you out of here."

"The door's open!" cried a young voice. "Let's go!" A chorus of agreement swelled behind those words, battering against Garrie much as the winds. Lucia stepped up on one side and Drew on the other, forming a barricade of not very formidable flesh. Garrie shored up her shields, recentered herself . . . and sent a warning breeze through the room. Enough for the spirits to notice; not so much as to incite them.

Far too many of them for that.

"I said, *hold off*," Beth repeated, her voice ringing over the clamor. "When it's safe to go, we will."

"It can't be safe to *stay*." That was the group's guide, vaguely familiar and just as flustered as all her charges. "I don't know what's going on here, Beth, but it's out of control!"

"Exactly," Beth said. "That's why we've got help."

"Someone already came to help," a derisive young man said from the middle of the pack—several families and several couples and a bewildered singleton clutching a brochure. The young man gestured toward the gleaming organ, where a mature woman dressed in silks and bangles sat, hands tightly folded on her lap. "She's been trapped here with the rest of us and all she's said is how angry the spirits are!"

"Hey, anyone can lock a door," a woman said, arms crossed defiantly before her.

"And the lights? And the hot and cold and the wind?"

"It's a setup," that same woman insisted. "It's for publicity."

"At the same time all this other stuff is happening in

the city?" The young man's face reddened; the whole conversation had the sound of a rerun.

"They *are* angry," Garrie said, head tipped slightly, eyes half closed as she searched out the most cohesive of the ghosts pressing against the circumference of safety she'd created. Looking for a spokes-ghost. "Hell, they're farking furious."

::Farking,:: Sklayne said, echoing her faintly. And then more strongly, ::Pick me up. Too many feet.::

Garrie scooped him up without looking, a bundle of fur and sinew and diffusely vibrating energy; he hooked his paws over her shoulder and tickled her cheek with his whiskers. "There," she whispered. "Do you see?" A ghost more solid than the rest, his outlines more distinct—too distinct, in fact, drawn with thick, crayonlike lines and filled with blocky, mismatched color that gave him the effect of an early colorized film. Especially the part where blood trails crawled around his body like living worms, squirming in and out of the gaping wounds that must have killed him. "Sixties?" she asked him, pretty certain the extreme bell-bottoms, snap fly, and painfully tight fit couldn't have come from any other era.

"Acid trip," he confirmed, clearly not really caring. "You said you'd help."

"*You* said you'd behave!"

"Who the hell is she talking to?" Someone new in from the tour group, a burly dad with his hands on his preteen's shoulders . . . Garrie saw him only vaguely, her sight attuned to the ethereal.

"Hard to say," Drew responded. "But don't mess with her, bro. Just marinate."

"Mommy!" The lone preschooler of the group pointed at Drew. "It's Shaggy!"

"See?" Lucia told him.

The sixties ghost scowled at Garrie alone, several blood worms gyrating with the energy of his anger—one so profoundly that it lost its grip on his body and splatted to the floor, manifesting visible spatter; the tourists drew back in horror. He said, "You took too long."

"Jeez," Garrie said. "I had things to do, so get a grip. I'm here, and we had a deal, and if you don't cool off and leave these folks alone, I won't be able to figure out what's really going on. Because I don't think it's starting with any of you."

"Death," intoned the medium, quite suddenly. Several members of the tour group gasped. "Darkness and death and sorrow . . ."

"Oh, *that's* really helping." Lucia planted her hands on her hips.

"Down below," the woman said, as if Lucia hadn't spoken. "It all comes from down below. The dying. The darkness. The—"

"Sorrow," Lucia said. "Right. Got it."

"No, she's right," Garrie said, feeling it—the wildness, the fluttering . . . a pull from below. Sklayne shuddered in her arms and hid his face against her shoulder; she rubbed light circles over his bony shoulder blades. "Krevata," she whispered.

The medium stood, focusing in on Garrie. She moved forward with strong, gliding steps and by golly everyone else got out of her way. She kept just enough distance to raise her arm and point, straight at Garrie and straight at Sklayne. "Demon child!"

Garrie splayed a protective hand over Sklayne. "Oh, I don't *think* so," she snapped. "How rude are *you*?"

And the medium looked sullen, and let her hand fall.

Except . . . Garrie didn't know, did she? She didn't have a clue what she held in her arms, only knew that he didn't consider himself a cat and he didn't have the energy of a cat and he didn't have the intelligence of a cat and he sometimes looked like a light with claws. *And he's desperate to help Trevarr.*

Trevarr, trapped somewhere in this house. Trevarr, hurt.

I'm coming, she told him, sending the thought out as if he could possibly hear her.

::Hurry,:: said Sklayne's voice in her head, smaller than usual.

"I have to find Trevarr," Garrie said, too aware of the angry swirl of energy in the room, and of how close it was to manifesting. Ghost poop would be the least of it. "He *knows* . . ." *If he's in any shape to deal with it . . .*

The sixties ghost scowled. He stepped up to her, his color vibrating—as close as he could push her barrier, and right through the medium while he was at it.

"*Oh,*" the medium said. "I . . . *oh.*" She looked down at Garrie. "You! You've stirred them all up."

"They've *been* stirred up," Garrie said, while the tour group turned on her with suspicious wariness. "And do you think you could possibly be less helpful? Do you have the first clue why they're so upset?"

Sixties Man made a derisive noise. "We've been shouting at her since she got here. And you might notice *we're tired of waiting for help.*" A nasty gust of ethereal rudeness caromed off her barrier, punctuation his words.

"Please," said a wispy little girl voice from the side. "Please?" Just as wispy as the voice, the spirit hovered not far away, bits and pieces of her form coming in and out of focus. A big hair bow, here and gone; the glimpse of long hair and wayward bangs, hair escaping from the bow. Prim shoes and stockings and a pretty little dress from days gone by. "Please."

It might well be the only word she'd be able to pull together. Polite, as she'd probably always been.

Garrie shivered and flushed at the same time; Sklayne twitched, uttering a little feline noise, and jumped from her arms. Dread bound internal hot and cold together, a painful knot. *Trevarr* ... And every moment she was here was a moment she wasn't *there*, wherever *there* was.

Except he'd made it so clear that he'd asked her to come in order to do just this. Handle the angry spirits. He'd deliberately kept her from his secrets, from the primary cause of things—of *everything*. And now she was supposed to fix it all? Stop the ghosts, stop the Krevata, save the innocents, save the not-so-innocent?

That, she thought, would be Trevarr. So totally not-so-innocent.

Didn't mean he wasn't worth saving.

"Please," said the girl, a bare whisper of sound.

Garrie tugged at her hair with both hands, eyes closed, breathing deep. She sent a quick, furious glance at the spirits who'd immediately crowded her barrier shield, warning them back with a stiff gust. Diplomacy only went so far. "Okay," she said. "You," she pointed at the tour group, "are going to leave me alone to work—"

"Oh, screw this," said the irate man. "The door's open. Honey, let's go. We'll find our way out of this place eventually, and then we'll sue their asses off."

His wife held their daughter close to her legs, a hand between the girl's shoulder blades. "I'm not sure—"

"Sir, *no*—" Beth said.

"Let's *go*," he snarled, revealing more of himself than he probably intended. He broke away from the crowd and stalked across the diamond-pattern floor toward the door, his complexion gone something akin to eggplant.

Garrie crossed her arms and waited. "There's always gotta be one." She tightened down the shields, strengthening them. *Here it comes* ... The lights flickered; a howl arose—so many of them, so angry ... even the tour group would hear that one. The medium cried out in alarm, and Garrie only watched as the spirits converged on the man. Letting it happen, because he'd earned that ire—and because denied it, the spirits might well lose complete control. As it was, they came close—plucking at him and shoving and pinching and leaving trails of slime down his arms, face, and legs—not to mention the blood worms contributed by their spokes-ghost. Slick ghost effluvia spilled across the floor; the tour group members made universal noises of dismay and crowded back, and the man—poked and prodded and pushed and shoved— lost his footing, scrambled for an instant on a floor suddenly as slick as ice, and fell heavily on his behind.

"Speaking of asses," Beth said dryly.

"Beth!" gasped the other tour leader.

"Oh, tell me you weren't thinking it." Beth scowled at him. "Do we not have enough trouble here already? Now they're all riled up again."

The young man who'd already spoken up now pointed, his jaw dropping open until he found words. "Look! Look at the floor!"

For although the slick, sticky ghost effluvia had quickly spread, an egg-shaped clearing around Garrie maintained pristine clarity over gorgeous parquet, half an inch of nastiness built up to make the border between safe and not-safe as obvious as it could be. The medium drew herself up, her eyes narrowed. "You!" she said, and this time with recognition— or at least, awareness.

"Imagine that." Garrie tried to keep her impatience to herself. "Okay, ready to listen now? Because in case you all haven't noticed, every minute you delay me is a minute I'm not doing something about this mess." Or finding and helping the man who could.

"Can you really—" started the young man who'd been so outspoken—but he stopped himself when Garrie snarled an inarticulate frustration, flinging her arms out wide.

"Aurgh!" she said again, still at a loss, and then finally,

"Be quiet! All of you! Very, very quiet! Or I'm out of here!"

Finally, silence.

"Good. Now. You know you're surrounded by furious ghosts, right?" She made a face at some of the blank expressions she saw. "Okay, unless you're in denial, you know it. Something's messing with them here in the house, and they want it stopped. The delay here is only pissing them off, by the way."

"Literally." Drew gave the floor a meaningful glance.

"So," Garrie said, looking at Sixties Man, "I'm going to come to an agreement with the ghosts to get you out of here, and then I'll go deal with the rest of it."

"Ohhh, no," Sixties Man said. "You go take care of things. We'll keep everyone safe here until you're done. It's the best place for them to be until then, anyway."

"Might well be," Garrie told him, ignoring the wariness of the tour group as she once again addressed that which they couldn't see. "But that's not how it's going to go."

"Please," the little girl whispered, barely a presence at all.

Beneath them, the ground rumbled. It rumbled big. The room shook; the chandelier jangled. A fierce rattly cry echoed through the room, moving so fast it left a trail of sound behind it.

"They're scared," Lucia said. "They are *so* scared." She didn't mean the tour group, either, although they'd quite suddenly grabbed onto one another. "This house has always been delightful, even if it confused them."

"Not anymore," Sixties Man said, underscoring her words. "Something is eating us alive."

"Eating you dead, you mean," Garrie said. "And as soon as you let them go, I'll do my best—"

"*Please,*" said the little girl.

"Mow!" said Sklayne.

"I want out!" shrieked one of the women, and suddenly the entire room echoed with it, ghostly cries of *out out out out!* so loudly even the medium heard it directly; Beth certainly did.

Within Garrie, something twisted. Hard. Pain bolted through her, flashing from just beneath her navel and shooting through her torso, splitting to burn up her arms and down her legs. She gasped; the room folded in around her, crumpling like discarded paper before springing back to its natural shape.

Sklayne sprawled at her feet. He looked up, catching her gaze with rich green eyes full of pain, his mouth opening on a soundless cry.

Clear enough. Time . . . running out.

Sound reverberated through the room; the gathering of spirits wailed a chorus of anger and fear and desperation, discordant spider web voices tangled in a mesh of barbed wire. The lights flickered; an ominous splashing noise renewed the fearful human cries.

"Garrie!" Lucia crouched beside her, making Garrie realize she'd folded in on herself, just as the room had folded around her. Only she hadn't sprung back into shape, and now when she tried, another wave of Daliesque surreality swept through the room and she cried out, crumpling around the lightning pain. So close to the gleaming perfection of the parquet floor, even with her watering eyes it was easy to see the ghost effluvia close in on them as her shields wavered.

::Trevarr,:: Sklayne said, deep within her head. ::Now.::

"Now," she agreed.

19

Helping everyone does not mean helping every one.
—Rhonda Rose

Destruction happens? What kind of motto is that?
—Lisa McGarrity

The Garrie straightened. Sklayne knew the effort of it, caught here in this vulnerable body; he felt a wash of unexpected pride in her. She caught her breath and stood, the Lucia person's hand on her arm.

She stood with such purpose that the room fell silent around her, leaving only the breathy moan of dimensions warping around them. The jagged motions of the spirits stilled, the energies momentarily quiescent; the noisy, clamorous tour group pulled into itself, barely breathing. The Drew person, his mouth open, closed it. The Garrie said, "I have to go."

"But—!" The Beth person turned to her, arms and legs full of awkward surprise. "You said—!"

"I *said* to be quiet. I *said* to let me work. And they didn't, and now I've run out of time. There's only one person who can stop this, and if I don't find him—*now*—then nothing I do here matters anyway."

Sklayne pressed against her leg, grounding himself. Trevarr's pain clawed through him, wreaking havoc on this form. Trapped here this way.

What if . . . ?

Then would it be forever . . . ?

Cat forever?

"Mow!" said Sklayne, although he hadn't meant to.

All around them, the room burst out into protest. Wailing and snarling, winds blowing up to batter everyone and form tiny rippled wavelets in the effluvia.

The Garrie ignored them, here inside her shielded space, her own steady breeze shaped and held with a control Sklayne hadn't expected of her. Not for this long, not through the filtered agonies that had reverberated between them. She turned to her people. "Lucia, Beth," she said. "Stay with them. Between you, you'll have a sense of what's going on. And remember they can hear you, even if you can't converse directly. Maybe that medium can help, if she *will*." She barely waited for the two to nod. The Lucia person trembled with the emotions battering at her, her face flushed, her pulse racing visibly at her throat.

Brave, the Lucia person. Sklayne wanted to blanket himself around her and eat up those emotions for a snack.

But no. Stuck as cat.

"Drew," the Garrie said. "I need you to come with me. I can target where I need to go . . . but *getting* there . . ."

The Drew person stood straighter. "Totally doable. Real action!"

"Drew," the Garrie said, more sharply. "I don't know what we'll find. I don't know if I'll be able to protect you."

The Drew person gave her a matter-of-fact shrug, ably ignoring the protest from the tour group. "If you can't protect me," he said, "then you won't be able to protect yourself, either. It's not like I'm taking any special risk."

The house gave a deep groan; the world around them echoed it. They heard it—they *all* heard it. ::Your city,:: Sklayne said. ::It comes apart at the foundation of the world.::

The Garrie gave him the sharpest of looks. For an instant, she suddenly looked weary. "Yeah," she muttered. "But I'm not sure I can stop it."

Neither was Sklayne.

* * *

"If not you, then who?" Lucia asked Garrie, and stroked a hand along her arm, a sisterly gesture before she stood back—taking herself out of the shields and out into the effluvia. A clearer signal, she couldn't have given.

Especially not when she dragged Beth out with her.

"No!" cried the outspoken young man. The spirits made way before him, allowing him to take up as their champion.

Sklayne sprang to his feet between them, suddenly puffed twice his normal size, suddenly scattering sparks from his coat. Teeth bared, warning growl vibrating between them, claws in gleaming evidence. Garrie could have sworn he'd gotten bigger; she could have sworn his fangs were absurdly long.

It stopped the man short, eyes first wide and then narrowed, gaze shifting from Sklayne to Garrie and back again, weighing his disbelief against the creature confronting him. "Demon," the medium whispered again.

Garrie grabbed Drew's hand, tugging him toward the door. "I could have fixed this," she cried, frustrated. *If you'd let me.* And she dragged him out of the room, closing her ears to the cries of dismay and protest behind her, to the slam of the ballroom door on ethereal winds just as Sklayne dashed clear.

She stormed down the hall. When a handful of spirits appeared before her, ill formed and inarticulate but building energy and intent, despair wrenched her throat. "Not now," she told them, pushing her voice past the choking point in her throat. "*Please,* not now—" But they didn't give way before her, and her hand tightened down over Drew's until he made a noise of surprise, slowing them both. She lowered her head, giving them a hard shove. "The only warning," she said, and her voice barely made it out that time.

They heard her. She knew they heard her. But she didn't need Lucia's liquid expressions to tell her how desperate they were, and she didn't need any warning as they dove in upon her, already braiding and twining their energies, returning to that which been so effective in the séance room before she'd realized how far they'd go, how fast.

But now she knew. She swallowed down the dismay and denial and choked out, "I'm sorry!" right before she scattered them with a wild gust of power. And then she clenched her fists and stomped her foot and wailed, "Why won't anyone *listen*?"

"*Hey.*" Drew surprised her by taking her shoulders and turning her to face him, giving her an earnest little shake. As if he'd ever even considered doing any such thing before.

Then again, she'd never wailed and threatened to baby-blubber in the middle of a reckoning, either.

"*Hey,*" he said. "You're right. They're *not* listening. None of them. They're just *wanting.*"

"This isn't—" she said, and couldn't finish that. Tried again. "It's not supposed to—" No, that wasn't going anywhere, either. "I should be able to—" No. No words at all.

::Helping everyone,:: Sklayne said, deeply in her thoughts, words she didn't expect to hear from him, ::does not mean helping every *one*. Dimensions quake. Beings die. Destruction happens.::

"Is that what this is?" Garrie turned on him, her throat still thick but already pouncing on that little slip of information. "Dimensions quaking?"

Drew's hands fell away. "Whoa," he said. "Dimensions?"

"Destruction *happens*?" Garrie repeated. "What kind of motto is that?"

"Sucks," Drew muttered, taken aback.

Sklayne didn't respond. Garrie smeared a hand

roughly across her eyes and gave a mighty sniff that wouldn't have been at home in polite society. "Down," she told Drew. "Over in that direction, but mainly *down*. I figure that's what you have to know first, right?"

Back to business. Drew took it well. He also took the lead. "Don't let me run into any mad ghosts," he told her. "Just being *near* all that ghost pee was enough for me." He led her in what seemed like swift circles, bypassing closed rooms, a hallway drop cloth weighted down with spackling and plaster buckets, a series of stained-glass windows, and several of the bathrooms. They crossed into a section of the tour path, made obvious by its extra gleam of spit and polish, and through a kitchen, and a smaller room and down several small flights. Ghosts peeked in on them but fled at her notice, finally taking her seriously. *Too late,* she thought sadly at them.

Sklayne bounded along at their heels, and if at times her sense of their goal ran counter to their direction, Sklayne never protested, never faltered—though he, like she, must be feeling those ever-flashing trills of pain and now sometimes even fear. *Trevarr, afraid.* She hadn't thought to experience that.

As if you've known him for longer than a couple of days.

But that wasn't right. Oh, it *was*, but . . .

So far they'd come, in those scant days.

"Garrie?" Drew stood with his hand on a black doorknob, old and round and set in a short gray door. "Here's the basement. It's a warren, but there aren't any more switchbacks—maybe a few steps up here, down there. I'm not totally sure where you're going, so . . ."

"Neither am I," Garrie said. "I just know I have to get there."

"But *why*?" Drew stood there, his hand on the knob,

effectively blocking the way—perhaps having forgotten the fate of the ghosts not long before.

She shook her head. "I barely know. *Trevarr* knows. And he's the one in trouble down here."

"How?" Frustration crossed his face.

The ground rumbled and the house groaned and creaked around them; they both instinctively ducked. Garrie tried to rein in the frantic in her voice. "He only ever said that if I handle the ghosts, he'll deal with the rest of it. The first clue I get, you guys will be the first to know. You can tell Lucia as much."

"Sure, I can—hey, wait a minute. You think I'm going back? You think you're going in alone?" Thunderous scowl, there.

"I know it," Garrie told him, as gently as she could. "You've already done what I couldn't—you got us here. Now I need you to go back, in case they get out—help them find the fastest, cleanest way out of this house."

"But what if—"

She cut him off, damned deliberately. "When Trevarr and I are through here, I'll find you. The ghosts will take me back—it's where they want me to be."

Drew scowled down at Sklayne. "Not me, but the cat goes with you."

"Hey," Garrie said, and gave him a smile. "If I leave him here, then *you* have to deal with him."

Sklayne turned to her with a lifted paw, toes spread wide and claws extruded.

"Yeah, yeah," Garrie muttered. She put her hand on the door knob over Drew's, not pushing.

After a moment—a moment of earth grumbling and house moaning and dust settling around them—he pulled his out from beneath. "I hope you know what you're doing." He took a step back, anything but convinced.

"I don't," she said. "But hey, this is what I wanted, right? Adventure? And I dragged you guys along. So now I've got to deal with it. That seems fair."

He gave her a strange look. "Not if we're a *team*."

That hit her hard, somewhere deep—but so mixed in with the dread and the sharp, twisting pains that she couldn't do anything more than wince as she opened the door. Wince and know that she'd have to face finishing this conversation before all was said and done.

Sklayne shot through the opening as soon as it was wide enough to admit him, feet light on the wooden steps. Limited by human eyes, Garrie fumbled around for the light switch—found it, and turned back to Drew. "Get them out, if you can," she said. "If the ghosts believe I'm working on the problem, they might give up their hostages. If they can finally believe that . . ." She took a breath, shook her head. "You might point out that I *could* have blown them away—"

"Literally," Drew said, his grin unrepentant.

"—Anytime I wanted. I didn't. That's because I really *am* trying to help. But we don't have time to coddle them." The rumbling earth underscored her words; from somewhere came that same stench of the glop from the café. Her voice dropped to a whisper. "*Please*, Drew."

She tried to pretend she didn't see the surprise on his face as she slipped through the door and closed it behind her. She thought he might follow—she listened for it, as she ran down the stairs and into the low space of the cellar, and wasn't sure if that feeling in her throat was disappointment or relief.

"Mow!" Sklayne demanded, a strangely muted sound.

"I can feel it just fine," she told him, just as muted. Skulk mode. And she could, too. Intrusive power, with the same flavor as Trevarr's but none of the heart. No, this was . . . rude and dangerous and threatening, and laced around the edges with familiar ethereal breezes.

Run, for sure. But away, or toward?

Pipes and joists brushed the top of her head but she straightened her shoulders anyway, lifting her chest, setting herself strong and grounded before moving forward, ducking the dim bare bulbs that lit the space.

Sklayne trotted along ahead of her—one room after another, sometimes with little rooms off to the side, always with the pipes and the stacks of neatly stored supplies from an age gone by, not to mention the occasional large object she couldn't begin to figure out. Coal furnace? Old ice box? Ancient torture device? What did she know of old mansion basements?

::Take care,:: Sklayne told her. ::Quiet, now.::

"I *am* quiet." She'd practically been tiptoeing at that.

::*All* of you,:: he retorted, and a faint sheen of sparks washed over his coat.

"I'm not—" Not sparking, she'd been about to say. But maybe to him, she was. And if to him . . . maybe to whatever awaited them down here. She stopped moving, checked herself—centered in, bringing her energies in tight. *Shields up and dark running!*

Not something she had practice with. Not something that ever mattered; not something, even, that Rhonda Rose had ever addressed, other than in matters of courtesy.

Garrie cast an inquiring glance at Sklayne, who offered approval with the mere twitch of his tail and continued on—but not as quickly. The intrusive power beat around them, thicker, heavier—filling her head with a pulse not her own and all but burying her sense of Trevarr. Now and then it surged slightly; a beat behind each surge, the earth rumbled around them.

::Warping,:: Sklayne said, his mental voice partially obscured by the noise of it all. ::Not for long.::

Relief brushed through her—until she realized. *Not for long* meant not that it would end soon, but that it couldn't maintain much longer.

As if fires blooming in the sky and unending earth-quake rumbles and belching ground and black ooze and beetles and Bob the Hulk hadn't been clue enough. All things that everyone had seen—not just the ethe-real, not just for Garrie's eyes. All things she hadn't been able to affect.

So what am I even doing here?

Because the man who'd come so suddenly into her life was here. And because he was the one who *could* do something—or so he'd claimed. And then she, mighty reckoner, could clean up the bothersome coincidental mess with the ghosts.

You'd better be right, she told him, cobbling thoughts together in spite of the throbbing beat and the way her entire being pulsed with it—expanding, collapsing, expanding again, a buzz of incompatible power turning into sandpaper against her nerves. *If I find you, you'd better be able to deal with this thing.*

And this *thing* . . . was just ahead.

She didn't need Sklayne's suddenly stiff posture to confirm it, or his tail sticking straight out behind him and slowly puffing up. She didn't even need the flicker-ing nature of the light ahead. The power . . . it told her enough. Pulsing, pounding . . . slamming within her. Her barriers, no matter how she strengthened them, did nothing against it. On impulse, she reached into herself for that which Trevarr had left behind—spinning it up, drawing breath against the alluring feel of it—and at-tempting, in some clumsy fashion, to shape it.

::*No!*:: Sklayne turned back to her, ears flat and fangs bared, soundless. ::They can feel that!::

Gah! Of course they could! Garrie floundered to re-lease what she'd built without losing the tight hold on the rest of her energy. "Sorry," she started to say, but stopped herself from that, too.

Sklayne relaxed, if only slightly. ::Think it.::

You're kidding.

::Not kidding.::

Great. And just how many of her thoughts had he been listening in on?

He cast her an annoyed look. ::Think it loud, then not my fault.::

Okay. Along with everything else she was trying to process in this moment, *think quietly* went onto the list. She swallowed the sudden wave of panic, the utter certainty she was about to drop all the unfamiliar pieces in play, and eased up to the thick timber frame of the doorless opening, where she saw . . .

Nothing.

Sklayne snagged her shoe when she would have taken another step out into the open. ::Not *nothing*.::

She looked more closely, though half the room was out of her field of view. This one, too, was taller than most of the space down here—tall enough so even Trevarr could have stood straight, had he been here. And no, not nothing. There, in the corner, she discovered a small bench, and around it a pile of ugly sacks, and on it a familiar satchel.

::Trevarr's.::

Trevarr's. They were right. They were in the right place.

::Krevata,:: Sklayne informed her.

She didn't see a thing.

::Semiethereal . . . seen as they want to be. Use the Trevarr inside:: Sklayne sounded reluctant, even obscured by the power slamming around in her head. She could only stare at him, more disoriented by the moment. ::Only a little bit of little,:: he told her. ::Call it up. See through it.::

Only a little bit of little. Right. Garrie withdrew, tucked up against the old stone wall and surrounded by the scents of damp earth and faintly musty cellar. She reached for the touch of Trevarr within . . . just the merest whisper of it, trickling in to tickle her low belly from the inside out. She closed her eyes to let it wash up through her, and when she felt she'd stabilized it, she dug deep for nerve and peeked around the corner again.

Lumbering beings washed in tones of mud and clay and viscous green, camel-nosed faces looming over barrel chests, arms bulky and legs on first glance stickish and bent all backward and oddly drawn in the flickering shadow of the light from she wasn't sure where. Some of them more distinct than others, some fading around the edges.

Garrie felt a squeak in her throat; she threw herself back around the corner and against the wall, both hands clapped over her mouth. For an instant, her gorge rose; she fought it back down. Retching, they'd hear for sure.

Sklayne sat beside her with his tail curled around his front feet, ignoring the trickle of dust settling between his ears. ::Strong, they are. Look again. Poison on those claws.::

Claws? She didn't remember claws. So she looked again, and wow . . . yes, there they were. Every one of those four fingers, tipped with a pointed nail that definitely counted as a claw. And a fifth, more of a spur— not a useable digit so much as a dedicated weapon. But what caught her eye this time was the jewelry. Some of it set directly into the thick hide between small eyes and below the sparse scattering of bristly forehead hairs, emphasizing the impressive sweep of the nose. Some of it in necklaces around exaggeratedly broad shoulders; some of it in belts below highly colorful vests. And then there were the loincloths, which weren't so much flaps as well-defined bundles with decorated rings securing them in place directly over those parts that darned well ought to be covered.

Way too much sharing.

::Vain,:: Sklayne agreed. ::But powerful beings. Krevata. Also stupid. See now, what they do?::

It meant another look; Garrie wasn't sure just how

many of these she'd get away with before one of them noticed her, but then again . . . their tiny little eyes didn't look terribly effective—she hoped. So she peeked again, this time looking for something stupid.

What she found was that which she'd seen nothing of the first time she'd looked and simply been unable to process the second time she'd looked.

A little pond in the floor. *No, not a pond.* From it burst little flares of energy, the source of the flickering light. No lightbulb here in this dead end of a room, she realized, just . . . this. The surface of the pond shimmered in a way her eyes declared simply *wrong*; even trying to focus made her nauseous, and she let her gaze shift away, taking in the rest of the room once more. The Krevata— in deep conversation over something, huddled together as close as their massive probisci allowed, their fat fingers moving in patterns that had to be part of that conversation and the rest of it done in some manner Garrie couldn't discern—took up the greater part of the space. There was the rickety bench that held Trevarr's satchel, and in the corner, a pile of what Garrie might have called duffel bags if they'd been a little smaller and a little more stylish and just possibly not made out of what appeared to be the badly tanned hide of some creature with lumpy porous skin.

No sign of Trevarr.

::There,:: Sklayne said, just enough of him appearing around the edge of the timber to point with a twitch of his whiskers before he withdrew again. ::Look not for something. Look for nothing.::

Oh, because that made so much sense. But Garrie obediently did just that. *Look for nothing.*

Whoa. Like the *nothing* there just on the other side of the threshold and toward the corner, barely visible from this angle but a distinct effect all the same. It diminished the quality of the hard-packed dirt beneath, of the stone wall beyond, of the very air it occupied.

All the way to the corner, she retreated this time, tucked away with her back up against the solid stone and her feet propped against the solid earth, feeling it rumble through her bones. "What *is* that?" she whispered, mouth forming words to which she gave no real voice.

::Trap-thing,:: Sklayne said, after a long pause during which his whiskers gave a hard-thinking twitch. He lifted his front paw for a quick series of token licks, then stopped himself and stared at the leg with some obvious annoyance. ::Not cat,:: he reminded himself. He redirected his attention to her and said, ::Nasty thing. Pocket of sucks-life. You need to go there.::

"Whoa, whoa, whoa!" Sound nearly slipped out on that last one; Garrie made the effort to regain self-control. *Nasty? Sucks life? And you want me to go there?*

::To get Trevarr.::

Crammed back in the corner, she spread her hands wide, balancing there in a half-crouch, indicating herself. "And just how am I supposed to do that? I can barely manage this weird energy *inside* my body! That was the whole point—I'm here to handle the ghosts, right? The rest is Trevarr's job."

Sklayne put his paw on her ankle, pushing. Pushing harder, while she glared. Finally, extruding deliberate claws. Garrie clapped her hands over another squeak, and Sklayne, apparently satisfied that he had her true attention, said, ::His job, yes. Take his things. He does his job.::

The satchel? "I take him the satchel, and he does the rest? How do you know he's even in any shape—?"

Sklayne withdrew his claws and looked away. ::Don't know.:: He looked back at her, deep green eyes unreadable. ::Hope.::

Cold reality clutched at Garrie. That's what it came down to, then. Dive headfirst into a nothingness from which she might or might not ever escape, for the sake of saving a city.

::A world,:: Sklayne said, breathtaking in eavesdropping audacity. Just as quickly, he slitted his eyes at her, and said defensively, ::Shouting!::

No, THIS IS SHOUTING.

"Mow!" Sklayne said, opening his mouth on a barely voiced cat-yelp. After a sullen moment, he admitted, ::Yes, shouting.::

"I was having a moment," Garric informed him. "A *private* moment. A little respect, please." For she hadn't finished the moment. She hadn't gotten to the part where she admitted to herself that it was all more personal than that. Save the city—the *world?*—but also . . . Trevarr. And if his pain had diminished, it was because the sense of him had weakened. Because *he* had weakened. "Oh, crap," she breathed.

Sklayne wisely said nothing.

"But the bag . . ."

::My job. Just be ready.::

"But how—?"

::It will take you.::

How reassuring.

::Be ready.::

Be wha—? Be huh?

"But—" she said. *How will it take me? Why will it take me? Would it take just anyone, or just me, or anyone who has the bag—?*

She found herself facing empty space. Alarmed noises came from within the room—or what she thought was alarm—and then the scuffling of oddly formed feet against dirt, a strange hopping movement . . . the Krevata lumbered out of the room, all fully visible—swinging their heads around, flicking great disks of ears . . . bent to avoid the lower ceiling, hop-loping on legs that belonged as much to a camel as the noses.

Garrie found herself rooted to the spot. Heavily rooted. Permanently, even.

The creatures scented her—their nostrils flared; they essayed rapid little huffing breaths and snorted out air, rejected—and then they turned to stare at her.

"Hey," she said. "You don't smell so hot, either."

A soft furry invisible weight hit her chest; she stumbled back.

::Get it!:: Sklayne told her, more than a hint of frantic there, bouncing away again and still invisible. ::In here!::

The satchel. Now just on the other side of the door, out of sight of the glowering Krevata. In between her and the sucks-life. *Go,* she told herself. *Go now.*

::Only way out,:: Sklayne pointed out, from somewhere inside the room, still impossibly invisible.

Right. The room was a dead end; the Krevata blocked the meandering maze, huge beings filling the small space. They inched closer, moving their enormous noses around to build a scent picture of her. And even as she steeled herself to move, she realized the significance of the rising musky smell—that the colorful loin bundles had suddenly taken on a life of their own.

"Oh, *no,*" she said, flat denial. "No, no, no. That is just not right. Stop that. All of you!"

::Krevata,:: Sklayne said, clear exasperation coming through. ::Not personal.::

"Damned right it's personal!" Garrie said. "They won't . . . surely they won't . . . I'm not even the same . . . *being!*"

::Power hunters, feel you.:: Sklayne might still be invisible, but Garrie thought she saw the flick of a barely there tail from the corner of her eye. ::Not suspecting you yet, poor lost human. Waiting for the big one to decide. Go!::

She watched the Krevata; they watched her. One of

them gave a little involuntary flex of his hips. *The big one,* she realized, and it wasn't a reference to height. The others responded with their own little demos of self, offering up little grunts of appreciation—and shuffling closer. Coming for her. *Power hunters.* Getting off on the mere scent and ethereal feel of her.

"Gahh!" she cried, and ran for it. She scooped up the satchel and she aimed at the *nothing* and . . .

She ran right through it and smacked into the wall beyond, hard enough to bounce slightly but not so hard she didn't immediately snarl an accusing, "Sklayne!"

Here came the Krevata, lumbering in to take up the whole of the room and leaving one to block the door. They bounced up and down on their bizarre legs and Garrie got the distinct impression that this passed for laughter; she cried out again, with somewhat less accusation and somewhat more frantic need. *"Sklayne!"*

::Push them,:: Sklayne said, somewhere inside the room and boy, he had to be quick if he'd avoided a trampling. ::Use the Trevarr and *push* them! Push the *nothing*!::

Braced against the old whitewashed brick of this section, Garrie gave them a panicked first push, just that which had first affected Trevarr—a stall tactic, while she reached more deeply for the other. They staggered back slightly—not so much, actually—and then they bounced up and down, the laughter movement. And other movements, as well.

::No, no! Use the Trevarr!::

"Okay, okay!" *Who knew?* She gathered her focus and drew hard on the foreign feelings within her, flooding herself with sensation even as she flung a hard gust at the Krevata. This time there was no laughter to their staggering—this time, two of them went down.

::Impressed,:: Sklayne said. ::Made them mad.::

"Yeah, that was totally my intent. Piss them off. Because what we had wasn't bad enough." Garrie clutched the satchel, feeling the hard objects within. That, too, was a mistake—the lead Krevata noticed for the first time that she had the thing at all. His disk ears swiveled around; his tiny eyes widened. He reached across his hunched shoulder and pulled out a machete-like blade.

"Oh, shit," Garrie said.

::Push the nothing spot!:: Sklayne commanded her, in a voice that meant all his fur was standing on end. ::Do, do, do!::

Garrie did.

The spot exploded into a fiery presence, no longer any sort of nothing. The Krevata exploded into angry snarling, slobbering grunts, rocking in a violent side-to-side motion; Sklayne shouted right into her head, ::Go! Go!:: and she shouted back, "But that's *fire*!" and then she didn't have any choice—no escape, they all had machetes, and oh, boy they weren't laughing anymore for sure as they hunkered down and charged her.

She had to run straight at them to reach the fiery sucks-life, and run she did, filling her lungs to bellow what should have been a battle cry but came out as pure girly *ahhhhhhhhhhhh!* Running at fire, running at lusty, musty, and furious Krevata, hoping not to collide directly with any of them.

Fire poofed out to engulf her, hot and full of brimstone; Sklayne shouted a victory and then faded as her failed battle cry turned to a scream. The fire scoured her from the inside out, grabbing her up for an instant of suspension that took forever—

And then spitting her back out again. Rejected?

Garrie tumbled to an undignified stop, losing any nimble recovery to the satchel she clutched close. There she sprawled, head spinning . . . assessing. Did she even have any hair left? Any skin? Hard to tell, with her senses so fried. Panting, she tried to orient—heard no

Sklayne, heard no sound of Krevata . . . smelled no Krevata.

Smelled leather and wood smoke.

"Trevarr?" Slowly, she unkinked herself, finding in this dim, diffuse light that she did indeed have her skin—unable to resist a quick pass over her hair to confirm its presence as well. She blinked, unable to find walls, unable to find a ceiling . . . unable, really, to find the floor. Only able to find where her feet stood in featureless reddish-gray mist. Vertigo seized her, sudden and ruthless, and dropped her to her knees and almost to her face. She closed her eyes, clutching the satchel tight.

After long moments, her perceptions settled. She opened her eyes cautiously . . . and this time didn't try to focus tightly on anything, using peripheral vision as she turned a slow three-sixty without getting up.

And found him.

Too late, too late, please not too late.

Nothing but a crumpled form in the distance; inexplicable energy smudges smeared the otherwise featureless mist around him. She scrambled to her feet, sprinting the distance, her body still not adjusted to this place—taking forever to reach him even though she ran with huge, flashing strides. Finally, finally she threw herself down beside him. "Trevarr!"

He didn't so much as blink, lying still as stone here where he'd quite obviously faltered from feet to knees and then sunk back on his heels and finally fallen, his legs twisted beneath and the leather coat splayed across the ground.

Or whatever it was.

"Trevarr?" She whispered it, a hesitant hand hovering over his arm. "Look," she said, nonsensically. "I brought your things. I met Sklayne, and we found the Krevata, and everything's falling the hell apart, and *what else didn't you tell me*?" She found no injuries on him, trembling hands passing over a body that had so quickly become familiar, muscle and bone and form. She tried to smooth away his troubled expression and couldn't—drawn brow, tension around his eyes, faint flare of nostril. The muscles of his jaw were hard; those of his neck corded.

She glanced up at those smudgy spots again—nothing there to clue her in; if they so much as drifted in this undefined fog of a backdrop, she couldn't perceive it. No natural breezes here, nothing for her to gather and shape. Only what she had within.

Better not waste it.

She flipped back the satchel flap. Some kind of leather, tough and nubbly and stained, the contents a rough jumble of disparate things. She caught the dull gleam of metal and found the disk she'd seen him use earlier—and beside it, another inexplicable device. She pulled that out, frowning at it—tight-fitting pieces with rounded edges, molded to fit a hand and inscribed with precision etchings, inset with spots of cloisonné color. *Right.* Whatever. She slipped it back into the bag.

The stout stick, she would have called a bludgeon—if it wasn't for the thick metal lines worked into the smooth wood, all of it polished by age, no rhyme or reason or pattern there. She could make no more sense of what she would have called a belt, had it been sturdier—as wide as her hand, made of intricately knotted string, a silky, fragile-looking piece that had no place in a man's things. Then a stone—deep blue and blooming all over with silvery lace, wrapped in metal inlay much as the stick. The glint of glass caught her eye—or she thought it was glass. A vial, thick, heavy, filled with something . . . when she reached for it, her fingers prickled.

She decided not to touch anything else, not even the gorgeous, gleaming flash of rainbow color that might have been enamel or might have been polished stone or might have been something else entirely. There certainly wasn't anything here that looked as though it could be of help—or if it was, she didn't recognize it and didn't know how to use it.

But Sklayne wanted him to have this.

"Trevarr," she said, following impulse to lay her head upon his chest, listening to the thud of his heart. Expecting the strong, solid beat she'd heard the night before and getting something more erratic, more shallow—it made her own pulse surge in fear. No wonder her perception of his pain had faded . . . so had he. "What have they done to you?" she whispered, not expecting an answer.

Not expecting, either, the spirit that suddenly appeared nearby, complete with a swoosh-and-suck that hit the silence hard enough to make Garrie jump. She hunched over Trevarr, but the spirit offered them no threat. She straightened, leaving her hand over his heart. "What brought you here?" she asked. "Did you come from the Winchester House?"

Even with blurry features and legs that forgot to finish up with feet and hands that were merely formed mittens, the spirit's terror came through to her. "Hehhh," it said, and she thought it might have been trying for *help.* "He-eh!"

"What's wrong? How did you get here?" If she could get it to focus . . . She hunted breezes to work with, any kind of energy she could use to bolster it—found nothing.

"He-ehp!" One of those unformed mitts reached out to her, grasping air—and then it dissipated, the remnants hanging there in the gray vagueness. A smudge.

Garrie jerked around to look at the other smudges—wildly, now, taking in the vast undefined space all around her. *Smudges, everywhere.* Dissipated ghosts, all of them.

No wonder the spirits had been so upset. They'd been trapped, and they'd become prey. Dissipated before their time, before their choice—and not because they'd gone destructive or turned their energies on the living. What the Krevata got from it, Garrie didn't know.

But she bet Trevarr would.

20

Maintain an appropriate demeanor at all times.
—Rhonda Rose

Holy farking crap!
—Lisa McGarrity

Sklayne hid in the basement corner, staying glass—so very hard, trapped as cat. Barely doable at all. Every breath in, he renewed the effect; every breath out, some part of him became just a little more visible. Toes this time, tail tip the next . . .

But the Krevata weren't paying attention just yet. The Krevata, who could do this thing, too . . .

The Krevata were too busy throwing a communal fit. Because they'd wanted the Garrie.

The Garrie, small person of much sweet power.

The Garrie, the one person who could save Trevarr, if anyone could.

So then Trevarr could stop the Krevata.

And he and Sklayne could go home.

Home.

Sklayne flattened his ears against the falling dust and mortar, squinting into it. Stupid Krevata, throwing a fit about the Garrie while this world tore itself to pieces around their ill-warded portal.

Starting here.
Starting . . .
Now.

Surrounded by ghost smudge and vast nothingness and kneeling there beside hope and fear and the balance of a world all wrapped up in one man, Garrie pressed both hands over her face and searched desperately for calm.

After all, Sklayne had brought Trevarr back once already. Okay, not from *this* exactly, but . . . still. Maybe she could do the same. She still carried the touch of him within . . .

Except she'd *hurt* him, that last time. There in the séance room—she'd hurt him badly. She'd been strong, boldly reaching out to shove back at ghosts run amok, and he'd gotten in the way.

So don't do that.

Trickle it, that's what.

She sat there another moment, gathering herself— trying to separate the rush and swirl of her feelings. *Yes, I saw monstrous creatures from who knows where. Yes, I'm in the* sucks-life *place and it's so totally not Kansas anymore.* Not to mention . . . no idea how to extricate herself. No idea if what had happened to that spirit would happen to her—or if it was already happening to Trevarr. But the cold heat and the yearning and the shivery impulses that rifled through her as steadily as her breath . . .

That's what she found when she paid attention. When she sat next to this man and *paid attention.* Still connected. That one thing, she could ground herself to. Focus on there

"Fine," she grumbled at him. "I'll deal." And then, so nothing would be lost into this void gray mass around them, she kept her hand his chest and channeled her trickle of energy there—giving of herself in a way she'd never done before. Never *considered* before. The passage of that energy pulled at her, brushing nerves as it passed by—an astonishingly pleasant sensation, as if some part of Trevarr had trickled back up the connection to touch her.

She lost herself to those sensations for a long, blissful moment before her eyes popped open and she gave herself a shake. A *not now* shake, a *not here* shake, and a *pay attention* shake.

Trevarr stirred; he groaned, deeply, and it sounded frustrated . . . words, stuck along the way.

"Hey there," she said, feeling his sudden deep breath, a changing awareness; his heartbeat strengthened beneath her hand. He shifted, a restless movement, one hand reaching out. She folded her fingers around his, around the old scuffs and scars and hard living there. His back arched briefly; he got his legs untangled. "Sah," she murmured, remembering how he'd once soothed her. "I'm sorry. I'm trying not to hurt you. But I have to . . . sah, sah . . ."

He rolled his head back; he lost his breath in a sudden huff and seemed momentarily stuck there, his chest trembling beneath her touch. She held her own breath until he finally drew in air, his hand tightening around hers.

"Okay," she said. "A little more. That's all. Just a—"

His eyes snapped open, instantly finding her.

"Holy farking crap!" she cried, and would have startled right away from him had his other hand not moved with blinding speed to trap hers at his chest. He grabbed her wrist; he rolled up to his knees. All feral, all power, all everything he'd ever been and then a hell of a lot more. Starting with those eyes. Bright in their tarnish-edged silver brilliance—bright enough so they seemed to . . .

No. She wouldn't think it. She wouldn't think the

word *glow*. Wasn't it enough that they were no longer round in pupil, but now distinctly slitted, a cat's eye in moderate light? *Cat's eye*. So no, she most definitely wouldn't think about the way they glowed.

Or about the way they looked at her while they did it.

"Are you . . ." she started—but, caught up in his regard, finding breath an elusive thing and fighting her own extremes, she suddenly didn't have any idea what words came next. Inches away, he was, the only compromise between her conflicting impulses. *Run. No, grab. No, run*— Oh, less than an inch, now, and that space between them practically vibrating.

Breathe, she told herself. Shaky but deliberate. Up this close, his eyes were no less alien, no less intense . . . no less predatory. He released her wrist, but only to twine his fingers through hers—holding her gaze while he did the same with the other hand, taking them both to run his hands down her sides, standing with her. Shaking with her.

"Wha—" she started, and this time he silenced her, a quick shake of his head—something pleading behind his gaze.

His cat-eye gaze.

He lifted her, and she didn't even think before wrapping her legs around him—would have reached for him, had she the freedom of her hands. He balanced her effortlessly that way, keeping her with his strength and with his gaze—until he pressed his cheek against hers, inhaling deeply of her neck—just holding her there. Absorbing, while she lost herself to his myriad subtle reactions—feeling the flutter of his ribs as he struggled for breath and composure, the tension in his arms that spoke more of restraint than effort, the faint tremor running through all. His hips shifted against her, seeking contact; she bit her lip and pushed back, wanting so badly to *touch*—

"No," he breathed—even as he pulled her closer, a little jerk of movement he couldn't seem to help. He groaned on it, and for a sudden blinding moment she thought—she *knew*—he was about to take them both to the ground, mindless and groping and completely lost to the moment and she *wanted*—

"No," he breathed again, harsh and strained and right at her ear. "*Atreya vo*, forgive." He ran his hands up her spine, cupping her head and kissing her fiercely, so fiercely she completely forgot all the little things she'd been thinking and clutched his arms and kissed him back, long and hot and hard while her thoughts soared and her body followed. And she thought she could possibly do this forever or until she exploded, whichever came first.

Except, quite suddenly, he ran his hands back down her spine, circled her waist, and set her on the ground. Or what passed for it. He smoothed her hair back—a quick frown, only a flicker and then gone while he pressed his mouth to her forehead and murmured again, "Forgive," before he stepped away. Not quite turning his back on her, but close enough, arms stiff and hands clenched at his side.

Garrie stood in disbelief. Her shirt all rucked up, her cargos twisted around her legs, every possible part of her throbbing and unfulfilled and crying out for more and he'd *put her down and turned away*? Speechless, she did the only thing she could. She made a sputtering, inarticulate noise and she stomped her foot.

He stiffened even more, if that was possible. And then his shoulders shook, and he turned his head away even more completely, and Garrie had a sudden horrible suspicion.

"You're laughing! *Again!*" Offended dismay filled her voice; she couldn't stop it. "Tell me you're *not!*"

He didn't answer right away; his head tipped ever so slightly . . . a more relaxed posture. "She was right about you," he said, more to himself than to her. "More than a match for me."

Garrie scowled at the inexplicable response—and then knuckled under to blinding revelation. All his previous little hints and comments . . . *good to finally meet you* . . . the way he seemed to know so much more of her than anyone receiving a simple referral from a past client could possibly know. The *familiarity*. "Oh my God," she blurted. "You knew Rhonda Rose!"

He half turned to look at her, and if he'd relaxed somewhat, the intensity still lingered on his face and the self-restraint stamped itself all over his body. He said again, "She was right about you."

"How?" she demanded. "When? *Where?*"

He finally turned back, his hands loosened, his shoulders relaxing. He crouched and scooped up the satchel. "*Atreya*," he said, "I am so very sorry, but we cannot stop to talk about those things right now." When he stood, he briefly touched the side of her face, passing his thumb over her cheek.

Garrie crossed her arms, unmoved. Or at least not that she'd let show. "Oh, I think we can. And what does that mean, anyway? *Atreya*. You've said it more than once."

"Short fiery person with unruly hair," he told her, pulling several objects from the satchel, redistributing them within the coat of endless pockets.

Garrie said nothing. Didn't move. Didn't demand. Didn't go, "Tre-*varr*," in irritated insistence.

Though she really wanted to.

He tucked one last thing into the front breast pocket. He took her hand, gently tugging it free of her defiant posture, tugging again so she took a step closer; he placed it flat over his heart. Beating strong and steady now, it was. "Heart-bond person," he said. "More or less." When she startled, pulling away, he held her there. "It is not an obligation. It is a one-way expression. Do you follow?"

"I . . . maybe." She gave him a patently skeptical look.

Regret flickered across his features. "I will not say it, then."

"No! I mean," Garrie added hastily, "I guess that's okay. If that's what comes to mind. I mean. Right."

Surely there'd been a sentence in there somewhere.

He looked like he might smile—so subtle, there at the corners of his mouth and the corners of, yes, *still* cat eyes. Amused again, at her. So she pulled her hand away. "And what is it with the eyes, and all the things in that bag, and what *is* this place, and by the way, just who are you really?"

"Ah," he said, and hefted the satchel strap over his shoulder. "Perhaps it is time for that, after all. But not here. To stay here is to die. For you, more slowly. For me . . . already this place steals what you gave me. That is its function."

Sucks-life. Garrie's impatience fled before understanding. "All these smudges—can you see them?"

The merest shake of his head, but he didn't seem surprised that she saw something. "Your ghosts," he said. "That which has enraged them so. To be trapped in this house . . . to be fed upon."

"But *why*?" Garrie frowned mightily. "I feel like the answers are finally right *here*—but dammit, I just can't put it together."

"No," he said, regretful. "Because you still miss pieces. The Krevata are feeding from the Winchester House ghosts, *atreya*, because they are collecting the energy to fuel the plasma portal that destroys your world."

Garrie blinked at him. Blinked again. Used Drew's inflection to drawl, "Well, shee-*it*." Remembered to breathe. Said, "World? Did you say *world*?" Sklayne had said *world,* too. She hadn't quite taken him literally.

She'd been in the middle of a moment. "Did you *mean* world? And did you notice you said *your*?"

Trevarr held out his hand. "We have to go," he told her. "Before I cannot."

21

I did warn you.
—Rhonda Rose

Rhonda Rose, you got some 'splainin' to do.
—Lisa McGarrity

Glass. Think glass. Sklayne tucked himself away. Trapped here. Not fretting overmuch if you didn't count *fear* for Trevarr and *fear* of Krevata and *fear* of this world ripping apart around him.

No, no, not fretting.

For a while there'd been relief—when waxing pain replaced waning Trevarr, and he knew the Garrie had done what needed doing despite the cost of it. The pain strengthened to brief agony to sudden awareness and then to an abrupt flare of that which Sklayne had feared the most—the awakening of that inner other.

And then quite suddenly it became too personal, even filtered by the dimensional cul-de-sac. Too private.

Often he rode Trevarr's thoughts during times of pleasure. But this . . . oh, it made him *want*. Home and self-form and sweet woods and his own curious, never sated kind. *Want.* But this . . . this belonged to Trevarr and the Garrie. Not to Sklayne.

Grumble. He pulled himself away. Just in time, too,

gone red-buff cat around all his edges, hair standing on end and whiskers straight out.

Eavesdropping, Trevarr had always said, would get him in trouble. *Not clever Sklayne, no.* But respect, he could give. Sklayne savored a last lingering intensity of that distant oh lovely deep swallow of feeling, and let it go.

He would look elsewhere instead, trapped here in this small room with Krevata filling the doorway and Krevata watching the portal and Krevata harvesting fearsomely warped illicit power at the portal, hurrying to finish their work here. Hurrying to leave this world in ruins, smug in their belief that Trevarr was dead or dying, the one who had come to rescue him inexplicably trapped as well. They would not understand how the Trevarr within Garrie had allowed her passage to the sucks-life, or what she could do once she was there. If they had discerned her true nature, they would have closed that trap, foregone the spiritual energy it tapped from this house, and finished their work.

They would have run away.

Sklayne waited to see their energies burn and flare when they realized it. So yes, he hunkered down for the waiting. Pretending to himself that he could do this forever. Glass. Unnoticed. Invisible. However long it took.

Pretending.

"But," Garrie said, reflexively extending her hand to meet Trevarr's and then changing her mind. *"But."*

He said, "Not here." He snagged her hand anyway, a quicker-than-Garrie movement that made her blink, and he brought from his many pockets the stone she'd seen in his satchel, all concentric blooming colors that shouldn't even be in rock at all.

"And what is that thing, anyway?" she demanded,

following his tug to move her in close as he held it up before them. "What kind of stone *is* that?"

He gave her a glance, one of those mere hints that a smile might well be lurking. "Not a stone," he told her, snugging her back against his chest and wrapping his arm across her body and boy, did that feel right.

But there was not a damned thing right about that way that stone spewed a sudden explosion of colors around them. Garrie stiffened as they expanded into a giant bubble of light and silence, her hands coming up to grip the hard muscle of Trevarr's steadying forearm. "Sah," he murmured, a trace of wry irony there, and then whatever he said vibrated between his chest and her back, the actual sound swallowed up by engulfing silence. Probably just as well, because when starbursts of black spattered across the color field and instantly expanded to tighten down in a swift blanket of nothingness, Garrie started to shriek.

She clapped her hands over her eyes and she filled her lungs and she screamed, endless long moments of imposed and unnatural silence during which something jerked unhappily inside her. She ran out of breath and started again, just in time for the silence to cut out and the sound to cut in—she clapped her hands from eyes to mouth.

The sound told her much in that instant of feedback, even with her eyes still shut. A closed-in space, but big enough for a faint echo. The faint scent of damp rock told her *underground;* the relative warmth seemed to conflict with this assessment. The air itself came with an overlying scent of spicy green; it made her think of wintergreen and tickled her nose.

It was a stronger version of that very faint scent she'd found on her nightshirt the evening before . . .

A fainter version of that very strong scent she'd found in her waking dreams and nightmares since arriving here.

"Where," she said, not quite sure she wanted the answer, "are we? And how did we get here? And how do you know Rhonda Rose? And—"

He shifted, close and to the side, looking at her. "You can open your eyes," he said. "This is a safe place."

"I doubt that," she said under her breath. "I don't think there's anything safe about you. Ever."

"That may be so," he agreed. "But this is my place, unknown to others. A place I have created to rest, when needed. Only a few moments, now. There are those who will know I have returned, if not my exact location. I cannot give them cause to look."

"Returned . . . *where*?" Garrie cracked open one eyelid . . . couldn't see much. Oddly, it still reassured her, simple because what it *wasn't*.

He must have felt her reaction. "Be easy," he said, stepping away from her.

"Don't—"

"Only to make light."

Warier without him, she listened to him move around, realizing anew how well he saw in this darkness and how little he needed the light. He confirmed it as he opened something with a latch, pulled out a few items, and worked swiftly. Garrie found dim soaring overhead outlines and a vague light source from the side; put together with her other clues and she was guessing *cave*, but where and how and why . . .

For that, she had no clue at all.

A sharp noise and harsh light made her squint away; in another moment he'd covered and adjusted it; it cast a cool silver-blue spectrum, and her eyes quickly settled out to discover just how right she'd been. A cave, and a small niche to the side of it, filled with the comforts of home. A cotlike bed covered in—okay, she wasn't sure she'd call those furs. One lone rug on the floor for luxury, and several chests and shelves, as neatly kept as she'd always wished she could do, and looking both solid and yet significantly aged. One of them bore a familiar symbol; she gave him a sharp look, confirming it—the same as the flat angled curves of his metal belt buckle. Off to the side, an unexpected rocking chair, all thick torqued wood shaped to suit, the seat woven of flat, wide strips of hide.

She claimed the rocking chair with more authority than she felt, finding the wood smooth and worn and substantial beneath her hand. She crossed her legs and rested her elbows on her knees. "Talk."

He sat on the cot. It was low for him; his knees jutted out. But he looked perfectly at home there. In fact, he looked more at home in this place altogether, more relaxed and yet somehow still more . . . intense, more chafing at the bit. Different than she'd seen him in Albuquerque, or on that plane, or in San Jose, where he'd been ever wary, ever on his toes . . . and possibly just always as though he expected some enemy to come flying at him from any direction.

Maybe he'd been right at that.

He said, "This is my home."

"You live in a cave," she said flatly.

"This is where I met Rhonda Rose," he said, without really answering. Nothing different about that. "She traveled; she found me here. I was . . . recuperating. She spoke highly of you."

"I *knew* it!" Garrie jumped to her feet, paced a few quick, hard steps, and forced herself to sit down again. "She wanted me to think she'd gotten tired, that she released herself to the beyond." She bounced in the chair, unable to help herself. "Oh, I *knew* it! She just didn't want me to know— She just let me think— Is she still here? Can I see her?"

Trevarr shook his head, a little bemused. "She is not."

Garrie burst back up out of the chair in frustration, found herself all the way across the cave-space and in front of him, taking advantage of his low seat to be as tall and even taller than he was. "Dammit, won't you just *tell* me?" She didn't expect him to take her by the hips—not the waist, but his hands spanning lower, familiar and confident and firm enough to draw an instant flush of warmth beneath and between them. Like throwing a switch, and she wondered if he could see the high color on her cheeks in this light and then knew of course he could.

"Garrie," he said, "this is not your world. The things you've seen these past days . . . they are not of your darkside. They are of this world. *Kehar.* You saw the Krevata?"

"I saw the Krevata," she said, too numb at his words to react . . . waiting for more.

"They use the energies of the Winchester House to fuel activities not allowed here . . . and for good reason. I was sent to stop them."

"So you used what Rhonda Rose told you about me, and you used *me.* You thought you could keep me all stupid and ignorant, playing clean-up with pissed-off ghosts while you stopped your bad guys."

"Not stupid," he said. "Never stupid. But telling you . . . would have complicated things."

"Right." She glared at him. "But kissing me, *that* was okay. That didn't complicate anything at all."

He looked away. For the first time ever, he broke away from her gaze. "That was wrong," he said, and tightened his grip on her when she would have jerked away, a proprietary touch. When he looked back at her he'd gone fierce, his eyes so definitely not . . . *say it* . . . human. "But not a mistake."

"We'll see," she said, her voice struggling to make it. "Sklayne said the world was warping. Because of the Krevata?"

"Because of the Krevata," he agreed, but his expression didn't match his mild words; his expression stayed where it was, holding her close. "They gather a type of plasma energy. They siphoned energies from your ghosts to create their portal—that is why they chose that house, with its abundant spirits. They store the energy here in this dimension. It isn't a stable procedure. It has created places where our worlds overlap."

"I dreamt of this place," Garric realized. "Not *this*, exactly . . . but outside." She looked toward the intruding glow of exterior light.

"Not a good place for you," he told her.

She mustered another glare. "As if that really matters. Has any of this been *good* for me? You tried to dress it up—you fed me what I was looking for. You never told me the true risks—you let me bring *my team* in."

"I couldn't risk . . ." he let the thought go unfinished, perhaps wisely realizing there was no good to come of it.

Indeed. "What, giving me the option to help with my eyes wide open? And speaking of eyes, what *is* it with yours?"

"Ah," he said. "My eyes."

"And those marks on your sides and up your chest. Not old tattoos, are they?"

"You saw those," he said, more to himself. Still in that private conversation, he gave himself a little shake; she could see him fighting the impulse to push her aside and explode into movement. That he didn't—that he sat there and let her crowd him, only betraying himself through the tension in his arms and the twitch in his hands—it touched something within her. His next words came with difficulty. "On my world, we have a greater variety of . . . beings. We don't generally intermingle. But sometimes—"

And there it was again. All the previous hints and tidbits and indications, leaping out to ambush her. His eyes might have been a final clue, but there had been others. His strength, his recovery from injury beyond what Sklayne had done for him. His truly impossible need for food. His reaction to the knife, nothing but a silver butter knife. His wild scent, rising with the moment. Tattoos that weren't, a cat companion who wasn't . . .

"You're not human," she blurted. She said it without thinking, with nothing but startled wonder behind it.

He stiffened; his hands tightened on her. "Not," he said, "entirely."

"That medium—there's one trapped in the house with a whole batch of tourists and now Drew and Lucia and Beth . . ." She stopped, shook her shoulders loose. Made herself breathe. "She said Sklayne was a demon."

Tense or not, distressed or not . . . Trevarr's mouth twisted slightly in wry amusement. "Sklayne would have liked that."

"But—"

"No," Trevarr said. "Or maybe yes. It depends on whether you think it valid for the people of your world to define the peoples of Kehar, or whether we may define ourselves." He drew his gaze back to hers with obvious effort. "Maybe yes."

She should have been shocked. Frightened, maybe. Or in complete denial. But instead she could only think of what it must mean in this place, to be *intermingled*. What he must have experienced, to respond to the subject as he did.

As if she hadn't been *other* all her life—and either trying to hide it, or trying to live with the consequences of people who knew she didn't fit in, even if they didn't know why.

"Trevarr," she said, and crowded him even more, framing his face with her hands and pushing back his hair—all loose from its tie, the shorter front strands falling briefly across cheek and brow and eyes, the hidden braids revealed to her touch. His features might have been cut from sharp ice, lines and angles with strength infused. His jaw twitched beneath her palm. She did what often happened around Trevan . . . she stopped thinking and she acted. Barren of words that mattered, she kissed him.

In that first instant, he barely acknowledged her mouth. But then he jerked her closer and kissed her the hell back, his fingers tightening down to the point of mild pain and his mouth acting as though it couldn't get enough of her. Instincts running on high, she took another guess—she gently pushed at him, using her own energy rather than reaching for the unfamiliar breezes of this world.

He stiffened; his hands spasmed on her hips and that gutteral sound, that groan . . . ha. Pure pleasure. Holy cow. He broke away from her; he gave a short laugh, a rare thing. His eyes had gone from pewter to bright, so obviously reactive along with everything else. "I see you figured it out."

"Oh," she said, "I *like* that." All his reactions to her light breezes . . . suddenly made sense.

In one swift motion he swung her off her feet and into his lap, all tensed muscle and knees jutting up from the cot. "I should have known."

"You should have," she agreed. "Since Rhonda Rose apparently told you all about me."

"Be careful," he told her, serious as serious and not talking about Rhonda Rose just yet. "With that. With what you can do. There are things within me that need to stay within."

"Fine." As if she didn't want to pounce on that and ask *what* and *why*—but knowing there were no answers there. Later, that's what. "Now tell me more about Rhonda Rose, please. Facts. Nice clean facts."

"She has nothing to do with this," he said, shifting his hold on her to allow his hand to roam her body. Gently, but obviously a proprietary touch. A man who felt he didn't need to ask.

She didn't think him wrong.

She thought him farking delightful.

"More," she said, and meant of everything.

He shifted her closer, resting his forehead against her brow. He breathed her in. Finally he said, "She stayed with me for a long time. A bad time . . . so I would not be alone. She taught me of your world, among others. Your language. She *showed* me those things."

"And me," Garrie said, stretching into his touch. She might have purred.

"You," he agreed. "She showed me much of you. Very proud, that one. And she then left, and time passed, and the Krevata moved into your world to escape the rules of this one." His hand quieted, resting on her stomach. Owning it. More pensively, he said, "Their portal . . ."

"Right. Destroying the world," Garrie said. She sighed, sliding her feet to the handwoven wool rug beside the cot. "What am I even doing here?"

"Understanding," Trevarr said simply. "Before we go back in. Recovering."

She gave him a sharp look. "Understand me this," she said. "Why you? Why only you?"

That brief expression might have been a grimace. Hard to tell, the way he hid it away so fast. Hard to tell in this light, period. "It is a matter of Blood Honor," he said. "The Krevata left my people—you would call them family—in hurt. A formal exile. This is what I do, this finding runaways outside of Kehar. It is another reason your Rhonda Rose gifted me so. I would have been sent regardless. But this time, if I bring them back . . . my people will survive."

"Survive?" Garrie repeated, startled.

He gave her a dry look. "Kehar is a harsh world, Garrie. Exiles do not last long."

"So you're a . . . what? A bounty hunter. And you're after the Krevata, and there's a big bonus if you get them, because you're feuding and they've messed up your family and this will set things to right."

She thought he might just cover his face with his hands, but he somehow restrained. "Close enough."

"*I owe someone.*" That's what he'd said. "You owe someone," she repeated, out loud this time.

"They took me in when no one else would," he said. "No child manages on this world without family, Garrie. Not even me."

She found herself baffled. "No one would . . ." she said. "But surely—"

"Mixed blood," he said flatly, "seldom survives on Kehar."

She would have reeled, had she been standing. "But—" she said, and then shut her mouth. She got to her feet and walked away from him, staring at the faintly visible entrance to this hollow space . . . breathing deeply of the spicy air. *Kehar.* A place that would have let this mixed-blood child die. A place that would now let his family die. A place of deadly creatures even now crossing over to her own world. A place of energies she'd never even imagined.

"I want to see," she said.

"No," he told her sharply, plenty of alarm there.

She slanted him a look back over his shoulder—*you think?*—and headed straight for the entrance. Or what she thought was the entrance. And she wasn't the least bit surprised when Trevarr took a mere handful of long strides to get there first.

"No," he said, and damned if he didn't sound just the slightest bit panicked.

She considered it. Then she said, "You aren't the boss of me," and stepped neatly around him. Not worried—not yet. She didn't think for a moment that the mouth to this hollow little sanctuary went straight to the outside terrain—and when she slipped through the narrow, sideways passage, she immediately saw she was right.

Trevarr navigated that small space with haste enough to leave rock dust on black leather. "Garrie," he said. "Your energy . . . it is not of this place. This place is safe; it has shields. Out there, they will come to you."

"Ah." She stopped. "So much better than trying to be the boss of me. *Explaining.* Imagine."

He loomed over her, sudden and close and fierce, and Garrie felt the impulse to quail back. She made herself stand her ground, fiercing right back up at him. Somehow she expected it when he took her head between his hands, looking down at her—looking hard and long. When he released her—a little extra emphasis, a little squeeze before he let her go—he said, "Follow me."

Kehar. Strange wild places and feet walking ground unlike any ever touched before and not-quite-human at her side and air she'd never been meant to breathe—

That was for sure. She coughed, coming out into it—thick and heavy and hot, more strongly scented than she'd ever expected. The cough turned into a sneeze, and then a combination of the two, and it was some moments later before she finally stood straight, half hidden in the entrance to the caves—she'd never find her way back without him—to smear a hand across watering eyes and look out onto this world. "one small step for Garrie," she said, "one giant step for Garrie-kind. Oh, for dignity and a tissue . . ."

But here she was, staring out over a nightmare dreamscape that had quickly become familiar, so casual. Taking a step back into Trevarr, only to stick her chin in the air and step forward again. She'd wanted this. Demanded it, in fact. A thin light cast over thick evergreens in lumpy, unfamiliar outlines and interlacing drooping branches, oval seed pods scattered heavily in the lower reaches . . . black fog easing along the forest floor. The terrain itself looked as though rock and earth had argued, winner undecided. It spewed both, jutting outcrops with plenty of sparkle built into the granitelike stone, and dark earth scattered over with damp growth and fungal patches. Branches shuddered as something moved through them, while chittering elsewhere suggested an encounter on the ground. Garrie thought of the energy in her dreamscapes—thought of Trevarr's energy, still lingering within her. Maybe forever lingering within her, for all she knew, changing what she had been into something she hadn't yet figured out.

She went looking.

"Not that," Trevarr said swiftly, and pulled her back into the cave. "Enough, now. You don't know how to protect yourself from what you just called."

"Could I learn?" she asked, more curious than alarmed. Trevarr seemed to think it was enough to sequester her away in here; she'd worry when he did.

"I do not know." He stopped once they were well within the cave. "Did you see enough?"

"Would it matter if I hadn't?"

"Not as much as you would prefer." He gave her a quick, hard kiss—one that seemed to take him by as much surprise as it did her. "But we have to go. The Krevata have caused much damage. I had planned to return to them last night."

"And then came Bob," Garrie said ruefully. "Was that really total coincidence?"

He shook his head. "The chakka was drawn by your energy. You are confection to such as it."

She gave the cave a wary eye—narrow here, with a wildly skewed ceiling and bubbly popcorn formations along the walls. She couldn't help it then—definitely had to ask. "But we're safe here, right?"

"Safe enough." He threaded his way down that natural hallway, and she heard his unspoken words well enough. *If we were going to stay.*

Which they weren't.

No, they'd had their moments of quiet—no one trying to kill them, no one sneaking up on them from the ethereal plane, no bizarre weirdness bombs dropped on their heads.

Must be just about time to charge back out into the fray.

Sklayne scraped claws against old packed dirt. *Stay glass*.

He'd better. The Krevata would rip this form to shreds just for being here.

But staying glass grew more difficult by the moment . . . and so many of those moments had passed since the Garrie had gone between dimensions to find Trevarr.

Sklayne wanted more than claws. Sklayne wanted sturdy scimitars. He wanted big ground-slapping paws, and the ability to slip between states.

Then the semiethereal Krevata would understand what it meant, ripping to shreds.

Trevarr had said *no*. Trevarr had wanted to gather them, to return them to Kehar where they would face tribunal truth-questioning. Only that would satisfy the Blood Honor—not just saving his people, but opening the door for Trevarr to return home unhunted. Sklayne, too.

Exiles.

It didn't have such a nice ring to it, that word.

He definitely wanted scimitars. Right there on the ends of his toes. He glared at them, imagining it—and just that quickly, slipped into visibility. His hair puffed out, spitting sparks. Unseen by preoccupied Krevata, he instantly pulled himself back in to visual silence. *Not yet*.

He pretended to not notice how much effort it took. No effort at all, usually. But trapped here in not-cat by the separation from Trevarr, the bond straining between them . . . the ground, enclosing him away from sun and radiation and all convertible forms . . . they weakened him. Oh brightly burning spark of Sklayne, always hungry.

His toes slipped; he got them back.

Distraction needed. He went hunting the Drew person, out in the halls of the angry house. The Drew person couldn't get lost; he should be back with the others by now. But the tug of the Drew person was nowhere near the ballroom.

Sklayne pulled his awareness in, found himself not far from the cellar door. *Drew person!* Tucked into a corner, such a small fetal ball for a tall person of lanky arms and legs. Ghosts beset him, and if the Drew person couldn't see them, he still knew of them. Whipped into a kinetic frenzy, they lashed his skin with heat welts; they released snapping blows against his exposed shoulder and sides, making him flinch.

"You guys are in *so* much trouble!" he cried—but he did it without lifting his head, and when the house rumbled around him with such vigor that the ceiling overhead sprouted a thick crack, he didn't so much as glance. His voice came thinner than usual, higher than usual. Fear rolled around the hallway, inciting the ghosts to greater effort.

They'd learned from the Krevata, it seemed. Semiethereal, skilled in applying the effects of one plane against the creatures of another.

The Krevata had to go.

Sklayne wanted to tell the Drew person that the Garrie had done well, even if he only now knew that they were gone from his awareness. Altogether gone. Leaving Sklayne alone in this room.

But not fearful. Not fighting to stay hidden, the only chance of survival. Not bereft and alone. Not helpless to do anything for the Drew person. *Not.*

Sklayne left the Drew person muttering imprecations and threats of dissolution upon Garrie's return, and he looked for the Lucia person. She might have calmed the ghosts; she had the medium. Between them, if they'd talked their way out—

But the Lucia person was still in the ballroom. The Lucia person threw herself against those walls, bloodying her fingers, clawing at that buffed and gleaming wood, howling in rage—unable to resist what the ghosts threw at her. The next moment she sobbed with their frustration, screamed with their fear . . .

Only the Beth person tried to help her, pleading with her, pleading with the ghosts. The imperious medium seemed dazed. Or comatose. Or simply hiding behind her closed eyes and murmuring lips while the Lucia person slammed her own head against the wall, so unexpected and fast that the Beth person shrieked in dismay and leaped for her, grappling with her to stop it from happening again. And Sklayne watched in dismay, unable to do anything for her. Still alone in the basement.

But not fearful. Not fighting to stay hidden, the only chance of survival. Not bereft and alone. Not helpless to do anything for the Lucia person. *Not.*

Scimitars. Slashing through ethereal and corporeal. Slashing through Krevata. Sklayne closed his eyes tightly and imagined them while the ground shook beneath him and the city cried out around him and chakka broke through into the streets and raged unopposed.

The Krevata had to go.

Oh, soon.

Very soon.

22

Back inside his bat cave, Trevarr dropped his satchel on the cot and pulled out a few select items, moving so swiftly in the low light that Garrie couldn't begin to follow his movement. "I can see why you need the sunglasses," she observed. "And the eye thing—how did you make me think they were normal for so long?"

He didn't even hesitate, distributing things among his duster pockets. A high inside pocket, a low inside pocket, one right to hand on the outside, none of them truly visible as pockets once he removed his hand from them. "It is a manipulation," he said. "A use of energy."

Memory flashed before her mind's vision—her insistence on seeing his eyes in the ice cream shop, that feeling he was hiding something. Boy, had she been right—and it hadn't been the color of them at all. That faint wash of energy . . . he'd put his mingled-blood eyes away behind innocuous round pupils, that's what. Just as he'd done after flashing them at that poor terrified pickpocket at the airport. Subtle when he wanted to be, for sure.

Toys hidden away, he closed the leather flap and placed the satchel at the head of the bed, and there was something about the way he did it—a reverence—that made her say, "Those things are important to you."

He gave her a sideways glance, a startling flash of the silvered eyes she'd only just been pondering. "They are everything. They are my history and my future and my honor. My people's honor. If I don't bring back the Krevata . . ." He didn't complete that thought. Instead he reached inside his coat, giving the inexplicable impression of a man reaching for a sword.

And damned if he didn't come up with one.

Not a long one, not a great whopping two-handed blade . . . more like a machete with style and a knuckle guard. But an unmistakable sword.

"You must be kidding," Garrie blurted. "Where the hell were you keeping *that*?"

"*Lukkas*," Trevarr said. "An old blade, also of my people. It is fitting that I use it now."

"But where did it *come*—" She stopped, trying to take in all the significance of it at once. "Waitaminute. You're going in with a *sword*?"

"I need to take them alive, but I must be alive to do it." He gave her a grim look. "Your breezes will not affect them; your world needs you for what you do, not for what I have come to do."

She skipped over the part where he seemed prepared to take them back into the middle of the Krevata and returned to the immediate heart of the matter, going up to him to pat the coat—for it should have fallen lumpy and misshapen from his shoulders instead of sweeping gracefully to swirl at his calves. She patted where she'd seen him store the items from the satchel, and she patted where there should be a scabbard to protect the coat, and she ran her hands along his sides—feeling only the warmth of his body and the lean form beneath, the frame of him a little too close to the surface. "Oh, come *on*," she said. And "But I saw what you *eat*," as if either of those two statements truly made sense without context.

Trevarr didn't seem to have any trouble with them. "Take care with this coat," he said. "The pockets are . . . *enhanced*. And I was not prepared for the trouble with the food. Something is missing there."

"You're kidding," she said. "All that food, and you're . . . what, *starving*?"

"Take this," he said, skipping any kind of response as if she wasn't going to notice, and removing the all-colors stone from one of the pockets that had patted flat an instant earlier, handing it to her. "It is called an Eye. The moment we return to the portal room, you must run."

"But—"

"No," he said, his eyes as hard as she'd ever seen, his features matching. He was rock. "This is for me to do."

"But—"

His hand closed around her arm. "Tell me you will run. Find your people and control the spirits in that place, make it safe for all."

"Fine, I'll run like a baby-girl," Garrie snapped, finally getting a word in. "*But*—I don't know what you expect me to do with this thing."

"The Eye?" He looked startled, if only briefly. "Hold it." He reached into his coat with his free hand, came up with a shorter blade—one that might have done service as a military knife if it hadn't had that strong sweep of the edge, the blade itself covered with shimmering watermark patterns. "My hands are full."

"So I see," she said dryly. "But—"

"Like this," he said, and stood behind her as he had before, crossing his arm across her upper chest as he had before—except this time she held the Eye before her and felt stupid about it.

At least, until he fed energy right through her, jarring her bolt upright and stiff and making her forget to breathe. Because even if the energy this time went *through* instead of *into,* it nonetheless flooded her with warmth and heady instant fullness of being—and then wonder, as the Eye instantly sucked it all up, Trevarr holding her close and warm and the knife in his hand so close to her skin and yet no threat at all, his knuckles resting against her collarbone.

"Run," he whispered in her ear, voice gone hoarse with its low and gritty tone.

She didn't even have time to reassure him before the stone became weightless in her hand, flushing out into colors—passing through her, passing through him . . . enfolding them both.

Maybe because she knew what to expect this time . . . maybe because his energy had come through her, grounding her to the process . . .

Maybe because it was just too cool to ignore.

Whatever the reason, Garrie didn't close her eyes; she didn't scream. She watched in fascination as the colors shifted around them, the starry black spots freckling and growing to suck away the light.

She might have clutched Trevarr's arm. Just a little.

The darkness fell away, shredding to make way for a new reality. The basement room, right back where she'd started. No sign of Sklayne, Krevata everywhere, the stone back in her hand and radiating warmth just the far side of pleasant.

Trevarr released her. He *pushed* her.

And she ran, because she'd promised. She skirted the burbling patch of sucks-life *nothing* that had caught her up in the first place, she dodged the two startled Krevata just turning away from the floor portal, and she dove past the equally startled Krevata watching the door.

And then she *stopped* running. She caught herself on the hallway corner as she passed it, and she slingshotted herself back toward the portal room. She'd done as promised and now she'd do what she wanted.

But she didn't go in, not with full battle under way. She'd only distract Trevarr; she couldn't risk it. Even if she'd never seen that kind of speed before, even if her jaw dropped at the way he used the blades—strike and block and slash, always in motion, keeping three of the surprisingly skilled Krevata at bay while two of them worked frantically at the portal, all of them too preoccupied to go invisible or even partly visible. Metal clashed against metal; metal clanged against stone. Trevarr's eyes burned silver-cold and bright, his face fierce in what seemed like his very own light.

She forgot to breathe. Again.

A reddish-buff cat popped into existence in the corner, yeowling an emphatic exclamation. ::*Free!*:: He poofed out into a faintly reddish-buff patch of amorphous inexplicability, emanating highly ticklish waves of shimmering energy—and then he pounced, a fierce high-pitched growl in Garrie's ears and mind as he enveloped the nothingness that had once swallowed her whole. There was a brief tussle; the nothingness imploded, sucking a belch of energy from the room and then spitting it back out. Sklayne bounced away, hitting the wall as inexplicable bare color and brief claws, bouncing to the floor as cat—rolling to a stop at Garrie's feet with his fur sparking and his whiskers standing on end and his expression nothing but satisfied smug.

The Krevata at the portal took up a choral howl, full of juicy grunt and snort curses. *Portal priests.* They cast vile glares at Sklayne, but the portal demanded attention, spitting black lavalike sunspots that sent the Krevata scrambling for the leather trunk not far away. They scooped out brightly colored stones that Garrie now knew weren't actually stones; oval, shaped into a shallow bowl . . . pretty trinkets.

Garrie knew better than that, too. She wasn't at all surprised when the Krevata arranged his awkward limbs just so, held the oval stone just so, and poised himself next to the portal with his partner to watch his back. There, with Trevarr fighting desperately at his back—*a parry, a strike, dark blood on his knuckles and a wicked nick above one eye*—and Garrie staring in stupified wonder from the doorway, he held the oval out over the portal. Closer, closer . . .

Not just any sunspot, not just any oval. The two met with a snap of power, snarling over the sound of battle. The Krevata achieved instant erection, colorfully emphasized; he jerked with it, paying no apparent attention to himself. Nor did Garrie, not once the earth growled an instant response to the new connection, a rising sound as the ground escalated toward full-blown earthquake. Garrie lost her balance, grabbed the wall to keep herself upright, and braced herself.

It was, she realized, the same position the Krevata had taken up. They'd known to expect this. They'd known they were tearing her world apart.

They just didn't care.

Above them, the house gave a mighty crack; bits of debris rained down. *Do something, then.*

But she didn't have to. Trevarr broke through the line held by the three he fought, slapped aside the half-raised blade of the portal guard-priest, and slammed into the back of the priest with the oval. Camel-like lips had the merest instant to form an *oh!* of surprise, beady black eyes opened wide—and then suddenly the Krevata hit fast-forward frantic, limbs flailing, colorful erection bobbing; he hung suspended over the portal in a Wile E. Coyote moment of impossibility before it sucked him in with audible force. He disappeared into the black power without so much as a splash.

Instantly, the earth calmed. Instantly, Sklayne shouted, ::Nonono don't *kill* them,:: although Garrie had thought it a perfectly good solution to the situation. Rip *her* world apart, would they?

But just as fast, the Krevata turned on Trevarr. Even as the second priest ditched his sword to grab up another oval from the leather trunk, taking up where his partner had left off, the others wielded fury at Trevarr—and Trevarr had left himself exposed, badly positioned and completely surrounded.

They could have killed him, then, had they come at

him all at once. Instead they batted at him—a pummel-punch that sent him from one into the blow from another; a lightning-swift kick that spun him to the ground. The knife clattered away; somehow he still held onto the sword Lukkas.

::Nonono don't *get* killed!:: Sklayne cried, adding a good yowl of emphasis. The second priest positioned his oval collecting device and woke the portal again, moving frantically—and Garrie could see why. For all he drew through that gateway, for all the intensity of the earth's complaints instantly escalated into tooth-rattling rumbles, the edges of the portal had tightened up slightly. The round puddle of darkness in the floor wasn't quite as round as it had been before. Bereft of the sucks-life, the thing was shrinking.

Garrie looked at the knife with some longing. A fierce longing—but not enough nerve and the hard knowledge that she would only make things worse. Staggering in the epicenter of the world's anger, she looked at Sklayne and demanded, "Do something!"

And Sklayne said nothing.

"You're his bond-partner! Help him—"

::I can't!:: Sklayne turned a glare of the highest power on her, green eyes glittering with the same sparks his coat shed. ::*His* fault! *He* did it!::

Barely coherent, clearly beside himself. Literally unable to help.

She'd promised to run. And she *had*. But now she was back, and she had no weapons, she had no skills, she had no strength—she had no breezes that would affect them, dammit.

Trevarr barreled straight into one of the Krevata, shoulder to gut. He fumbled at his coat, staggering back, his hand bleeding and swollen and obviously not working quite right, and before he could find the pocket he wanted, another of the Krevata grabbed him up from behind and swung him into a wall with a thump that would have shaken the foundations had not the portal activity already been doing just that. "Stop it!" Garrie screamed at them, complete nonsense and she knew it and still couldn't keep her mouth shut. "Leave him alone!"

No breezes to affect them.

Oh, but wait. No breezes to *hurt* them. She couldn't dissolve them, she couldn't shove them around . . .

But she could damned well *affect* them. And it might be all the break Trevarr needed.

Supposing he could even still think. He'd slid down against the wall like a limp cat, dark and powerful and altogether battered; now he came to his hands and knees, Lukkas still loosely held in one hand, loose hair hanging over his face—but not so much that she couldn't see his expression, finding him dazed, that predatory light gone from his eyes. His face swelled around one eye and cheek; one arm didn't quite seem to work right.

She could damned well affect them, but . . .

She wasn't sure it would be worth the price he'd pay. She wasn't even sure he could afford to pay it.

::Ysss,:: Sklayne said, a hiss that went beyond language. He braced against the movement of the earth; beside the portal, the priest leaped into a happy dance, oblivious to the unstable ground and the groaning house overhead and the bits and pieces of house now raining down upon them. The black sunspots danced with him, leaping over the still narrowing mouth of the pond and exploding in silent bursts of power over the surface of the coruscating darkness. The oval stone seemed to have a life of its own, shuddering in time with the Krevata's hooded erection, the metal latticework and colors glowing with preternatural intensity.

Not that the other Krevata paid attention to any of it. They closed in on Trevarr, reaching for him. Arrogant bastards, they were playing with him now. He raised his poorly functioning arm in a futile attempt to ward them off, and Garrie snapped.

The Krevata had forgotten, maybe. Garrie couldn't hurt them, but . . .

::Yesss!:: Sklayne cried. ::Do this thing!::

With the angry, turbid storms of energy in this house, she had all the resources she could possibly ask for. She opened herself to it, drawing so hard and fast that breezes whispered through the halls, stirring the corporeal world with the power of her touch. One great big inhalation of power, harvested from the roiling currents around them.

Sklayne gave her a startled look, his hair standing on end and his ears flattening back, and yowled, ::Nonono changed my mind!:: but too late for that. She slung power into the embattled room—slung it so hard it bounced back and mixed and roiled around.

She got their attention, all right.

The portal sputtered with enthusiasm, spewing a gout of black plasmic energy as its borders widened out again. The earth shook around them, splitting the far wall in two. The Krevata grunted and gestured and straightened, every line of their bodies shouting of startled glee. Yes, every single line.

But Trevarr cried out in surprise, an anguished shout; his body twisted and fell out from beneath him. Writhing there, beyond all endurance, his shoulders pinned and his back arching and his lingering cry of pain nothing human at all.

"No!" Garrie wailed. "No, not like that! Trevarr!" It shouldn't have been that hard, not that bad. He'd handled it before. "I'm sorry! I'm sorry!"

::Waiwaiwaiwai!:: Sklayne wailed, as blasted as any of them, and he ran blind full speed across the hallway to hit the cement block wall and crumple into a boneless heap on the spot.

The Krevata didn't care. Not about Trevarr, not about the portal spreading across the floor—if you didn't count the fellow who was now gathering up energy as fast as he could, whimpering, his body quite clearly torn between orgasmic influences.

The Krevata exchanged a single unified gesture and charged at her, a lumbering stampede of face and nose and colorful bobbing parts. Sklayne was still a heap, Trevarr had collapsed, chest heaving, hands clawing aimlessly at air and floor. Garrie channeled Lucia and yelped, "¡Aiee, caray!" and did the only thing she could think of, which was to dive *for* the three Krevata, as small as she could be, hip slamming into the doorway on one side, into hard leathery skin over honkin' hard muscle and bone on the other. She squirmed the rest of the way through on her hands and toes, falling forward when she broke free and scrambling ahead even then.

By the time the Krevata got themselves turned around in that low hallway, Garrie's hand had closed around the rough leather-wrapped hilt of Trevarr's sword; by the time they returned, she'd climbed to her unsteady feet beside him, legs braced and heavy sword drooping.

The Krevata crowded at the doorway, their swords drooping, too. All of them. A mistake to call them stupid or easily fooled; Garrie wouldn't make it. They'd responded to instinct, overwhelmed by what she'd thrown at them. She didn't think they'd do it again.

Besides, she had nowhere to go. No convenient coal chutes, no dumbwaiters, just an oddball little room in the back corner of the basement, built taller than most, its original function lost and its current function not doing anyone any good at all.

::Bad idea,:: Sklayne said, a loopy and dazed version of his usual mind-voice.

"Do something," Garrie told him, a desperate and

high-pitched version of her usual throat-voice. "Do something *now*."

::Told you. Can't.::

"You said you couldn't *hurt* them," she corrected him, eyeing the distance to the bench, to the satchel, to the portal, and to the Krevata priest frantically harvesting the black plasmic energy—hunting everything that might help, finding nothing. Beside her on the floor, Trevarr made a rough noise. "Listen to him! Do something!"

::No need,:: Sklayne said, and though he sounded stronger, his voice had gone dry, dry, dry.

"Plenty of need!" Garrie said, ascending to a squeak. "Need everywhere!" She hefted the sword up, trying to look as fierce as Trevarr. Lifting her lip in a little snarl, just in case it helped.

::Facial tick,:: Sklayne told her, the whiskers of him alone visible at the edge of the doorway. ::Not fierce.::

"Shut up!" she cried. Trevarr groaned again, rolling over on his side, wood smoke gone to ash. "If you're not going to help, you should just shut up!"

::In there with their portal. Need my help why?::

Okay, maybe not a bad point. The portal had reacted to her energy. Not in a *good* way, but then . . . she'd thrown a great big heaving ghost ball at it. She'd blown a huge gust down its proverbial throat. What if she . . .

Inhaled.

"There's a limit," she told Sklayne, and she didn't know if she was warning him or pleading with him.

::Plenty of need!:: Sklayne said, mimicking her.

"I'm going to kick your furry little ass," Garrie said, a pretty bold statement considering Sklayne was on the freedom side of the Krevata and she was trapped as they closed in around her, their bold noses sniffing out the details of her.

::Live first,:: Sklayne advised.

Garrie cursed under her breath with great feeling.

Trevarr made an uncoordinated attempt to find his feet, aiming for a crouch. She put a hand on his shoulder, felt him fairly vibrating with the pain she'd put him in—*again*—on top of what they'd already done to him.

Inhale.

She targeted the area around the portal. Everything she'd thrown at it, however inadvertently, she now took back. The portal hissed and sputtered a protest; the Krevata priest sputtered along with it. The others gibbered in confusion quickly turning to alarm. All those disk ears went flat at once, all those tremendous camel noses wrinkled along their significant lengths, arms gesturing wildly and other body parts in complete retreat.

She *inhaled* again, and the portal shrank noticeably, the earth rumbling around it. And again, and the living black substance retreated, sullen and dull. And again, but her head reeled and her chest felt stuffy and in truth it was hard to breathe at all. "Whoa," she said, clamping her hand a little tighter on Trevarr's shoulder.

The Krevata looked at the little punctuation mark that was left of their fine strong illicit plasma pool, and at the stunned priest staggering from the loss of that energy influx, and they decided. They snarled in gutteral unison, raised their blades . . . they began to stalk. Slow-mo and deliberate.

This is gonna hurt.

She dared a quick glance at the minimized portal. If she could pull in just a little more energy . . .

Bursting at the seams already. Lightheaded, barely connected to ground, swaying. Her ears buzzed, her skin tingled, and specks danced in her vision. She barely felt Trevarr shuddering beneath her hand, and she realized quite suddenly that even if she could do this thing, even if she could close the portal, there was nothing she could do with any of this energy to save herself. To save Trevarr.

Sklayne . . . she thought, pure pleading desperation, braced against the weight of Lukkas and the ground shuddering beneath her feet. A pebbly bit of something pinged off her shoulder.

::Can't,:: he told her, misery personified—standing behind the Krevata, tail lashing, completely exposed and completely ignored.

Then at least distract *them!*

Silence. Either he couldn't, or he wouldn't, or he didn't know how. But with slow-motion Krevata gurgling gently to themselves, advancing in a slow, stylized form, she didn't have time to waste on him. It was a dance, she thought, with gestures and blades held just so and synchronized movements and complete and utter focus on . . .

Her.

No, somehow she had to swallow down the energy already in her system and take in what remained, closing the portal. And she had to do it without releasing what she'd already gathered.

With the portal closed, the city would be safe.

With the cul-de-sac gone, the spirits here would settle.

Lucia and Drew would escape this place with its howling spirits and its shuddering earth.

And if she couldn't do it? Everyone would die. Even Trevarr's people, lost in exile when Trevarr didn't return with the Krevata.

"I'm sorry," she told him, her strained voice barely audible. "I mean, I'll try, but . . . I'm sorry."

Krevata feet shuffled against packed dirt, moving in unison. The gibbering sounded more like a chant now, broken only by the frantic snuffling from the priest.

All that energy. She couldn't let them have that, either.

"Well," she said to no one in particular. "I *was* looking for excitement."

She reached for the portal. She *inhaled.*

The Krevata cried out and rushed her.

::*Mowaiowaiowai!*:: Sklayne dashed through the middle of them, all his energies held tightly to himself, his feline form winding sinuously between their feet. Giving her the space to draw in the power, giving her what little chance she had—

And Garrie hiccuped on internalized ethereal breezes. *Farking hell!* She lost a bubble of energy from her overstuffed self, energy that slipped away and splashed gently against the walls, the Krevata, the portal. Against Trevarr. The portal sputtered, the Krevata stumbled around Sklayne, and Trevarr . . .

Trevarr lifted his head. His little shudders grew suddenly audible, until Garrie realized with numbing shock that he hadn't been trembling, shivering, or shuddering at all.

He'd been growling.

She took a dazed step away.

The Krevata stuttered to a stop.

Sklayne poofed out into something vague with more claws than usual, poofed back into the cat, and ran between Trevarr and the Krevata. ::Nonono, don't kill! Thinkthinkthink!::

Garrie didn't get the impression that Trevarr was doing any such thing. Pupils slitted cat-narrow, eyes silvered bright and glowing . . . when he stood he seemed *bigger* somehow; more than he'd been. The backs of his hands bore the same markings that had been along his sides, darker and distinct and she could have sworn there was even texture. He bared his teeth in a terrible warning, and damned if he didn't suddenly have fangs. Not saber-toothed tiger fangs, but canines and secondary canines all the same. His features had hardened, from strong and angled to something harsher, almost leonine.

And they held none of the regard she'd seen in them so recently, none of the tempered strength.

They held blood lust.

::Thinkthinkthink!:: Sklayne pleaded.

There was no thought in those eyes.

He had only the knife. He had only one arm in working order. He was up against four of Krevata, each of whom outweighed him, who would have towered over him had they been able to stretch to full height.

He shouted a battle cry and charged into the midst of them.

"You, um, want Lukkas?" Garrie asked the very thin air where he'd been standing. "Because, you know, I'm doing so much good with it?"

::Stophim stophim stophim!:: Sklayne squirted out from the tangle of them, staggering slightly.

She gestured at the sweeping blade of the short sword, frustrated. "Because, *you know,* I'm doing so much good with it?"

::Some other way!:: Sklayne reared up on his hind legs, stopping himself just short of putting a pleading paw on her leg. In the scramble, metal clashing but the fighting too close and dirty for much of it, Trevarr snarled a wordless curse and black-red blood spattered the floor. He dumped a Krevata over his back, slammed his elbow into the nose of another. ::If he kills them he can't return them!::

"Oh, shee-it," Garrie said, truly understanding those rules for the first time. Not dead or alive, this particular bounty. And the only weapon she had would do nothing more than distract the Krevata—give them an instant Viagra effect at most. *Even as it took Trevarr down again.* And so she targeted the only option left. "The portal." *But I can't—*

"Mow," Sklayne said, an unhappy sound. Agreement. And then he did put a paw on her leg, and he said into her mind, ::Permission?:: Trevarr leaped at a Krevata, right inside the creature's guard, plunging his knife deeply into its nose. It wailed in agony. Sklayne's mind-voice took on a frantic note. ::Permission!::

Permission, *what*? "I'm trusting you," she warned him, implied permission of a sort. Two Krevata hauled Trevarr off the third and slung him hard against a wall. Garrie expected *crunch* and she expected blood and maybe even a little gore, but as Trevarr slid down, he also flailed out, already struggling to his feet. "But hurry!"

She barely noticed it at first, so gentle was Sklayne's touch. But suddenly she didn't feel so full, not so light-headed. Sparks grew at the ends of Sklayne's reddish hairs; his tail puffed out to twice its normal size. On the other side of the tight room, Trevarr took a hard blow to the cheek from a sword knuckle guard and laughed it off.

Not the sound of a man in control.

Garrie asked Sklayne, "Then why didn't *you*—"

::Different,:: Sklayne said with impatience, not waiting for her to ask him why he hadn't bled energy off the portal this way. *::Permission.::*

The priest reached for another collection device. Trevarr skidded across the floor on his shoulders, flipped back to his feet, and charged into the fray. One of the warriors slammed against the wall, gone limp; the contents of his belly flopped out onto the floor. Sklayne made a moaning, yowling noise. ::No breaking them!::

Garrie *inhaled*. The portal shrunk back down; the priest looked wildly around until he spotted her, reaching for his sword. She reeled back, percolating with energy, her vision all gray and sparkly.

::Slower!:: Sklayne said, sounding frantic. ::Can't help . . . already full. Took the *sucks-life* door.::

Swallowed it whole, as she dimly recalled. No wonder he had indigestion. But she couldn't go any slower.

Once that priest reached her . . . she had to be done with it by then, the portal closed—or it would never be closed at all.

She thought she'd found the wall at her back. She thought she'd slid down it, her shirt not sliding quite as easily, leaving skin bare and exposed. Her spine against the wall picked up the heady rumbling of the ground, a disturbance so deeply under way that reducing the portal hadn't calmed it. Maybe closing the portal wouldn't even do it. Maybe it was just too late.

Priest, looming large. Garrie took a deep breath, focused on the portal, and breathed it all in. Every bit of the energy keeping that abomination open, she took into herself. Every bit. Surely it was closed. Surely. *Oh, wow, man.* Talk about a trip. Disconnected from her arms and legs, swirling through her torso, head floating several feet above her body . . . Priest's arm drawn back, ready to strike, and Sklayne's distant mind-voice crying, ::Run! Crawl! *Do*!:: as his claws flashed out, lightning fast, to slash across her ankle.

She felt that. It woke the reality in her, and the fear, and the crystal-clear image of the Krevata looming over her, intoning some camel-nose gibberish. *No room to move . . .* Not even an extra inch in which to wield the unfamiliar sword still in her hand. And it seemed like a very, very good time to scream.

Very, said her distant memory in her own voice, exquisitely dry and pinpointing the exact moment that had led to this one, *only weakens your meaning.*

Better just to scream—not even sure if she'd done it, only knowing she couldn't hold so much as a whisper of additional energy and she'd run out of time and Trevarr was letting them rip him to shreds because of what she'd done to him and even if he lived he'd never get home because he was killing the Krevata, too—

::*Listen!*:: Sklayne shouted in the background, not to her. ::Listen to her!::

The priest struck. Reflex saved her—Garrie shrieked and dove between his awkward legs, torquing herself around to bring the sword down on his hamstring—a hard impact, the grim slice of sharp metal through flesh, and the leg gave way above her.

Suddenly not such a good idea.

She had a mere instant of *oh, shit* before the Krevata fell on her and rolled aside. Ton-of-bricks, obliterating her breath, her thought, and her half-formed cry of alarm. The energy broke through her control, broke wild—flaring into white nuclear hot heat, eating her up inside.

::The Garrie!:: Sklayne shouted, still not to her. ::*Come back!* Listen to the Garrie!::

White sparklies mixed with fade-to-white. Inner whirlies wrapped up with pain, an inside-out ice cream cone swirl of flavors covered in one musky, stinky Krevata who writhed beside her. She slapped at the floor, groping for freedom, thinking, *Tell me! Just tell me if I did it!* Tell me if my friends are all right . . . tell me if Trevarr will make it home . . . *tell me!*

The weight, too profound. The Krevata, blade still in hand, wrenching around to bury it in her. Sklayne, yeowling terribly. And all of it fading, the foreign energy within her turned consuming, the whole of it too much for one small person of much power to bear.

Sklayne couldn't hurt the Krevata. Couldn't even act against them. Nothing but watching. *Not right.* Watching while the Krevata priest floundered around beside the Garrie, his ruined leg flailing so he couldn't regain his balance, portal energy convulsing inside her.

Not right.

Trevarr couldn't hear him. Raging in a different kind of convulsion, the uncontrollable aspects of his being released—the part of him that others always feared. Two essences in the same person . . . made him strong, gave him skills neither halves of his lineage could match, but always the danger that the war between them would go wrong.

So wrong.

Sklayne couldn't reach through. He shouted as if at rock. Feral, raging, damaged rock.

Not allowed to help Trevarr. *Not right.* Not allowed to help the Garrie. *Not right.*

Sklayne gathered himself, buzzing with energy, buzzing with fear. Defy the geas shackles, then what? How hard, then?

But how much harder for the Garrie? The Garrie, who burned to save the world.

Do it. Risk it.

Sklayne leaped. High and strong and true, feet reaching, claws extending to land and latch.

Right on Trevarr's shoulder.

It was red-black with slick blood and clear Krevata gore, but not immune to those claws—nor the ear to that feline yowl. So sensitive, those ears, when the uncontrolled part of Trevarr took over. The eyes, the patterning of feathery scales along torso and arms and shoulders—diamond-hard protection. More quickness, more strength . . . less thinking. Much less thinking.

Truly, no thinking at all.

But plenty of hearing. Plenty of *feeling.*

Trevarr spun, trying to dislodge him; he slashed a Krevata forearm open along the way. They weren't stylized in their movement anymore, those Krevata. Stupid, they'd been, to underestimate either Trevarr or the Garrie, so full of *we win* that they hadn't killed Trevarr when they'd had the easy chance. So full of energy and theft and guile that their brains didn't quite connect the big picture.

Krevata by definition.

They realized it now, with one of them dying on the floor, all of them sorely wounded, the priest floundering around at the wall and the portal so threatened. All they wanted now was to get away from this madman.

Sklayne gave them their wish.

Sort of.

He dug his claws in deep, hind legs scrambling along Trevarr's back. And while he yowled out loud, with his mind-voice he cried, *::Feel the Garrie!::* and he threw himself open as a conduit, ramming the Garrie's blind-white pain and incoherently fading thoughts straight into Trevarr. Unable, yet, to touch anything of Trevarr himself, but after so many years . . . *::Feel the Garrie!::* There, the Garrie's terror for Trevarr, her wild need to know him safe—her wild need for his presence.

Trevarr faltered. He flooded Sklayne with confusion; with dim and abrupt awareness of how much his arms suddenly weighed and how rubbery his legs had become and the overwhelming realization that he'd left the Garrie alone against the priest. Sklayne jumped lightly to the floor as Trevarr whirled around to her, the Krevata instantly rallying at his back.

Now the hard part.

Sklayne . . . not allowed to hurt. Not allowed to act. But threat with no intent? Startle with no sharp behind the claw? Maybe.

He bounded at the clustered Krevata, stiff-legged. He whirled in midair, front paws spread wide, claws extruded—grabbing hugely at invisible air-prey, face snarling horribly. Bounce, leap, twist, roll. It held them, if only for an instant. Long enough for Trevarr to drag his sorry Keharian ass to the floundering priest and clamp a hand around the arm about to strike the Garrie. To wrench at the sword there, yanking the priest off-balance and away and instantly following through with the sword, ramming it like a spear through the priest's shoulder.

Long enough for Trevarr's regret and fear and oh

something new, deep and tearing, to rush through Sklayne and leave him reeling with it.

But not much longer.

Sklayne gathered himself, hiss and spit and spark, *keep them back* and leap into the air with paws armed and outstretched, a wild feint. If it went beyond what was allowed . . .

The geas struck back, a deep disemboweling slash of pain; he dropped out of the air as if gravity had suddenly discovered him, crouching stunned and bewildered. Only a smallish cat shape after all, the spark blown out of him.

One of the Krevata kicked him across the room.

"*Atreya*." Deep voice, that. With the rumble behind it. With a catch behind it. Pain everywhere, hers and his and Sklayne's. Just that, and the floating inability to ground to the world, the distinct impression that she would fly apart into a million disparate pieces—dissipated, just as she did to problematic ghosts.

Problematic Garrie. That was her, all right.

"Sah, *atreya*," he told her, his head bent close to hers and his arms sliding around her in. He lifted his head to snap something in an unfamiliar language—speaking to the Krevata. Warning them. *Not all dead, then.* Was that good or bad? He set something on her stomach and stroked the side of her face. His breathing wasn't good; his arm didn't move right. His words seemed to come with effort. No longer controlled by the darkness, but still battling it. "Hold on, *atreya*. We have yet to finish this."

The portal, she wanted to ask him, but her thoughts were in no way connected to her mouth. Barely connected to her body. She pointed at it, but if her hand so much as twitched in response, she'd have been surprised.

He must have seen it. Somehow. Those keen eyes.

He lay his hand over hers. "Closed," he said, to her immense relief. She'd done it. She'd killed that portal dead. Surely that's what he meant when he added emphatically, *"Gone."* And then he picked up whatever he'd put on her stomach and his body thrummed with tension and his voice, when he spoke, had darkened again. "Now," he told the Krevata, for all they might understand him. "Now we finish this."

Mistake.

Big mistake, to have gotten caught out in this form. In this body. Unable to switch before hitting the wall.

Broken again. Stunned and powerless. Red-buff fur piled together in no particular order, punished by geas and damaged by foot.

Easy to drift out and see beyond. There he found the halls in an uproar, cyclonic winds driven by ghostly rage and retribution. Spirits riding the winds, scraping the walls with kinetic energy, raising welts in wallpaper and scorch marks on painted plaster, leaving smoke trails behind them.

The Drew person huddled in his corner, battered and marked and crying out, spirits piling atop one another in their efforts to reach him.

The Lucia person flung her head back and screamed, her remaining voice little more than a creaky whisper in a room literally dripping of ghostly disdain. The tour group huddled off to the side, screaming over the convulsing body of a child; the medium rocked back and forth on the organ seat, her eyes rolled back in her head and her fingers digging into her own arms. "They die, they die, they die," she chanted, a moan of words strung together until they barely had meaning, the house jerking and groaning around them, ghosts shrieking in the just-audible, edging on ultrasonic range from all corners of the room, and one barely formed little girl ghost crying, "Please! Please!"

The house began to lose its battle, dropping ceiling in the quake-damaged section, cracking walls throughout Black fog leaked from the cracks, filling the house with new stench; the swarm of beetles scuttled from those cracks and began hunting—scenting prey and heading for it.

For the tour group. The ballroom. The Lucia person. The Beth person. Some of them peeling off to find the Drew person.

Not that any of them would notice, once the chakka found a host. Or the swamp chimera broke through the door and started crunching bones. Or any of the things suddenly emerging from the connection between two dimensions gone twisted and wrong.

Sklayne pulled himself back. Effort, that took. Back here, the Krevata priest pinned to the ground by his own sword driven deep, tears staining his down-furred face. Here, one left dead. Far too late to bring them all back alive.

And back here, Trevarr, almost himself—the eyes still full of unearthly glow, but that happened sometimes. Teeth still a little fangsome, but that, too, happened on occasion. The feather-scales receding, faded marks on the backs of his wrists. His knife close at hand; the sword gently recovered from the Garrie's limp hand.

Still alive, the Garrie. Limp, that one hand twitching as though it wanted something, eyelids flickering. So completely bursting with energy that it blurred her edges.

Sklayne gave a mental squint. Unless she really *was* blurring at the edges . . .

Help her.

That's what he'd told Trevarr, and Trevarr had used it, focused on it . . . pulled himself back from the brink of undoing. But Trevarr helped the Garrie simply by being there. By touching her. By murmuring his words to her while he prepared the Gatherer.

Sklayne could not help her so easily. Especially not from here . . . and this body didn't seem likely to go anywhere else. Every last bit of power she'd given him, gone—slammed out of him by the geas, leaving this body as vulnerable as any to the damage it had taken. *Bodies die.*

The surviving Krevata made no attempt to flee, or to reach for their weapons. Disconsolate, broken . . . draped around their compatriots. Except that one. Staggery, standing there, reaching in his belt pouch for a . . .

Where had the Krevata acquired a *gun*?

There was none such on Kehar. Too easy to tamper into explosiveness. But there was no one here to tamper, not with Sklayne in his furry heap and the Garrie in her ethereally based semicoma, growing bright and bright to Sklayne's inner eye. Way too bright.

Hurry, he told Trevarr, though his mind-voice didn't reach outside his head. *O hurry.*

But Trevarr fumbled the Gatherer, and the gun spoke so loudly the room shuddered with it. Whitewashed cement block spat chips beside Trevarr, starting instant runnels of dark blood trickling down skin—cheek and neck, strong straight nose. Sklayne found himself crawling—inching, no more, every twitch an agony—particularly intent on the vulnerable soft spot between the tendons of the Krevata's fetlock.

After all, geas had already done its worst. *Hadn't it?*

Another shot hit the cement. Awkward hands at the trigger, no evident experience—but if a very poor shot at this short distance, the Krevata was at least consistent.

Soon enough, it would correct its aim.

Sklayne won another four inches, panting. He peeled back his lips, made sure his jaws still worked.

The Krevata steadied its hand. It tipped its massive head sideways slightly, refining the aim of nearsighted eyes.

Trevarr stopped what he was doing—normally the work of seconds—to look up, to smile the most terrifying smile, cold and predatory and daring. *Ready.* Too late, but ready. *Aim corrected. Trigger pulled.*

The third bullet hit home. Trevarr jerked with it, eyes widening—but his cold fierce smile barely faltered, and he lifted the Gatherer to pull the Krevata in. *Cold fierce.*

Krevata, half ethereal and half corporeal, choosing whichever suited them most, whenever it suited them until the Gatherer took over. It yanked this one to the ethereal, shedding energy in a flare of pale green light. Sklayne stopped crawling, panting, and lifted his wobbling head to the sweeping, sweet taste of energy exchanged and power used. A conduit to Kehar, the Gatherer, attuned to the tribunal holding area. Straight to those who had been waiting, straight to their questions—to those who set Trevarr to this task and held his very life as the reward. *Do this or never come home. Do this or know your people will die.*

Some of the Krevata were broken. Some dead. Maybe it would still be enough.

This one wailed and tried to run even as the Gatherer shifted him. This one knew the consequences of such a capture. Not just Trevarr, angry Trevarr, coming for revenge. Oh, no, the Krevata had been noticed by many more, their activities condemned by all. No one cared about this world in any great fashion, but to destroy it so carelessly would reverberate through dimensions, bringing interdictions and consequences to even the most powerful on Kehar.

So Kehar policed its own, using the tribunal. They sent the mixed-blood bounty hunter with the best off-world collection record and the best reason to get the job done. They gave him more reason yet, and turned him loose . . . not even knowing of Rhonda Rose or the Garrie.

Now the second Krevata went with less dignity yet, trumpeting a nasal lament as it made what might be considered a mad lumbering dash for the hallway. Trevarr caught it in midstride. So went the next, a wounded creature unable to do more than crawl, and then the priest, and by then Sklayne had gained a few more inches on his torturous path to reach the Garrie's limp shining form draped over Trevarr's legs, and by then Trevarr had slumped against the wall into grim determination and much blood.

It hadn't stopped the scream of the earth around them. It hadn't stopped the scream of the spirits in this place. It hadn't stopped the assault of creatures living and ethereal on either this land or this house or the people within.

It hadn't stopped the slow glowing death within the Garrie. It hadn't stopped Trevarr from sinking down, fighting the final insult of flesh ravaged by that bullet. And Sklayne, somehow, had stopped moving altogether, not quite within reach of either the Garrie or Trevarr.

Trevarr's eyes rolled back—dull, they were, tarnished unto darkness—and he struggled back with a groan, his hand leaving a bloody smear over the Garrie's bare belly skin. He caught Sklayne's eye as a ceiling joist above them gave a mighty crack. "Fark," he said. "Damned well farking *hurts*."

::Hurts,:: Sklayne agreed.

"Garrie—?" It was as much as he could gasp out on that particular breath.

::Hurts,:: Sklayne said. ::Broken.::

Trevarr's head tipped back; he battled it. "No," he said, even if the word barely came out, just a scrape of vocal cord. "Not like this, Sklayne. Not her. Not—" His hand tensed against the Garrie's skin, smearing the black-hued blood they'd once tried so hard to hide from her. A few quick, panting breaths, and he managed, "Not any of us."

::Broken,:: Sklayne said, and this time it was apology. He could do nothing, not for any of them.

"Don't," Trevarr told him, a harsh word edged by desperation.

Sklayne understood. After all these years, he understood. No apologies, that's what. But he wished he was there, not here, these inches away. One not-cat paw touching. That's all.

But then Trevarr got that look.

Sklayne knew that look.

Sklayne had sometimes hated that look, but right this very moment he loved that look. Stubborn. Rule-breaking. Risk-taker look. About-to-do-something-that-someone-would-be-sorry-for look.

"The plasma—" Trevarr stopped, closed his eyes; shifted his legs in restless pain. "Can you take—?"

::*Any* energy,:: Sklayne said, proud of it. Even with his mind-voice fading.

Trevarr opened his eyes, working hard for focus. Finding it—finding it with such purpose that Sklayne followed his gaze.

The leather trunk. Full of collection ovals. Like the Eye, like the Gatherer . . . attuned to Kehar, but physically present here. Had the priest been carrying them, they all would have gone . . .

But he hadn't. He'd left them behind to attack the Garrie.

Across the room. Might as well have been on Kehar after all.

But Trevarr took several deep, hitching breaths, and he moved the Garrie off his legs—so carefully, as if jarring her might make her explode.

It just might.

His hand trailed down the side of her face as she rolled limply to her back, and then he got that look again. The good look. Mostly it covered the desperate fear he had for the Garrie.

Mostly.

He tried crawling, but instantly clutched his side, rolling over to mutter singeing words. The ceiling rained dust and debris in his face and he pulled himself back to his belly and forward, not trying to get up this time. Leaving a long smear of blood across the dirt floor.

At first Sklayne was confused, for Trevarr didn't aim for the leather trunk. He came the short distance to Sklayne himself, and with great effort and no explanation and no hesitation for the mew of startled pain he invoked, he slid Sklayne over beside the Garrie. Right beside her. Touching.

Oh. This *was* better.

Sklayne drifted away there, his nose resting against the Garrie's arm, his whiskers caressing her skin. Vaguely aware of grunting in the background, of a particular gasp of pain, and of a quiet string of tight, hoarse curses. *Farking.*

And then there it was.

Right in front of his nose.

Smeared with dirt-gritty blood, held in a hand that lost its strength and grip.

But right there.

"Snack time," Trevarr said, and passed out.

23

Avoid abuse of your advantages.
—Rhonda Rose

Superpowers aren't all they're cracked up to be.
—Lisa McGarrity

"I don't . . ." Garrie said.

And "Wha—?"

::Not dead,:: said Sklayne's voice in her head, oh so helpfully.

"I can't . . ." Think. See. Feel.

Warm hands closed over hers. Sticky, gritty hands. She felt that. She knew those hands. She was afraid she knew why they were sticky.

"Do something for him!" she told Sklayne, hazy recollections of explosive gunfire in her visceral memory, of ponderous but inexorable Krevata out to kill.

::Already,:: he told her. ::What I could.::

"*Atreya*," Trevarr said, "it is you for whom we must *do something*."

::And the house, and the others.:: Sklayne's voice sent dread down her spine. She felt that, too. That must be good, right?

"The house is failing," Trevarr said. "Your city is failing, and after it the world."

But the portal . . .

She hadn't said it out loud. She was sure of it. But with Sklayne there . . . who knew who could hear what? Because Trevarr said, "Yes, closed. And the Krevata . . . home. But not soon enough."

::Have a plan,:: Sklayne said, full of smug.

"You took in too much," Trevarr said, urgency in his voice. "Give it back to your world."

"No!" Too much emphasis on that word . . . she floated away for a while. When she came back it was to find Trevarr's hand warming her again, warming her fiercely, resting there just below her belly button, spanning the gap between her hip bones. Oh, she felt that, too. "I can't let it loose," she whispered. "What it does to you . . . what *I* did to you . . ."

Garrie came back to herself far too suddenly, screaming into blinding, burning light. No more numb, no more distant. Right in the middle of fire raking every bone, every muscle. Full force, an alien sound, so profound as to be disconnected from body and thought.

"Take this!" A strong hand closed around her wrist, inexorably tugging it away from her writhing body. "Use this!" She fought him and his incomprehensibility, full of kick and scream; her foot landed somewhere yielding and he made a strangled noise and doubled over.

::No, no, no.:: Sklayne's voice, as disapproving as she'd ever heard it. ::Already leaking there. Not to hurt *more*.::

Not that it mattered. The words meant nothing, just more noise in the fiery extremes that surrounded her and ripped through her and literally—*literally*—tore her apart.

Trevarr said no more. He simply took her wrist and extended her arm and plunged her hand into . . .

Coolness. Hungry darkness. Suckingly hungry darkness, damp and welcoming and instantly pulling on the energy going nova inside her—demanding it. She dug her fingers into that darkness; it crumbled around her hand, but still craved more, a welcome parasite.

Her vision went from nuclear white to a something less intense; she felt her toes again. The fire in her joints faded until she could feel individual joints and not one huge aggregate of pain. She found gritty packed dirt beneath her body; somewhere along the way her shirt had ridden up to expose most of her torso, where the skin turned oddly tight and dry. Trevarr lay close behind her, cradling her, his breath gusting at her neck, his grip on her wrist loosening.

All this energy . . . how . . .

::It goes to the earth,:: Sklayne told her. ::It heals your earth.:: But he corrected himself. ::Starts to.:: He nudged her other hand open with his cold little nose and rolled an object into it.

Garrie recoiled—or tried to. Nowhere to go, with Trevarr at her back and his hand tightening at her stomach, so possessive there. But she knew what this was, even with her vision still awash with watercolor dapples and light. She'd never held it before, she'd never felt it before, but she *knew*—

"No," she said, horror coming out even in her cracked and feeble voice.

::Yes,:: Sklayne said. ::Conduit. Must. *Through,* not in.::

She pushed it away—the bright rainbow colors of the scooped ovals the Krevata had been using at the portal, full of pulsing alien energy. Utter denial prevented her from forming words; utter terror prevented thought. When Sklayne pushed it back at her, she panicked; she pulled her hand back, flinging dirt everywhere; she bucked against Trevarr, fighting for freedom in earnest.

His arm tightened around her, both caressing and restraining; he captured her hand. The side of his face pressed just behind her ear. "Sah," he murmured, but some part of her was gratified by his breathlessness and she only fought harder. She could almost see now; she thought she might even be able to stagger away from this place, bouncing off walls if that's what it took. She'd gather up Drew and Lucia and—

::Look,:: Sklayne demanded, and if she'd thought

she had any kind of true connection with him before, now she learned the difference. He blew away the restrictions he'd allowed her, coming in through Trevarr to make of them all a muddy swirl, and he plunged her into *seeing*.

San Jose, buried in a swarm of darkness, full of screaming and destruction and creatures that never belonged on this world. Glimpses of terror, glimpses of death, a city folding in on itself while the earth buckled and tore around it. Here in this house, glimpses of madness. Drew sobbing, beset and battered, trapped in a corner while ghosts howled around him and the hallway fairly bulged with the sudden onslaught of more— drawn by the energies, the activity . . . the anger and the chance for retribution. Revenge against the Krevata and their chains, their spirit-sucking trap and their theft. *Drew, no—!*

Ghosts didn't often kill. But they could.

They were about to.

::They *have*.::

Not Lucia! Not—

And there they were, the tour group in the ballroom, clustered under the swaying chandelier, no longer fussy about ethereal effluvia on the floor but focused on the fallen medium . . . on a fallen child. Ghosts circled the room in a counterclockwise charge, tightening the energies around every living being there—not just the sensitives, with Lucia running against the flow of them, her beauty lost in utter insanity and her forehead streaming blood. She ran into a corner full speed, making it very clear where that injury had come from. And while Beth stood in the center of the room with her fists clenched over her ears screaming, *"Stop it! Stop it!"* another tourist fell.

And beetles that *weren't* emerged into the room from all directions, heading straight for the tourists. The beetles that burned and digested and ate . . .

::Watch them die,:: Sklayne said. ::Or not.::

Atreya. Trevarr's thought, muted and diffuse, reaching across some great distance. Nothing more than that, just a hint of his ferocity, the smooth stroke of his understanding. The tightening of his hand on her flesh.

::They die,:: Sklayne said, taking her in closer—a sharpening of focus, enough to see the flashing legs of the skittering beetles, to have no doubt that the medium and the child were already dead.

Lucia stopped her wild run, her hair tangled and her face flushed and her hands searching the air around her as if she could no longer see through her eyes at all. "Garrie!" she wailed. "Garrie, *please!*"

"Pleeease," echoed the little ghost girl. "Pleeeeaa . . ."

Garrie sobbed into that empty hand of hers. "Not Lucia," she cried. "Not Drew!"

::Both. All.::

Trevarr knew her decision before she did. Even as she reached out her trembling hand, he eased his hold on her, turned it into reassurance.

Sklayne nudged the oval back into place. For a moment it was only a strange, smooth rock, the central bowl cool and a little oily beneath her thumb. And then Sklayne *nudged* it a different way and the energy flooded through her and Trevarr slammed her other hand back into the earth—not this hard dirt floor with its coating of use and time, but freshly exposed, untainted earth. Deep earth.

Garrie threw her head back and howled. Too visceral, this. Too primal. Too encompassing, unable to pass through her without taking most of her along the way. No longer too bright to see but dark and swirling, coruscating almost-seen color painting her in its own image.

I have you, Trevarr said, even that deep in her thoughts—the taste of Sklayne clinging to him, bringing him there. *Stay with me.* More than the depth of his voice, the depth of what he was. All his pain, sketched out and transferred to her, from his damaged arm to the deep burning high in his gut to strains and bruises and slashing cuts. All his conflict, the two parts of his nature straining against one another. All his emotions. Raw and unfettered and wild, all hidden behind that cold, hard restraint. Living hard, a fierce life that gave him nonstop temporary intensity but never *this*. Never her. Never what she invoked in him.

She clung to that sense of him while the harvested power coursed through her and into the earth . . . healing. Cleansing through the city to calm the shuddering earth, to wipe away the darkness. Blasting through the house with unfettered power, a hurricane roar of silence that shredded the invaders and flung the jailed and freed the trapped.

Beguiling power cloaked in peaceful fury, deep surging waves of darkness, encompassing fire and fluttery wings, and just as it faded, Sklayne pushed a new source into her hand and broke it open and started it all over again and she watched the power carry little pieces of herself away except . . .

She felt his hands. She felt his truth. She felt where it connected within her.

She clung to it.

And Sklayne pushed a new source into her hand and broke it open and another and another, until only one tiny piece of Garrie clung to all of what held between them.

Until finally she heard Trevarr's voice, inexorably firm. "Enough."

That she could hear it at all meant something to her, in a vague way. That she could hear Sklayne's response, too. ::Needs more.::

"No." Trevarr leaned over her, movement that seemed an effort; his hand left her stomach and flicked away the source lingering in her hand. He tucked her in close, turned her over, and brushed his hand against her face, grimy as it was. Somehow it didn't surprise her when he bent close and kissed her—deep and lingering, full of firm warmth and unspoken words.

It didn't even surprise her that she kissed him back. Limp, wrung out, not even sure if she was still what she had once been, she farking well kissed him back. Long and deep and lingering, returning full warmth and unspoken words.

::Not sharing,:: Sklayne said plaintively.

Trevarr's mouth smiled against hers. His chest rumbled against hers as he spoke. "Good to know I can still block you."

::Maybe the Garrie," Sklayne suggested hopefully.

"Don't even try it," Garrie told him, voice so faint it hardly counted. She could feel herself again, toes and fingers and tingling spine. The perfect medicine. Trevarr stroked that spine—not smoothly, not with his usual strength. She followed him for an instant when he pulled back, and he apologized with a kiss to her brow, lingering there, too. As much an affirmation as anything.

Except then he said, "*Atreya*, I have to go."

Garrie had been thinking about the fact that she was still alive, or at least that she thought she was still alive, and that she was here in the basement of Winchester House making out, so inappropriately, with a man who might or might not be half demon. She'd been thinking about all that energy and what it might have done to her, and about what it might have done for the city, and about whether she'd felt truly that Lucia and Drew were free. She'd especially just been *being,* here with him. "You . . . what?" Surely not. "No," she decided.

"*Atreya*," Trevarr said, as gently as she'd ever heard him speak.

::Broken,:: Sklayne informed her briskly. ::Can't fix here.::

It took her a moment, and then suddenly all the clues

fell into place—everything she should have noticed already but had been too caught up in . . .

Well, in being a vessel of pure energy to notice.

She stopped reveling in her toes again, and in her fingers, and in the very lovely sensation of being tucked up so closely against him. She opened her eyes and pulled herself half upright, looking around the room—Krevata gone, recaptured. The cul-de-sac trap closed off. The portal shut. The ground, no longer shaking; the house no longer ripping itself apart. The ghosts, silent. She looked at her hand—covered with dirt, grime lodged deeply beneath her nails, knuckles bloodied. Over at the wall, several of the foundation blocks were missing; dark loamy earth spilled out and over the floor. "How—?"

Sklayne showed her in shorthand, inserting a quick image of himself—refreshed by plasmic energy, *ploofing* out into his vague and formless version, taking advantage of bullet cracks to slip in behind the blocks and blow one outward. ::Me,:: he said. ::Sklayne. I did it.::

"You certainly did," she agreed. She twisted around, found Trevarr propped against the wall behind her. "Ohhh, no," she said, and shook her head in denial. "No, no, no. Tell me you haven't really been—" But she couldn't say it, because it was quite obvious he *had* been. Distinct round hole in his shirt. Distinct fan of his dark blood from that hole. So helpfully, Sklayne showed her that in her mind, too. The widened eyes, the jerk of his body . . . the way his predator's smile hadn't faltered. "How could you—all this time—you *kissed* me."

"Yes," he agreed, and if his battered face was set in weary pain, there was nonetheless a spark behind his eyes. Pewter-bright cat's eyes. *Demon-touched eyes.* "Sklayne helped me. But the bullet . . . it interferes."

::And it hurts,:: Sklayne said, sitting in prim mode with his tail wrapped around his feet and no apparent awareness that his short reddish hair spiked off in every direction, rather like Garrie's hair on a particularly bad day.

Trevarr frowned at him. No more than a faint narrowing of his eyes, a slight tip of his head and hardening of his jaw. "You are like a child with that which should not be said."

"First thing that should be told," Garrie corrected. Hesitant, she leaned forward, hand hovering over his bruised face . . . over the bullet wound, over the arm he held protectively to his side. Then she gave up. "Fark."

He said, "You healed a world, Garrie. You need to go find your friends, care for them. Take them back to your home in the desert. But I must go."

"Is it safe for you there?" Strange how her voice came out in a whisper again. It *had* been fine, just like the rest of her. Playing power line had left her physically whole, rushing the power through her and not making it *of* her. She had the feeling it wouldn't be that simple for long, but for now . . .

No, her voice failed her for entirely different reasons.

Trust Trevarr to tell her the uncomfortable truth. "I don't know."

"Can't we . . ." she couldn't find the words at first. "Can't we pay off some doctor? Can't you—" She stopped herself; the flicker of pain on his face had been all too real, as was the regret.

"For all reasons," he told her, "I must go."

Panic was unbecoming. That's what she told herself. She'd saved a world; he'd said as much. She'd held a blazing universe of power beyond imagining and she'd survived. She could handle this. No problem.

Yeah.

Complete and utter panic, no doubt about it.

Trevarr fumbled in his coat—more than just a coat, she knew that now.

More than just a man, she knew that, too. And so much more than just a client.

She half expected it when he pulled out the Eye, replete with its impossible gleaming rich colors. "No," she said, and then clapped her hand over her mouth. She could see how much effort it took just to retrieve the damned eye. She'd somehow come to think of him as more than human—and so quickly, *more* than more than human—but even a man with startling strength, one who'd come back from near death once already in the past few days, who'd managed to defeat every impossible thing standing in his way . . .

Even a man such as that did not absorb a bullet so readily. Even a man such as that could still die.

She wasn't quite ready to get up. Toes and fingers attached, yes; perfectly functioning, who knew? She reached for his hand—carefully, this time, aware of his pain—and pulled it up to her cheek. He ran his thumb over her mouth, but then he winced and stiffened, and Garrie's missing courage—what she needed to let him go—suddenly found her.

She put his hand down and moved away, giving the Eye room to work even as Sklayne sauntered right up to sit on Trevarr's leg. She took a deep breath as the shimmer of color began—and only then, because she'd just plain stupid-been-assuming, did she think to blurt, "Will you come back?"

He met her gaze, held it—extraordinary eyes, once impenetrable, now a direct connection. And so her stomach was already bottoming out by the time he answered—the colors falling around him in a thickening curtain, swifter than she'd remembered, his expression flickering regret and uncertainty and *oh my God he's frightened, too.* All those things, as he looked at her and said, "I don't know."

And the colors took him away.

24

Give ease where you may.
—Rhonda Rose

Rhonda Rose, did you even know what you were doing?
—Lisa McGarrity

Garrie's face was entirely out of her control. It stared at
the spot where Trevarr had been—where dark blood
had collected in a frightening pool—and it crumpled in
the most amazing way.

Just for an instant. A quick, hiccuping sob and then
another, and then she covered her face with her hands
and turned around—as if that was going to do any
good.

But it did. It gave her a chance to take a breath, and
then another, and then for thoughts to come crowding
in. *Drew. Lucia.* Getting out of here. Clearing up any
remaining troublemakers and going home. *Home.*

*Rhonda Rose, did you even know what you were
doing?* Keeping a wounded man company, from the
sound of it—and Garrie had the feeling that Trevarr
wrecked himself up just about as fast as he healed.

"What did you even tell him?" Garrie wondered out
loud, finding her voice cracked and incomprehensible.
She cleared it. Whatever it was, Trevarr had remembered. He'd learned what Rhonda Rose had given him,
and he'd held onto it, and he'd found Garrie already
knowing who and what she was.

And to think, Rhonda Rose had never so much as
hinted to Garrie that there were other dimensions. That
she was headed off to travel instead of passing beyond.

"You'd *better* run," she mumbled, an imaginary threat
to someone who wasn't even there. Then she sighed,

wiped away tears, and faced the room again. Much better, in this direction. In fact . . .

She reached down to the little leather trunk, found it not quite empty—several of the collection ovals remained, nestled in a silk lining. And there, over on the floor . . . Trevarr's knife. How badly had things gone, for him to just *leave* it?

But second thought told her. He'd left it for her. A *remember me* token. "Damned well don't want it," she muttered at his absent self, but she picked it up and sliced through the satin with such buttery ease that she instantly handled it with much more respect.

She tied the corners of the lining together and had herself a hobo bag without the stick. A silk hobo bag full of collected alien plasmic energy too powerful to handle. Right.

With that, she climbed to her feet, surveying the room for other things that shouldn't be left behind. Nothing she could do about the various spots of gore, or the thing that looked like a severed finger. The trunk would be a mystery, but nothing that would gain any notice after what else had happened in this house, this city, this day. Garrie hefted her hobo silk, kept a careful awareness of the knife's edge, and headed out of the basement.

She didn't look back. Not at the mess, not at the broken-out block where she'd clutched raw earth and healed it, not at the blood so much darker than any human blood. She settled her shirt, she settled her shoulders back, she took a deep breath, and she went.

The house stayed silent around her. No ghosts pestering her as she climbed the basement stairs. No breezes washing against her awareness. None of the oppressive anger and distress. Her feet felt like someone else's; her body didn't quite respond normally to gravity. She made it up the stairs; she politely closed the basement door behind her, muttering an apology to no one when the brush of Trevarr's knife sliced a neat peel of paint from the door. A sheath might be in order. A rolled-up newspaper. *Some*thing.

Still cautious, she headed for the ballroom. Or hoped she was heading for the ballroom. It had seemed so easy when Drew brought her down this way . . .

But ah. Drew himself hadn't gotten very far. Ghosts begone, but Drew still huddled in the corner, his lanky limbs pulled in tight, arms covering his head, every muscle tense unto quivering. She hesitated, wanting to run to him, not wanting to startle him. Finally, keeping her distance, she said softly, "Drew."

"Garrie?" Cautiously, for sure. He lowered his arm, raised his head. Welts and streaks and trickles of blood marked his cheeks; he had a fat lip. Tears glistened across his skin. He seemed to realize it; he employed a hasty scrubbing hand to erase the evidence. Garrie said nothing more, just rested a hand briefly on his shoulder and walked on. After a moment, he scrambled to his feet and followed.

Another moment and he said, "Uh, it's this way," and she rolled her eyes and backtracked to follow him.

They approached the ballroom with mutual trepidation in a hallway dark without electricity or windows; just outside the door she stopped him, hesitated on the right words, and finally said, "Drew, it's bad in there."

He nodded. He didn't ask her how she knew. He opened the door.

Sobbing, that's what they found. Huddled tourists in distinct groups, one of whom bent over a body too small to bear. Not far away, the medium lay on the floor, hands crossed neatly over her stomach and her silk scarf placed over her face. Beth sat cross-legged beside her, her long face drawn with sorrow.

"Beth!" Drew said, and ran in to her. She had reached her feet by the time he got there, and threw her arms around him.

I thought so.

Beth quickly pulled away, moving to Garrie, taking her arm with a less than gentle grip. "I didn't know," she said, as if in confession. "I didn't know they could do anything like this."

"Not just them," Garrie said, but didn't try to explain. Not now. Not with those small legs just barely showing from behind those who cried together. She forced her gaze away, taking in clean floors and clean walls and clean ceiling, everything sparking as it had been . . . effluvia blasted away by her cleansing storm. "Where's Lucia?"

Beth didn't seem to hear her. "Can't you . . . I don't know . . . *help* somehow?"

Garrie snorted. "Do I look like I can—" She cut herself off. She wouldn't say *resurrect the dead* where the others could hear it.

Beth raised both eyebrows, giving Garrie a look that meant something without offering any other clues. Drew came to join her, his eyes on the dead woman, shaking his head, his mouth forming the infamous word of wonderment. *"Shee-it."*

"What?" Garrie asked Beth. "And where's—"

"Don't you know?" Beth asked, giving her a new look that meant something even more.

"What?"

"Shee-it!" Drew said it right out loud, taking his first good, hard look at her, here where the stained-glass windows brought in some light.

Garrie narrowed her eyes. "I have a knife," she said. "It's Trevarr's. It's very sharp. I could shave that soul patch right *now.*"

Drew took a startled look around. "Hey, where *is*—"
"Later."

"Your hair," Beth said. She raised a hand, passing it beside Garrie's head—not quite touching. "Where it used to be blue . . . now it's . . ."

"Still blue," Drew said. "But it's . . ."

Garrie would have thrown her hands up if she hadn't been holding that knife. Well, and enough stored power to leave this place a smoking crater in the ground. "Later," she said once more, if that's all it was. As long as no one had said *you've grown a third eye!* or *your nose splits in two!* "Where's—"

Never mind. There she was. Huddled in the foot well of the organ, face hidden in her hands, rocking back and forth and back and forth, her hair a snarled mess and her shirt twisted.

"Lu!" Garrie said, and ran for her. When she got closer, she could hear the muttering, an endless stream of nonsense words—no punctuation, meaningless . . . frightening. She crouched, shoving the knife and silk bundle aside, hands hovering over Lucia's, not quite ready to pull them away.

Beth came up behind her. "She tried. She tried really, really hard. She tried to protect us from their emotions, but it was too much. In the end she couldn't even begin to protect herself."

"We should have been together," Drew said, an odd note to his voice. "Everything would have been different if we'd stuck together. And then you sent me away, and it didn't do anyone any good anyway."

Garrie kept herself from turning to snap at him. "It kept you *alive,*" she said, and ground her teeth on anything more. With all the energy still coursing around in her body, affecting her reactions, affecting who knew what, she was in no position to lose control of herself.

With Trevarr gone, leaving her with no promises and a damned knife, it would be far too easy to do that.

But Drew didn't get it. Drew was stuck in the hallway. "Better than being alone out there?" he snorted. "I don't think so."

"You have *no idea,*" Garrie muttered, drawing her hand back. She couldn't touch Lucia, not like this.

"No," Drew agreed bitterly. "How could I?"

She closed her eyes. She took a deep breath. She didn't think about the Krevata, intent on killing her, intent on killing Trevarr. She didn't think about Trevarr, in so much pain and still holding her, still getting her through what it took to heal this world. She didn't think about the energies still swirling within her, the indelible stamp of Trevarr on her body and soul, the sight of a strange world and just how badly it had wanted to suck her in. She didn't think about a pink elephant while she was at it.

"Drew," Beth whispered, making no real attempt to keep it from Garrie—only from the others in the room. "*Look* at her. Can't you see—?" She stopped, blew out an exasperated breath. "Maybe not. Maybe that's one of those *sensitive* things. But look at her *shirt*—"

"Stained," Drew said, sounding sullen. "Basement. Big sur—"

"Blood," Beth interrupted. "Can't you tell? I know it doesn't look right, but—"

"Trevarr," Garrie said from between her teeth.

Quiet hands touched hers. Gentle hands. Cool. And a whisper of noise. Garrie's eyes flew open to find Lucia, startled at her own lack of voice, drawn out in response to Garrie's pain. Didn't it just figure. So deeply in hiding to protect herself, ravaged by the terrorized and terrorizing spirits of this place, and yet so alert to someone else's need. "Lucia!"

Lucia nodded, eyes bright and reddened, nose reddened, cheeks full of emotional rouge. For an instant they stared at one another, and then as if on cue they fell together in a fierce girlfriend hug, patting each other's backs and sniffling in each other's ears.

When they pulled apart, Lucia was already digging into her waist pack for tissues. She handed one to Garrie and said, without sound, "Let's get out of here."

Garrie was all for it. She gathered up her things in one

hand and held the other out to Lucia as she stood, and then they were all together again, and it took Beth two seconds to arrange for the original guide to stay here with the bereaved families and the victims of the ghostly extremes while she led everyone else out and Garrie brought up the rear, keeping an eye for trouble.

They left the room subdued and quiet and drained, and as Garrie crossed the threshold she heard the faintest of familiar voices, the little girl's voice. No real sign of her here, nothing more than the lingering presence of all the ghosts—she'd blown this place out good and clear. Just enough left behind to leave a sigh of words on the ethereal breeze. *"Thaank youu."*

25

Dissolution is a last resort.
—Rhonda Rose

Really, I just blew them all away.
—Lisa McGarrity

"You *killed* them?" Bob said, popping up right in front of Garrie as she ran on the hotel treadmill.

Garrie pretended he hadn't affected her in the least with that trick. New spirits were especially fond of it, and they all assumed they were the very first to think of it. It'd wear off.

She hoped.

Besides, she'd felt him in the area. Taking her by surprise before her inner woo-woo had been supercharged by plasmic energy hadn't been easy in the first place. Now . . .

She wasn't sure it could be done.

"Hey," Bob said. *"Boo."*

She'd have thought she'd be exhausted. Too tired to worry about the uneasy settle of energies within her, and completely ready to sleep for a week. Which seemed to be about how long Trevarr had reserved their rooms, paid in full. Instead, she'd slept for . . . well, a day. A day in which San Jose still buzzed with excitement and dazed confusion but had largely recovered itself, left only with minor quake cleanup. Nothing new about that. A day in which the news media beat its frustrated communal head against hard objects due to the inability of any camera, anywhere, to capture images of recent events.

That, Garrie had to admit, was damned convenient. She'd give anything to ask Trevarr about it.

She'd give anything to ask him so many things. What was it with her hair and skin? What was she supposed to do with the stunningly beautiful collection of devices tucked away behind her clothes in the hotel drawer? How long had he been doing this bounty hunter thing? How many different worlds and dimensions had he been to?

And would he maybe take her to see them, too?

Going back to slow-mo reckoning . . . if it had been paling before, it seemed unbearable now.

She wasn't sure Drew felt the same. Or Lucia. They'd slept for two days, both of them—getting up only long enough to stumble into the bathroom, eat a few bites of the food she'd made available, and fall back into bed. Processing. Recovering. Lucia looked a little better each time she got up. Drew . . . got a little more quiet. And then he'd gotten up, called Beth, and disappeared. Lucia, too, had disappeared—to shop. She'd padded Garrie's minimal remaining wardrobe—so many shirts lost to blood and battle—and she'd chosen clothes that Garrie would have picked herself instead of poking at her sense of personal style by bringing back designer I-don't-think-sos. Then off she'd gone, perusing more than buying but not about to lose the opportunity.

Exactly why they were still here, Garrie wasn't sure. Only that none of them seemed quite ready to go.

"Seriously," Bob said. "You're giving me a complex."

"Sorry," she said. "I was thinking. How's this? *Eeek!*" No one else in the room, always a plus when talking to a ghost.

"Ha-ha. You've been at this for days. Do you ever stop?" He mimed running with his fingers.

"I don't know," she told him. "I've never been in this particular position before."

"Do you think he's coming back?"

"I don't *know*," she told him, and let slip a small breeze, giving herself a little personal space.

Bob didn't take offense; Bob was in the spiritual classification of *golden retriever*. In your face, enthusiastic, everything was cool and nothing bothered him much.

That last was kind of a shame. "You sure you don't want to, you know, figure out what's keeping you here and find some resolution?"

"Hey," he said, putting on an offended face. "That wasn't subtle." But golden retriever mode was set to full force, and only a moment later, he said again, "You *killed* them?"

"Technically," she pointed out, breathing easily between "they were already dead." She'd picked an easy long-distance pace for the day, put the exercise room TV to the HBO feed, and settled in for a movie. Bob, of course, had muted the sound upon his arrival. He was learning fast, all right.

He put a finger on the treadmill computer; the pace suddenly hit *sprint*. Garrie avoided nasty road rash with a wild twisting windmill of arm and torso, and then let the belt carry her back far enough so she could jump off, straddling a foot on either side of the base. "Don't," she said. "If you think I'll even hesitate—"

"To what?" he challenged, stopping the treadmill altogether. "Blow me away, too?"

"That's *all* I did," she told him, exasperated. "You're the one who assumed otherwise. But I didn't take them apart. I blew them elsewhere. I cleared the house." And clear it was, too. She'd done a number of surveys of the house since then, and found only a stray spirit or two, newly wandered into the house as it did what it had always done . . . enticed ghosts and led them in circles of illogical architecture.

"Really?" He brightened. "I thought . . ."

She reached for her sweat towel. "I would have, if I hadn't had a choice. And I won't say I think they're happy about how things turned out. But they made their choices, too." She gave him a pointed look. "So do you."

"Give it up. I'm having fun. My life prepared me perfectly for my death."

She couldn't argue that. She picked up her sports bottle and headed back for the room . . . he'd follow her, or he wouldn't.

Once there, she threw the bottle on the bed she still shared with Lucia, and stood in the doorway of Trevarr's room.

It still smelled like him.

She stood there a long time, the sweat of exertion drying on her body, eyes closed, just . . . inhaling. Not thinking too hard about it, because she'd learned fast not to do that. And then, when her throat had tightened down into a painful knot and her stomach felt hard and her spine had tightened to painful tension, she turned away. Right before it got to be too much. She'd learned fast how to calculate that, too.

She ended up in front of the mirror. Looking again at

what that day had wrought. Normal Garric, in a public-ready sports bra nonetheless covered by a crop top—cropped by her own hand, so not exactly straight, either. Tight and tiny workout shorts. Same-old, same-old. Body by austerity budget—too short, too scant. Nothing lush about it.

Except the way it had felt when—

She turned away from that, too. Fast learner. Right.

But it wasn't all the same. Not her skin, which—in just the right light, in just the right places, had a new sheen to it. Not a normal sheen. Not a *human* sheen. Silver overlay, the faintest shimmer in the sun . . . over her collarbones, over her shoulders, over her cheeks and nose . . .

Good thing glimmer dust was in. For now, anyway.

The hair was a little easier. She'd played with colors and streaks for years, after all. Just because her fading blue streaks had gone silvery gray, just because it now seemed to come from the root in those spots . . . well, really. The least of her problems.

Because she couldn't help but wonder—if the energy had interacted with her body to make these small surface changes, what had it done down deep? And at what possible worst time would she discover those other changes?

She knew whom she wanted to ask, all right.

She headed for the shower. She didn't worry about the shampoo versus the hair dye.

Okay, that part was kind of nice.

She came out to the sound of voices, a small bundle of dirty clothes in her hand and dressed in bumming-around sweats and ready for dinner. They knew her, down at the hotel dining room. She was the only one of them who'd eaten all her meals here, when she hadn't eaten in her room.

The voices turned out to be Lucia, hanging up her cell phone, and Drew, draped over a chair while Beth sat on his bed. Lucia, her fading bruises expertly covered with makeup, her espresso-dark hair sleek and shiny again, thumbed the hang-up button with ceremonial flair. "Chicalet," she said. "That was Quinnie. He's got a lead on something in Arizona. He thinks it got stirred up by recent . . . events." She shrugged. "Who knows. But . . . old girlfriend, you know? Asking for help. He wants us to meet him there."

"There, where?" Garrie said absently, shoving her bundle of dirty clothes in the drawer beside the bundle of intense extradimensional beauty and power.

Lucia exchanged a glance with Drew. "Sedona," she admitted.

"What?" Garrie threw her hands up. "No!"

"It's very pretty," Lucia said, by way of admonishment.

"It's *insane.* You know it's insane. All that energy whipping around, all the woo-woo hounds—"

"We are woo-woo hounds," Lucia pointed out.

Garrie opened her mouth to argue—and slowly closed it again. Sedona . . . her worst nightmare. Those with half a talent would peg her for the real thing right away, drawn to her . . . fascinated by her. Or else they'd spend all their time trying to prove themselves more woo-woo than thou. And the pretenders . . . they would scorn her, trying to trip her up, getting in her way. Disproving her would be the only way to validated themselves.

But Quinn had asked. And Lucia clearly wanted to go. And she owed them all.

Drew cleared his throat. "Maybe not me," he said.

Lucia snorted genteely, swinging her leg back and forth over the side of the bed, a sandal dangling from her toes. "As much as any of us," she said. "More."

"No, I mean . . ." He glanced at Beth, who offered silent encouragement, and then he looked at the floor. And by then Garrie knew.

He wasn't coming with them.

"Drew . . ." she said.

"Look, you know I'm not doing so hot with the university thing. I don't fit their mold. I know too much about stuff I can't prove I know anything about. I don't follow their neat rules and patterns and linear thinking."

Garrie's throat, still tight from her time in Trevarr's room, barely let her say, "But you love archaeology. I can't believe you'd give that up."

"What?" He gave her a startled look. "No! I mean . . . I'm just looking to go freelance, maybe. You know, do advance work for folks who want to up the odds of their success on a dig. Get out in the field—and what with Stanford and all, this place has opportunities. You should understand that . . . you were stifled, back in Albuquerque with nothing going on. Well, this has all made me realize . . . me, too."

Imagine that. Not a badly used slang term in the mix.

Lucia had lost her composure, her swinging leg stilled. "But Drew . . . we're a *team* . . ."

He sent Garrie a wry look. "Not so much as we should be."

"But—"

"It's okay, Lucia," Garrie said, forcing the words; they came out a little rushed, a little harsh. "I get it. I mean, I don't like it, but I get it." She swallowed, hard. "I hope you change your mind, Drew. I really do."

Beth stood up, overly cheerful in every movement. "Well, you've got a couple more days on this room, right? Time for everyone to think?"

As if she didn't want Drew to stay. Couldn't have been more obvious.

Drew, too, rose from his chair, heading for the open doorway. "I'm thinking I'll take this room," he said. "It's stupid to leave it empty when we're splitting this one three ways." He glanced over his shoulder at Garrie. "I mean, it's not like he's coming back."

Oh, why not just complete the misery? "You don't know that," she told him, voice catching on the words. When he just looked at her, she said, "You *don't*. And hey . . ." She narrowed her eyes. "You *shaved*."

Beth gave a pleased nod. "He certainly did."

Oh, God. It *was* serious.

"You know what?" she told him. "Whatever. Seriously. Your choice. I'm just gonna call the airlines and see what it would take to change those tickets so we land in Phoenix." If she turned around fast enough, he might not even see that she'd finally lost the battle and started leaking the tears she'd been fighting off for days now, and she had the feeling that if she started, she'd just never stop.

"Oh," Drew said, and his voice had gone strange. "Oh. Er. Never mind. I like sharing. Sharing is good." He backed out of the room. Slowly. So very casual.

Sklayne's voice rang in Garrie's mind. ::Share *your* room. This is *mine*.::

And Garrie knew.

Garrie stopped leaking tears.

Garrie whirled around and propelled herself into the adjoining room, not slowing down until she ran right into the wall of Trevarr—a collision, it would have been, had he not been perfectly ready for it, turning all that momentum upward. If he thought lifting her would slow her down, he was so very wrong. She wrapped her legs around his hips and her arms around his neck and commenced to kissing the hell out of him.

He did quite a fine job of kissing her back.

So much so that it took several moments before Garrie registered the conversation behind her, and Lucia's wickedly dry voice. "Hey," she said. "Seriously. No need to be shy around us. We certainly never suspected."

Garrie stopped with the kissing—right there, still clinging to him, her mouth still connected to his. "Oops," she said, through the kiss.

He pulled back slightly, that faint smile at the corners of his mouth. "No need for *oops*."

She relaxed her legs, slid right down the front of him, careful of the belt buckle. "Good," she said. "Because I'd like to do that as often as possible. Are you back? Are you *all right*?" In sudden frantic realization, she patted down his torso, looking for bandages, wondering if she'd hurt him. He caught her hands and looked at the doorway, where the others had gathered. Once more, behind the invisible line.

"A few more days," he said. "But all right."

"And . . . and your people?"

At that, he looked away.

"No!" she cried. "That's not right! You brought back the Krevata!"

"Damaged," he said. "Dead. In tribunal eyes, that was indulgence. My instructions were to return them whole, to face punishment."

"But you did it for me! For this world! You could have gone at any time, don't tell me you couldn't! You didn't need to stay, or to get shot, or to bring me back or to heal this world—" It's not as if she hadn't had plenty of time to think it out.

He didn't respond, not at first. He just looked at her. And when she went to throw her arms around him again, he opened his own and took her in, and that was answer enough.

Don't die in order to live. —Rhonda Rose

Life, full speed ahead! —Lisa McGarrity

I'll be back. —Trevarr

TOR
ROMANCE

Believe that love is magic

Please join us at the website below for more information about this author and other great romance selections, and to sign up for our monthly newsletter!

www.tor-forge.com